YOU MUST REMEMBER THIS

A NOVEL OF WORLD WAR II HOLLYWOOD

MARTIN TURNBULL

This book is dedicated to

SUZIE PERKINS

because Thursday mornings wouldn't be the same without you.

Copyright 2023 Martin Turnbull

All rights reserved. No part of this e-book may be reproduced in any form other than that in which it was purchased and without the written permission of the author. This e-book is licensed for your personal enjoyment only. This e-book may not be re-sold or given away to other people. If you would like to share this book with another person, please purchase an additional copy for each recipient. If you're reading this book and did not purchase it, or it was not purchased for you, please purchase your own copy. Thank you for respecting the hard work of this author.

DISCLAIMER

This novel is a work of historical fiction. Apart from the well-known actual people, events and locales that figure into the narrative, all names, characters, places, and incidents are the product of the author's imagination or are used fictitiously. Any resemblance to actual persons, living or dead, events or locals is entirely coincidental.

❦ Created with Vellum

1

The radio room of the USS *Lanternfish* reeked of sweat and grease. Dozens of instruments glowed and ticked. And Ensign Luke Valenti could still taste the canned corn chowder he had wolfed down for lunch three hours before. Or was it four? It was hard to know for sure when a guy was trapped in a space that had been built for one but was now housing him as well as the radio operator.

They sat, back pressed against back. The heat of Sparky's spine seeped through his rumpled chambray shirt.

Luke pushed the headset halfway off his ears. "Got the time?"

"What did you do, Warner Boy? Lose your watch overboard?"

Like it or not, almost every enlisted man in the Navy got branded with a nickname. All radio operators were called Sparky. No exceptions. And when Luke had let on that he'd worked at Warner Brothers, the crew had pounced on it.

"It fell off my bunk," he replied. "Sugar was asleep, so I wasn't about to risk my life."

One of the cardinal rules aboard a sub was to never wake a sleeping man. But with only eight inches of space separating one bunk from another, it wasn't always possible. If roused prematurely, the *Lanternfish*'s cranky Chief of the Boat transformed into an ogre who devoured sailors for breakfast.

"Wondering what your girl's doing right now?" Sparky asked.

It would soon be three years since Luke had kissed Nell Davenport goodbye. Usually, it felt like hardly any time had passed since he'd felt her tear-stained cheek against his. On tough days, though, it felt like a dozen lifetimes. It probably wouldn't if he'd heard from her, but he had received no letters, no cards, no V-mails. Nothing. Ever. Probably just bad dumb luck; most likely, they had gone astray in the vast military postal service. After all, he'd frequently moved around. It would've been hard to keep track of him.

But what about the three months he'd spent at the Navy Language School in Colorado learning Japanese? Hadn't that been enough time for the mail to catch up with him? If it hadn't been for that Hollywood Canteen broadcast, he might have dropped into a pit of despair. Hearing Nell sing a song she had written using their special secret code had flooded Luke with relief. Her V-mails hadn't reached him, but at least she'd been getting his.

"Might she be at that fancy nightspot you told me about?" Sparky asked. "What's it called again? Simon's?"

"Simon's is a drive-in hamburger joint. You're thinking of Ciro's."

"She could be puttin' on the Ritz with Clark Gable or Ronald Colman."

"They're not Warner stars. If she's out with anyone, I'd hope it was Bogie."

Sparky squirmed in his seat. "I blow a gasket every time I think about how I know someone who's pals with Humphrey Bogart."

"He's a regular guy," Luke said. "Likes to play chess, likes his whiskey, likes to read, and he especially likes to sit in the steam room at Finlandia Baths on Sunset Boulevard and shoot the breeze with Peter Lorre."

Just then, a crewman appeared in the doorway of the radio

room's newly installed watertight door. "Lookouts on the platform have sighted a mast. Jap merchant ship. Five miles, give or take. Doesn't appear to be moving."

Luke patted his earphones. "We need to get in much closer before this prototype I'm testing will kick in." He needn't have said anything. Combat procedure was straightforward: all enemy vessels must be fired on. At least Japanese merchant ships had no torpedoes.

"We're submerging to the deckline to lower our profile, but your antennas should be okay."

The dense air in the radio room congealed even thicker. The *Lanternfish* had approached the enemy before, but most recently as part of a pack. This time, however, it was alone.

"Anyhow," Luke said, as he continued to monitor his set, "when you come visit, I'll take you to Finlandia Baths. We can relax until we're puddles of sweat. Deal?"

Sparky studied a photo of the Brooklyn Bridge he'd taped to the only empty square foot of wall space. On their first day out from Pearl Harbor, he'd mentioned to Luke that he'd prefer the Marine Parkway Bridge to remind him of Rockaway Park, where he was from, "but Brooklyn Bridge gets all the attention, so I'm making do." The two men had discovered they had grown up ten miles from each other. Back home, it wouldn't have raised an eyebrow, but five thousand miles away in the middle of the Pacific, it meant a great deal.

"I'll see if Bogie can join us at Finlandia," Luke said. There was no reply. He turned to see Sparky staring at the Brooklyn Bridge, barely moving. "Christopher?"

Sparky jumped. Nobody used real names, which, he had confessed during a long night watch, bothered him. "It makes me feel like nothing more than a number. Once in a while, I'd like to hear someone call me by my actual name."

"Yeah, yeah," Sparky muttered now. "Norwegian Baths. Bogie. Count me in."

Luke had noticed the haunted look in Sparky's eyes the last time a Jap ship had pinged the *Lanternfish*'s radar. "It's my job to send out continuous maydays," he had told Luke that night, "until the end."

Luke raised a finger at the photograph on the wall. "Thinking about home?"

Sparky ran a hand over his sandy-blond crew cut. "I used to bike from Ninety-Seventh Street to Rockaway Beach Boulevard, ducking in and out of traffic, old ladies shaking their walking sticks at me, dogs barking. I'd pedal all the way to Breezy Point Tip."

"Must have taken you all day."

"That's what summers are for, right?"

"What kind of bike did you have?"

"Schwinn. Red with chrome trim. And you?"

Luke pictured himself coasting along Argyle Road, his feet off the pedals, en route to Aunt Wilda's, where there'd be rich cream cakes, a new record album to play, and a wild story involving a Levantine diplomat or a contortionist from Saskatchewan. "Sun Racer. Dark green. Black trim."

"If we knew each other back then, we could've ridden from Brighton Beach to Greenpoint."

"From Bay Ridge to Jamaica Bay!"

Static cracked and popped in Luke's headset for a full minute before subsiding to a dull hum. Chatter, low and indistinct, rose in its place. As the *Lanternfish* glided closer to the enemy, inarticulate murmuring grew crisper and clearer. Luke upped the volume. Oh, yes. Definitely Japanese.

A voice, older and deeper, spat out instructions. Do this. Do that. Check this. Double check that. The other voice, younger and efficient, responded. Yes, sir. Copy that. Confirmed. Understood.

Then Luke heard a command he wasn't expecting: Flood tubes one and two.

Flooding the tubes was the first step before a submarine fired torpedoes. How was that possible? Merchant ships were armed with only machine guns on the decks. Maybe he'd misheard?

There it was again: *gyorai*.

The Japanese word for 'torpedo' sounded nothing like their word for machine gun.

Luke ripped off his earphones and threw himself through the hatch and into the command chamber, his heart thudding against his ribs. "Captain, I've picked up chatter on my prototype. They're flooding torpedo tubes one and two."

Captain Polk, a rational man with flinty blue eyes that rarely blinked, pulled his face from the periscope. "Are you sure?"

"Positively."

The captain reached for his phone to address the entire crew over the boat's loudspeaker. "All hands. Battle stations. Secure all watertight doors except the com. Clear the bridge. Dive! Dive! Dive! Periscope depth. "The enemy has torpedoes, probably in a sub hiding on the far side of that decoy *maru*. They've already readied their fish, which means they'll be coming out from cover real soon." He swiveled to his right. "Jigs, see anything yet?"

The *Lanternfish*'s chief radarman stared at his circular screen. "The ship hasn't moved this whole time."

"Estimated distance from target?"

"Twenty-one hundred yards and closing."

Torpedoes had at least a five-thousand-yard range, but the best shots were within one thousand, and could take a minute or more to swim that distance. It wouldn't be long until the *Lanternfish* reached that point. Luke tried to swallow, but his saliva had turned to concrete.

"BRIDGE!" Every crewman froze in place as Jigs roared his warning. "Confirming a second craft."

"Sub?"

Tense seconds crawled by until Jigs could be sure. "Jap sub, aye."

Polk picked up the phone connected to the loudspeaker. "The

enemy has detected us. They have the advantage of surprise and will be launching their fish before we can launch ours."

Luke took his seat as the *Lanternfish* leveled off.

Sparky gawked at Luke, eyes fogged with apprehension. "Remember our pact. If one of us doesn't make it out alive, the other one—"

"No defeatist talk," Luke fired back. The voices in his earphones fell silent.

Jigs called out their distance. "Nineteen hundred yards . . . fourteen hundred . . . eleven hundred . . . reaching a thousand in four . . . three . . . two . . . one . . ."

A high-pitched voice split the air. It was Dipper, the sonar guy. "Confirming two inbound fish."

"All hands," Polk boomed into the intercom, "brace for impact."

Luke gripped the edge of his tiny desk and braced his feet against the deck. As the *Lanternfish* cruised through the water, the only sound was Dipper's voice piercing the dank air like an arrow.

"One hundred yards . . . fifty . . . twenty . . ."

Luke held his breath and closed his eyes. Nell's face appeared in front of him. *It'll be okay*, her tentative smile assured him. A breeze blew a lock of hair across her left eye and—

A deafening clang tolled the length of the *Lanternfish*. Metallic ripping sounds followed. The boat shuddered a moment or two before righting itself.

"It's a dud!" Sparky let out his breath. "It hit us, though."

"Forward torpedo room," Polk called out. "Report your damage."

A voice Luke couldn't identify shot out over the intercom. "Bow plane gone. Torn a hole in the hull. Forward torpedo evacuating now."

"Blow ballast," Polk ordered. "Take 'er up."

The forward torpedo room held fourteen men trained to clear out in under fifteen seconds. The *Lanternfish* could still fire on the enemy with aft torpedoes, but without a functioning bow plane, they were now stuck on the surface.

The captain gave his next order. "Swing ninety to starboard for a tail shot. Flood stern tubes. Open outer doors."

Their torpedoes were fitted with gyros that could guide them through ninety degrees, toward the enemy, which saved the *Lanternfish* needing to rotate a full one-eighty. Not an ideal situation, but far from hopeless.

As the deck beneath Luke's shoes swayed, the earphone voices started up again.

The merchant ship captain was now talking about how his cargo was packed shoulder to shoulder. What were they transporting? Cows? Luke leapt from his desk when he heard the word *horyo* and approached the captain again. "Sir, the enemy is carrying POWs."

Polk winced. "It's a hellship." The Japs had been freighting POWs as they pulled back to the Home Islands. "Did they say where?"

"Amidships, sir. There must be lots of them packed into the main hold because they're, quote, shoulder to shoulder."

The captain dropped his chin to his chest. "Those sons of bitches know they're screwed, but determined to take as many of us as they can."

"Also, sir." Luke hated the wobble he heard in his voice. "Their skipper stated that he's prepared to scuttle his *maru* if he has to."

Polk alerted the boat. "The enemy is holding POWs. Our objective is to cripple, not sink. With the forward torpedoes gone, I know this is a tall order, but I want you to remember that many Allied lives hang in the balance."

Sending Luke back to his station, he asked for their current position from the boat's navigator, who confirmed they had completed the ninety-degree turn.

Dipper called out, "The enemy has fired a second pair of fish."

"Fire seven!" Polk boomed. "Fire eight! Fire nine! Reload seven. Reload eight. Reload nine."

Luke felt the vibration through the soles of his black shoes as the *Lanternfish* thrust three torpedoes into the Pacific.

"All hands brace for impact."

Luke found Sparky staring at him, eyes round as marbles. *Don't say it,* Luke wanted to tell him. *We know your job is to send out a mayday while the crew hotfoots it topside.*

A deafening explosion reverberated the length of the boat. The *Lanternfish* lurched and rolled sideways, almost jolting Luke and Sparky from their seats. The Japanese fish had struck the aft torpedo room, gashing it with a massive hole.

A fatal blow.

Water would be pouring in now, the room littered with bodies, any surviving crew entombed behind sealed doors.

A shrill alarm rang out. Every man on board knew its meaning. The *Lanternfish* was dead. Time to abandon ship.

Sparky hunched over his telegraph set—three dots, three dashes, three dots—followed by their coordinates. Luke pressed a hand to Sparky's shoulder, but he shrugged it away. "Save yourself." He turned back to his microphone. "Mayday! Mayday!" he said. "*Lanternfish* disabled. Will report ongoing status."

Another explosion rattled the sub. Luke hurled himself toward the scrum of crewmen heading for the ladders to the deck. The screeching alarm drilled deep into his skull as his arms and legs flailed for purchase on the ladder's slick rungs.

The cool sea air whipped Luke's face as he scrambled onto one of the gun decks.

Pop! Bang!

A bullet whistled past his right ear.

Pop-pop! Bang-bang!

The *maru* lay silhouetted against the reddish-orange disk of the setting sun. It was closer than Luke had imagined, less than the length of a football field. Close enough that he could see Japs manning machine guns on their deck. Close enough to shoot or be shot. He grabbed the machine gun he'd been allotted to play with during drills.

Rat-a-tatta-rat-a-tatta-rat-a-tatta-rat-a-tatta-rat-a-tatta.

He lost track of how many bursts he fired. Four? Seven? Ten? He was going to hammer away until he ran out of ammo.

A thunderous blast exploded in his ears as rounds splattered above his head. Shreds of bullet and boat rained down, sharp and searing hot, singeing his hair, scorching his shirt and skin. Bullets zipped and zinged, whistling past him. He kept firing as the last strands of daylight dissolved in the west.

Dizzy and disoriented, he felt his knees buckling and he hit the deck hard, aching, burning, as he crawled to starboard. Rubber rafts and chunks of debris bobbed on the ocean's surface. As he struggled to stand, a second boom, louder than the first, felt like it came from the conning tower behind him. Luke's breath whooshed from his lungs as he lost his footing and tumbled.

Dropping from the cigarette deck, he hit his head against something rigid, metallic, and unforgiving.

Sharp, agonizing pain filled his skull.

Then nothing.

2

Nell Davenport flung her feet onto her desk in the Warner Bros. PR department and fanned herself with the final draft of a press release she had been working on for *Mildred Pierce*. As soon as word had leaked out that Joan Crawford and Michael Curtiz were conjuring movie magic, Jack Warner had ordered PR to pull out all the stops for its September premiere in a couple of months' time.

Nell's boss, Robert Taplinger, favored soft-soled shoes, so she didn't catch sight of him, or his giraffe of a guest, until they were standing next to her. She handed him the release. "Hot off the presses."

Taplinger took her draft. "I want you to meet Buzz Bryant," he said, indicating the stony-faced man behind him. "Buzz, this is Nell Davenport, who's been keeping your desk warm while you were laying your life on the line in Iwo Jima." Taplinger turned to Nell. "You know that photo of our boys raising the flag on Mount Suribachi?"

Of course she did. It would probably end up being the most famous photograph taken during the entire war.

"Buzz was the Marine who carried that flag up to the peak."

Ah, so *this* was the storied Buzz Bryant, king of movie PR, who had been with the studio since the early talkies, and whom everybody had discussed in reverential tones during the whole two and a half years Nell had worked in PR. He was so masterful at creating buzz that he'd taken it on as a nickname. Nell had imagined a cross between St. Francis of Assisi and Thor, God of Thunder, but this florid-faced shmuck, tall but underfed, standing at attention, was not what she'd been picturing. Still, Nell couldn't guess how it must have been to slug it out, day after day, trudging through the shifting sands amid the stench of sulfur and bodies piling up on all sides.

"I'm glad you made it out in one piece," Nell said.

Bryant's version of a nod was a curt bob of the chin. "Do it all again if I had to."

Nell managed a tremulous smile. As rumors in the press of the inevitable invasion of Nippon grew louder, Nell hoped that Luke, wherever he was, could keep himself safe until the Japs were forced to cry uncle.

"And now he's ready to return to work." Taplinger sounded as proud as a father.

Nell was unsure what to say. It was news to her that her desk had been Bryant's before the war. Was she expected to vacate it? And go where? To the lone desk next to the men's room?

Taplinger handed Nell's press release to Bryant. "Feel free to make any improvements."

Bryant glanced at the headline. "The new Crawford picture?"

"Better than anything MGM gave her. Nell can bring you up to speed."

I've reworked, rewritten, refined and revised that announcement, Nell thought. It's word-perfect, highly polished, and ready for printing. No improvements necessary.

"Oh, and by the way"—Taplinger affected a phony nonchalant tone—"Buzz will be taking over *Mildred Pierce*."

Hold your cotton-picking horses. "He what?"

11

"I'm also giving him *The Corn is Green* and *Pride of the Marines*."

In other words, Taplinger was turning over three of the year's biggest pictures to this unsmiling, taciturn stinker. Bryant had fought in one of the bloodiest battles in the Pacific theater, so handing him *Pride of the Marines* made sense. But *Mildred Pierce* and *The Corn is Green*?

Nell was still formulating a convincing argument when Taplinger added, "You won't be sitting around twiddling your thumbs. I'm giving you *Danger Signal* and *Christmas in Connecticut*."

Danger Signal was a half-baked B picture about a psychopath and faked suicide notes, and would disappear from theaters the same week it landed. *Christmas in Connecticut* was fluffy nonsense, but at least it starred Barbara Stanwyck, Dennis Morgan, and Sydney Greenstreet.

She was supposed to thank her boss for his largesse, but the best she could manage was a tepid smile.

"My secretary is in Portland burying her grandmother," Taplinger told Bryant. "Her desk is free for the next week. That'll give us time to play musical chairs."

Was Nell expected to be grateful for not getting kicked to the bathroom desk? She fiddled with the carriage release lever on her typewriter. *Casablanca* and *To Have and Have Not* had been big, fat hits. And hadn't the *Hollywood Canteen* movie been Warners' box office champ of 1944? Not to mention that Christmas broadcast from the Canteen. Not only had millions of people tuned in that night, but it had also garnered acres of press coverage. Every last one of them had mentioned Warner Brothers in glowing terms. Did Taplinger think it had all happened by magic?

But, Nell told herself, you've always known that when the boys came home, they would expect to pick up where they left off. You can't blame Buzz Bryant for that. Naturally, Taplinger is going to give guys all the jobs because they have wives and children and mortgages, and all the things single girls don't have. You have no cause to be surprised now that it's happened.

But still, the props department was short-handed. Couldn't they have stuck him in there? Gosh darn it all. It wasn't fair. Nell Davenport had been demoted, and the humiliation stung.

* * *

She had been brooding like a Brontë heroine for hours. What she needed was fresh air, a July breeze through her hair, and summer sun on her face. *Danger Signal* would have to wait. She fled the office without a word and marched to Stage Seventeen where Betty Bacall was filming *Confidential Agent*.

With Luke away at war, it had been a fun distraction to watch Bogie and Betty fall for each other during the shooting of *To Have and Have Not*. She'd have liked to have attended their wedding, but they had held it in Ohio to avoid turning it into a circus. And now, although they were giddily ensconced in their home above the Sunset Strip, Warners had lumbered poor Betty with a silly movie. The reality of being a studio actress had socked her right in the kisser. Nell figured Betty needed as much cheering up as she did.

Nell knocked twice, then once, then twice again—their secret knock.

Lauren's gravelly voice rang out. "Get in here."

Warner Bros.' newest sensation wore a knitted sweater the color of dirty dishwater that registered as elegantly gray on a black-and-white screen. "Help me rehearse this tripe." She tossed a pair of pages toward a small radio playing a Chopin piano concerto and they floated to the floor.

"How's Mr. Boyer treating you?"

"His usual Europeanly debonair self." Betty dropped onto a white, tufted loveseat and took a drag on the cigarette that had been smoldering in a brass ashtray. "I wouldn't mind so much if Bogie were on the lot and we could eat lunch together. But now that he's finished

The Two Mrs. Carrolls, he gets to putter around the house while I'm here pretending to be a bored rich socialite helping a concert pianist obtain coal for the Spanish rebels. It's all so ludicrous."

A member of the kitchen staff arrived with a bowl of chicken broth, a cheese-and-tomato sandwich, and a glass of milk. Betty thanked the girl and waited until she had left. "I have no appetite. Help yourself."

Nell merely stared at the plates.

"What's up?" Betty asked. "You look like I feel." She puffed harder and harder at her cigarette as Nell told her about the shuffling of PR projects. "What a louse!"

Nell shrugged. "Taplinger gets to call the shots."

"I was talking about the other guy. He should know how it feels to have primo movies pulled out from under him."

"What should I have said? 'Sorry you had to withstand all those banzai charges, but *Mildred Pierce* is mine.'"

"So it isn't just stars who are only as good as their last picture?" Betty leaned onto her elbows. "Can you imagine if *Confidential Agent* was my debut? My career would've been dead in the water. Thank God *The Big Sleep* is coming out before the public can get a whiff of this stinkeroo."

"Maybe *Christmas in Connecticut* will end up being bigger than *The Corn is Green* and *Pride of the Marines* combined!" Nell deadpanned. "Who'll have the last laugh then?"

The idea that Bette Davis's Welsh teacher and John Garfield's blind Marine could be outdone by a magazine writer impersonating a farm wife was preposterous. The two women burst out laughing.

Betty handed over the sandwich. "I'll take the broth, and we can share the milk."

Hungrier now than she realized, Nell accepted her offer. "This almost feels like the good old days when we were roommates."

"These current days ain't so bad." The playful smile of a

newlywed curled Betty's lips. "Bogie and I fit together like jigsaw puzzle pieces. We enjoy the same radio shows, dislike the same phonies, and laugh at the same absurdities. Last night I came home to a pile of books wrapped in bright red paper. He'd been at that bookstore you took me to that day you picked me up at Union Station."

"What did he buy for you?"

"*Brideshead Revisited, Four Quartets*, Ernie Pyle's *Brave Men*, and something about being nothing by Jean-Paul Sartre."

"Heady stuff. Will you read them?"

"Sure." The bell chimed from the radio on her vanity ahead of the one o'clock news. Betty raised the volume. "It might be a while till I get to Sartre."

"You're listening to KFWB, broadcasting to you from the Warner Brothers studios on Sunset Boulevard in Hollywood, California. Turning to the war first, information has reached us that US naval forces have lost their fifty-third submarine."

Nell met Betty's unblinking eyes.

"The exact location is unknown," the newsreader continued, "but estimates put it around the Ogasawara Islands, six hundred miles south of Tokyo. The US crew mounted a heroic fight, with Japanese losses far exceeding our own. We shall continue to keep listeners informed as further details come to hand. All we can confirm for now is the name of the downed submarine: the USS *Lanternfish*."

A gasp flew out of Nell.

That was Luke's sub. Or had been the last time she'd heard from him. But that had been six months ago. They could have reassigned him to a different one. Or re-stationed him at Pearl Harbor. He could be in a cab rushing to the studio this very minute to surprise her with news of a weeklong shore leave.

Betty took the plate from Nell's trembling fingers and deposited it on the side table. "Let's not get ahead of ourselves."

She was right. It was a preliminary report. And a sketchy one, at that.

But still.

Nell knew the name of only one US sub, and it had sunk to the bottom of the Pacific.

3

*A*n agonizing pulse throbbed the back of Luke's skull. He tried to open his eyes, but the light through the wafer-thin cracks between his eyelids was too bright. Too painful.

His hands had contracted into fists, the bedsheets twisted in his fingers. The taut skin stretched over his knuckles slackened as he let go.

He took in a deep breath. It didn't hurt, so that was good news.

Should I try opening my eyes again?

Gingerly, he parted his eyelids once more. The light that slipped in was stark and antiseptic, but bearable. Just.

Go on. A little bit more.

The mottled ceiling needed a fresh paint job.

Chatter surrounded him. Laughter. A Bronx cheer.

"Nurse!" somebody shouted. "NURSE!"

The chattering stopped.

Bandages encircled his head and left ear. He hurt all over, but mostly his left hand throbbed like a tom-tom.

"Warner Boy!" the voice bawled. "He's waking up!"

Warner Boy? That's me. He turned carefully to the right. *Sonar guy. What was his name?*

"Can you talk?"

Luke licked his lips. Rough as sandpaper. "Where am I?"

A new face hovered over him. Blonde hair. No lipstick. Professional smile. "You're on a hospital ship, Ensign, heading for Pearl Harbor. We passed Wake Island an hour ago. Soon we'll be waving at Johnston Atoll."

"Johnston? How long have I been out?"

"Three days. Got yourself one heck of a concussion. I expect you have a formidable headache?"

Luke nodded.

She laid a hand on his forearm. "It'll be monstrous for a while."

"Nurse Holden's leaving out the best bit!" Dipper piped up. "You're the hero of the *Lanternfish*."

The events of that night came tumbling back to him in a foggy jumble. "It didn't sink?"

"Sweet Jesus, it sank, all right. But not before twenty-eight men jumped clear."

More than half the crew. What a relief.

"Remember those POWs? Get this: a hundred thirty-nine of 'em were jammed into the hold like junkyard dogs. A hundred and nineteen of them survived. Because of you, Mr. Valenti."

Luke struggled to raise himself onto his elbows, but the effort was too much. "How do you figure?"

"We woulda sunk them Jap bastards, lock, stock, and geisha girls. But after you alerted the skipper, we only winged their *maru* so they couldn't go no place. Our deck guns held them off until the *Abbot* came charging in. All told, you saved a hundred forty-nine lives."

Luke's eyes glazed over at this news. "I was only doing my job."

"You went above and beyond."

"What about Sparky?" Luke asked. "He made it out okay, didn't he?"

A crushing silence followed.

"Sorry, Warner Boy." Dipper lowered his voice. "Spunky ol'

Sparky stayed at his post until the *Abbot* picked up his mayday. We never saw him again."

Luke closed his eyes. He could remember hearing Japanese voices in his earphones. *Gyorai,* torpedoes. *Horyo,* POWs. The "a-ooga" klaxon ringing through the sub. But what had been his last words to Sparky? Luke drew a blank. Even worse, he struggled to conjure Sparky's face.

"And what have we here?"

Captain Polk stood at Luke's bedside, flanked by a snowy-haired man in a white coat and a much younger guy in his thirties with a Catskills-comic smile. Luke tried again to hoist himself onto his elbows. The doctor pulled him forward and added an extra pillow, allowing Luke to sit up.

"We're mighty glad to see you awake, Ensign." Polk leaned on his metal walking stick.

"I hope you won't need that permanently, sir."

Polk's smile curdled. "I twisted my ankle. Nothing to write home about. But what about you? Feeling okay?"

He was alive, so that rated more than "okay," didn't it?

The doctor lifted Luke's left hand and cradled it in his. "How's this?"

A tight bandage encased his middle finger. "It hurts."

"Sharp pain or throb?"

The blood pulsed up Luke's finger. "Throb."

"You were bleeding from it when they hauled you aboard," Polk said. "Sorry, Valenti, but you've lost the top half."

Luke examined his swaddled finger more closely. It was distinctly shorter now. "How?"

"Stray bullet, most likely."

"Yeah!" Dipper said. "But you gave as good as you got. Jumped onto that .50 and fired away like you was at the O.K. Corral. Remember?"

Luke nodded, but he had no recollection of any of this.

"We've been joking about how you can't give anyone the

middle finger no more," Dipper continued. "Hey, Halloran, maybe that can be your headline."

The guy by Polk's side extended his hand. "Nate Halloran, stringer with the Associated Press. The Navy brass has given me full run of the ship to dig around for human-interest stuff." He fiddled with his striped bow tie. "And the hero of the *Lanternfish* is precisely what the doctor ordered."

The pounding at the base of Luke's scalp ratcheted up a notch.

"You'll be going home with one hell of a war record." Polk reached into the back pocket of his white trousers and withdrew a presentation box containing a heart-shaped medal hanging from a ribbon. "Ensign Valenti, I present this Purple Heart for your brave and decisive actions in the face of the enemy." Luke felt the heat of a furious blush redden his cheeks as Polk opened the box and placed the medal in his good hand. "I have reports to file, so I'll leave you to it."

Dipper waited until the captain had hobbled out of the ward. "Finally!" He was now holding up a Purple Heart of his own. "Polk was going to pin yours to your pillow, but we insisted he wait until you woke up." Luke looked around. Each of the men held their Purple Hearts aloft. "Welcome to the club, Warner Boy—uh, I mean Ensign Valenti, *sir*."

"Thanks, fellas." Luke ran a thumb over his medal. "A mighty fine club to be a member of."

Halloran dragged a chair from across the aisle. "And now it's my turn to interview the hero of the *Lanternfish*."

"You won't call me that in your article, will you?"

"Are you kidding?" Halloran flashed his unctuous smile again and faced the other patients. "Get a load of Mister Modesty here." He returned to Luke. "Let me explain. Victory was declared in Europe two months ago, right? Americans want this war to be over. We've got those Japs on the run now, but we need to bolster morale. My job is to provide the news services with feel-good stories."

Luke wasn't against being an uplifting story, but how many questions could he answer when he scarcely recalled anything from that night?

"The thing is, Valenti, Navy brass is hell-bent on the *Lanternfish* being the last downed sub of the war. No more losses, period. You're the guy who helped save a hundred fifty men, and that makes you a symbol of the coming end. Now, look." He lifted a note pad and pencil out of the breast pocket of his shirt. "You've woken up out of a coma, you've lost a finger, your captain's awarded you the Purple Heart. It's a lot to take in. I get it. But that's what'll make my article so poignant. Your thoughts, your impressions, your reflections—they'll be as real as it gets. Folks back home'll be reading about you in Kansas City, Spokane, and Detroit, thinking, 'I can make do reusing this morning's coffee grounds. I can stockpile my gas rations and walk to work. I can fill the hole in my shoe with newspapers until all the Luke Valentis out there can finish the job.'"

How was Luke supposed to say no to such a stirring speech, delivered like Halloran was Jimmy Stewart in a Frank Capra movie?

Luke lay back deeper into his pillows. "What do you want to know?"

Halloran licked the tip of his pencil. "First up, is there a special gal keeping the home fires burning for you?"

Luke pictured Nell sitting at her dining table with the *Times* or *Examiner*, squealing when she read his name. She wasn't the squealing type, but it wasn't every day her boyfriend got called "The hero of the *Lanternfish*."

"Her name is Nell Davenport," he said. "And she's a peach."

4

*N*ell checked her wristwatch. Not even ten a.m. yet. Plenty of time until Lieutenant Commander Whitley from the Navy's Radio and Motion Picture Liaison Office arrived to drive her to Long Beach for the big reunion.

Meanwhile, "The Girlfriend" reuniting with "The Hero" meant that her outfit needed to be feminine, but sensible. Flattering, but not showy. Appealing, but not vulgar.

After years of rationing, Nell had re-stitched, re-darned, re-patched, or re-dyed every last piece of her decent clothes. Desperation had been setting in until she'd had the ingenious idea of looting the wardrobe department. Costumes used for personal use was off-limits, but as her Costuming pal, Tristan, had pointed out, "We have seven thousand pieces in the women's section. Who's going to miss one little frock for a few hours?"

She pulled out a two-piece dark green suit with burgundy buttons. "What about this?"

Tristan looked up from a sapphire strapless cocktail dress he'd been debating over for Ann Sheridan in *Nora Prentiss*. "What does the label say?"

"Dvorak."

"You've got Ann's coloring, but it'll broaden you across the hips. And we can't have that. Not if there's a gaggle of photographers at the wharf."

Nell would have preferred a private reunion, but fat chance of that. Not with the *Lanternfish* hero. "Who should I be keeping an eye out for?"

"Glenda Farrell or Jane Wyman. Stay away from Ruby Keeler and Joan Blondell."

Nell continued flipping through ballgowns, honky-tonk dresses, and dowdy spinster-aunt shawls. Out of seven thousand choices, she was bound to find some outfit or other that would fit the bill—and her hips. She recognized an Eleanor Parker outfit from *Between Two Worlds*.

"Just the girl I'm looking for."

Nell turned to see Hoagy Carmichael in the doorway. She had first met him on the set of *To Have and Have Not*, and had ended up performing a song they had written together on a big Christmas broadcast. "For me? How come?"

"I did a week at the Rhythm Room, testing out new material, new orchestrations."

She pulled out a gaberdine suit of dark crimson with extra-wide white lapels. The collar read '*Wyman.*' "I wish I'd known."

"I do, too. On most nights, someone requested I play 'Every Fifth Word.'"

Nell held the dress to her waist. "Isn't that something?" Flaring the generous skirt, she called out to Tristan, "I think this'll work."

He needed only a quick glance. "You got hat, gloves, handbag, and shoes to match?"

"I do."

"In that case, it's perfect."

"I can see you're busy," Hoagy said.

"Luke's ship is due in at Long Beach this afternoon."

"I read about him in the papers. You must be beside yourself."

"Trying hard not to be." Yes. This Wyman suit was exactly

what she'd been looking for. "The Navy press officer warned me to expect a dockside madhouse."

"I want to plant a seed for you to think about."

Nell wondered if there were fitting rooms nearby. "What type of seed?"

"We should take 'Every Fifth Word' into the studio."

For the first time in over a week, all thoughts of Luke's arrival flew from Nell's mind. "A commercial recording?"

"Full orchestrations, twenty-piece orchestra, the whole nine yards. And you'll sing lead vocals."

"ME?!" The crimson suit almost slipped away. She caught it before it sagged to the floor. "Wouldn't you want Dinah Shore, or Betty Hutton, or even the Andrews Sisters?"

"That song became yours the moment we stepped on the Canteen stage."

"Oh, Hoagy, that's terribly flattering. Honest it is. But I'm not a professional singer—"

"You could be."

Professional?

He kissed her on the forehead. "Good luck this afternoon. I'll call you in a few days."

Nell's mouth was still gaping open when Hoagy disappeared through the exit.

***

"That's quite a fetching outfit you're wearing."

The neighborhoods past downtown slipped by Nell's window as the Buick—navy blue, naturally—headed south. The closer they drew, the more sharply her nerves clawed at her innards. Fortunately, Hoagy had provided her with an intoxicating diversion.

Hoagy Carmichael thinks I'm good enough for a professional record. With full orchestra. That people would plunk down cash for. To hear me sing. ME!

"Thank you. It's—" Nell smoothed out the skirt. *It's what? Stolen? Snuck out of Costuming? Illegally borrowed?* "I hope gabardine isn't too hot for this August weather."

Whitley was a pleasant-enough sort, with a broad, open face, and a head of thick black hair that reminded her of Luke's. She'd get to run her fingers through his soon. "Those ocean breezes will keep you cool."

I'll make it clear to Hoagy that if I don't cut the mustard, he's free to call Dinah. No hard feelings.

"Do you think there'll be many people at the dock?" she asked.

"Luke is one of three hundred and ninety-eight returning servicemen, so I'm expecting a considerable gathering to greet them. Plus press, photographers, and newsreels."

They passed a huge sign: LONG BEACH NAVAL SHIPYARD. "What if he can't see me?"

Whitley smiled at her a tad indulgently. "You let me worry about that."

* * *

They circumvented the public parking lot and headed into a smaller one signposted OFFICIAL VEHICLES ONLY. Nell didn't hear the cheering of the throngs and the oom-pah-pah of the Navy band until she swung open her car door. Brightly colored pennants hung from lamp posts and flags flapped in breezes fragrant with briny sea air.

A white hospital ship docked at the wharf possessed a single funnel displaying a huge red cross painted at its center and sported a matching red stripe running from bow to stern. Sailors jamming the main deck launched streamers to civilians—mostly women in their best Sunday hats—crowding the pier.

Whitley led her to a roped-off walkway that paralleled the water's edge and guided her toward a bank of newsreel cameras and press photographers.

Oh, boy. Here we go.

Nell had dreamed so long about this homecoming. How she would feel when she saw him. What his first words might be. The sound of his voice. Gathering him in her arms and pressing him close. Ever since Whitley had called her, she'd known this moment would play out in front of hundreds of people. But now she was here. So many faces looking at her, dozens of cameras pointing at her.

"What should I do?" she asked Whitley.

He prodded her shoulder so that she rotated to face the gaggle of press. "Smiling would be nice."

Easy for you to say. Your whole body isn't trembling worse than a shrinking violet at her first formal ball.

"Nell! Hey, Nell!"

I know that voice!

She should've expected Fox Movietone News would be here. Thank heavens it was good ol' reliable Reggie Bloom. She rushed over to him. It had been his footage in Colorado that had helped Nell track Luke down. What a relief to see a familiar face among feverish wives, mothers, and girlfriends.

"How are you feeling?" he asked.

"Overwhelmed would be an understatement."

"Can you do me a favor?"

"Anything."

"Step back about ten feet. Keep your right foot forward, and angle your body to the left. Not too far, otherwise it'll look awkward."

"Who are you?" she asked, breaking the tension with a laugh. "John Huston?"

"Trust your Uncle Reggie. You'll be slimmer for the camera." She followed his directions. "And . . . wave."

Three deafening blasts boomed from the ship's horn. Whitley touched her elbow. "The men are ready to disembark."

A gate opened at the top of the gangplank. Nell raised her

hand, shielding her eyes from the sun. A sailor in a chambray shirt and white Dixie cup hat steered a wheelchair down the ramp. His charge wore Navy-issue khaki. His garrison cap sat a little crooked, off to the side and back. She could see the whites of his teeth as he smiled through his dark, bushy beard.

Whitley stepped closer. "I put in a request for the hero of the *Lanternfish* to be the first one off—"

Nell bolted ahead. Etiquette be damned. Protocol be damned. Decorum be damned. Luke was in a wheelchair. Had he been badly injured? Could he not even walk anymore?

"Luke!" she called. "LUKE!"

His head shot up when he heard her voice. He waved, then spoke to his escort, who bent over to listen.

She reached the end of the gangplank seconds ahead of him. He slung his white canvas seabag aside as he struggled to his feet. The gold insignia pinned to his cap glinted in the sunshine. He looked so thin. His khaki uniform, creased and baggy, seemed to engulf him, and the garrison cap was slipping off his head. A thick bandage swaddled the middle finger of his left hand. His eyes had lost their sparkle. After everything he'd been through, she should have guessed they might.

"Come here," he said to her. His hands felt sandpaper rough, but warm and dry. That beard! Tears she hadn't been aware of blurred his face.

"Your wheelchair! I got such a fright!"

He brushed away a lock of her hair. "It's the concussion. I'm still not fully recovered, so it's Navy regulations." His voice quivered like a hummingbird. But she would have known it anywhere.

"So you can stand? And walk?"

"And run and dance. But we'll leave the singing up to you."

Oh! There was so much to tell him! She brushed her fingers against his beard. "What's all this?"

"With no women around to impress, daily grooming falls by the wayside."

She nodded. "The Navy has booked you a hotel."

"Just me? Or us?"

She gave that awful wild beard a gentle tug. "Someone needs to shave you."

As sailors streamed off the boat, she stared into his soulful hazel eyes until she could no longer keep herself so far from him. Not when six inches felt like six miles. She hurled herself at him again, wrapped her arms around him, and pressed her lips to his. He tasted of salt, smelled of starch.

He'd come home to her at last.

At long last.

5

Luke burrowed deeper into his bed at the Biltmore Hotel. So soft. So comfortable. Or was it a regular mattress with ordinary sheets and he'd become used to Navy bunks that were sometimes firm, sometimes saggy, but rarely exactly right? He breathed in the bedsheet's subtle lavender scent. Who, exactly, was paying for this plush suite?

Nell's eyelids fluttered, her breathing slow and steady.

Yesterday at Terminal Island. Good God, what a circus! Newsreel cameras, press photographers, all those reporters calling his name. He now knew how it felt to be as famous as Bogie. Without Whitley from the Navy press office taking charge, he might still have been stammering answers to their endless questions. The minute he'd flopped onto the Buick's back seat, he had asked if they could stop at Simon's Drive-in at Wilshire and Fairfax, where he'd chowed down on a double order of everything as Nell caught him up on the last three years: her promotion to PR, shepherding Bogie and his new love toward matrimony, writing and performing that "Every Fifth Word" song, which she would soon record with Hoagy Carmichael.

The raw throbbing at the back of his skull abated if he lay on his left side. It also allowed him to drink her in some more. What a cute little nose she had. Why hadn't he noticed it before?

The schedule stretching ahead of them was almost too much to contemplate. His mind wandered farther into the future.

All this "the hero of the *Lanternfish*" commotion would be over in a week or two. Where would he be then? Did Bogie still have a job for him?

Did he even need it? His thoughts flew to his inheritance. All thirty-one thousand nine hundred and eighty-eight bucks of it. The staggering amount had been too overwhelming to think about when he'd first learned of it, so he'd pushed it from his mind. Easy to accomplish out at sea with no idea when he'd get home. Or if. That New York lawyer had told him it'd be a while until the courts had processed his grandfather's estate. How long was "a while"? One month? Six? A year?

Nell yawned and opened her eyes. "I can't believe you're back." She sandwiched the palm of his left hand between her warm fingers. "Your missing finger—does it hurt?"

"The missing bit doesn't."

A girlish giggle bubbled out of her. What a tonic it was to hear again. He'd never get sick of that sound.

"The doctor who stitched me up said the pain will subside, but it'll take time. Compared to Tony, I have no cause to complain."

"He wanted to be there yesterday, but he's got his hands full with our Cole Porter biopic."

"Hands full? Doing what?"

A flicker of confusion clouding Nell's face gave way to a you'd-better-brace-yourself grin. "Your brother works in Hair and Makeup."

The concussion throbbed even harder. Would it ever give him a break? "Tony? The roofer who enjoys an ugly-drunk bar fight more than he ought to? He's now working at Warner Brothers? In *Hair and Makeup?*"

"Did you know he fixes Audrey's hair?"

Luke pictured Tony's wife, the envy of Bensonhurst housewives with those elaborate hairdos that he'd always assumed had taken her hours to complete. All this time it had been Tony?

"Oh, and that's another thing. Audrey and Carol live out here now."

"They left Brooklyn? Jesus! Anything else?"

"Yes. Avery Osterhaus."

"My uncle? What's he done?"

"Gone legit. Works at Warners, too, painting backdrops. He's been helpful for your brother. After losing his leg like that, it took Tony ages to come good again. But now he and Avery are pals. Everything's rosy all round."

Luke massaged the base of his middle finger. Sometimes it helped with the pain. But not today.

"But enough of everyone else." Nell raked her nails through Luke's hair. "Ensign Valenti, I have questions."

He pulled her closer until she wrapped her naked body around his. How many times had he lain on a bunk and dreamed of this? "It's Lieutenant Junior Grade Valenti now."

"A promotion?"

"Halfway between Pearl Harbor and here." Luke leaned in for a long, tender kiss. "Just so that you know, I plan on wearing those lips down to nubs." He settled back into the pillows. "Okay. Shoot."

"Montauk, Boulder, Sea of Japan. Fill in the blanks."

Montauk's wide, wind-swept beaches conjured themselves in Luke's mind. Untamed expanses of North Atlantic. Clumps of pungent seaweed. The lone lighthouse. What a halcyon time it had been.

"Montauk was everything I hoped. It was long hours, and I was often alone, sometimes all night, but I didn't care. We were doing important work monitoring German communications, trying to break their codes. But every time we did, they'd realize it and switch to a new one. Boom. We're back to square one. Working as a crippie was thrilling."

"Crippie?"

"Slang for cryptanalyst."

"So you were the right man for the right job at the right time in the right place."

"I guess so."

"I know so."

"Anyway, one of the chaps wanted me to quiz him on his vocabulary. He'd applied for the Navy's language center in Colorado and was finding it tough going because Japanese is—" Luke whistled "—it may as well be from another planet."

"But," Nell interrupted, "your photographic memory soaked it all up. In the end, he threw in the towel, and you were the one sent to Boulder."

"That's pretty much it, yes."

"Which is where you met Reggie Bloom."

"You know Reggie?"

"Your newsreel ran ahead of *Heaven Can Wait*. Tristan and I nearly leapt out of our seats. He got me into Fox, where I tracked down the guy who shot the footage." She unleashed those enchanting giggles he used to replay in his mind as he drifted off to sleep. "Did you see Reggie at the dock yesterday?"

"Yesterday was . . . a lot."

"In that case, you'll need to brace yourself for what's coming up today."

Oh, yes. The parade. Couldn't he skip it?

Luke had started on his second cheeseburger when Whitley had laid out today's agenda. Marching bands, girl scouts, returned veterans, and anyone they could conscript to troop along Broadway to City Hall for speeches and a ceremony. And who would be sitting in a convertible, waving at the crowds as he brought up the rear? Ugh. As if his skull-cracking headache wasn't bad enough already.

"Tell me"—Nell's voice was softer now—"what's a sparky? You kept repeating it in your sleep, saying it over and over."

"The Navy is big on nicknames. The radio operators are always called Sparky. They put me in with him so that I could test some new equipment. He was a real nice guy."

At least, from what Luke could remember. He could recall boarding the *Lanternfish* in Pearl Harbor. And the day-to-day grind as they sailed toward Japan. Most of the names and faces of his fellow crewmembers. The bunks—too soft. The biscuits—too hard. The bathrooms—too communal. He could recall the funny incidents, the ribald humor. But the closer he got to the sinking, the less he could recall.

"What was his actual name?"

Luke would have given anything to be able to answer, but his memories had huge, yawning gaps. It wasn't a short name. Lawrence? Jeremiah? Anderson? Sparky's name would come to him one day. Hopefully.

Knuckles rapped on the door. "ROOM SERVICE!"

"You ordered breakfast?" Luke asked Nell.

"I suspect Whitley did. That guy thinks of everything."

Luke scooped up the bathrobe draped over the foot of the bed and went to open the door. "I hope they have marmalade. Only once in a blue moon did the Navy—"

"Surprise!"

Bogie stood behind a chrome cart laden with enough food to fuel the entire crew of the *Lanternfish*. A stunning young woman with wavy hair and flashing eyes hovered next to him. He wished he could see colors because this looker would be even more alluring.

Luke stepped aside to let them into the room before Bogie pulled him into a bear hug.

"I can't tell you how this warms my heart." Emotion choked Bogie's words. "Safe and sound, healthy and intact."

Luke held up his left hand. "Almost."

"Christ almighty, Valenti. A few inches over and—yikes."

The shock of seeing Bogie had intensified the pounding in Luke's skull, but he wasn't about to let it spoil this moment. "I've been luckier than a four-leaf clover growing out of a rabbit's foot surrounded by a horseshoe."

"You're not the only one." Bogie clapped a hand to Luke's back. "Allow me to introduce the best thing that's ever happened to me."

The knockout flashed her vivid eyes. "Outside of a single malt Scotch whiskey, that is."

"This, Luke, is my wife, Lauren Bacall."

"Terrific to finally meet you," she purred. "But I'm only Lauren Bacall for business purposes. I'm really just Betty from Brooklyn."

Nell greeted the pair and then announced that the party from the mayor's office was due at ten, and seeing as how it was nearly nine, they should eat while they could. They drew up four chairs around the room's little dining table and dug in.

An hour later, another knock interrupted the convivial session of "And then what happened?"

When Luke opened the door, he found Lieutenant Commander Whitley alongside a rotund gent with a beer belly and a whiskey nose. Whitley introduced Luke to Mr. Ackerman, the head of the Los Angeles Chamber of Commerce and the usual phalanx of flunkies, and the two men stepped into the room.

"We know who these two fine people are," Ackerman said, winking at Bogie and Bacall, "but who's this young lady?"

Luke gulped. It was unacceptably improper for an unmarried couple to spend the night together, especially when one-half of that couple was about to get a parade. They should have dreamed up a cover story.

Nell stepped forward, confident as a cheerleader. "Pleased to make your acquaintance, Mr. Ackerman. Nell Davenport, with the Warner Brothers' PR office. I'm here to—to—"

"I think the word you're groping for is 'nursemaid.'" Bogie

nudged Ackerman. "You know us actors. Can't be trusted out of our cages for a minute."

Introductions taken care of, Ackerman outlined their plans for the day ahead.

"The parade kicks off at eleven. It'll take about an hour to get to City Hall, where Mayor Bowron will be waiting to present you with a key to the city."

Luke's gaze drifted through the tall windows overlooking Pershing Square, where a shuttered booth stood among the shrubs. A weathered sign read BUY WAR BONDS HERE! DO YOUR PART! BE A PATRIOT! My part was more dicey than I bargained for, he thought, but I got through it. Can't I just get back to my regular life?

"Did you hear that, Luke?" Nell asked. "The key to the city!"

He plastered a smile on his face. "That sure is something."

"Excuse us a moment." Bogie hauled Luke into the bathroom and kicked the door shut behind them. "I can read you like a billboard. You were the only Jap speaker on that boat. If you hadn't alerted the skipper that torpedoes were on the way, the loss of life would have been much higher."

Luke found he couldn't meet Bogie's eyes. "Half the crew lost their lives. All I lost was half a finger. It just doesn't seem right that I'm the one getting a parade."

Bogie leaned against the wall, pretending to be low-key and casual, but Luke could tell it was window dressing. "All this hubbub today isn't about you. It's for the mothers and fathers, the wives and girlfriends who'll never get to hug their boys, or attend their weddings, or wrap their Christmas presents. You're standing in for all those guys. You joined the Navy to defend your country, and you rose to the occasion in ways none of us ever imagined. I'm so proud of you I could bust apart at the seams."

Luke took in Bogie's earnest expression. "No fooling?"

"When you left us, you were still a goggle-eyed kid. But now you've seen life and faced death." He grasped Luke's hand, being careful not to jostle the bandaged finger, and raised it in front of their faces. "And you've got the war wound to prove it."

"Jesus, Bogie. Who wrote that speech for you? The Epstein brothers?"

Bogie landed a playful slap to Luke's shoulder. "This parade will go faster if you enjoy it."

* * *

The black visor on Luke's service dress cap shielded his face from the unrelenting summer sun. Whitley sat up front alongside the assigned driver.

Bogie's advice—*It'll go faster if you enjoy it*—bounced around Luke's skull as they pulled out of the parking lot at the southern end of downtown. By the time the Packard had reached Twenty-Fifth Street, the doubts plaguing him like belligerent vultures had scattered, chased away by the cheers roaring from Bogie's mothers, fathers, wives, and girlfriends. They called out his name and yelled "Bravo!" and "Welcome home!" over the Naval Academy Band's "Fairest of the Fair" and "Hands Across the Sea."

Bogie was even more on the money than he knew, Luke realized. It was a downright honor to be the person these people looked to for comfort and reassurance. Okay, sure, he'd be enjoying this if he weren't suffering from such a wearying, pernicious headache and a half-finger that burned white hot. But the Navy chose you, Lieutenant Valenti, so do your job and wave until your arm drops off.

Luke spotted a little girl out front of the United Artists Theatre dressed in a starched white dress and waving her American flag for all she was worth. With her board-straight hair and gleeful eyes, the little dickens was a miniature Nell.

Bogie's voice rang in his ears. *I'm so proud of you I could bust apart at the seams.* Was Nell proud of him, too? He hoped so. What about his family back in Brooklyn? Had he done something they could brag about to their friends and neighbors?

As the car passed the little girl, Luke noticed she was standing in front of her father, who had the sun-ripened face and crewcut sandy hair of a freshly discharged sailor. Luke couldn't picture Sparky, hear his voice, or recall a single detail about him, but earlier that morning, a glimmer had flashed through Luke's mind. However, this was neither the time nor place to ruminate on that. He had a job to do. Forget the throbbing pain. Forget the burning finger. Hey Sparky, this one's for you.

Luke's convertible pulled up outside City Hall, where officials had set up a stage adorned with red, white, and blue bunting. A high-school marching band caterwauled an unrecognizable tune as Luke approached the dais where the mayor stood, a camera-ready beam propping up his sagging face.

With his thinning gray hair and rimless glasses, Fletcher Bowron resembled everybody's grandpa, fresh from a folksy Norman Rockwell painting. After vigorously shaking Luke's hand, he positioned himself at the microphones and motioned for the bandleader to wind down his melody.

"Ladies and gentlemen, boys and girls, honored guests, and my fellow Angelenos, welcome to this afternoon's stirring ceremony."

As the mayor yammered through his speech, Luke scanned the throng. Bogie and Betty had taken off after everybody exited the hotel, reluctant to steal his thunder. Nell had assured him she'd catch up with him at City Hall, but neither of them had counted on there being several thousand people to wade through. Spotting her was like trying to locate a buoy in a hundred square miles of ocean, so he gave up searching.

"In closing"—Bowron took a box covered in blue velvet from a hovering assistant—"I have the boundless pleasure of awarding Lieutenant Junior Grade Luke Valenti this key to the city of Los Angeles." He flipped open the lid and passed the box to Luke.

A ten-inch brass key glowed in the sunshine. Its head featured the official LA city seal bookended with angels; a miniature replica of City Hall filled the tip. It wouldn't unlock anything, but it was, nevertheless, an impressive piece of hardware. Luke held it up to the audience and hollered into the microphones how grateful he was for this inspiring honor. But where would he put it? He had no home.

"And now we have a surprise for our esteemed guest." Bowron took an abrupt step back to make way for a new, yet familiar face.

Luke had first met Captain Keaton Vance in the boardinghouse Luke had lived in before the war. Vance had been the occasional overnight visitor of his neighbor, Beatrice. It had been Tristan who had dubbed the strapping career naval officer Captain Stamina.

Luke snapped to attention and saluted.

Vance smiled as he returned the salute. "At ease, Lieutenant."

"It's good to see you, Captain."

"Likewise." Vance tapped on the sleeve of his dark-blue, double-breasted dress uniform. A thick gold band had replaced the four half-inch stripes of a captain.

Luke saluted again. "Congratulations, Commodore."

Vance pivoted to face the microphones.

"Due to his superior language skills during the July thirteenth attack by Japanese forces on the USS *Lanternfish*, then-Ensign Valenti determined his submarine was facing imminent attack while also discerning that the enemy ship held a large number of Allied prisoners of war. His quick thinking saved one hundred and forty-nine lives that night, and so for distinguished devotion to duty, extraordinary courage, and disregard for his own personal safety, it is my deep honor to present you the Navy Cross."

Luke staggered half a step backward. The medal—a gold cross with a sailing ship at its center—was the Navy's second-highest valor award, presented only to sailors who had distinguished themselves during combat. The Purple Heart had been one thing. Everyone who'd suffered injury during action got one.

Thousands of people cheered their appreciation as Vance pinned the medal to his chest next to his Purple Heart, Pacific Theater and victory ribbons, and the submarine combat pin, then offered a firm congratulatory handshake.

Bowron's assistant steered Luke away from the podium, and Mayor Bowron introduced Archbishop Cantwell, who trumpeted a fervent blessing for the war dead, "to commemorate the lieutenant's gallant shipmates and martyred POWs who made the return voyage to our Heavenly Father the night the *Lanternfish* was sunk."

As Luke stood off to the side of the dais, the mayor's assistant pointed to a line of two dozen uniformed men. "There's just one more thing to ask before you depart. We'd like to give you the opportunity to greet those men."

Many of them were as skinny as bamboo, and looked as though they'd been dribbled into careworn, poorly fitted uniforms cobbled together from the racks at Western Costume. More than one or two of them tottered from the strain of standing at attention.

"You should know," the assistant said, "each one of them requested to be here today."

"Who are they?" Luke asked.

"Some of the POWs from the Japanese merchant ship."

A strangled cry caught in Luke's throat. That explained the anguish haunting each hollowed-out face.

"They want to thank you personally for saving their lives."

"They deserve the Navy Cross, not me." Luke could barely raise his voice above a whisper. "What do I even say to them?"

The assistant prodded Luke toward the line-up. "Anything to help them regain their humanity." He pried the two velvet boxes from Luke's grip as they approached.

"Hello, there." Luke felt the bones poking through the blistered skin of the man's offered hand. "Very glad to meet you."

6

*N*ell sauntered into the Bogarts' kitchen, wondering if a substantial breakfast like the one Bogie was wolfing down would settle her nerves or aggravate them. Would scrambled eggs, French toast, silver-dollar pancakes, half a grilled tomato, half a grapefruit, and a gallon of coffee fortify her? Or weigh her down?

The big day had dawned. In a few hours, she would be recording "Every Fifth Word" with the twenty-piece orchestra Hoagy had promised.

There's no reason to be nervous. He's rehearsed the arrangement with you over and over. All you have to do is stand there and sing. She slid into the breakfast nook. *Yeah. Easy as pie.*

Betty was still grinding through *Confidential Agent*, but Bogie wasn't filming anything, and Luke had no job at all. Did any of them remember what was happening today?

Bogie was the first to look up. "Coffee?" She nodded. "You're looking a mite peaked," he said, filling her cup.

"You are, at that," Betty said. "Didn't sleep well?"

"Just a busy day ahead, is all." Nell splashed cream into her cup. Now that she was sitting next to Bogie's full plate, all that food seemed like a terrible idea. "I've struggled to talk *Women's Day* into an interview with Tony."

With Betty now living with Bogie above the Sunset Strip, Nell had their Beverly Hills apartment to herself. Luke couldn't move in since he and Nell weren't married, so he'd taken up the Bogarts' offer to live in their guesthouse.

"Why him?" Bogie asked.

"He loses a leg at Guadalcanal and ends up showing John Garfield how to use two rifles, a .45, and a machine gun on a tripod in *Pride of the Marines* while also working in Hair and Makeup. I figure it would interest their readers."

"Especially seeing as how Garfield is one big slab o' stud," Betty said with a wink.

Are none of them going to ask how I'm feeling about today? "But I'm having the devil of a time convincing them."

"You should tell them that Tony is the brother of the *Lanternfish* hero," Bogie said. "Between those newsreels heralding his return, and newspapers covering his City Hall ceremony, a guy can't go ten minutes without seeing this goober's mug." He showed them a page from his *L.A. Times.* "Luke's parade was a week ago, and they're still taking about it."

Luke read the article's headline—*SUBMARINE HERO'S LEGACY FOR FREED POWs*—as he massaged his wounded finger. She often caught him rubbing his thumb up and down what was left of it. "I thought your boss took you off *Pride of the Marines.*"

"He did," Nell admitted. "But I'd been pitching the idea at them long before Bryant the Bore rode into town."

Betty looked up from her *Life* magazine. "He's a bore?"

"He's forever talking about carrying that damned flag up Suribachi. Its weight, its shape, the terrain, his boots, the weather, handing it over to his CO. I know it was a big deal, and he was part of history, and all, but jeez, bub, give it a rest."

Her conscience panged with guilt for criticizing a Marine

who'd survived the nightmare Iwo Jima had been. She sympathized with what he must have endured. But he told the same story again and again, obsessing over ever-more infinitesimal details. Yesterday it had been the texture of the sand halfway up the hill.

"Come on, Davenport." Betty plucked a silver-dollar pancake off Bogie's plate. "We should be going. You boys behave yourselves."

Nell planted a kiss on Luke's cheek. She received a smile in return, but she could tell it took some effort.

* * *

Nell flicked the *Women's Day* editor's business card across her nails. Would he change his mind if she told him who Tony's brother was? Tony's experiences should be enough to make a compelling story. But a connection with the hero of the *Lanternfish* might goad the editor over the line—even if *Pride of the Marines* was no longer one of her babies.

She snuck a glance at Buzz. There he was, staring vacantly into the rafters. Again. She had noticed Luke's face taking on the same blankness every now and then. *Don't ask*, that faraway look seemed to say. *Leave me with my thoughts.*

The office clock glared at Nell. It's nearly noon, Miss Davenport. In an hour, you'll be standing in front of a microphone. Isn't it time you started getting nervous?

She told the clock to shut up and picked up the telephone. If this "hero of the *Lanternfish*" angle didn't work, she'd give up.

* * *

She dropped the receiver in its cradle. "I'll be damned!"

"You will?" The question came from Taplinger's secretary, Paisley, who had parked herself at Nell's desk.

"*Woman's Day* agreed to a story I pitched for *Pride of the Marines*."

"Weren't you taken off that picture?"

"Yes, but—" Nell tilted her head toward Buzz, still lost in his personal Never-Never Land.

"Taplinger just shrugs and says, 'It was Iwo Jima.'"

The two women watched him for what was longer than polite until Nell said, "Does Taplinger want to see me?"

"No. You were on the phone, so Hoagy Carmichael called me instead to let you know that recording the *Mildred Pierce* score has run into difficulties and that the studio won't be free until four o'clock."

What a relief. She wouldn't need to get nervous for another couple of hours. Meanwhile, she now had time to break the news to Tony.

When she walked into the makeup department, she found him working on Alexis Smith and Joan Leslie for *Rhapsody in Blue* publicity photos. "I have exciting news!"

"For me?" Alexis asked. "Or Joan?"

"For your makeup artist."

Tony looked up from his row of powder puffs. "Me?"

An incredulous smile blossomed across his face as she filled him in on her magazine pitch. But the whole time she was laying out what Tony could expect during his *Women's Day* interview, Alexis and Joan were giggling worse than a pair of high schoolers.

Nell crossed her arms. "Spill it, you two."

They looked at Tony, who brushed powder from his hands. "To tell you would spoil the surprise."

"I don't particularly enjoy surprises." Strictly speaking, that wasn't true, but it felt like the mean girls were taunting her again in the McKinley Elementary School playground.

"Okay, fine, but you didn't hear it from me." Tony ran a brush through Alexis's hair. "This afternoon, when you're recording that song, you'll have a rah-rah-rah squad to boost your spirits."

"Made up of who?"

"Humphrey Bogart, Betty Bacall, and your very own personal war hero."

Those rotten little sons of bitches, sitting at the breakfast table, acting as though nothing was going on.

"Luke and Bogie have been hanging around Betty's dressing room until she finishes filming," Tony said. "I helped with her hair this morning. She said she should be done by lunchtime."

He went to continue, but Nell was already gone.

* * *

She thrust open the door to Betty's dressing room. "YOU DIRTY SKUNKS!"

Bogie's right hand froze in mid-air, a cigarette lighter gripped between his fingers. Luke stood at Betty's basin trying to rub out a stain on the cuff of his khaki shirt. "We were waiting for Betty to finish her scene," he told her, "and then we were planning to tippy-toe over to surprise you." He dried his hands and squeezed her shoulders. "I figured you could do with a cheer squad."

"You rats let me stew through breakfast thinking you'd all forgotten."

"Yeah, yeah, we're a bunch of stinkers," Bogie said. "You nervous?"

"Somewhere between 'clammy hands' and 'breaking out in hives.'"

"Would a slug of that help?" Bogie side-eyed a bottle of Four Roses sitting on Betty's vanity.

They were soon clinking shot glasses.

"To our little songbird," Bogie said.

The bourbon burned Nell's throat, but if she gave it a second or two, a warming backwash would—ah, there it was. "I've managed—barely—to keep my jitters in check all morning, but—"

A long, uninterrupted blast from a car horn cut through the air. Another one joined it. Then a third.

They scrambled onto the balcony of the star dressing rooms building. Below them, a cluster of secretaries clung onto each other, letting out joyful whoops. Four women in matching diner waitress costumes of white dresses and yellow aprons held hands as they skipped along, chiming out the same five-word phrase, but the chorus of screaming klaxons, pealing bells, and humming kazoos drowned them out.

Nell, Luke, and Bogie dashed down the stairs and stopped the first person to cross their path. It was Don, one of the montage editors who had worked on *Casablanca*. "Haven't you heard?" he asked. "Truman's been on the radio. The Japs have surrendered! Unconditionally!"

"It's official?" Nell cried out.

"They haven't signed on the dotted line, but yes—this lousy doggone war is OVER!" Unable to contain himself any longer, he screamed out that last word as he melted into the swelling crowd.

Relief washed over Nell as she, Bogie, and Luke clutched their hands into a bunch the size of a pineapple. She let the tears drip down her face. The moment she had longed for—that everybody had longed for—had arrived at last. Oddly, she felt ill-prepared.

A gang of crew members emerged from the *Night and Day* soundstage, cheering and waving handkerchiefs. Bogie yelled, "STAGE SEVEN!"

They negotiated an obstacle course of jubilant revelers throwing confetti, streamers, hats, office memos, and script pages until they raced onto a living room set filled with unbridled pandemonium every bit as tumultuous as the uproar outside. Cast and crew alike were hugging and crying, dancing and hollering, "It's over! It's all over!"

"Betty?" Bogie's voice harpooned through the commotion.

A hand waved above bobbing heads. "Over here!" They jostled through the crowd until they reached her. "Can you believe it?" Betty was still dressed in her *Confidential Agent* costume—white blouse with small black polka dots, matching skirt, and in full filming makeup. "I've been working my way up to our big emotional scene, but of course that went out the window!"

They threw themselves into a group hug and held on tight until someone switched on a radio.

"This is KFWB broadcasting live from the corner of Hollywood and Vine, where Carmen Miranda is wowing the crowds with an impromptu concert from the backseat of some lucky driver's convertible."

Loud crackles and splutters filled the speaker before Miranda's unmistakable voice sang the opening verse to "Happy Days are Here Again." As she chirped about the skies being clear and songs of cheer, electricians joined sound editors, script girls and costumers embraced assistant directors and costumed extras.

In among the mayhem, Nell watched unalloyed joy and relief peppering Luke's face. Maybe his restlessness and distracted moods had been a natural process of re-adjustment. With the Japs surrendering and Carmen warbling the perfect song for this precise moment, Nell threw herself into the celebrations and sang along in the loudest voice of all.

7

Luke hadn't been in the taxicab more than a minute or two before the driver asked him the question he was asked most often: "So, buddy, where'd you serve?" A nebulous response like "The Pacific" was never enough. People wanted places, ships, service, rank, training.

Their curiosity was understandable. He hadn't mustered out yet, so he was always in uniform, especially now that the brass had seen fit to promote him to full lieutenant. Whitley had hinted that he wasn't likely to receive his discharge papers as long as the Navy had use for the *Lanternfish* hero.

"In the stretches of empty ocean between Pearl Harbor and the Japanese Home Islands," Luke replied.

"No kiddin'?" The doughy driver with the thick glasses turned left onto Sunset Boulevard. "I got me the worst peepers in the world; otherwise, I woulda signed up to the Navy the same day them Jap bastards rained hellfire on us. What did you sail on?"

Luke was thankful that this wasn't a long taxi ride because they were only two questions away from the guy recognizing him. "Submarines."

"You a bubblehead, huh? Ain't that su'um. I don't know that I could stand being cooped up in one of them tin pipes. Not without going crackers, anyways."

This fellow was at least fifty pounds too large to have been in the submarine service. With so little elbow room, the Navy preferred the lithe and sinewy. "How long till we get to Breneman's?"

"You're not the usual type o' passenger I take to Breneman's this time o' the morning. Dowdy housewives and middle-aged spinsters—they're the ones who listen to *Breakfast in Hollywood.*"

Apprehension over his first radio appearance had robbed Luke of a restful night's sleep and had encouraged a third cup of coffee. It might have been nice of Whitley to mention he'd be facing an easy-to-please audience of housewives and spinsters. Maybe this wouldn't be such a nerve-wracker, after all.

"There'll be nobody under forty. Guaranteed," the cab driver said. "Can't vouch for their ten million listeners, though."

Luke gripped the arm rest. "Ten *million?*" What else had Whitley failed to mention?

"It's the biggest morning live broadcast in the country." The driver braked at a red light out front of Hollywood High and eyed Luke in his rearview mirror. "You're who I think you are, ain't you?"

And here it comes. "I'm not sure—"

"You got the key to the city from Bowron and the Navy Cross from some admiral. The hero of the *Lanternfish* is riding in my cab. Wait till I tell the missus tonight. She won't believe it!"

The lights changed to green, but the driver was too distracted to notice.

"I have to be at the studio by seven."

He wished he could dodge these sorts of encounters. Everybody wanted to hear the experience he recalled so little about. Most of the time he escaped with generalities, which was what he spouted to his excited cab driver now. But he was going to be interviewed by a professional. The hair along his forearms rose in clammy waves the closer they grew to the Vine Street restaurant, where Tom Breneman broadcast to—gulp—ten million people.

* * *

Breneman, a man with a genial face and a well-fed waistline, declared, "So glad to have you aboard, Lieutenant." He peered at the Purple Heart and Navy Cross standing out among the ribbons on Luke's jacket. "Do you have your key to the city? When I asked you to bring it along, you probably wondered, 'How can I do a show-and-tell on the radio?' but it'll impress the old ducks in the studio audience. They'll ooh and aah, which our sound guys'll pick up, so it adds atmosphere."

"I'll keep that in mind. Anything else I need to be aware of?"

Breneman checked his dark-blue necktie in a nearby mirror. "Be yourself. Have fun. Call me Tom or Mr. B. Your choice. Oh, and I know how you salty sea dogs cuss as often as you blink, but this is a live broadcast, so you'll have to can the swearing for the next ten minutes."

* * *

Luke paced the backstage area as Breneman greeted his studio audience and radio listeners with lighthearted banter. After running through a smattering of current affairs, his tone turned serious.

"Now listen, folks"—he lowered his voice to a more resonant timbre—"normally, we let fly with more gags than a Marx Brothers convention. But today is different. In a few hours' time, Fleet Admiral Chester Nimitz and General Douglas MacArthur and their Japanese counterparts will sign the official terms of surrender!"

He paused as the audience broke into thunderous applause.

"For such a history-making day as this, I've invited someone who has witnessed the horrors of the enemy first-hand—and triumphed over them. You might have seen him in your newspaper or in newsreels when he was the central figure of a grand ceremony at LA City Hall. Let's give a big, warm *Breakfast in Hollywood* welcome to the hero of the *Lanternfish*, Lieutenant Luke Valenti!"

Luke walked on stage expecting to be blinded by the blazing lights he'd grown used to in film production. But the lighting was surprisingly low-key; he remembered that, on radio, looks counted for nothing. It was all about the sound. He looked around. The restaurant accommodated around eighty women, all of them well north of the forty-year cut-off his cab driver had predicted. They gazed up at him, maternal smiles lodged on their faces.

"Welcome, Lieutenant!" Breneman jostled Luke closer to the microphone.

"Thank you, Mr. B. This is my first radio appearance, so I'd also like to thank your audience for their hospitable reception. It's helped make me a little less jittery."

"Get a load of that, ladies," Breneman addressed his flock of housewives. "The hero of the *Lanternfish* is nervous about getting up in front of us. I tell you, the modesty of this guy—it warms the cockles of our hearts, doesn't it?" An approving round of applause spread through the crowd. "Now, Lieutenant, you were aboard what was destined to be the last sub of the war to be lost when your boat engaged two Japanese vessels." He faced the sea of gray hair and strands of pearls. "This is where it gets dire, folks. You," he said, addressing Luke again, "were on duty when it became apparent the enemy was hiding a sub of its own."

"I was."

"And subs are armed with torpedoes, aren't they?"

"That's right."

"Which you learned when they . . ." Breneman gestured with a circular motion.

Oops. I'm not talking enough. "When I heard the Japanese word for 'torpedo.' We did our best to prepare, but we had very little time. One of them missed, but the other one took out a bow plane, which hampered our ability to move up and down."

"But you could still go forward?"

"Oh, yes. Undaunted, we plunged into the fray."

"That must have been frightening, Lieutenant."

"Our job was to engage the enemy. Retreat was not an option."

"So you forged ahead with no regard for your own personal safety?"

"We needed to fire on them before they fired on us. And we would've except that I heard the Japanese talking about how they were holding a hundred thirty-nine POWs in the hull amidships."

Breneman turned to his hushed audience. "So hitting the Jap sub would have meant drowning them."

"Exactly right. So instead of sinking the *maru*, our tactic was to cripple it."

"A trickier maneuver, no?"

"Far more difficult, but so many lives hung in the balance."

"So then you fired on them?"

"We fired on each other."

"I have to confess, listeners. My heart is in my throat. Tell us, Lieutenant, what was the next sound you heard?"

Luke stared blankly at his host. *The next . . . sound?* A stabbing pain shot up the stump of his missing finger. He had to swallow hard to stop himself from gasping. They had arrived at the point where Luke's memory faded to a blank screen.

He'd been half-expecting something like this. Knowing that the *Lanternfish* hero couldn't have no tale to tell, Luke had cobbled together a storyline from his scant memories, along with newspaper reports and what the guys on the hospital ship and at the Navy Cross ceremony had told him. Luke had rewritten and refined a hodgepodge of other peoples' accounts until he had shaped it into a plausible chronicle that he could memorize. It used to be that he retained anything with his photographic memory. These days, however, it took effort. Luke had repeated his version out loud over and over and over until he knew all the images, all the scenes, by heart.

But . . . sounds. He stared at Breneman. None of the newspaper articles, nor any of the sailors' accounts, had mentioned sounds. Theoretically, he knew he could say anything: scraping, banging, twisting, shouting. Other men in other parts of the boat doing other jobs could have heard a different sound, so there was no wrong answer. Why, then, could he not push a single syllable from his mouth?

Because I have no idea what I heard next.
Or what happened next.
Or what I did next.
Because I'm a big phony who's making it all up.
I don't deserve these medals pinned to my chest, or the key to the city in my pocket, or any of this attention.

The shooting pain along his finger stump intensified. Sticking it into a lit candle couldn't have hurt worse than this. And now Breneman was staring at him, goggle-eyed, beseeching him to respond. Anything was better than dead air.

Tears pricked his eyeballs. "It—it was more than one sound."

"Every crewman had a job to do," Breneman prompted him.

Luke swallowed hard. "The captain is hollering orders. Men are shouting their responses. Metal slams against metal. Periscope up; periscope down. The radio operator is on his set, calling for assistance."

"So much is going on all at once." Breneman tempered his narration to a soothing monotone. "But you have to stay cool. Keep your head clear. Do your job like your life depends on it."

"Everybody's does!"

Sparky's voice echoed in Luke's head. *Mayday! Mayday!* He could hear Sparky talking faster and louder. Too rapid to understand, but Luke could hear the tremor in his voice.

"Lieutenant Valenti?" Breneman held a Western Union telegram in his hand. "We have a message from your family."

A single word—"Brooklyn?"—was all he could manage.

"As soon as you came on the air, they cabled us." The radio host held the message at a distance so that he could read it without glasses.

WE'RE ALL LISTENING TO YOU STOP
OUR HEARTS ARE FILLED WITH ADMIRATION STOP
WE ARE OVER THE MOON THAT YOU ARE
SAFE STOP
YOU ARE OUR HERO AND WE LOVE YOU VERY
MUCH STOP
SIGNED YOUR PROUD FATHER

No member of his family had telegrammed him when he had found himself stranded in Los Angeles. Nor when he had joined the Navy. Nor when he'd been awarded the key to the city or the Navy Cross or been lauded as the hero of the *Lanternfish*.

If this is what it took, Luke decided, that was okay. As lingering resentment melted away, Luke felt lighter, bigger, happier.

And then he burst into tears.

* * *

Luke swallowed his first shot of Old Forester in a single gulp.

"Jesus, Valenti, did it even touch the sides?"

Luke slammed the glass onto Bogie's wet bar. "Hit me again."

"Tough day, huh?"

Luke savored the burn down his throat. "Don't stop now."

Bogie called out to Betty. "Do we have any more Old Forester?"

She walked out of the kitchen holding a platter of Belgian endive spears arranged around a cheese ball the size of Joe Louis's fist. "If there's one thing this house is never short of, it's booze."

This new wife of Bogie's possessed an appealing down-to-earth saltiness that Luke guessed kept Bogie on his toes. It was one of the many reasons he liked this spunky girl. He waited until Bogie had refilled his glass before he waved toward the gang gathered around the Bogarts' Aero-Vane Motorola.

"Hey!" he called to Tony and Audrey, who had joined his uncle Avery and his mother's best friend, Violet Beaudine, on the couch. "Did any of you bawl your eyes out on national radio today?"

"Nope," Tony responded. "Just you."

Luke dumped the bourbon down his throat as though nothing would quench his thirst. He'd been waiting for this moment ever since he had stumbled out of Breneman's restaurant, still blushing from having made a fool of himself.

"You've got nothing to be embarrassed about." Bogie filled the seven shot glasses he'd lined up along the bar.

"I agree." Violet was by Luke's side in four strides. It was the first time he had met this larger-than-life woman who, earlier that evening, had drawn him to her ample bosom, crying, "Lily! I can see my darling Lily in your face, hear her in your voice. The stories I have about your mother!" Luke wanted to hear them, too. Every one of them. But not now. Not tonight.

"For you it may have been mortifying," Nell said, "but for the rest of us, it was one of the most touching broadcasts we've ever heard."

"Didn't you hear all those old ducks?" Avery asked. "All that sympathetic ooh-ing and aah-ing and henhouse clucking."

"Multiply that by—say, how many people tune into *Breakfast in Hollywood*?" Audrey asked.

"Ten million." Luke tipped the remaining booze into his glass.

There was barely enough left to fill it. The burn was more like a comforting glow now. "I was representing the Navy. Decked out in my uniform. Ribbons. Medals. All the trappings."

"—that you drowned with all those big, fat, blubbering tears." Audrey thwacked Tony with a rolled-up *Look* magazine. He snatched it from her and tossed it behind him. "I never got no telegram from our folks, and I lost a goddamn leg at that fucking island!"

Luke still couldn't believe Pop had sent it. *You are our hero and we love you very much.* Who even knew Pop could string ten words together, let alone say them to Western Union?

The booze percolated around Luke's edges. Fuzzy, warm, delicious. "You can pretend you're their favorite son, but we know it's me now."

Tony hurled a cushion at Luke. It fell short by a few feet, confirming that Tony had started drinking before they'd arrived; otherwise, it would have hit its mark.

Betty crossed over to the radio set. "They're starting." She twisted the volume all the way up.

The foul weather that had delayed the signing ceremony had cleared up. The commentator described the scene aboard the USS *Missouri* anchored in Tokyo Bay, noting how casually the Allies had dressed. MacArthur's and Nimitz's open-necked khaki shirts contrasted with the stiffly formal uniforms of the officers, and the black morning coats of the Japanese officials.

The Bogart living room fell silent as MacArthur approached the microphone.

"It is my earnest concern," the general proclaimed, "and indeed the hope of all mankind, that from this solemn occasion, a better world shall emerge out of the blood and carnage of the past. A world founded upon faith and understanding, a world dedicated to the dignity of man and the fulfillment of his most cherished wish for freedom, tolerance, and justice."

Luke squeezed Nell's hand as he stared, unblinking, into her eyes. It had been a tough day. Bone-wearingly exhausting. But now it was over.

She dropped her head onto his shoulder. "I know."

At long last, he could put the war behind him and look forward to the future. Their future. Together. And he couldn't wait for it to begin.

8

*H*oagy Carmichael greeted Nell at his front door. "Welcome to the house that 'Stardust' built!"

Nell stepped into the foyer. "Cute line, but is it true?"

"Nah, but it makes for a fun opener." He led her through a wood-paneled living room filled with floral upholstery, and into a spacious study where an upright piano stood under a standard lamp that would have looked more at home in a Booth Tarkington novel.

Nell set her purse onto an octagonal coffee table in a bay window. "I'm surprised you don't have a grand piano."

Hoagy tapped a fingertip on the upright. "Our baby grand is in the front parlor where I can play it for dinner guests."

"I guess it's only natural to expect the host to knock out a few tunes when you're a guest of *the* Mr. Hoagy Carmichael."

She knew she was sounding testy, but she couldn't help it. It had been a week since Luke's appearance on *Breakfast in Hollywood* and at that party at the Bogarts', where he'd drunk himself into a determined stupor. Not that she had minded. Everybody had built up steam in the months leading to the end of the war. Listening to the ceremony on the radio had acted as a collective release valve, sending them all plumb loco. Not just at the Bogart house, but across LA.

After his colossal hangover had ebbed, Nell had expected to see a return of the Luke she'd fallen in love with. But more often than not, he was silent now. Almost brooding.

"Being the party ivory thumper comes with the territory." Hoagy picked up some papers from the pile at his elbow. "I've been thinking about our song, and how it's a blessing we didn't get around to recording it." He fanned his face with the "Every Fifth Word" sheet music. "It did its job. You needed to get a message to your beau. But now that the war's over, we no longer need to stick to the same lyrics."

She felt the floor beneath her feet shift. Writing "Every Fifth Word" with Hoagy and singing it to a worldwide audience on the radio hoping Luke would hear her was one of her most cherished accomplishments. It had also helped her parents see her in a whole new light. Her father wrote to her regularly now, a situation she could never have foreseen, and all because of that song.

"You want to change it?"

"Make it more commercial." He sat on the piano bench, leaving room for her to join him. "Those three lawyer names—Bell, Amiss, and White—we had to cram them in places they didn't need to fit. Look at these lines. 'But I listen more closely than ol' Alexander Graham *Bell*,' and 'Let me tell you, dear, that your assumption's quite *amiss*.' They work because we shoehorned them in, but to stand a chance of turning it into a hit—"

She looked into his earnest, narrow face. "You think it can be?"

"Why else would we be going to all this trouble?"

A commercial hit? Nell felt her heart beat a little faster. "I see."

His eyebrows furrowed together. "It's not too late to call it all off. Or I can ask one of those other gals you suggested."

"NO!" The word flew out of her with such force it caught her by surprise. "Don't you dare give it to them!"

"Attagirl."

"I'm sorry if I've been coming across like Tepid Tammy." She blew a short raspberry.

Hoagy gave her a sideways glance. "The girl next door to us in Indiana used to make that sound whenever she had boy trouble."

"Am I that transparent?"

"It's one of your charms."

Nell tucked away that veiled compliment to revel in later. "You're right. It's Luke. He hasn't been the same since he got back. He's moody, and silent, and preoccupied."

"He spent weeks, maybe even months, trapped inside a sub, and nearly lost his life. What makes you think he'd come out of the war the same way he went in?"

Somewhere in a distant room, a cuckoo clock chimed the hour. It seemed to mock her for being so boneheaded.

"You're one smart hombre, Señor Carmichael."

He dismissed her observation with a single-shouldered shrug. "It's my job to absorb what's going on around me, discern how people feel, individually or societally, and distill that down into a song I can serve back to them."

If she could have, Nell would have driven straight to Luke and told him, "I get it now. You're not the same man I fell for. But that's okay. I love the new version, too." But she and one of America's greatest tunesmiths had a song to improve, and they would be recording it the next day. She took a deep breath and forced herself to focus on the sheet music in front of her.

"I'm rather attached to the Alexander Graham Bell line," she said, "but you're right about 'assumption's quite amiss.' We can do better than that."

Hoagy picked up a pencil from the music stand. "Any suggestions?"

"Bliss?"

"This?"

"Abyss?"

"Hiss?"

"Reminisce?"

The two looked at each other.

A-ha!

* * *

The twenty-piece orchestra was more intimidating than Nell had pictured. Was it because she would soon be standing in the middle of it?

"I hope you're not nervous."

Hoagy wore an expensive suit of dark brown that he'd contrasted with a butter-yellow silk necktie. She blinked. "You have a tie with fives painted all over it?"

"Five is my lucky number." He swept a hand across the assembled musicians. "If you'll excuse me, I have a couple of last-minute notes for the orchestra." She nodded and watched him walk over, brandishing a sheet of paper.

The Carmichael family cuckoo clock had struck six by the time they'd finished rewriting. She had marveled at the care Hoagy had taken to ensure each word fitted in the right place, and that no other could do a better job. Their new version was a tremendous improvement, and she had full confidence he would orchestrate it masterfully.

Of course he would. He had written "Stardust" and "Georgia on My Mind" and "Heart and Soul." And today he had assembled musicians skilled enough to play a sophisticated score by Max Steiner or Erich Wolfgang Korngold, note-perfect, from start to finish, in one take.

Meanwhile, there's little me. This is the big time. The World Series. Who am I to be swinging my baseball bat with all these Babe Ruths?

When a voice inside her head answered her question, she let loose a slight yelp. "Why not you?" it volleyed back at her. "He could've asked Dinah Shore, or Betty Hutton, or the Andrews Sisters. But he didn't." She pictured a knitting needle in her hand, wielded it like a dagger, and used it to stab at the bubble of doubt ballooning in her chest. She almost heard it pop.

Hoagy beckoned her to join him. "And this, gentlemen—" he draped a lanky arm across her shoulders—"is our vocalist, Nell Davenport. I want Nell to hear the new orchestrations before we do a take."

"We can do more than one, though, right?"

"Mind if we watch?"

Nell turned towards the door, where Bogie stood with his hands buried in the pockets of his double-breasted charcoal pinstripe, a friendly, encouraging smile on his face. Betty stood to his left, looking as fresh and radiant as she always did—*How does she manage it?*—and Luke hovered behind them, glum and resentful. It was plainly obvious that Bogie had talked him into joining them. Nell forced herself to recall Hoagy's wise words about coming through the war unchanged. He'll steady his boat in time, she told herself.

"I can't tell you how happy I am to see you here!"

"Try to keep us away." Betty nudged Luke. "Right?"

"Right!" His smile pinched at the edges. "Let's hope history-making events don't overtake you a second time."

"Nell making her first professional record *is* a history-making event," Bogie said.

"And so is *Confidential Agent*," Betty added. "History, I mean. Filming wrapped at goddamn last, which means the four of us are going out to celebrate when you're done."

"Nell?" Hoagy called from the piano. "We're ready for you."

"Wish me luck," she told her cheer squad.

"What do you need with luck when you've got talent?"

Nell would have preferred a morale-booster from Luke, but Humphrey Bogart himself was no shabby second place.

* * *

The four of them clinked their champagne coupes over the votive candle flickering inside the rose-colored glass jar at the center of their table. The maître d' at Mike Lyman's Grill, south of Hollywood and Vine, had installed them in a corner booth.

"Here's to One-Take Davenport!" Bogie exclaimed.

Nell giggled. "Oh, stop it!"

"New lyrics, new orchestrations, and you nail it on the first try!" Betty said. "The band didn't think it was nothing. Not if their standing ovation is anything to go by, and I'll wager a hundred bucks it is."

"It was sensational to watch," Luke said. "I'm so glad I was here to witness it."

His words lacked gusto, but he was trying.

"I'm still in shock," Nell declared. "I'll never forget Hoagy's reaction when I finished that final note."

She had held it for as long as she could. When she had looked at Hoagy, his eyes had been wide with astonishment. It would be a good, long while before the memory of the orchestra's applause faded away.

Bogie sipped his champagne and winced. "I'll be mighty glad when the proper stuff starts flowing again from the Continent. But if French fields resemble the ones I saw in Italy, I'm not holding my breath."

Betty whispered into her glass, "We've been spotted. Hair bun approaching fast. Get out your autograph pen, husband o' mine."

The middle-aged woman nearing them wore the tentative but eager look of a Bogie fan who could scarcely believe her luck, and who wouldn't forgive herself if she didn't say hello.

Bogie arranged his face into a professional smile. "You're marginally famous yourself, sweetheart."

"Please excuse my forwardness," the woman said, "but aren't you Luke Valenti?"

Luke's head jerked up. "Do I know you?" His voice was barely audible above the din.

She plucked at the narrow lapels of her careworn jacket. "When I saw you on the Fox Movietone newsreel last month, I couldn't have dreamed I'd get the chance to thank you personally."

Luke shot Nell an apprehensive glance, then returned to the woman. "For what?"

"My name is Mrs. Velma Allenton, and my boy, Aaron, joined the Navy right after Pearl Harbor. I was terribly proud of him, naturally, but he was captured in the Philippines."

Nell slid her hand across the pale pink tablecloth. As she laid it on top of his, she could sense his fingers tremble.

"I worried and fretted as any mother would," Mrs. Allenton continued, "but we had a happy ending."

"I'm so glad," Luke replied. "What happened to him?"

"He had the good fortune to be a POW aboard the *Toyotomi Maru*."

She dropped the name as though it were a pebble into a pond. When the ripples hit Luke, he slotted his fingers between Nell's and squeezed them as hard as he could. He opened his mouth to speak, but the words refused to emerge.

"I guess you could say he was in the right place at the right time," Nell said to fill the heavy silence.

"He and all those poor souls were on their way to Japan." Mrs. Allenton's voice quivered from the effort of holding herself together. "He was undernourished and so dreadfully frail. He wouldn't have survived that prison camp. He'd given up hope. They all had. Until you came along."

"Oh, gosh, Mrs. Allenton, no. I was just—"

"Please, Lieutenant, let me get this out." She bit down on her lower lip to still her wobbling chin. "You came along. On the *Lanternfish*. You learned what—whom—the Japs were transporting. Your captain would have sunk the enemy ship. Those were his orders. But all those lives were saved. My darling boy is only twenty-two. Got his whole life ahead of him. Because of what *you* did."

Her face crumpled; she pressed it into her gloved hands.

Luke leaped up to wrap his arms around the woman. He tilted her head into his shoulder and let her weep into the collar of his uniform until she was able to pull herself together.

"And Aaron?" Luke asked. "How is he?"

"Just yesterday, he was released from the naval hospital at Pearl Harbor. He's due to ship back to the mainland on Friday."

"Where he can feast on his loving mother's home-cooked meals, right?" Luke patted her cheek. "And when that happens, tell him I said, 'Welcome back, Aaron.'"

"I will, I will. Thank you." Mrs. Allenton smiled at him, then gave a little start when she noticed who else was sitting at Luke's table. "I'll let you get on with your evening." She gave his hand a final squeeze and then weaved her way through the tables and out the door.

Bogie struck a match along the Mike Lyman Grill matchbook and lit a Chesterfield. "What do you say to all that?"

Luke stayed silent, choosing instead to watch Bogie's match as it sputtered out in the glass ashtray at his elbow.

Nell clamped her fingers around his wrist. "That was very touching."

He shuddered, gave a slight shrug, and tried to respond, but gave up before he could voice his feelings.

No, Nell decided, I need more than that. A popular Hollywood restaurant might not have been the ideal place, as emotions were almost guaranteed to run high, but this was her chance to press harder.

"I need to hear how you feel about what happened, Luke. For that matter, how you feel about everything."

"Come on, Warner Boy," Bogie said, smoothing his voice to a soft silkiness. "Bottling it up doesn't work. Believe me." He pinged a fingernail against his empty coupe. "I've tried."

Luke stared at him in dead silence for an uncomfortably long time.

Nell watched him, her heart in her mouth. *Say something. Anything. Give us a little morsel. The tiniest smidgen of what's plaguing you.* Out of the corner of her eye, Nell spied their waiter approaching the table, but she waved him away. "What is it they say about a burden shared?"

Luke's response barreled out of him. "Guilty," he said in a strangled voice. "So guilty!"

Nell, Bogie, and Betty stared at each other. He had saved nearly a hundred fifty lives—and yet he felt guilty?

"About what, darling?" Nell asked.

"Sparky," Luke blurted out.

"What about him?" Bogie asked.

"I can barely remember him."

"There was so much going on—"

"I recall nothing from that night." Luke looked Nell in the eye, his face now distorted in torment. "Tiny scraps, here and there, but that's all." He picked up Bogie's matchbook and flipped it over and over. "Every so often, a sudden flash comes to me. Anything can set it off: smells or voices, words or sounds. And every time it does, I think of Christopher."

"Who's Christopher?" Bogie asked.

"Sparky's real name was—Ohmygod!" Luke felt his throat go dry. He forced down a heavy swallow. "Sparky's name was Christopher."

Nell smiled gently as she squeezed his hand. "It's finally come back to you."

Luke could only stare at her. *Of course it was Christopher. How could I have forgotten that? We had a whole conversation about—*

"The two of you became good pals?" Betty prompted.

Luke nodded, but not convincingly. "I assume so. But I can't even remember what he looked like, which makes me a terrible friend."

"Honey," Nell gripped his wrist a little more firmly, "you suffered a serious concussion. Didn't the doctors say—"

"That whole night is one long, black void."

"But, Luke," Nell said, "at your ceremony, in front of those newsreel cameras, on the radio, you've talked about it over and over."

"All I've done is regurgitated other reports. What else could I do? I have no memories of my own."

"Apart from this Sparky guy," Betty said, "what memories are you left with?"

Luke's face slowly blanched. "A vague suspicion that I've let him down." He went to sip his champagne and found his coupe dry. "I'm so wracked with guilt I can't stand it."

All four sat in silence, each of them staring at the fluttering candle in the glass jar, until Betty said, "You know what I think?"

"Please tell me," Luke begged. "I'm at my wits' end."

She turned to Bogie. "You told me once about what it was like to serve on a Navy ship during the Great War, and how friendships formed in almost no time."

He nodded. "That must be doubly true on a sub where men are living cheek by jowl."

She swung back to Luke. "You and this Sparky guy shared the tiny radio room, right? You must have buddied up real close. He didn't survive, whereas you were rescued, you recovered, you found yourself hailed as the hero of the *Lanternfish*. Suddenly you're getting medals and keys to the city. You're in the papers and on newsreels. Exciting as all get-out, I'm sure, but you haven't had a chance to do what you've needed to do."

"Which is what?"

"Grieve for your friend."

The last dregs of color drained from Luke's face as he absorbed Betty's theory.

"She might be onto something," Nell said.

He dropped his gaze into his lap. "Could be."

"What about a remembrance service?"

"For someone I can barely remember?"

"Let that be part of it."

"We could do it out on the Pacific," Bogie said. "It's the same ocean, so it's connected. What do you say, chum?"

Nell held her breath as Luke turned the idea over in his mind. She didn't let it out until he looked up, his eyes searching hers. "I'd like that very much."

"Oh, Luke!" She planted a kiss on his cheek so firm that it left an outline in lipstick.

A smile surfaced on his face, the first genuine one in ages. "I'm famished. Where'd that waiter get to?"

Nell shot her hand into the air and called. "Yoo-hoo!" across the bustle of conversation. "We're ready now!"

9

Standing at 235 South Hill Street engulfed Luke in memories of the night Bogie and Lorre had driven him into downtown to hand over the forged birth certificate to Vance. He had yearned so deeply to win his place in the Navy that when Vance had called him "Ensign," he had scarcely been able to take it in.

He stared at the sign in the building's directory—*UNITED STATES NAVY DEPARTMENT*—and fantasized about warning the Luke Valenti from 1942 to prepare for the unexpected.

Like last week, for instance. There he'd been at Mike Lyman's Grill, celebrating Nell's remarkable recording session, when that woman had thanked him on behalf of her son. That night, Luke had dreamed of Aaron Allenton crowded into the hold of the *Toyotomi Maru* while he had frantically searched for a hatch to open before the air ran out. Sparky had been there too. Or his voice, at least. "Try that one, Luke! Or that one!" Luke had scrambled all over the deck in fading dusk light as the sub rocked on choppier and choppier seas. None of the hatches had budged.

Lieutenant Commander Whitley emerged from the

skyscraper's glass-and-copper doors in a tailored blue uniform that Luke guessed had been custom-made by one of the studios. His French-cuffed shirt and knotted silk tie contrasted with Luke's standard-issue coat and trousers, which couldn't hold a decent press after a few days' wear.

"Walk with me." Whitley barely broke his stride as he headed down the sidewalk. "I got called up in late forty-one and sent out here to the eleventh district, where I've been with the Radio and Motion Picture Liaison Office ever since. And all this time I've never ridden Angels Flight. Have you?"

Angels Flight was a brightly painted funicular connecting Hill Street with Olive Street. Luke hadn't ridden it either. Why had Whitley mentioned it?

Since the day after Luke's hospital ship had docked at Long Beach, all their communication had been by telephone. Whitley had been friendly, but professional. Approachable, but always by-the-book. This request to meet him at his office had been unusual, and this resolute march, shouldering their way along crowded sidewalks, felt out of character.

Whitley didn't speak again until they arrived at the Second Street corner. "I'd give anything to be your age and in your shoes."

Luke wasn't sure how to respond to the abrupt left turns in this guy's soliloquy. "You would?"

"I didn't see any combat in the Great War, and have had a pretty easy time of it in this one." Whitley recoiled slightly, as though his confession had pained him. "I've been wined and dined, schmoozed and flattered by all those Hollywood types who needed the cooperation of the Navy for their war movies." A bitter laugh hiccupped out of him. "Not one of those cigar-chomping blowhards with egos the size of an aircraft carrier cottoned onto how they didn't need to take me out to Ciro's or Mocambo, or introduce me to starlets. They were making the propaganda films we wanted them to make."

The red light changed to green; Whitley bounded off the curb.

"Sounds cushy." A bland response seemed like the best way forward until Luke could figure out why the guy was spilling his guts.

"Too damn cushy," Whitley snapped. "The expensive champagne. The black-market filet mignons. Real cheese, real coffee, real sugar, all the cigarettes I wanted. I'm as red-blooded as the next American. If I get to the end of a date with some pretty girl, I can tell if she's thinking, 'Invite me back to your place. I'm going to say yes.'" He slapped his hands against his sides. "What else would I do? Put her in a taxi? Hell's bells, I may be forty-six, but those fires aren't ready to be banked yet." They were at the Hill Street funicular station now. He inserted a pair of nickels through a slot in the glass box. "I'd almost convinced myself that I was one of the fortunate ones. And then you come along."

They climbed aboard. Whitley chose a weathered wooden bench halfway up the car.

"You sailed into the heart of the Pacific. You faced off the enemy and you triumphed. You're a goddamn war hero now. I even envy your missing finger. Meanwhile, what have I got to show for the past three and a half years?"

Luke smelled the brandy on his breath. No cheap brand, either.

"For starters," Luke said, "my finger aches like hell the whole time—including the bit I lost. And let's not forget how I cried on national radio as though I was Barbara Stanwyck in a women's weepie. Some war hero I am."

"Are you kidding?" Whitley let his head fall backward against the window behind him. "Most war heroes come across looking like they jumped out of a comic book. Not you, though. You weren't afraid to show the world that you're a regular guy. My superiors all the way up the chain loved it."

The irony made Luke squirm on the wooden slats. He had

spent the following week reliving that ghastly moment over and over until his only respite had come from a near-full pint of Old Cabin Still whiskey that he'd found under his bed in Bogie's guest room. And yet this brandy-soaked moaner was *envious* of him?

"Which is why," Whitley said, "we're stepping up the PR."

A cold stone of disappointment sank into the pit of Luke's stomach. "I was hoping you'd called me in to discuss my discharge."

"Sorry, Lieutenant. The brass has deemed you too valuable to be released back into the wild."

"What does 'stepping up the PR' mean?"

"It means that when an interview request came in from *Life* magazine, my CO agreed to it without consulting me. And then he asked, 'Valenti still works for Warner Brothers, doesn't he?' When I told him you don't, he said, 'That's a problem. He can't be any kind of loafer. Why isn't he back there?'" The bell attached to the front of the Angels Flight car clanged. "So why aren't you?"

"I wasn't employed by the studio," Luke replied. "I worked for Humphrey Bogart."

"How come you're not working for him again?"

Because I have a stupefying amount of money coming to me that would set me up for life if I'm smart about it. And if I knew when it was going to arrive, I could plan accordingly. But I don't. So here I am, stuck in limbo. "His circumstances have changed."

The funicular trundled up the steep incline, passing rundown mansions jury-rigged into seedy boarding houses. Sun-blanched paint curled and peeled; rotted wood hung from rusted nails. Luke caught sight of a gray-whiskered geezer in a grimy undershirt, who stared at Luke as they rambled past his open window.

Luke wanted to slap himself. He'd wasted so much angst obsessing over one single night that he couldn't recall. He needed a reason to get up in the morning. By the time their carriage reached the top of Angels Flight, he knew he had the perfect one in mind.

* * *

Luke stared at Nell banging on her Remington for nearly a minute before she looked up.

"Your powers of concentration are impressive, Miss Davenport."

"Sitting in the middle of this cacophony, a girl needs to be. What are you doing here?"

He pulled a spare office chair closer to her desk and sat down. "I need a job." *Was that relief washing over her face?* "Otherwise I'll go stark raving mad."

"Here in PR?"

Luke shook his head. "Didn't you say Props was short-staffed?"

"Woefully."

"What about that guy I had to deliver the hollow Maltese falcon to?"

"Simon Kovner." Nell grimaced. "Bogie and I bumped into him about a year ago. Good lord, what a mess. Bogie said it was a severe case of battle fatigue."

"So, who runs the department now?"

"A revolving door of changing faces. They need someone reliable—" She snapped her fingers. "Great idea!"

Whether or not he nabbed a job, it had been worth the expensive taxi ride to see her chirpy expression. So often lately, all he seemed good for was to etch worry lines deeper into her wide-open face.

"Who should I butter up?"

"It's a department head, so . . ." Her enthusiasm withered a little. "Head of production."

"But isn't that—?"

"You're in uniform." She stood up, hooked her elbow through his and walked him to the exit. "He's a sucker for that kind of thing."

"Any advice?"

They stepped outside, where the September sun had lost the worst of its summer sting. She kissed him on the cheek. "You're a smart guy. You'll figure it out."

* * *

Jack Warner wiggled an expensive fountain pen between manicured fingers. "I feel as though I should know who you are."

Did the guy not even watch his own newsreels? "You might have seen me around the studio before the war."

"Your name?"

"Valenti, sir."

"Why, you're our *Lanternfish* hero! Take a seat." He waited until Luke had settled into one of his guest chairs. "Tell me, Lieutenant, what was your role on that sub? Officially speaking."

"I was a cryptanalyst trained to break the Japanese code."

Warner's eyebrows shot up. "Crippie, huh? Can't have been a cakewalk."

"The job required a certain sort of mind. Organized. Methodical. Systematic. Thorough. Every time they determined we were onto them, they dreamed up a new code."

He slotted the pen into its brass holder. "I have a meeting in ten minutes. Get to the point."

"Your props department." Luke said. "It ran like a Swiss clock when Simon Kovner was in charge, but he's not coming back any time soon. Meanwhile, you've had a string of people doing their best, but it's not good enough."

"You can do better?"

"I cracked the Japanese military code five times." It was only three, but Jack Warner wouldn't know that. "I have what it takes to run your props department."

Warner ran his eyes down Luke's khaki uniform. "Did you wear that to impress me?"

"No, sir. I'm still in the service."

"How come they haven't mustered you out?"

In a perfect world, Luke would have preferred to land this job without mentioning the *Lanternfish*, the war, his crippie job, the Navy, or his recent rise in fame. But the world hadn't been a perfect place before Pearl Harbor, nor was it one since hostilities had ceased. People got jobs exploiting whatever ace in the hole they had at their disposal, so why shouldn't he?

"It appears the Navy values my—" Luke groped around to avoid using the word 'heroism' "—wartime experience in terms of public relations."

"And they call the shots, huh?"

"I'm happy to serve my country, but meanwhile, I prefer to stay busy."

The secretary buzzed the intercom. "Mr. Warner, your three o'clock is here."

Just keep yakking, Luke told himself, till you've talked your way into this job. "From what I hear, the person running Props doesn't even know where they store the Maltese falcon. It's time you got someone who is organized, methodical, systematic, thorough. I'm familiar with the entire studio and how it's run. Furthermore—"

"Yeah, yeah, yeah." Warner waved away the rest of Luke's pitch. "What salary are you asking for?"

"I'm still on the Navy's payroll."

"So I don't have to pay you a dime?"

It always, always, always came down to money. "No, sir."

"You start tomorrow. Now, get the hell out of here and let me run my studio."

* * *

It was like pulling on a forgotten sweater he'd found at the back of the closet, breathing in a lungful of cedar, mothballs, wool, and smoke, and thinking, "It's nice to be home."

The props department was bigger than he remembered. Had they added space now that movie production was at an all-time high, and profits for the coming year were expected to reach an astounding twenty million?

Memorizing the layout and location of the thousands of lamps, tables, irons, portraits, golf clubs, and myriad other objects would have been a piece of cake before the war, when Luke's photographic memory had been infallible. Nowadays, though, not so much. But that was okay. It would make for an invigorating challenge. It might even help stimulate those defective brain cells.

He picked up a pencil and tapped the eraser end on his desk. His watch read one fifty-four. That reporter was due to arrive in six minutes.

Whitley had yelled out, "Perfect!" when Luke had told him where he was working. "That'll make great atmosphere for your *Life* magazine interview with . . ." The sound of flipping papers had rattled down the other end of the line. "Maxine Waterford. She'll have a photographer, so be sure to press your uniform. Remember: you work at a movie studio, but you *represent* the Navy."

The front door swung open to reveal a woman teetering on the edge of forty, with dancing eyes and a lively mouth gaping a wide O. "My heavens! There's quite a Santa Ana blowing today." She lifted the black straw hat in her hands. "This expensive little number nearly went swimming in the river."

Luke had been picturing someone more buttoned down, looking for all the world like a county librarian on a day pass. He rounded his reception desk. "You must be Maxine Waterford."

"From *Life* magazine. This week, anyway. I'm freelance." She drew a circle in the air around his Purple Heart and Navy Cross ribbon before tilting his sterling silver combat patrol pin toward the light. "Please tell me you brought the key to the city."

He tapped his pocket. "I assumed a photographer would be accompanying you."

"Steve'll be along soon. He wanted to get some atmosphere shots of the studio." Waterford swiped a lock of hair out of her eyes. She possessed a head of thick, black coils, except for a single ash-gray maverick sprouting over her forehead. "I expect that wicked wind has left me looking a fright."

"Not at all." He led her to the spot where two club chairs most recently used in *Old Acquaintance* sat in front of Sam's *Casablanca* piano. "I thought we could talk here."

Waterford's green eyes lit up, and she pressed her hands to her bosom. "That song! I hummed it for weeks."

Luke sat on Dooley's bench, lifted the keyboard lid, and played the opening bars to "As Time Goes By." He smiled to himself when she murmured, "Oh, my, my, my!"

"I was on the set of that movie." What an idyllic time it seemed to him now. No concussion, no narrow escapes from death, no missing fingers, no memory gaps, no ceremonies, no enormous crowds, and no magazine reporters.

He heard the click of a camera and looked up to see an older gent, sixty years or more, with a half-burned cigarette dangling from the corner of his mouth. The guy wiggled a black-and-silver Leica, one of those new models that had replaced the clunky old Speed Graflexes.

"That'll be a nice one," he said.

After Waterford introduced them, she blithely told Luke to "forget he's even here. Steve works better when he's free to creep around all stealthy and ghostly."

"We can walk and talk," he suggested. "This place has plenty of interesting doodads and whatsits to show you." Sam's piano wasn't the only prop Luke had staged in various locations.

Waterford withdrew a spiral notebook and pen from her alligator-skin purse. "According to that AP article from the hospital ship, you learned to speak German and Japanese in a matter of weeks. How remarkable!"

Luke had laughed when he'd read Halloran's piece. He had captured the skeleton of Luke's wartime experience, but had exaggerated almost every fact. "Remarkable, yes; true, no. I already knew German, and I learned Japanese at the Navy language school in not weeks but months."

Waterford paused her pen above the notebook. "Helped by your photographic memory, no doubt."

Luke picked up a fan of ostrich feathers off an Empire-era table. "Bette Davis used this in *The Private Lives of Elizabeth and Essex*." He waved it in her face. "Under all those hot studio lights, you can bet Miss Davis needed it more than Elizabeth ever did."

Waterford gave it a perfunctory glance. "Japanese is a tough language to master, isn't it?"

Would it be bragging if he told her that of the twenty-two guys who had started with him in Boulder, only five had graduated? Yes, it would. "There was a motivating sign posted in our dorms. It said, 'Every day the Japanese code goes unbroken is another day they have the upper hand.'"

"You have a knack for languages." Waterford followed him into a large room that held Renaissance, medieval, and Dark Ages artifacts. It was where Luke had lain Errol Flynn's bow and arrow across a ship's table used in *The Sea Wolf*. "I imagine when the Japs were talking to each other, they must've been speaking a mile a minute. And you still deciphered what they were saying."

He scooped up the enormous bow. "Do you remember seeing this in *The Adventures of Robin Hood*?" He plucked at the string; it made the flat pinging sound that accompanied clumsy cartoon characters when they fell on their keester.

She flipped the cover of her notebook, closing it with a soft slap. "The *Casablanca* piano, that bow—you've been using them as distractions."

She wasn't laughing at him as he first guessed. If anything, the sympathetic concern etched across her face was almost maternal.

Luke replaced Errol's bow on the table. "I haven't been a good interview subject, have I?"

"Reluctant war heroes rarely are. Not that I would know," she added. "I usually get palmed off with the fluffy stuff. Pretty chorines whose sugar daddies have done the director a favor. But when I heard this one was up for grabs, I campaigned my editor for it. That Whitley guy at the press office, he said you were happy to talk about anything and everything. Told me, 'The guy's an open book.'"

"Sorry to disappoint."

"Au contraire!" She playfully slapped him across the shoulder. "I was expecting a puffy-chested, swell-headed grandstander who I planned on skewering with a well-aimed question."

Luke hadn't intended to be so evasive and uncooperative. His middle finger no longer throbbed quite so badly as it had before, and after that encounter with the POW mother, he hadn't been dreaming about being trapped on the *Lanternfish* nearly so often. Now that he'd nabbed this job, he felt as though the ground beneath his feet was growing more stable day by day. On the other hand, appearing in *Life* magazine was a big deal. All morning his newfound confidence had been draining slowly away.

"We can start over, if you like," he suggested. "I'll be the anything-and-everything guy."

"Absolutely not. Reluctant heroes are far more interesting."

He caught the sincerity in her eyes. "Why is that?"

She spied a Victorian-era sofa upholstered in velvet and led him to it. "You, sir, did an extraordinary thing. How you feel about it is almost irrelevant. Fact is, the *Lanternfish* embodies American bravery and American spirit, fighting for the American way. So tell me—" she patted his knee—"if you don't think you're the hero of the *Lanternfish*, who is?"

"Sparky."

Waterford opened her notebook again and wrote down the name. "Why him? Can you give me specifics?"

That's the whole problem, Luke thought. I can't.

But this reporter had been so kind, she deserved a halfway decent answer.

"That last hour on the sub," he began, then halted, gathering his thoughts. "It was all such a blur. Time sped up and slowed down all at the same time. I managed to get out, but Sparky's job was to keep sending out the mayday until the *Abbot* responded. Thank God it did, but too late for poor Sparky. Without him and his dedication, we might have been picked off by the Japs, one by one."

"Were you good pals?"

"We worked back-to-back—and I mean literally. How could we not be?"

"You remind me of my brother," she said, twisting the top of her pen into place. "He was with the Army. Ended up fighting in the Battle of Aachen, where he palled up with a fellow trigger-puller. Turns out he and Duane went to the same high school and were both in love with their English teacher. My brother came through it fine, but he was standing right next to Duane when the poor guy took a sniper bullet direct to the skull. Dead before he hit the ground. For six months my brother refused to say his name."

"How is he now?"

"Better, thanks. But every time he brings it up, I can see the guilt bleeding from his eyeballs. He keeps mentioning how he wants to visit Duane's parents, but they live in Oceanside, so it's a little far to drop in."

"Isn't Oceanside south of Long Beach?"

"No, sweetie. The one in New York. Near that new airport at Idlewild, out past East Rockaway."

Waterford went on talking about her brother, but Luke paid little heed.

Rockaway Beach.

Luke had seen Sparky's full name—Christopher Walsh—on the KIA list in the newspapers. But those lists didn't include where the fallen men hailed from. Had Luke remembered a legitimate detail? Or was his jumbled mind pulling a fast one?

Rockaway Park and his old neighborhood of Bensonhurst were next to each other, so was close enough good enough?

The Walshes must be grieving right now, he knew. I should write to them and describe how dedicated their son was. But first I'd need an address. Christopher's family might have a telephone. In which case, they'd be listed in the New York phone book. The library in downtown LA had telephone books from all over the country.

"Rockaway Park?" Waterford asked. "Is that where you're from?"

Luke didn't realize he'd said it out loud. "Brooklyn. But I think it's where Sparky hailed from."

"Does everybody get a nickname in the Navy?"

"Yeah, pretty much."

"Did you get one?"

Luke smiled. "Warner Boy."

Her lively eyes lit up. "That's going to make great copy. Don't be surprised if it ends up a photo caption. Right, Steve?"

The *Life* photographer stood next to a suit of armor, his zoom lens fully extended. Luke had forgotten about him. Steve launched into a story about being at Wrigley Field in Chicago the year the Cubs won the pennant in nineteen-thirty-something-or-other, but Luke thought only of running over to the PR department and telling Nell that a memory had resurfaced! Maybe. Sparky was from Rockaway Park! Possibly. Rockaway was close to Brooklyn. Was that why they'd become pals?

"Would you like to see the Maltese falcon?" Luke blurted out his question before he realized Steve hadn't finished his baseball story. "Sorry to interrupt, but it's through here and I'm sure you don't have all day."

"*The Maltese Falcon* is my favorite Bogart picture."

"Then let's go visit him."

This Maxine Waterford had been nice and all, but the room after that would take them back to the foyer, where he could wrap things up and send them on their way.

10

*N*ell halted in front of Wallichs Music City at Sunset and Vine, unexpectedly breathless.

"You're coming in, aren't you?" Luke asked.

"I've been looking forward to this ever since Hoagy called to tell me our record's release date. Now it's here and I'm—I'm—"

"Nell, honey—" Violet gave her chin a comforting squeeze— "the day 'When My Boy Helps to Liberate Gay Paree' came out, I was jumpier than a box of frogs, too."

Nell untwisted her fingers. "It's not just me?"

"You're no different from any first-time recording artist," Beatrice said, swinging open the glass door. "Now, get in here before we have to drag you in."

Four long rows of racks stretched the length of the room, each packed with records. Ten enclosed listening booths ran along the far wall. Over the loudspeakers, Kitty Kallen sang, "It's Been a Long, Long Time."

"They keep the new releases this-a-way." Violet marched to a rack near the cash registers and flicked through the records until she came to the final one.

"Not there?" Beatrice asked.

Luke suggested maybe they'd sold out, but Violet shook her head. "By eleven in the morning on release day? Let's check out Popular Music." Nell's recording wasn't there. Nor was it in Big Bands, or Female Vocalists.

"This is ridiculous!" Beatrice announced. "It must be somewhere."

"Leave it to your Auntie Vi." Violet strode to the main counter. "Hiram, honey," she said to the young man. "We're looking for the new Hoagy Carmichael tune due out today. You got it?"

"You won't find it out on the floor. It's been flying off the shelves."

Luke kissed Nell's hand. "You hear that?"

Exhilaration filled her chest. *Flying* off the shelves?

Hiram reached below the counter and produced a disc in its paper sleeve. Nell read the label in the center.

WAITING FOR YOU ON THE PIER
Words and lyrics by Hoagy Carmichael
Lead vocals: Hoagy Carmichael

"Oh . . ." The sound leaked out of Nell like she was an old squeaky toy.

"No, sweet pea," Violet said to Hiram, "I'm talking 'Every Fifth Word.' Have you—"

Hiram flipped the record over.

EVERY FIFTH WORD
Words and lyrics by Hoagy Carmichael
Lead vocals: Nell Davenport

. . .

So it was the B-side? She gave in to sinking disappointment, but only for a moment or two. Don't be so ungrateful. He's Hoagy Carmichael, for crying out loud. *Of course* he got the A-side. Being the B-side to someone as famous as him was hardly a consolation prize.

"Marvelous!" Nell announced. "I'll take ten copies."

"We only have seven left. Until we get new stocks, it's one per customer. Manager's orders."

"This gal here is the singer," Violet said. "You can let her have a few."

Hiram shook his head. "One per—"

"What if we each buy one?" Luke cut in.

"But aren't you all together?"

"We bumped into each other out front—"

"It's okay. We don't want to get Hiram into trouble." Nell pushed the record toward him. "Can we use one of the listening booths?"

"Once you've bought it, you can play it anywhere you like."

The booth had three walls made of double-paned glass to block out the din. It was not, however, designed to hold five people, so they squeezed in as best they could.

"Decca should have sent you some," Luke said.

"Even if they relegated you to the B-side," Violet added.

Nell gingerly placed the record—*her very own record!*—onto the turntable. "This is a one-off, so better a B-side than no side at all." She lowered the needle onto the edge of the disk.

Tristan twisted the volume to the maximum setting. "We need to hear it full blast."

The lush harmonies of Hoagy's six violins soared skyward as

the melody escalated to top C. Nell waited for the first line of the lyric.

"You think I don't listen when you prattle and ramble..."

Oh, my heavens! I sound like THAT?

After her remarkable one-take recording, the booth engineer had played the track through the loudspeakers. She had been delighted with how she'd sounded. But that was on a huge soundstage. Crammed into this booth with the four people whose opinions mattered most, it was as though she were singing only to them.

"But I listen more closely than ol' Alexander Graham Bell..."

She glanced covertly at their impassive faces, her heart in her throat. Weren't they enjoying it? At all? A ferocious blush crept up her neck and bloomed across her cheeks.

"You assume I only hear every fifth word you say..."

Hoagy would have been well within his rights to ask Dinah Shore or Betty Hutton, but could any of those women have poured more heart into those lyrics?

"But I catch every meaning your words can convey..."

Nell felt the heat of Luke's body pressed against her own. Shoulders, arms, hips, knees. He was staring out across the store, tears pooling in his eyes. He had worn a similar expression the day of the *Life* magazine interview, when he had deluged her with words she had been powerless to stop. She still wasn't clear on how the reporter had helped him remember Sparky was from Rockaway Park, but the 'how' didn't matter as much as the 'what.' He had recovered a precious fragment of the memory he'd lost when he'd hit that unforgiving steel deck.

He must have felt her eyes on him because he turned to face her as the song arrived at her favorite verse: "We started out so happy, when talking wasn't any chore. Let's get back to good times, the way things were before..."

"Wow," he mouthed. And again, "Wow."

***

They squeezed out of the cubicle, laughing at Tristan's wisecrack about how they looked like the Keystone Kops toppling out of a telephone booth. Suddenly he became serious again and uncertainty flickered across his face.

"Say," he said to Nell, "that guy in the Classical Music section. Didn't he work at Warners?"

Luke spotted him before Nell did. "It's Gus O'Farrell!"

Nell had last seen Gus a couple of Christmas Eves ago, slouched over the Cocoanut Grove bar, drinking alone. He had consigned his thuggish bully of a father to an asylum, and his mother had chosen to view life through the bottom of a Hennessy bottle.

But this Gus O'Farrell, in his caramel-brown herringbone suit and cream shirt, a natty pea-green ascot knotted at his throat, was a whole different person. He greeted them with a wide smile as they approached. "You—" he tapped Luke on the chest—"popped up in a Fox Movietone newsreel when I went to see *State Fair*. I nearly fell out of my seat!"

"Is that newsreel still making the rounds?"

Gus turned to Nell. "And as for you, little Miss Hollywood Canteen broadcast song siren." For such a thick-necked tank of a man, Gus emitted a bubbly lightness that Nell wouldn't have guessed possible. "I thought, 'I should track those two down.'" His smile beamed wider. "And here you are."

"We're here to buy this." Nell held up her record. "And now we're going to celebrate at Melody Lane. Care to join us?"

Nell saw no sign of the Gus O'Farrell who had once badgered her around the studio. That Gus would have scoffed at the idea of a group date. But this new version said yes as soon as the question had left her lips.

***

The booths lining the northern wall of the Melody Lane at Hollywood and Vine weren't designed to accommodate six adults, but nobody seemed to mind.

"We'll be fine," Tristan declared, "as long as none of us needs to breathe and eat simultaneously."

"Gosh," Gus said, "the last time I was here, the news broke out about the Japanese surrender. I was eating at the counter when suddenly every car in earshot was blasting its horn. We all ran outside—including the waitresses! Some passing motorist told us what had happened and we just about lost our minds."

"There'll never be another moment like it," Violet said.

"But you were right here!" Nell said. "In the thick of it."

Gus nodded. "I felt as though I was standing at the center of the world."

"The KFWB reporter said Carmen Miranda gave an impromptu concert."

"On the back seat of a convertible, wearing the cutest little matching two-piece outfit, and she sang her heart out."

Their waitress arrived with an armful of menus and told them she'd return to take their orders in a few minutes.

"I hope you kept up with your reading practice," Luke said to Gus.

"Not long after we put Dad away, a pal of mine was about to start building a house on Catalina Island and needed a hired hand for six months. I said yes in a flash and packed two suitcases. One for clothes, and because there's nothing much to do at night, I loaded the other one with every book I could lay my hands on." Gus beamed like a first grader who'd just learned to tie his shoelaces. "I've now read F. Scott Fitzgerald, Zane Grey, H.G. Wells, Edna Ferber, and Ernest Hemingway. I even tackled *Crime and Punishment*."

"Dostoevsky, huh?" Luke tipped his Navy cap to Gus. "I'm impressed."

"Yeah, but did you understand it?" Tristan asked.

"Not a damned word. But I kept hearing my father's voice in my head. 'Give up, you crummy good-for-nothing. You'll never finish that book.' I told myself how glad Luke would be to know that the time he took to teach me my ABCs set me on a path to Dostoevsky, of all people."

Luke reached across the table and grabbed Gus by the wrist. "I couldn't be more proud of you."

Gus blinked. "So imagine the look on my face when I'm sitting at the Fox Westwood and up you pop in the newsreel about Colorado. I nearly dropped my popcorn! After that, I started keeping a scrapbook. I have every mention of you in the press."

Luke's mouth hung open. "You do?"

Nell lifted her menu to cloak her face as she studied Gus. *Look at the way his eyebrows arch toward the middle of his forehead. Look at how hope fills his eyes. Does he realize his hero-worship is showing?*

"Where are you living now?" Gus asked. "I can come over and show you my scrapbook."

"In Humphrey Bogart's guesthouse. I think it's high time I moved out, though, and gave the honeymooners some space."

"You know what?" Tristan slapped their table. "I live in a block of garden court bungalows in Burbank. Real cute, real friendly, real quiet, near Warners. A neighbor of mine has applied for a job at the El Cortez Hotel in Las Vegas. If he gets it, he'll be moving, which means there'll be a vacancy."

Nell shifted her gaze to Luke and held her breath as he mulled over the opportunity. *It's time you got on with your life. This is exactly what you need.*

"Sounds perfect," Luke said. "If you could put in a good word with the manager—"

"Sure I can!"

"Wonderful!" Nell snatched up her menu. "I heard this place is famous for their Little Thin Hot Cakes, so that's me decided. What's everybody else having?"

11

When the letter arrived, it took Luke by surprise. "Whoa," he muttered to himself. "It's happening."

"What is?" Bogie kept his impatient eyes on the toaster.

Luke joined him at the counter and laid the sheet of paper in front of him.

Bogie scanned the "Bell, Amiss, and White, Attorneys-at-Law" letterhead, then whistled at the mind-boggling figure confirming Boris Osterhaus's estate had been settled and a check would soon be forthcoming. "A number that big makes a man stop and think."

"Evidently, dear ol' grandpa was a world-class bastard who couldn't be trusted to keep his word." At the Melody Lane lunch a few weeks back, Violet had told Luke stories about Boris Osterhaus, none of them flattering. "I assumed there would be a hidden catch or expired deadline, and all I'd get is 'Due to a legal technicality, you won't see a dime. Oops. Sorry. Best regards.'" But now that an honest-to-goodness check would soon be on its way, he found himself unprepared. "I don't want to be one of those numbskulls who comes into a pile of dough and burns through it all so fast they're penniless by Christmas."

"You're not the burn-through-a-pile-of-dough type. You'll be fine." Bogie extracted his breakfast from the toaster. "Have you seen that bungalow in Burbank yet?"

Tristan had called Luke a few days after their lunch at Melody Lane to tell him that his neighbor would be moving out after Thanksgiving. When Luke broke the news to Bogie and Betty, neither of them had protested "We'll miss having you around!"

"I can inspect it as soon as the tenant leaves."

Bogie tapped the letter. "Why rent?"

"Having this new place means I won't make the mistake of buying the first house I see."

"You're not the buy-the-first-house type, either."

The figure was almost hypnotizing. Big-time money. Life-changing money. Do-what-you-want, buy-what-you-want, be-what-you-want money. All he knew for now was that until it no longer had the power to make his hands damp, he'd be smart to put off any substantial decisions.

"What are you thinking about?" Bogie asked.

"Avery." Luke turned his back on the letter. "He was Osterhaus's son. I can't help thinking he deserves this more than I do."

"Even though you were his grandson?"

"Illegitimate. Socially unacceptable. Given away at the earliest opportunity."

"Like most super-rich people, the guy was a grade-A asshole. But don't forget, he convinced your aunt to keep an eye out for you. So he didn't abandon you altogether."

Luke missed Aunt Wilda at the most peculiar times. It wasn't only when he heard a favorite song of hers or someone with her laugh. Sometimes birdsong triggered a wave of love mixed with regret and longing. One night in Boulder, when he was trying to pound Japanese military terms into his mutinous brain, he noticed a full moon outside his dorm window. Before he knew it, he'd spent ten minutes reminiscing about the day she took him to the foot of the Brooklyn Bridge. She had pointed across the East

River to the soaring Manhattan skyline and told him, "That could be your oyster, Luke. Don't settle for anything less."

The door to the Bogart manse slammed shut. Betty's voice called from down the hall, "We have booze!"

"And sandwiches," Nell's voice chimed in. "Sandwich ingredients, anyway. Enough bologna to feed the Pacific Fleet." The girls set their over-filled shopping bags on the tiled counter and took in the guys' faces. "What's happened?"

Luke shook the letter like it was a semaphore flag. "It appears I'm about to become a fat cat with more money than I know what to do with."

Nell read out loud the colossal figure and punctuated it with a sharp whistle. "I had my doubts this money would ever come through."

"You and me both."

"The whole 'don't count your chickens' thing?" Betty said. "I was the same way before Howard cast me in *To Have and Have Not*." She planted a loving smooch on Bogie's cheek. "But everything turned out fine for us. And it will for you."

"We have two reasons to celebrate this afternoon." Bogie pulled out a huge bundle of bologna wrapped in white butcher paper. "The sooner we make these sandwiches, the sooner we can get on the water."

* * *

When Bogie had bought a fifty-foot schooner from Dick Powell, he'd suggested that the four of them take the *Sluggy* for a fare-thee-well cruise to Dana Point. Bogie could have chosen any of his closest pals: John Huston, Nathaniel Benchley, Peter Lorre, Nunnally Johnson. But he'd passed them all over for Luke and Nell, a gesture that had touched Luke so deeply that he had still been trying to find the words when Betty had proposed they hold a remembrance ceremony for Sparky. He had found the Walshes' address in a New York telephone book at the library and had written to them, but hadn't heard back.

Halfway to the Newport Yacht Club, they were approaching Huntington Beach when Nell announced, "We need to make a stop!"

Bogie tsked from the front seat. "Can't you hold it till we get there?"

"Not that." She slapped the back of his head. "Today's *Saturday Evening Post* is serializing a new novel called *The Unsuspected*. The scuttlebutt at the studio is that we might option it. If we do, I want to pitch Taplinger first to make sure that Mister I Carried the Flag at Iwo Jima doesn't nab it."

Nell was still the same spunky girl whose glass was nearly always half full. But since that day at Wallichs, Luke had noticed the extra zing enlivening her step, coupled with a radiant glow that had only dimmed after Taplinger had demoted her to B pictures. Whatever was going to happen with "Every Fifth Word," the experience had boosted her confidence, and now she was making plans to get in on the ground level of a project that might not even come to Warners. He had to admire her pluck—and he did.

He wished he could brush off the tiny niggling doubt that had been pestering him since the afternoon he had watched her in the recording booth. If he'd known that Nell would incorporate their secret code into a song that she'd write with a famous musician and sing on a broadcast, he never would have started sending her coded messages in the first place. Sure, it had led to his being able to claim his inheritance, so he wasn't about to complain. But sending coded messages about where he was and what he was doing was the biggest no-no in the Navy's No-No Manual. Breaking it was grounds for dishonorable discharge. Or worse: court martial.

The war was over, so he was probably worrying about nothing. But still, of all the songs she could have recorded, did it have to be the one he wished would fade away?

When Betty noticed a newsstand filling part of a rest area, Bogie pulled off the Pacific Coast Highway. Nell hopped out, promising she wouldn't be long.

"Funny how you bumped into Gus O'Farrell the other day," Bogie said. "I hope that kid got out from under that meat-headed father of his."

He and Betty had been out when Gus had come around, so Luke and Gus had sat undisturbed in the kitchen nook, poring over Gus's scrapbook. Luke had had no idea how far his story had spread until he'd leafed through page after page filled with articles Gus had cut out of every newspaper between Oregon and the Mexican border.

"He's doing fine," Luke replied. "After he helped a friend build a house on Catalina, he got a job working construction for a developer who says we're heading into a housing boom. He thinks that in twenty years' time, blocks and blocks of houses will replace all those citrus groves and lima bean fields in the San Fernando Valley."

"It's hot out there," Betty commented. "Especially in the summer."

"Gus's boss claims that by 1950, LA's population will have doubled. All those newcomers have to live somewhere."

Nell had kidded Luke about Gus's hero-worship. He hadn't noticed it across the crowded Melody Lane table, but it had been obvious in the Bogart breakfast nook. That loyal puppy-dog look in his eyes, the giggly tone his voice took on when describing how he'd located another mention of Luke in the *Sacramento Bee* or *Denver Post*. He had even offered to give Luke the scrapbook, but Luke had turned him down, saying that he had only so much space in Bogie's guest room. In truth, he felt owning such a book verged on narcissism, and he'd seen too many of those personalities to get sucked into the same trap of self-admiration leading to unfettered self-absorption.

"Is it true you taught that guy to read?" Betty asked.

"Just his ABCs. I went off to serve, so he learned the rest himself."

Betty reached over and tapped Luke's knee. "You make it sound as though it were nothing, but you—"

The passenger-side door flew open and Nell jumped in, two folded magazines in her hand. "You'll never guess what!"

"Sold out of the *Post*?" Bogie asked.

She unfurled a copy of *Life* magazine; a demure photo of Ingrid Bergman filled the cover.

"Hardly surprising," Betty said. "She's got three big movies coming out this year."

"No, not her." She flipped the pages until she came to the cause of her bright pink cheeks. "THIS!"

Luke stared at himself seated at the *Casablanca* piano with a dreamy smile as his fingers played a chord. That interview had been two months ago. The reporter—what was her name? Melody? Madeline? Mavis?—had admitted that she didn't know if they would even publish her article. "It's all up to the editor," she had said. "Don't get your hopes up!" And so Luke hadn't.

"You didn't mention a photographer!" Nell exclaimed.

"He floated around like a shadow." Luke took the magazine from her and read the photo's caption: *Lieutenant Luke Valenti, war hero and accomplished pianist.*

In retrospect, it had felt less of an interview and more of a meandering stroll while chatting about this, that, and the other. How could he have given her enough material to fill an entire article? All he had was a variation of the crazy quilt of facts and figures he'd stitched together for his *Breakfast in Hollywood* appearance.

Bogie huffed a melodramatic sigh to rival anything Joan Crawford had ever put on film. "Has the egomaniac finished staring at himself yet?"

Luke handed over the magazine so that he and Betty could see. "Were you actually tickling the ivories?" Bogie asked.

"Would you believe I was playing 'As Time Goes By'?"

Bogie exploded with laughter. "Well, if that don't beat all." He swung his car back into the sparse Sunday morning traffic.

Betty rolled down her window to let the sea breeze whip through her hair. "I dunno," she said to her husband, "maybe *you* should do something important."

He roared again. "Get a load of Miss Harper's Bazaar here."

As the two slung zingers at each other, Nell stroked Luke's knee. "I should have bought more copies to send to your folks."

Over the previous months, they had joked and marveled in equal measure at the unexpected turnaround with their families.

Nell regularly heard from her father these days. The man who had always been impossible to please packed his letters with how the Notre Dame football team was faring now that the boys were coming home; an enormous owl he'd tracked in Pinhook Park; a fiftieth-anniversary party he and Mother had attended at the Morris Park Country Club. Few of the names he mentioned were familiar to her, and she had no great interest in the fate of the Fighting Irish football team, but she treasured each letter, nonetheless. And ever since Luke's folks had sent that telegram during *Breakfast in Hollywood*, a steady stream of picture postcards, letters, and photographs of family gatherings had been arriving.

"*Life* magazine is available in Brooklyn, y'know."

She pinched his earlobe affectionately. "They could show off an autographed one to their neighbors."

"You could start getting fan mail at the studio," Bogie cautioned. "Brace yourself, is all I'm saying."

"And if you receive more than he does," Betty added, "he'll slug you right in the puss. You know those movie-star egos. There's no controlling them."

"I'll happily put my ducking skills against Humphrey Bogart's slugging skills any damned day of the week and twice on Sunday."

* * *

Luke hadn't anticipated the sharp nip in the November breezes. The open-necked seersucker shirt he'd donned that morning was no match for the chill of the late-fall sun. But the water was reasonably calm when Bogie cut the engine and announced they were ten nautical miles off Laguna Beach.

Luke braced his legs against the stern of the *Sluggy* and stared into the endless blue of the Pacific, thinking about the time Bogie had decided to treat his unanticipated fear of deep water. Whatever had caused his anxiety that day had long since melted away. Living for months in an underwater tube was enough to cure anyone of thalassophobia.

"I'm not sure what to say," he told the others.

He wanted more than ever to give Christopher the valediction he deserved. That stealthy photographer had captured a flattering image, and the Valenti clan back east would get a kick out of it. But parallel to that eddy of surprise and pride ran a second riptide of conflicting emotions that Luke struggled to pinpoint.

He was already uncomfortable standing in the heat of the limelight, and this *Life* article only intensified those feelings. But there was something else lurking in the background, staining this moment.

"You can't go wrong speaking from the heart," Betty prompted. Nell took his hand. "Just a few words are all you need."

"This might help."

Bogie held up an old microphone, chipped in places, dented in others. "I found this beauty cleaning out the garage last weekend. When I was in the Navy at the end of the Great War, we had a few funerals at sea. They'd slide the wrapped body into the water and we'd all watch it sink. Your pal was a radio operator. His equipment probably didn't look like this, but for the purposes of this exercise, a microphone is a microphone."

Luke took it from him. Tarnished over time, it was around eight inches across. Sitting on a half-circle stand, it had a series of concentric circles on one side and the brand name—*Little Wonder Microphone*—embossed on the back.

It also provided Luke with the words he needed.

"I wish you had made it out that night, and that you could be with us here today. I'd give anything to watch you receiving medals and appearing in magazines. I can't change how it all unfolded, but here's what I can do, buddy. Everybody called you Sparky, but I'll remember you as Christopher from Rockaway Park. I'll never forget you. Not ever."

Luke dropped the Little Wonder into the water. It thwacked the surface and sank without a trace. He felt one hand on his left shoulder, another one on his right, as a third one patted his back.

A gust of briny sea air blew along the deck as a pair of seagulls glided into view and landed on the water. "Thanks, guys," he said to the three behind him. "I needed that. The weight has been unbearable. But now—" he about-faced "—oddly, I'm famished. Is that wrong? Who's ready for a juicy bologna sandwich? Is there any beer aboard the Bogart bucket?"

12

Nell pulled Betty's old Plymouth to the curb. Technically, it was Nell's now that Betty had spent some of her *Confidential Agent* money on a new car to make herself feel better after critics had written off her performance as "amateur."

The vaguely Spanish Mission-style garden court bungalows were painted a pale terracotta with dark green window trim, and each had a front patio big enough to fit two chairs and a café table. A line of three bungalows faced each other over a central fountain; a couple more stood at the rear.

"Oh, Luke! What a cute block this is!" Nell pointed to the row of purple, yellow, and white flowers running along the sidewalk. "And those darling crocuses."

"The manager gives Tristan a break on the rent to maintain the garden. He alternates them with geraniums and nasturtiums."

"And only eight blocks from the studio? If you don't take this place, I might."

"The hell you will, Davenport," he said. "Back off."

Nell smiled to herself. Betty's idea of a nautical memorial service had hit the mark. He'd been so different on the drive home from Newport that day. Lighter, somehow. Brighter. Almost as though he'd stumbled across an electric switch inside him.

It had been a fun couple of weeks watching him return to his old self. A picnic in Griffith Park, dancing at the Palomar, chicken dinners at King's Tropical Inn. Her favorite had been that walk along Santa Monica beach followed by a marathon heavy petting session in the last row of the El Miro as some Betty Grable musical played out in glorious-but-ignored Technicolor. And if these bungalows were as charming on the inside as they were on the outside, they would make a much more cheerful spot to show Luke the telegram that had arrived earlier that morning.

She opened the car door. "First one there gets first choice—"

He shot out of the Plymouth like his tail feathers were on fire. Happy to let him win, she was still panting and giggly by the time he'd retrieved the key from beneath a pot of orange marigolds.

The front door opened into a square living room. Around twelve feet by twelve feet, it was big enough for the loveseat and coffee table, as well as an easy chair that would need a throw blanket to cover an amorphous stain on the brown velvet upholstery. With windows on two sides and a high ceiling, there was plenty of space for one person. And the odd overnight visitor.

The doorway on the right opened onto a kitchen painted in lovely pale yellow with corncob-pattern drapes framing the window. Not that colors meant much to him, but there was a cozy, welcoming feeling to the room. A small table for two sat in the corner opposite a spotless stove.

"I could be happy here," he said.

Nell toyed with the top button of her blouse. "Let's check out the bedroom." She suffused that last word with a breathy shamelessness to test the waters. If it was as darling as the living room, he would be in high spirits.

The bedroom was smaller, but had enough space for a double bed, a pair of black-lacquered side tables, matching lamps, and a wardrobe. A framed painting could cheer up the sun-faded cream-and-blue-striped wallpaper. Breezes wafted in through the open window, lifting the lace curtains as it brought with it a melody playing on the neighbor's radio.

"I think I should—"

"Do you hear that?" She dragged him to the window.

More than a month had passed since Decca had released "Every Fifth Word." Content with being the B-side to Hoagy's A, she had watched with mounting delirium as the record climbed into the top fifty. On the astonishing day it reached the top twenty, *Billboard* had listed "Waiting for You on the Pier" as the B-side and Nell's song as the A. Nell had jumped on the phone to ask Hoagy who they should call to have this error corrected. He had replied with a good-natured chuckle. "*Billboard* didn't screw up. It's not me those buyers want. It's *you*."

Luke kissed the backs of her hands. "I hear it all the time on the radio."

"You know what I think?" she asked.

"It's a sign I should move in?"

"Laugh all you want, but yes."

"What if the bathroom resembles Dracula's dungeon decorated by Frankenstein?"

She prodded him toward the door. "When you're done, you'll find me right here because I doubt I'll ever get sick of hearing myself on the radio."

She popped open her pocketbook to ensure the telegram was still tucked inside. Naturally, it was. Where else would it be? She wouldn't have needed to reassure herself if her colleagues' reaction to her news hadn't been so dispiriting.

When she learned NBC had invited her to appear on *The Lucky Strike Program Starring Jack Benny*, Nell had showed the telegram to her co-workers, squealing, "Me? On *The Lucky Strike Program*? With Jack Benny! Can you believe it?"

They couldn't. A couple of them mumbled their congratulations, but hadn't bothered to put any oomph behind it. The rest of them had stared mutely at her. Their reaction had been underwhelming enough, so she was uneasy about how Taplinger was going to react, considering his iron-fast dictum: PR people *spread* the story, but they must never *be* the story. She had broken that rule once over the infamous Hedda Hopper–slapping incident, but now it had happened again. Would he be so forgiving a second time around?

No. He wouldn't. "That sure is something," had been his tepid response. "However, it can't interfere with your work."

A breath of warm afternoon breeze drifted in as her song reached its last verse. Perhaps she should knock back the *Lucky Strikes* offer, let the record run its course, and fade into obscurity. Settle down with Luke, mingle with the Bogarts and their orbit of movie elites, and every now and then talk about the winter when she had one of the most popular songs in the country. It was hardly a meager consolation prize.

But her heart sank at the thought of it.

Was it so bad to admit she was enjoying her moment of fame? She had loved the process of recording the song. Not long after the *Sluggy*'s final excursion, Hoagy had asked her and Luke to dinner with his wife at Perino's, a classy restaurant she couldn't afford on her own. Whenever people approached the table to say hello, Hoagy always introduced her and Luke, transforming the evening into one long, continuous thrill.

She might have relished it even more had it not been for the twinges of guilt dimming her delight. Guilt about what? She had been too caught up in the thrill of sitting at Perino's center table to answer that question. But later, it had come to her: Luke couldn't wait for his own celebrity to subside. Later that night, when she and Luke had talked about it, she made out like she felt the same as him, and that she would've preferred Hoagy hadn't made a fuss.

An odd noise floated in from the bathroom. Why was Luke taking so long? "Is Frankenstein's taste as bad as all that?"

She found him sprawled out on the tiles, face down, between the bathtub and the toilet, his eyes closed, his forehead glazed with sweat, retching with dry heaves.

"LUKE!" She threw her purse aside and crouched next to him. "What's going on? Luke? LUKE! Can you hear me?"

A tear leaked out of his right eye and plopped onto the tile. He tried to speak, but the words left his mouth in breathy wheezes. "Blah," he panted. "Blee . . . chuh . . ."

Bleach? Was that what he said? Nell sniffed at the air. Someone had given the place a thorough cleaning. Wasn't that a good thing? She hooked her elbows under his armpits. "I can't get you to the living room alone. I need your help."

She helped him to his feet and steered him to the loveseat.

"What was that all about?"

He took several deep breaths. "I felt like I'd been hit in the face with a sack of wet jellyfish. And then a nauseating feeling of panic swamped me."

"From the bleach?"

"It was so strong, so overwhelming."

It seemed the usual amount to Nell. "What happened after that?"

"I couldn't see straight. Couldn't think straight. I guess my knees buckled because the next thing I knew, the cold bathtub was pressing against my face and my stomach was churning."

"How is it now?"

"Gone." He took a deeper, cleansing breath. "Mostly."

"So . . . this place? You taking it?"

"I was ready to sign up, but oh brother, that bathroom." He shook his head ruefully. "What a cream puff. I mean, it's just bleach. I grew up in a house crammed with men; Mom used it constantly."

"I can rinse everything down with hot water."

"Would you?" He kissed her cheek. "That'd be super."

Outside in the courtyard, they heard a familiar tinkling laugh.

They slipped off the sofa and went to the front door, but stopped themselves from calling out when they caught sight of Tristan walking toward the street with Gus O'Farrell. And not any old regular walking. There was something awfully cozy to the way their shoulders grazed each other, and how their pinkie fingers momentarily snared each other.

Nell looked at Luke. "I don't want to jump to conclusions, but—" she returned to the sight of the two men practically floating down the path "—are we seeing what I think we're seeing?"

Luke craned his neck until they had reached the sidewalk. "I think so, yes."

"Tristan and Gus? They're . . ."

"Together?" Luke let out a low whistle. "I did not see that coming."

"So Gus is—I mean, Tristan, sure. You'd have to be deaf, dumb, and blind not to know about him. But Gus? *GUS O'FARRELL?*"

Luke looked at Nell with as much wide-eyed incredulity as she felt. "I can barely wrap my head around it."

"But it's a good thing, right?" Nell said. "It's hard enough to find a decent guy in this world, but when you're a guy yourself, it must be—"

Luke took a half-step back from the doorway. "Should we pretend we didn't see anything?"

"You saw the way they were with each other just now."

"You're right," he said. "He's our friend and we're happy for him."

They waited until Tristan had reached Luke's porch. "Well, helloo-oo!" Nell called out, marching out of the shadow.

Tristan shielded his eyes from the late-afternoon sun. "Been inspecting the joint? Moving in? Will we be neighbors soon?"

When Luke told him yes, yes, and yes, Tristan invited them into his own bungalow for a "celebratory sherry, brandy, port, or pick-your-poison." His living room was overloaded with a sewing machine, three dress forms, bolts of shot silk, chiffon, and

Donegal tweed, baskets of ribbons, and boxes of lace. He cast an appraising eye at them. "I assume you saw the parade?" He poured them each a glass of Spanish dry sherry and told them to take a seat on his sofa. "It appears I have a love life. And I couldn't be more surprised."

Nell wasn't a great fan of sherry, but it seemed a shame to spoil his buoyant mood. She took a sip. "How long's this been going on?"

"Since Melody Lane. He played footsies with me under the table. At first, I thought it was accidental. Then I decided he was jeering me with the usual 'torment the faggot' scenario, until it dawned on me that he was flirting! One thing led to another, and we ended up back at my place. And here we are, six weeks later."

"You're having a romance," Luke said.

"I am!" Tristan slapped his hands to his chest. "I guess you must be, too—with your adoring public. I hear they've been inundating you with scads of fan mail since your interview in *Life*."

Nell exhaled a silent breath of relief that the three of them had negotiated what could have been an acutely awkward moment without much discomfort.

A sour expression passed over Luke's face. "Bogie predicted I would. I laughed it off at the time, so I nearly passed out when they dropped off three bags filled with mail."

"Are you really that surprised?" Nell asked. "I thought the reporter did a masterful job of wallpapering over how you couldn't give her many concrete details."

"Yep," Luke conceded, "she did."

"Then why do you look like you've been force-fed a quart of castor oil?"

"I've been looking forward to the day when this spotlight moves on to someone else, but it keeps getting brighter."

"My goodness!" Nell jumped up. "With all the drama, I left my purse behind."

"What drama?" Tristan asked.

"Luke can fill you in." She stepped outside, where the deliciously tangy scent of sage filled the clear December air.

The early moon shone through Luke's new living room window, giving her enough light to find her way to the bathroom. The purse lay on its side. She pried the clasp open and pulled out the *Lucky Strike* telegram.

She could already picture Luke's expression if she told him she was accepting the offer. He'd see it as inviting fame to move even closer, make the spotlight shine brighter. He'd been through enough. She wanted to lighten his load, not add to his misery.

She ripped the Western Union envelope into halves and tore the halves into shreds. When she was done, she tossed the pieces into the trash can next to Tristan's porch. "I'm back!" she shrieked. "Let's toast to you two becoming neighbors."

13

*L*uke rapped his knuckles on the polished teak lining the edge of Bogie's new schooner, the *Santana*. "This sure is a step up, Cap'n Fancypants."

Bogie's grin hadn't left him since Luke and Nell had arrived at the Newport Yacht Club. "I was fond of the *Sluggy*, but it doesn't come close." He ran his eyes up the main mast jutting into the sea air. "I can't wait to take her out."

"Why are we still tied to the dock," Nell asked, "when we could have the wind at our backs, dolphins leaping at the—what's the front bit called?"

"The *bow*," Betty told her. "If you don't get the basics down, Captain Fancypants'll toss you overboard."

"Nell's got a point." Luke stretched a hand toward the open ocean. "Aren't you just itching to sail out there?"

Bogie rolled up the sleeves of his red flannel shirt. "I will not risk taking my baby out until I've learned how she works in every situation, weather condition, and emergency."

"Gee, Bogie." Nell faked a yawn. "I had you pegged as a learn-on-the-job type sailor. I didn't realize you took it all so seriously."

Bogie pensively tied a length of rope into a reef knot. "An actor needs something to stabilize his personality, to nail down what he really is, not what he's pretending to be."

"Y'know—" Betty stretched her legs over Bogie's "—we haven't talked about that *Hollywood Reporter* article."

Luke's face fell. He had been hoping that the four of them might enjoy an afternoon on the *Santana*, the water rocking them gently, champagne to toast Bogie's beloved new toy, and leave behind all talk of Hollywood, Hollywood, Hollywood. Did oil people and banking people and grocery people discuss and dissect their industry as much as Hollywoodites did?

"From the look on Luke's face, perhaps we shouldn't," Bogie said.

"Nah, it's fine," Luke said. "It did get us the table beneath Gable and Lombard at the Vine Street Brown Derby." Caricatures of famous faces covered the restaurant's walls; the bigger the star, the more desirable the location. "I've always wondered how it felt being a big movie star."

But for him, the *Life* magazine piece had been more than enough of a sip at fame's soup bowl. Here they were, weeks later, and fan mail continued to overwhelm his work area. The bulk of people had written to thank him for his brave service to his country. He was happy to reply to as many of their heartfelt letters as he could, even though it had become a second full-time job.

What kept him going was the hope that the next letter he opened might be from Christopher's family. But no such response had arrived, and his hope was waning. If the Walshes didn't read *Life*, they wouldn't read *The Hollywood Reporter*.

"El Primo muckamuck service takes some getting used to." Betty let out a throaty laugh that most of America couldn't get enough of. "But how did Kathryn Massey figure out that your song was written about and sung to the hero of the *Lanternfish?*"

"We have Joan Crawford to thank for that," Nell said. "Kathryn had been interviewing her about her *Mildred Pierce* success. They were in Joan's dressing room when my song came on the radio.

Joan mentioned I had written it for Luke. The next thing I knew, Kathryn was standing at my desk insisting on an interview, which was awkward because my co-workers aren't exactly enamored with me right now. But I couldn't tell her to shove off, so we went to the commissary and had a long cup of coffee." She drained the last of her champagne. "The calls and telegrams I've been getting—it's been the most marvelous whirlwind, hasn't it, darling?"

Luke nodded.

It has been, he thought, for *you*.

He didn't want to be the sourpuss who ruined the party, and was genuinely glad she hadn't let the jealous killjoys she worked with dampen her spirits. After all, it had to have been awful for her to find him sprawled out on the bathroom floor, clammy, dry-mouthed, and nauseous. And he'd happily sat on the sidelines and watched how her success filled her with a radiant sparkle. Why begrudge her time in the spotlight when fame was a fickle bitch who would ultimately decamp for someone else?

Seeing himself in *Life* magazine had sent a frisson of excitement up his spine, mostly because he knew how proud his family would be. Frankly, though, it had been enough. This *Hollywood Reporter* article had splashed some of Nell's spotlight onto him, and now he wished he could rinse it off the way Nell had scrubbed off that overpowering bleach.

Bogie tossed the empty champagne magnum into a nearby trashcan. It clattered against the metal sides loudly enough to disturb the pair of gray petrels resting on the rail that followed the curve of the bow. "That's all the bubbly we brought. Beer from here on out." He reached into an oval tub of ice and pulled out four bottles of Lucky Lager. "Did anyone see my bottle opener?"

"In the drawer next to the sink," Betty said. As he made for the door that led below decks, she asked him, "Can I tell them our big news now?"

"Which one?"

"How many have you got?" Luke asked.

Bogie waved for her to go ahead as he disappeared into the galley.

Betty now had a gleam in her eye the size of the Hope Diamond. "A neighbor of ours runs the West Coast office of *Billboard* magazine. This morning, as we were getting ready to come down here, he presented us with this!" She reached behind her pink-and-white polka-dotted cushion and pulled out the latest edition, featuring Perry Como on a burgundy-red velvet sofa. She flipped it open to an early page and held it up. The headline read MUSIC POPULARITY CHART.

"Look who's sitting at Number One."

Three columns divided the chart: "National," "East," and "West Coast." The same song occupied the top position in each category.

EVERY FIFTH WORD
Nell Davenport

Nell squealed. A pair of teenagers who'd been necking in a nearby rowboat looked up and waved. She waved back and turned to Luke, her eyes blazing. "All three markets? Can you believe it?"

Her spotlight just got brighter, but that's okay. It'll all be over soon. Nobody's going to connect your V-mails home to Nell and the most popular song in the country. Yes, you did the wrong thing, but nobody's looking. Nobody cares. So quit worrying and don't be a wet blanket.

"All *four* markets." Luke kissed her cheek. "You're number one with me, too."

"Being in the top twenty was exciting enough." She lifted the magazine out of Betty's hands and kissed the page. "But this?!"

Bogie reemerged on deck, a filled ice bucket in his hands. "We should have saved the champagne for Nell's news." He popped the cap off each bottle of Lucky Lager and handed them around. "Couldn't happen to a more well-deserving kiddo."

"I'm lightheaded!" She crushed the magazine to her chest.

"Meanwhile, I have some news, too," Bogie said. "More of an announcement, I guess." His sun-bronzed face took on a dreamy glow, blotting out any residue of the streetwise hoods and hustlers he had played for years. "I'm planning a jail break."

Luke looked at Betty, then Nell, then back to Bogie. "In this scenario, jail is Warners?"

"I give them *Casablanca*, *To Have and Have Not*, and *The Big Sleep*, and they say thanks with *The Two Mrs. Carrolls*. I'm bound by shackles and chains."

"You sound like a man with a plan," Luke said.

"I'm starting my own production company." Bogie couldn't have sounded prouder if he'd learned he'd soon be a father. "And I'm going to call it—" he rapped three times on the teak trim "—Santana Productions." He crossed his arms over his chest, almost as though to keep himself from busting wide open.

"You absolutely should have far more say in your career," Nell said.

"You've earned the right to pick your projects, your directors, your—" Luke flickered a glance at Betty "—co-stars."

"You're all for it?" Bogie asked Luke.

"Absolutely."

"Good." Bogie clinked his lager to Luke's. "Because I want you on board with me."

The *Santana* seesawed from the ripples of a passing motorboat. "On board . . . how?"

"Beats the hell out of me. The higher you go in this business, the more toady, boot-licking sycophants you attract. Everybody's in it for what they'll get out of it. I want to jump into this venture with someone I can trust."

"You have trustworthy friends," Nell said.

"Friends who know the trade better than I do," Luke added.

"Correct on both counts. But I need the right friend I can trust in the right way."

"And that's me?"

"You've had a great deal of fame thrown at you, and I should have said this sooner, but I admire how you've taken it in your stride. Most guys would have let it go to their head, strutting around the Cocoanut Grove and Ciro's like they're General fucking Patton—'scuse my French, ladies."

"I have a theory," Betty announced, giving Luke a pointed glance, "that you haven't been enjoying your celebrity."

Luke wondered if he was this transparent to everybody, or whether Bogie's new wife was just especially perceptive. "It hasn't been all bad. Some aspects of it have been exciting."

"It's different for me," Betty continued. "I went after it whole hog. Who the hell knew I'd hit it big right out of the gate? But it's not what you signed up for."

"No," Luke admitted. "It isn't." He turned to Bogie. "You want me on board because I won't hog the spotlight?"

"It's one of a whole bunch of reasons. We can go through them—"

"That won't be necessary." How could Luke say no to this opportunity? Why would he? Why would anybody? "Let's do it."

14

*N*ell and Luke were fifteen feet from Romanoff's restaurant when she hooked the sleeve of his rented tux and bared her teeth to him. "Any lipstick on my teeth? I think I can taste it."

He angled her toward the streetlight. "I see more lipstick than teeth."

"What?" She was halfway through peeling off her glove when he laughed. She swatted him across the shoulder. "Fink!"

"What are you so nervous about?" he asked.

"Who's nervous?" *Gosh, Nell, that didn't sound defensive at all.*

He responded with sardonically raised eyebrows.

She had no answer for him. Not one that she wanted to speak out loud, at any rate. "Come on. They're probably waiting for us."

When Betty had called to invite Nell and Luke to see in the new year at Romanoff's, they had already made plans with Beatrice and Keaton Vance. "Six is better than four," Betty had told Nell. "Bring 'em along!"

Beatrice had been thrilled to hear they'd be spending the evening with the Bogarts. A conspiratorial whisper quickly followed. "Keaton's got an upcoming assignment of global proportions. I can't tell you about it, but while he's here, what he needs is fun, fun, fun. Capeesh?"

Luke moved aside to let a trio of starlets in strapless gowns of sparkling tulle step past them. "What is it, then?"

Telling him "It's nothing" would be unfair. But what could she say? "When was the last time you saw Captain Stamina?"

"Apart from my ceremony?" Luke thought for a moment. "Before I went to Boulder, so it must be close to three years. Why?"

Because you've been so happy-go-lucky since that day on the Santana. "I'd imagine a couple of war veterans like you two would have a lot to chew over, but I'm wondering if it'll spoil an otherwise fun New Year's Eve."

He kissed her on the forehead. "Trust me, war is the last subject I want to talk about." He opened the Romanoff's door. "And for God's sake, remember: it's now *Commodore* Stamina."

* * *

Beatrice and Keaton were waiting for them in the foyer, claiming they had "arrived only seconds ago," but Nell suspected they were a little too intimidated to introduce themselves to Hollywood's current "It" couple. Perhaps not. Would a movie star daunt a seasoned officer who had faced years of maritime warfare? Then again, Luke and Tristan had referred to him as "Captain Stamina" for so long that Nell had built up an image of a barrel-chested titan with a lantern jaw and he-man voice. Seeing him at Luke's ceremony looking more like one of Luke's POWs had surprised her. Whatever he'd done during the war had plainly taken its toll.

Betty looked ravishing in an emerald-green silk dress whose bateau neckline cut across her collarbone. She and Bogie were saying goodbye to Dick Powell and June Allyson when the four of them arrived at a roomy table on the edge of the dance floor, where Abe Lyman and his orchestra played a jaunty version of

"For Me and My Gal." Introductions were made, drink orders taken, and cigarettes lit.

Nell snuck a peek around the place. All eight people in Alfred Hitchcock's party were rubbernecking in their direction. Even Greer Garson and her conspicuously younger husband were having trouble disguising their fascination.

The band finished off with a flourish of cymbals. Lyman, a slick-haired, pale-skinned man in his forties, stepped to the microphone. "Ladies and gentlemen, we're fortunate to have among us the talented chanteuse whose vocal stylings occupy the number one slot atop *Billboard's* Music Popularity Chart." Nell belched out a conspicuous yip. "I'm hoping that with sufficient encouragement, she might favor us with a rendition of her song."

As applause deluged her, Nell gaped at Luke—*Should I?* He replied with a silent blink. *I don't think you've got much choice.*

When she stepped onto the stage, she squinted in the glare of the spotlight. "Good evening, everyone. My name is Nell Davenport." She heard Betty's distinctive baritone whooping. "This is spontaneous, so forgive me any flubs."

Sitting at the white piano positioned somewhere off to her right—*Honestly! How can performers bear not seeing anything past the end of their hands?*—Lyman said, "Nod whenever you're ready."

When she took a breath to calm herself, she found, to her surprise, no nerves that needed settling. Was this how it felt to be in the eye of a twister?

She nodded.

Lyman called out "A-five, six, seven, eight," and led his orchestra into the opening chords.

The melody of the last line was an almost-two-octave run up from D above middle C to the B below high C. When she had sung "Every Fifth Word" at the Hollywood Canteen, reaching that final note had taken every scintilla of concentration. But not this time, not this evening, not this stage. Carried along by the electricity galvanizing the air, Nell filled her lungs, opened her mouth. "The couple of the Y-E-A-RRRRR!"

The applause lifted her up as though she were lighter than an autumn leaf. On the night of the Hollywood Canteen broadcast, Martha Raye had counseled her, "The savviest performers are the ones who know when to make their exit." She waved her thanks to Lyman, blew the audience a double-handed kiss, and shielded her eyes so that she could step off the stage without falling into an ignominious heap.

She used to dread singing for people so much that she would ride her bicycle deep into the woods on the outskirts of South Bend to avoid getting up in front of a crowd. *And look at me now.*

Luke leapt up as she approached their table and planted a kiss on her cheek as she acknowledged their appreciation with a wave.

"My goodness," Keaton said as she settled into her seat. "That was quite the thrill."

"You sure wowed us!" Luke's enthusiasm made her relive her regret over ripping up that *Lucky Strike* invitation so rashly. It hadn't taken long before her misgivings had begun to nip at her like summer skeeters. She had made the decision herself, so she had nobody to blame. But oh brother, if she had a dollar for every time she wished she could go back and accept the offer. But now it sounded like Luke had come around to the idea of this singing business. She had no plans to take it any further, but it was nice to know he might be supportive, if only in theory.

"Thank you, darling!" She raised her empty coupe. "Which one of you lushes drank the rest of my champagne cocktail?"

"Alleged lushes," Beatrice insisted. "Nell, honey, you downed that baby before you stepped up to the microphone."

This whole evening was turning into a starry-eyed blur. Casting around for their waiter, she caught sight of a pair of faces seated at a table two rows back. "Who's the guy sitting with Kathryn Massey?"

"Marcus Adler," Bogie said. "He heads up the MGM writing department. They got hitched a few months ago."

"Don't you remember?" Betty asked. "We met him at the Garden of Allah when we bought those"—she lowered her voice to a stage whisper—"black-market nylons."

"*That's* the guy she married?" Nell stole a second peek to confirm he was who she thought he was. "He struck me as being on the swishy side."

"He is," Bogie said matter-of-factly. "But he needed to hedge his bets after that tawdry roman à clef came out."

"*Reds in the Beds!*" Beatrice stabbed out her cigarette with more force than necessary.

All the reviews Nell had read about it had dismissed the book as a shoddy time-waster. "Is it as bad as they say?"

"Atrocious character assassination from start to finish."

Betty sliced a red varnished nail across her throat. "Whoever wrote that piece of trash sure has it out for those two."

"I know them from the Garden," Bogie said. "They're sterling people and don't deserve this treatment."

"I'm surprised they're showing their faces," Beatrice said. "And on New Year's Eve, no less. Talk about fearless."

Nell had been around Louella Parsons and Hedda Hopper when they'd been at fancy restaurants. Those two old crones spent more time table-hopping and celebrity-elbow-rubbing than dining. But Kathryn simply sat at her table, steadfastly focusing on her conversation with her husband.

How awful did a book have to be if it had cornered them into getting married?

Nell stood up. "Order me another champagne cocktail."

"Where are you going?" Dismay laced Bogie's question.

"To say hello."

"They're social lepers right now."

"You said yourself that they don't deserve this treatment. Come with me."

"I've already had the stink of communism flung at me like dog dirt. I'm sorry, but—"

Nell didn't stick around to hear the rest of Bogie's disappointing reply. If it hadn't been for Kathryn Massey, Taplinger probably wouldn't have agreed to reinstate her after everybody had believed Hedda Hopper's "Nell Davenport slapped me!" whopper.

"Good evening," she said. "I thought I'd stop by to wish you a happy new year."

"You were terrific up there," Kathryn said. "Was it really on the spur of the moment?"

"If I had known Abe was going to pull that on me, I'd have warmed up in the ladies' room."

"I want you to meet my—husband, Marcus Adler."

Nell pretended not to notice Kathryn stumbling over the word 'husband' as she laid a hand on the cuff of his tux. "We've already met." The edges of his eyes crinkled through his horn-rimmed glasses. "It was at your friend's apartment at the Garden of Allah. We were there to buy her—ahem—merchandise. You walked in with an atlas because you wanted to locate a Pacific atoll. I forget the reason why."

Marcus's round face lit up. He turned to Kathryn. "Remember when Hedda was publishing messages from servicemen to their sweethearts? One of them made no sense, but it mentioned Johnston Atoll, which neither Gwennie nor I had ever heard of, so I fetched my atlas."

Nell didn't need to scour the room for the lingering, judgmental gawping; she could feel it pressing in from all sides. She couldn't hear the disapproving whispers behind oversized menus, but she knew the tone. If this was anything like the stink of communism Bogie had talked about, maybe she had made a mistake.

Nell was still trying to think of a facile exit line when she smelled Bogie's aftershave.

"Well, if it ain't Mr. and Mrs. Adler."

"Don't you start," Marcus said with a droll twist to his words. "Keeping up this pretense is bad enough. And as you can see,"—he circled the air with his index finger—"everybody is so very thoroughly convinced."

"We were wondering if you'd care to join us."

Nell stole a glance at Bogie. He lobbed back a remorseful eye roll. *Ah, so Betty insisted.* "We can fit two more people, easy as pie."

"Are you sure you don't mind being seen with us—"

"Screw 'em," Bogie cut in. "Screw 'em all."

When Nell returned to their table, she found eight filled champagne coupes lined up in the center. She scooped up the nearest one. "Here's to a bright and peaceful 1946."

"Between the endless sunshine and blinding key lights," Bogie said, "this burg has always been bright. But peaceful?" He shook his head mournfully. "Hollywood hasn't had a tranquil moment since the day DeMille arrived to film *The Squaw Man*."

"Can we at least hope for cheerful?" Nell asked.

"By all means." Bogie made a point of clinking glasses with everybody at the table. "So, ol' sport," he said to Marcus, "how is it being the top dog at MGM?"

"Last time I looked, Mayer was still top dog."

"Doesn't every picture start with the script?"

"I'm new to the job, but I must admit it's nifty to have a big say in choosing our pictures." Marcus turned to Luke. "I've been following your story. Between the newsreels, magazines, and papers, it's hard to avoid you."

Luke squirmed in his seat. "The spotlight sure has been blinding."

"Your story would make a terrific movie." Marcus set down his drink, earnest as a monk. "Not only the terrible sinking, but your battle to get into the Navy. Stirring stuff. A picture

Michael Curtiz would direct if he were to find himself at MGM."

Nell studied this round-faced guy to see if she could pick up any clues that would explain his peculiar statement. Every person in this restaurant knew that Michael Curtiz was Warners' most valuable director. No way in hell would they permit him to work for anyone else. Under what possible circumstances could Curtiz "find himself at MGM"?

It was a moot point, she decided. Luke wanted *less* fuss, not more, which was what he'd have to face with a movie featuring him as the lead character.

"That's an interesting idea," Luke said. "I'll keep it in mind."

Nell's head jerked around. *YOU WILL?*

"Please do," Marcus said, "because I would love . . ."

The opening bombast of Lyman's "I'm Beginning to See the Light" drowned out the remainder of his reply.

"Luke, darling?" Nell jacked her thumb at the dance floor. "You promised me the first lap around."

He hadn't, but he could recognize a cue when he saw it. He swung to his feet and straightened his tux jacket. She took his offered hand with a dozen questions already marshaling on the tip of her tongue.

15

Luke hefted the cardboard box marked *Report from the Aleutians* onto his workbench. It was unusual for the studio to construct props to promote a movie, especially a documentary, but someone had crafted them with such care it seemed a shame to toss them away.

He withdrew a ship's compass, a large pair of binoculars, and a handful of headshots of some of the real-life pilots featured in John Huston's documentary. The compass's brass casing gleamed in the overhead lights. It could be used in a war film. Maybe on a submarine in the Sea of Japan at the end of the conflict...

Luke's mind wandered to the set they might build for a movie based on his experience. It would be tricky to construct an accurate rendition of the *Lanternfish*, considering it was lying at the bottom of the ocean. But her sister boat, the *Viperfish*, was still around somewhere off the Philippines' coast. How much detail would they include? A cutaway version of the entire sub. Nah, probably not. Maybe the main cabin with the periscope and conning tower. And, of course, the radio room.

For the umpteenth time, he worked to conjure it in his mind.

Was there a typewriter or telegraph set? Did it make any sounds? Were the chairs wooden? Metal? Were they comfortable?

The binoculars were weightier than he'd expected. He looked through the eyepieces. The mirror at the top of the five-drawer chiffonier against the far wall sharpened into view.

He marked them on his inventory sheet and made a mental note to look into getting a pair for Bogie's Christmas present.

He pulled out two roughly hewn signs and set them down next to the compass. One of them read THE FINAL STEP TO VICTORY BEGINS AT THE FIRST STEP.

Was it weird he hadn't even so much as mentally spend none of that inheritance? Probably. But he wanted to avoid being the type of numbskull who came into a ton of dough and squandered it on terrible investments or junk he didn't need, or found he was a soft touch for greedy relatives. Better to leave the whole danged lot alone. For now, at least.

He picked up the other sign. Someone had daubed ADAK ISLAND on it in black paint.

When John Huston had joined the Army Signal Corps to film Report from the Aleutians, Bogie had brought an atlas to work. They found Adak was one of the westernmost islands in the Aleutian chain, which put it closer to Russia than the US.

Below ADAK ISLAND was a grouping of Cyrillic letters. He assumed they said the same name in Russian because below them, even smaller, was a line of Japanese characters that phonetically spelled out ADAK ISLAND.

Down near the bottom, four words were scored into the wood: IT'S A BIG OCEAN.

Those words rang in his ears, in a voice rasping from too many cigarettes and whiskey shots. Like Bogie's, but younger, and with a sigh of resignation, as though to say, *Why fight it? It's too big. Only a fool would think he could win.*

Was this Christopher's voice? Luke struggled to picture the guy's face. Was it round? Square-jawed? Wide forehead? Low hairline? Widow's peak? Wavy hair? Dead straight? Kinky or curly?

The telephone in the adjoining room rang. What was the use of forcing a mental image? Christopher was gone and with him all clear memories.

He crossed to his desk and snatched up his telephone. "Props department."

"Luke? Thank God you picked up!" Tony's voice was hoarse with panic. "There's been a terrible accident on the set of *Humoresque*."

"Oh, shit! Joan Crawford?"

"Avery. He was putting the final touches on a large backdrop when his scaffolding collapsed."

Luke dropped onto his stool. "Don't tell me he's—he's not—"

"No, but they've taken him to Saint Joseph's. I'm pulling double duty on *Humoresque* and the *Of Human Bondage* remake. I won't get out of here till late."

Luke grabbed his uniform coat. "I'll call you if I can."

The doors of the hospital elevator closed with a quiet ping.

Nell slipped her hand into his. "I hope to God he's conscious."

The assistant director on *Humoresque* had told him Avery's scaffolding had been holding him fifty feet in the air before it collapsed into a horrific tangle of metal pipes and splintered wood.

The doors pinged again as they opened. Luke held them open for Nell. "Hoping for the best is—"

The funk of bleach walloped Luke in the face. His knees buckled slightly. He thrust out a hand to the wall for support as the corridor rotated. He fell against the cool plaster and tried to swallow. No go.

The *ADAK ISLAND* sign swam into view as a wave of nausea

churned his innards. Where the hell did *that* come from? Adak Island lay thousands of miles from the *Lanternfish*'s northernmost position. He'd think about that later. For now, staying upright without choking on the stench of this bleach was taking all his energy.

Nell rested a comforting hand on his back. "What's going on?"

The nausea receded; the dizziness subsided. He let go of the wall and straightened himself. "Let's find room three-seven-eight."

Avery had the room to himself, not that he knew it. His head swayed from side to side. His lips moved, but no sound came from them. His left arm lay on top of the covers, unscathed from what Luke could see, but thick bandages swathed his right hand.

A stout nurse with her hair pulled under her cap bustled into the room. "Are you family?"

"I am," Luke told her. "What's the prognosis?"

The nurse checked his pulse and noted it on the chart hanging from the foot of Avery's bed. "The X-rays showed most of the bones in his hand have been shattered. Regaining full use is unlikely."

The wispy bleach fumes out in the corridor were still making Luke woozy. He wrapped his arm around Nell's waist to steady himself. "He needs full range of motion. He's an artist."

The nurse shook her head. "Not anymore."

An excruciating wail harpooned out of Avery. "Why is my hand bandaged? Why can't I feel it?"

"You've been through a terrible ordeal, Mr. Osterhaus," the nurse said. "Now's not the time—"

"What do you mean 'Not anymore'?"

Luke stepped up to his bedside. "It's probably not as bad as it sounds."

Avery raised his left hand and pounded the strip of mattress beside him. "No! No! NO!"

"Calm yourself, Mr. Osterhaus," the nurse admonished. "You might aggravate your injuries—"

But Avery kicked his legs to loosen the covers. "I'm entitled to know. And I want to hear it now."

"I'll have to sedate him," the nurse muttered, "otherwise he could make matters worse."

She asked Luke to help steady Avery as she emptied a syringe into his arm. Avery calmed down almost immediately. His breath was still jagged and his eyelids fluttered like overwrought butterflies, but his limbs and torso settled into an uneasy truce. "It's best to leave him alone for a bit," the nurse told Luke and Nell. "Take a walk around the grounds and come back in half an hour."

* * *

A side door opened onto a narrow gravel path that led to a circular loop around the main building.

The bracing air helped clear the last vestiges of the bleach from Luke's head.

How strange that he'd think of the Adak Island sign at such a moment. The *Lanternfish* never ventured as far north as that. And this quirk with the bleach—what the hell was that about? It made no sense.

But he could worry about that some other time.

Most of his bones? How does anybody recover from that? Let alone a painter. What on earth was Avery going to do?

Luke and Nell followed the path as it curved around to a row of slender cypress pines reaching for the overcast sky.

"Penny for your thoughts?" she asked.

"The inheritance."

She stopped and angled her body toward him. "What about it?"

"I know Boris and Avery didn't get along."

"Wasn't he an utter bastard? It's no mystery why Avery wanted to get out from under him."

"I would've done the same."

"So, what are you thinking?"

"It doesn't feel like it belongs to me." Luke confessed.

"The money?"

They arrived at a weatherworn concrete bench. Luke sat on it and waited for Nell to join him. "I know Boris left it to me, fair and square, but he gypped his own flesh and blood. And that's not fair, no matter how you look at it. And now Avery won't be able to work again. Thirty thousand is enough to keep him comfortable till the end of his days."

"But what about till the end of *your* days?"

"I'm only twenty-five. I've got the rest of my life ahead of me."

"Are you saying that you're giving it to him? The whole lot?"

"I think maybe I am. If he'll accept it. I hope he does. I'd feel so much better." A trio of sparrows alighted on the tallest cypress and chirped at each other in spritely bursts. He let a couple of hushed minutes tick by. "You think I'm nuts, don't you?"

She didn't respond.

She's trying to find a nice way to point out that I could do so much with that money, but I'm giving it away, which makes me the biggest fool south of the Arctic Circle and she wants nothing more to do with me—

Nell raised her face to meet his eyes. "I honestly don't know how I could love you more than I do right now."

He folded her in his arms and hugged her to his chest as a massive weight lifted off his shoulders. He squeezed out a whispered, "You don't think I'm nuts?"

"Far from it."

"Maybe just a little?"

"If you're a little nuts, then everybody should be." She put a finger on his temple and coaxed his face around until his mouth met hers. They kissed, hungrily, longingly, until they became self-conscious that they'd been making out at a hospital. "Let's pick this up again later. We should tell Avery the good news. Assuming he accepts."

Luke looked up at the third floor. "We won't leave until he does."

* * *

Luke didn't see Bogie sitting on his porch until he was almost at the steps.

Tristan jumped up from the rickety chairs Luke had found in the toolshed out the back. "Is Avery okay?"

"He wasn't badly hurt, was he?" Bogie said.

When Luke and Nell had reached Avery's corridor, his doctor had stopped them to confirm what the nurse had said about Avery's hand and warned that recovery might not go so well, physically and emotionally.

Luke let the two men inside and poured them double Wild Turkeys. "He's a mess of cuts and bruises and broken bones."

"Tough break," Bogie said. "Where's Nell?"

"She's got a big day tomorrow, so she went back to her place." Luke cracked the first smile in what felt like an eon. "It's very thoughtful of you to drive all the way over here to see how Avery's doing."

Bogie tugged at his ear sheepishly. "I didn't find out about Avery's accident until Tristan heard me knocking on your door. We'd only started chatting when you pulled up."

"Why are you here?"

"I spent the afternoon with my lawyer setting up Santana Productions."

Luke had heard many people in Hollywood say all sorts of things for a whole range of reasons, so he'd taken Bogie's plans with a grain of I'll-believe-it-when-I-see-it salt. "How'd it go?"

"Here's something I didn't know: Putting together a production company takes a hell of a lot more dough than I had assumed, and more ready cash than I have on hand. My accountant has tied up most of my money in inaccessible investments."

The sun had almost slipped behind the horizon; Luke's living room had sunk into twilight darkness. He flipped on the standard lamp with the frilly pink shade that had come with the place. "What's your plan?"

"I'm here to ask if you would consider investing your inheritance. We'd each go in fifty-fifty, sharing the upfront costs and splitting the profits right down the middle."

If only Bogie had come to him the day before.

Avery had somewhat calmed down when they'd returned to the room, but he'd been a bit moony, too, with a languid smile and a faraway look in his eyes. All that ended when Luke made his offer. Jackknifing upright in his bed, Avery had protested that it was too much, too generous, too reckless. But Luke laid out the reasons why he should give it and Avery should take it, and had been on the verge of declaring "And that's all there is to it!" when the bell announcing the conclusion of visiting hours had rung through the PA system. Avery had repeated over and over that he could never repay Luke's kindness, and hadn't stopped until the nurse had shooed Luke and Nell from the room.

"Should I take it that's a 'no'?" Bogie asked. Luke went to respond, but Bogie hoisted his hand. "Making movies is a colossal gamble. Sure, the payout can be huge when you hit big, but only because the odds are steeper than Half Dome. You ever been to Yosemite? The drop on that rock is straight down."

Luke let Bogie ramble for a while about national parks and wilderness hikes until he'd run out of steam. "The stark truth is that Avery has lost the use of his hand."

"But isn't he a painter?"

"His career ended today, which is why I'm giving him my inheritance."

Tristan gasped softly, but kept quiet.

Bogie took his time pouring himself another double, and held it up to the light to study. "I see."

"Doctors don't always get it right," Luke said. "His hand might not be as banged up as all that. But you should've seen the gratitude and relief in his face. I'd feel terrible backing out."

Disappointment pulled at the edges of Bogie's eyes. "Don't give it another thought. You did the right thing, and I'm proud of you."

"I appreciate you saying that." Luke held up his drink so that they could clink glasses.

Bogie kept his whiskey where it was. "I've always been proud of you. The way you fought to get into the Navy. How you handled yourself at war. I'm glad to call you my friend."

First Nell's declaration, and now this. There'll be days when you'll question the wisdom of your decision, Luke told himself, but all you need to do is look back on this conversation. He felt the sting of tears prickle the backs of his eyes. He blinked them away and tapped his nightcap against Bogie's. "There's nothing in the ice box but pickles and a weird-looking radish, so if you're staying for dinner, one of us'll have to make a run to the Jewish deli on Riverside."

16

Nell tried to whip up a modicum of enthusiasm for the *Three Strangers* promo stills. The studio hoped to duplicate their *Maltese Falcon* success by filming another John Huston screenplay, whose action also revolved around a statue—a Chinese goddess of fortune and destiny instead of a bird. It was a bargain-basement rip-off, which is why Taplinger had dumped the assignment on Nell's lap.

It was bad enough that Taplinger had awarded Buzz *Humoresque* and *Of Human Bondage* to shepherd along the PR conveyor belt. But did he have to hand over *The Two Mrs. Carrolls* as well? It was a Bogie movie. She, not Buzz, socialized with Bogie and Betty. If anybody could get promotion-shy Bogart to cooperate with publicizing the movie, it was her.

But no. Buzz was awarded Bogie and Stanwyck; Nell got three strangers chasing a Chinese idol.

A Western Union messenger stopped at her desk. She tipped the kid a nickel, and stared at the envelope. What were the chances that this was a cable from Jack Warner on vacation in Europe insisting that she handle *The Big Sleep*?

She cut along the edge with her silver letter opener.

. . .

CAUGHT YOUR PERF AT ROMANOFFS STOP
LOVED IT LOVED YOU STOP
OFFER OF GUEST APPEARANCE ON MUSIC FROM HOLLYWOOD RADIO SHOW STOP
CALL HO-3738 STOP
SACKVILLE HOBBES PRODUCER

Music from Hollywood was the program Nell and Luke would listen to if they were home on a Friday night. Neither of them was skilled in the kitchen, so they had taught themselves how to cook while listening to the show. It was one of the qualities she most admired about him: he wasn't a slippers-pipe-newspaper guy. If he had been, he wouldn't have given away his inheritance with no regrets.

Down deep, though, she still lamented saying no to that *Lucky Strike* offer. Whenever it bobbed to the surface, which was more often than she cared to admit, she'd dismiss it with a breezy "No regrets, Davenport. You made your choice."

It worked—most of the time.

But not today.

Gosh, oh my. *Music from Hollywood*. It didn't have a star like Jack Benny, but it was a national show, which meant South Bend would hear her.

If interested, call Hollywood 3738.

She picked up the receiver and dialed.

* * *

Nell rapped her knuckles on Taplinger's doorjamb. "Got a minute?"

He nodded. Drafts of lobby cards for *The Big Sleep* lay strewn across his desk.

"They rarely hold off releasing a picture for an entire year and a half," she said, stepping closer. "Don't tell me it's finally got a release date?"

"End of August."

The lobby card in his hand featured close-ups of Bogart and Bacall against a vivid red background. Their names were the same size. Equal co-star billing in only her third outing! Nell couldn't wait to tell Betty this exciting tidbit.

"Ever heard of Sackville Hobbes?" she asked.

"Sure." Taplinger cast aside an awful lobby card in which someone had tinted Bacall's dress the color of lime Jell-O. "Radio producer. Met him at one of Cagney's Christmas parties. Why?"

"He's invited me to sing 'Every Fifth Word' on *Music from Hollywood*. I told him I'd have to clear it with you first."

"What you do on your own time is your own affair."

Nell ached to yell, "My song sat at the top of *Billboard*'s chart for three weeks. Would it have killed you to stop by my desk and say, 'Well done. I'm so happy for you.'?" But that was too much to expect from a small-minded, jealous little crumb-bum.

"*Music from Hollywood* airs on Friday nights, so they'd need me at the studio by two p.m. for rehearsals. I'd have to leave work around noon."

"On a Friday."

"That's right."

"Anything else?"

Don't stop now. Get it over and done with.

"As a matter of fact, they're looking for a regular girl singer and if I go over well, it could turn into a weekly appearance."

Indignation dented his forehead. "You'd want *every* Friday afternoon off?"

"I thought I could make up the time by putting in a full Saturday instead of the usual half-day."

"What if a problem arises that needs fixing right away?"

Oh, please. What possible crisis could come up on Shadow of a Woman, *starring nobody, directed by nobody, based on a book written by nobody? And don't get me started on* The Beast with Five Fingers.

"Let's not get ahead of ourselves," Nell said, careful to set an appropriately cheery tone. "Hobbes could give the job to Janis Paige instead."

Taplinger snarled an inscrutable grunt that sounded like *They'd give it to Janis if they had any sense*, but she let it slide.

"So, about this Friday off?"

"*This* Friday?"

"Only the afternoon."

Taplinger slapped the lobby cards onto his desk. "Look here, Miss Davenport." *Uh-oh, so it's 'Miss Davenport' now?* "I don't mean to throw a wet blanket on whatever singing ambitions you may hold, but one song does not a career make."

"I understand—"

"You can't straddle two careers any more than a jockey can saddle two thoroughbreds in the Kentucky Derby."

"I'm not—"

"Are you a singer or a publicity agent? I have a busy department to run; I deserve to know if your intentions lie elsewhere."

"I'm only asking for an afternoon, which I'll offset the next day." It wasn't an outrageous request. She refused to blink until he'd made a Sarah Bernhardt–level performance out of sighing and telling her yes, it would be okay, but she had better think long and hard about where her priorities and loyalties lie, young lady.

She fled his office before he could change his mind.

* * *

Nell parked her car in the lot opposite the CBS Columbia Square radio studios. She jammed on the brakes harder than she needed to and pitched forward, falling against the horn. It barked out a harsh yelp.

"Damn you, Valenti. You had to pick a fight? Today? Of all days?" She groped around inside her purse for a handkerchief. "You knew I'd be nervous, but you went ahead and said what you had to say."

She could find only an orphaned glove to blot the sweat coating her forehead. The tan suede wouldn't do the job, but she couldn't very well walk in with her face shining like a bowling ball. She peered into the rearview mirror. "Oh, crap. I look redder than a barber pole." She mopped her hairline with the glove, then used it as a fan to cool her face. It was woefully inadequate at either job, but it was the best she could do.

But at least she had fifteen minutes to compose herself. She wound down the window to let the chilly winter air gust through the Plymouth.

She should have seen this fight coming a few days ago when they'd met at the Smoke House restaurant across from the studio. He had kept his face parked in stony neutral as she'd told him about her powwow with Taplinger. When she'd finished, he hadn't said, "What a jerk!" or "You'll find a way to get what you want and keep him happy, too." He had merely opened the menu and commented on the French onion soup. If she had slapped it out of his hands, they'd at least have gotten everything off their chests.

"How could you agree with Taplinger?" she demanded of the imaginary Luke in her rearview mirror. "Where is the sign saying 'One Career Per Customer'?" She twisted the orphaned glove through her fingers. "My PR job is dying on the vine. All the Buzz Bryants are back and reclaiming their jobs. I always knew it would happen, but I figured by then I'd have proven myself."

She swatted her glove against the steering wheel. It made such a satisfying thwack that she did it again.

She hadn't needed Luke to explain she'd be throwing away a

steady full-time job for a once-a-week appearance. She would decline the weekly spot if they offered it to her. But what had made her want to rip her hair out was Luke's attitude that she should stick with the mundane, the ordinary, the predictable. Please tell me he's not already turning into an old fogey?

* * *

"Miss Davenport!" Sackville Hobbes, a fit-looking forty-year-old with a tennis tan, was dressed in a dark-blue double-breasted pinstripe that fitted and flattered so skillfully that Nell suspected it was a bespoke suit from Sy Devore's. "I'm pleased as rum-spiked punch that you were available to join us." He walked her up the corridor to where jazzy, upbeat music spilled through an open doorway. In the studio, a dozen musicians lounged on scattered chairs improvising runs. The show's resident band leader, Arlo Nash, greeted her with a level of enthusiasm that matched Hobbes's. When he introduced her to the band, they stood up as one and blasted her with a "TA-DA!" chord.

"We'll need you in about half an hour." Hobbes guided her to the far end of the stage. "Your dressing room is through here." Someone had written Nell's name on a square card and had pinned it onto a flat block of cork glued to the first dressing room door. "Enjoy your surprise visitor."

She perked up. Oh, my! I'm such a louse, she thought. I should've given Luke the benefit of the doubt. He'd had time to think about how poorly he's behaved, and how he wants to make it up to me.

Nell threw the door open.

"Oh," she said flatly. "It's you."

"Is that the reception I get?" Betty shrieked. "I said no to drinks at the Beverly Hills Hotel with Slim Hawks—and she was paying!"

"That came out all wrong." Nell dropped her purse on the vanity. "I'm so relieved you're here."

"Uh-oh. Boy trouble?"

Nell nodded. "Our first fight."

"Oh, no. We haven't had ours yet. I'm dreading it. Want to get it off your chest?"

"I do, but they'll be calling for me soon. I'll have to fill you in while I fix my face."

Dressed in only a plain black-and-white-striped blouse and pewter-gray A-line skirt, Betty had mastered the art of looking every inch the movie star. She kicked off her high heels. "I have two patient ears and all the time in the world."

"Good," said Nell. "I need all of the above."

* * *

Unlike the Hollywood Canteen and Romanoff's, there was no need to drench the stage with bright lights, so seeing two hundred people in full view had caught Nell off guard. Some members of the audience mouthed the words to the song. Others swayed to the rhythm of the music. Most of the women had chosen their nicest Sunday hats, and the men sported expensive silk neckties. But every last one of them had worn a wide, toothy smile that said, "Entertain us!"

My boss may have decided I can't handle PR on our A-list movies, Nell had soothed herself, *but I can deliver "Every Fifth Word" better than anybody.*

By the time Nell had walked up to the mike and quipped off-the-cuff banter with Arlo Nash, she felt like one of those lighthouses Luke used to sketch: bright and strong and capable of withstanding anything. Maybe it was knowing that the South Bend folks were huddled around their Philco. Or maybe it was the comfort of knowing this was a one-time-only deal. But when Nell opened her mouth to sing that first note, she knew that she had what it took to go out on top.

Her head was still ringing from the clamorous applause as she tottered off the stage.

She had knocked it out of the park, right? Maybe she'd even wowed everyone enough to tempt Sackville Hobbes and Arlo Nash into offering her a regular slot on the show. Because of all the bother it had caused with Taplinger, she wouldn't think of taking it, but was it such a crime to *want* them to ask? She needed a second opinion. Shoot-from-the-hip Bacall fit the bill because in this town, a friend who spoke the unvarnished truth was more precious than an Oscar.

She sashayed through her dressing room door. "So how did I —Violet!"

"Sweetheart!" Before Nell was three feet inside, Violet had enveloped her in the Coty L'Origan perfume she always wore.

"I didn't see you in the audience."

Violet plucked at the sleeves of her indigo silk blouse. "I had a flat tire outside RKO. Lucky for me, a coupla he-man types came to my rescue, but the auditorium was more packed than a burlesque palace on half-price night, so I convinced the stage door guard that I'm a pal of yours. I walked in and found *this* vision of loveliness as they were introducing you."

"You were wonderful," Betty said. "Not only the singing part, but that repartee between you and Nash—it was fresh and fun and bubbly."

Nell's heartbeat was starting to slow down. "Nobody told me I'd be expected to joke with him."

Betty flopped back down on the sofa. "You played off each other as though you've been kidding around since before Moses was a boy scout."

As the post-performance frisson of exhilaration tapered off, Nell crash-landed next to Betty. "That's a relief to hear."

Violet took the chair in front of the vanity. "You did very well." Nell braced herself for the inevitable 'but' as Violet hunched her shoulders. "May I be honest?"

"I hate for you to be anything else."

"As good as you were—and you really were wonderful—I feel there is room for improvement."

What a relief! "I've never had a proper singing lesson in my life, so there's always room for that."

"Look at how far you've come on your own. Imagine how much further you could get if you put yourself in the hands of a trusted singing teacher. And I know exactly the right person."

But, but, but, Nell wanted to tell her, I don't plan on turning this lark into a full-time singing career. This whole "Every Fifth Word" episode was a fluke. Without Luke's inheritance, without Hoagy Carmichael being cast in *To Have and Have Not*, without the Hollywood Canteen broadcast, and without a dozen other happy coincidences, she wouldn't be sitting here in a CBS dressing room having sung her heart out to God only knew how many listeners.

"Doesn't that sound marvelous, Nell-Bell?" Betty wasn't the gushing type, but right at that moment, she looked like a teenaged co-ed whose beau had just pinned her. She turned back to Violet. "Who do you have in mind?"

"My singing teacher." Violet produced a card from her black patent leather purse. "Her name is Cora Maddox. Now, I'll warn you that she comes across as eccentric, but make no mistake. She knows her stuff—and then some. Cora can teach you the proper techniques. The results will amaze you. I guarantee it."

Nell took the card. Even if she didn't pursue singing professionally, one lesson wouldn't hurt.

Two purposeful knocks on her door rang out. Sackville Hobbes called out, "Are you decent?"

She told him to come on in.

He strode in with Arlo Nash trailing behind. "Glorious Miss Davenport! I do hope you were as happy as we are with how the show went."

"Take 'happy,' mix it with a cup of 'thrilled,' and top it off with a dollop of 'wow'!"

"We're so pleased that you're so pleased," Nash declared.

"So pleased, in fact," Sackville said, "that we've come to make you an offer."

Nell slipped Cora Maddox's card face down onto the counter. "You have?"

"We'd love you to become the next featured resident vocalist on *Music from Hollywood*. And so I've taken the liberty of preparing a contract." He pulled some folded papers from his inside jacket pocket. "Twenty-four weeks at two hundred dollars a week."

In the back of Nell's mind lurked a bunch of sensible reasons a one-day-per-week job didn't sound appealing. But twenty-four weeks meant six months. Stretch that over a year and it meant their salary offer was—Nell executed some mental gymnastics—three times what she was currently making.

"That's most generous." She wished her voice hadn't turned kewpie-doll.

"You're very talented, Miss Davenport," Nash said. "We had such great on-air rapport, don't you think?"

"I do."

"Audiences lose interest when they sense performers are faking it, but they adore it when they know it's genuinely spur-of-the-moment."

Hobbes placed the contract on the vanity counter and flattened out the sheets. "It's the standard arrangement, same as Alice Faye's."

Nell's eyes found Betty's. *They're asking me to fill the shoes of Alice doggoned Faye, for goodness' sake.*

"Can I think it over?"

"Naturally." Hobbes guided Nash toward the exit. "Call me with any questions you might have."

"Thank you, Mr. Hobbes."

"My friends call me Sacky." He bid them all adieu and bustled Nash from the room.

Violet closed the door with a click. "If you don't sign it, *I* will."

"You should take it home and read it through," Betty said. "I wish I'd done that before signing with Howard Hawks."

"Does Bogie have a lawyer? Maybe I should get him to look it over."

"He does, and you should."

Nell steadied herself against the counter's edge.

Twenty-four weeks.

Two hundred dollars per week.

That'd sure buy a lot of hot fudge sundaes at C.C. Brown's.

17

*L*uke stood in front of the cabinet that held the three Maltese falcons. Staring at them brought him a degree of comfort. Especially when one of his headaches hit. Despite the Navy doctor's assurance they would abate over time, they were assaulting him more often these days. Their throbbing pounded the back of his head; nausea churned his innards. Sometimes they were so wretched, two packets of Goody's headache powders didn't help.

A few weeks ago, he'd been standing at what he called "The Maltese Falcon Cabinet" restocking a bust of Franz Schubert used in Bette Davis's *Deception* when an especially vicious headache had seized him. He had gripped the shelving and tried to breathe away the pounding. It hadn't worked. His eyes fell on the falcons lined up along the shelf. Had it been a coincidence? Was he suffering from that condition an article in *The Stars and Stripes* had mentioned? He'd never heard the word "psychosomatic," but the gist of it seemed to be: *It's all in your head, kiddo.* Whatever the reason, the longer he stared at the falcons, the better he felt.

Maybe he was resentful at being hidden in among the props, keeping track of lampshades and restocking vases while Nell's singing career was taking off. He ran his finger up one side of the middle falcon and down the other. He could tell by its heft that it was the primary bird they'd used in production. Secretly, he thought Nell was crazy to leave her steady job to sing on *Music from Hollywood*. But could he blame her for saying yes to a much fatter paycheck? No, he couldn't. And he didn't. But it would keep her busy for only one day a week. She wasn't the type of girl who loafed around her apartment, but Hollywood was a town where a mere taste of success had seduced otherwise sensible people.

The resin falcon weighed a couple of pounds, so it was easy to toss from one hand to the other. There was something about the steady rhythm—back and forth, back and forth—that helped dull this damnable headache.

"There you are! I've been calling your name—" Tristan eyed the bird. "What are you doing?"

Luke slid the prop back onto the cabinet shelf and closed the doors. "Here on business?"

"I'm working on costumes for Joan Leslie and Janis Paige in *Two Guys from Milwaukee*. It's a knock-off *Road* picture, so I'm bored and restless. But that's neither here nor there." He rapped a knuckle against the gray metal cabinet. "You avoided my question."

"I was... sometimes I find myself..." Luke couldn't think of a plausible explanation, so he let the sentence trickle away.

Tristan leaned his head against the cabinet. "I call it 'Going to Nostalgialand.' Life seemed happier and more sparkly before the war, didn't it?"

Luke's headache began to dissipate. Was he suffering from nothing more than good, old-fashioned nostalgia? "Why would you want to go down that road? Hasn't your career been on an upswing since Orry-Kelly left?"

"It most certainly has."

"Your romance with Gus isn't on the wane, is it?"

"Au contraire. We're compatible in practically every way that matters."

"So why are you hankering for the past?"

"I could ask the same of you, Valenti of the Newsreels, Mister *Life* magazine, Lieutenant Hero of the *Lanternfish*, adored by one and all."

The two men stared at each other, not blinking, not speaking, barely even moving, until Tristan asked, "Does feeling this way make us a pair of idiots?"

"I hope not. I visit Nostalgialand at least twice a week."

Tristan snapped his fingers. "I've got an idea that might clear out our sentimental blues. Meet me at knock-off time at Gate Two."

"Where are we going?"

"It may not work, but what the hell?"

* * *

Luke and Tristan stood at the edge of the enormous expanse of bare earth where their boardinghouse had once been. The only sign of life was a clump of weeds that had sprouted in the space the front door had occupied.

"Do you ever think about our boardinghouse days?" Tristan asked.

"Sure I do." Luke had felt no hint of a headache or nausea since Tristan had revealed their destination. "Especially on those long nights at sea."

"Me too. More often than what's probably healthy,"

"Sometimes I worry that I'm wearing rose-colored glasses when I look back." Luke picked up a half-buried stick and flipped it over in his right hand. "Which is weird because I arrived in LA the morning of Pearl Harbor."

"On the actual day?"

"The country was at war, but I only remember the good times.

Sitting on the *Casablanca* set. Coming home to our communal dinners."

"Not to mention having to listen to Beatrice and Captain Stamina go at it for-ev-errr."

"What about Seymour and Minerva? I never did figure out how she could change costumes so fast. Not that I looked too closely. Sometimes you have to preserve the magic."

"You're right about those meals." Tristan kicked a pine cone. It hurtled clear across the desolate lot and bounced off the sagging back fence. "I don't know how talented Edith Maine was as a movie actress, but she was a darned good cook. Even Sabine thought so, and she was all 'I've eaten in the finest restaurants of Europe, but our landlady's beef bourguignon is—" Tristan pinched his lips, kissed his fingertips, then released, splaying his long fingers. "—mwuh! *Köstlich!*"

"Poor old Edith. She was lucky to survive the fire. I don't suppose you've kept in contact with her?"

"For a while. She was in a bad way, but I visited her until she told me the visits were too taxing. I let a bunch of weeks pass by before checking up on her. The nurse said that she'd moved into the Motion Picture Country Home."

"Is she happy there?"

"It's way out in Woodland Hills. I called on her a handful of times, but she wasn't the same. She died about six months later. I feel terrible that I didn't tell you about it."

Luke shoved his hands into the pockets of his Navy uniform trousers. "There was a lot going on."

Gus's heavy footsteps slapped the sidewalk behind them. "Now that they're making cars again, have you guys noticed how much harder it is to find parking?" He drew alongside them. "All this time and they still haven't built anything."

"You have to wonder why they're dragging their feet," Luke said.

Gus crossed his arms. "Would you two have preferred to discover new apartments, or is it good that this lot is still empty?"

It was an insightful question Luke hadn't considered. "At least something's remained the same."

"Yes," Tristan said pensively. "I thought coming back here was going to help, but now I see it's a mistake to look to the past."

The three of them stood in silence as they gazed out over the deserted patch.

"So let's look at the future," Gus said.

"Any suggestions?" Tristan asked.

"Let's go somewhere new."

"Such as?"

"I've never been to the Formosa Café."

The boardinghouse's block looked so desolate and neglected, Luke wished they hadn't come. "Me either," Luke said. "I hear they make a mean Singapore Sling."

* * *

Long tassels hung from two-foot Chinese lanterns of black-lacquered wood. A vaguely Oriental melody played through the loudspeakers as the Formosa's bartender listlessly polished highball glasses in the corner.

All of this Luke was expecting. What came as a surprise, however, was to find Marcus Adler seated at the bar. When Adler spotted Luke, Tristan and Gus walking in, he chuckled.

"Here for the Slings, I assume?"

"You know we are." Tristan kissed Adler lightly on the cheek and ordered a round from the bartender.

"Mr. Valenti." Adler said. "Nice to see you again."

Tristan did a double take. "You've met before?"

"New Year's Eve at Romanoff's," Adler said. "My wife and I were feeling like nobody's children until Bogie invited us to join the table."

"And how do you know each other?" Luke asked.

"Marcus and I have been saying hello around the pool table at a bar called the S.S. Friendship at—dare I say it—the mouth of Santa Monica Canyon." Tristan playfully slapped Marcus's shoulder. "The last I saw you there was the night that female impersonator put on an impromptu show. She had a clever name, but I don't recall it."

"Remy Brandee-Whyne," Marcus said. "She's now knocking 'em dead at The First Step."

Tristan cupped his hand to the side of his mouth and stage-whispered, "Not a class of bar that a feller such as yourself will ever likely have visited, if you catch my drift."

Luke needed a moment to tumble to his meaning. He wasn't sure how to respond, and was saved when the bartender delivered their drinks. A toast seemed in order. "Here's to friendship. S.S. and otherwise."

Gus clinked his glass to Luke's. "You're such a good sport. I was a fool to not spot that right away."

"Don't fret, Gussie," Tristan cooed. "You caught on."

"As a matter of fact, I want to talk with you," Marcus said. "It's business, though. A joint like this feels unprofessional."

If this was about how Luke's life would make an excellent movie, Luke knew he could nip it in the bud before they had finished their Slings. "Here's as good a place as any."

"You remember our chat on New Year's Eve?"

"I do."

"I was dead serious about the idea."

"I didn't hear back from you, so I put it down as party talk."

"Far from it."

"How far?"

"I'm prepared to make you a handsome offer."

There was still no way on God's green backlot that Luke would sell his story to a rival studio, but the words 'handsome offer' never bored anyone to death.

"Keep talking."

"I'm authorized to offer you twenty thousand dollars for the rights to your story—"

"HOLY FUCK!" Tristan's outcry shot across the Formosa, causing the pair of genteel dowagers in expensive felt hats at the far end to tsk their disapproval. "Sorry, ladies! Won't happen again!" He turned back to Marcus. "Do go on."

"Twenty thousand," Marcus repeated, "plus an extra three for a 'Technical Consultant' screen credit."

"Like what Tony got for *Pride of the Marines*?" Tristan intruded again.

Luke pictured how it would look on the screen.

TECHNICAL CONSULTANT
LT. LUKE VALENTI

He took a long sip from his cocktail. Although this deal fell a few grand short of his inheritance, twenty-three thousand was still a hell of a lot of money. Enough to help set up Santana Productions?

"I'm shocked!" Marcus said.

"Why?"

"I assumed you'd turn me down flat. If for no other reason than you work for Warner Brothers."

Luke tapped a finger against his cocktail glass. "When we were chatting that night, you said something about Michael Curtiz being at MGM."

"I said '*if* Curtiz found himself at MGM.' Emphasis on 'if.'"

"OHMYGOD!" Tristan clutched Marcus's arm. "Curtiz defecting to MGM will give Jack Warner the biggest conniption fit in the history of conniption fits."

"No, no, no!" Marcus waved his hands like a stranded castaway trying to flag down a passing ship. "This is how rumors get started. I was playing 'What If.'"

He might have gotten away with it had a furious blush not betrayed him. He struck Luke as a reliable, stand-up guy, so whatever secret he'd almost spilled, he deserved the benefit of the doubt.

"You still haven't said no," Gus pointed out.

Twenty-three thousand dollars was an awful lot of cabbage that could buy an awful lot of excitement. Keeping one's options open wasn't the worst piece of advice in the world.

"Put it in writing and I'll give it some thought." Luke flipped over his coaster. He took the pen Marcus produced and scribbled his home address.

"It might take a while," Marcus said, slipping the coaster into his jacket pocket. "Studio lawyers can be infuriatingly nitpicky."

"I'm in no rush." Luke raised his hand to attract the bartender's attention. "Tell those two ladies at the end of the bar we're buying their next round. And put it on the tab of Mister Gutter Mouth."

18

Cora Maddox lived in the upstairs apartment of a Spanish duplex nestled among a grove of twenty-foot banana palms in a side street not far from the Fox studios. The dark crimson paint job was an arresting choice. Or maybe not. Violet had described Cora as "a singing teacher with an uncommonly checkerboarded life."

Nell followed the garden path lined with lavender and orange asters and mounted the stairs to a small balcony. She came face to face with a bronze eagle-beak-shaped door knocker and banged on it.

Her thoughts turned to Luke's reaction to the news of her *Music from Hollywood* offer. He'd *seemed* supportive. He'd *said* the right things, like "The decision is all yours." But was he actually kind of miffed?

The front door swung open to reveal a woman who held herself like a regal ballerina. The black hair, parted down the middle and woven into a tight braid, was obviously dyed, and her heavy makeup and thick eyeliner made her appear as though she had stepped off stage moments before. Still, she possessed a faded-rose beauty that made it easy for Nell to imagine she must have been a head-turner in her day.

The tiny vestibule gave way to a spacious living room painted in a dusky pink, with blood-red velvet drapes framing the picture window facing north. Ornate posters for *Rigoletto*, *The Magic Flute*, *Tosca*, and *La Traviata* filled the opposite wall, interspersed with handbills in ornately carved frames advertising appearances at Boston's Strand Theatre, the Orpheum in Memphis, and the Palace in New York.

"You played the Palace, Miss Maddox?" Nell asked.

"You may call me Madame." She tapped a lacquered fingernail on a handbill for the Hippodrome Theatre in Baltimore.

OPERA STAR MISS CORA MADDOX PRESENTS
TEN FAMOUS ARIAS IN TEN MINUTES

"And headlined in vaudeville?" Nell asked. "How thrilling."

"It was a comedown. But that's what you get for carrying on with the director of the New York City Opera, whose wife was a leading socialite with a vindictive streak wider than Fifth Avenue. The ten arias in ten minutes was merely a gimmick." She pulled a rueful grimace. "I did well out of it—until vaudeville died, of course." Her grand piano stood on a Persian rug that featured an intricate pattern of interlocking leaves and petals in teal and gold. At its center, a threadbare patch bore the telltale sign of previous students. She took a seat at the keyboard. "I shall play a note and you will sing it. After that, we'll move on to scales."

In the backwoods of South Bend or in front of a raucous Hollywood Canteen crowd, Nell had only ever opened her mouth and warbled to her best ability. Hoagy thought it was enough. Sacky Hobbes and Arlo Nash did, too. But this woman was not the easy-to-please type. Nell squeezed her palms together as she followed Madame's commands.

Did she hit the right notes? Was she in key and on pitch? God forbid Madame should reveal her thoughts until after Nell's armpits had grown dank with sweat.

She retracted her long, bony fingers from the keyboard. "I'm more impressed than I expected."

This glacial woman struck Nell as the type who rarely handed out compliments. Nell slid her hand onto the piano for support. "You are?"

"For someone who's never had a lesson, yes." Madame sucked on her teeth. "Where do you want to sing, Miss Davenport?"

"I've been invited to perform on the *Music from Hollywood* radio program."

"Congratulations."

Madame had a way of making a single word sound like 'How utterly dreadful.'

"They want me as their new resident vocalist."

"I suppose you'll be singing popular music." Madame glided to a large tan leather attaché case and scooped out a thick handful of sheet music. Returning to the piano, she deposited the pile in front of Nell. "Do you know any of these?"

The songs ranged from comic novelties—"There's a Song They Sing at a Sing Song in Sing Sing"—to torch songs—"Willow Weep for Me"—and Gilbert and Sullivan light operetta. Nell wasn't familiar with any of them. She continued to dig through the offerings. *Please, please, please have something I already know.* Flip, flip, flip. *I don't think I've got the nerve to tackle an unfamiliar number in front of this imperious woman.* Flip, flip, flip. *Oh! Thank God!* Nell pulled the perfect song from the pile.

"Interesting choice." Madame took it from her and opened it onto the music stand.

"I worked on the movie. It's also where I met my boyfriend, so we consider it 'our song.'"

It occurred to Nell that *she* thought of it as their song, but did Luke? Not that it mattered at that particular moment because Madame showed no interest in hearing about Nell Davenport's history with "As Time Goes By." Without hesitation, she played the opening chord.

Nell had sung it a hundred times. Maybe as much as two hundred. Confident as a tightrope walker, she sang the first line. What, in God's name, was that? The phrase came out like a bullfrog preparing to mate. Madame didn't miss a note. Nell pushed forward, singing about how a kiss was still a kiss. She sounded a little better, but still off-key, with every lyric wobbling badly.

When Madame reached the part about moonlight and love songs, she called it quits. "I'd have preferred you to choose a song you're acquainted with."

"But I am." Nell wished she could use her pocketbook to camouflage her mortification over having slaughtered her favorite song. "Can we start from the top?"

"Why were you holding back?"

"I wasn't aware that I—"

"You have a fine voice, Miss Davenport, but—" Madame wrapped her hands around her own throat "—you're strangling it. We need to know why; otherwise, all this is a waste of my time and your money. You and your boyfriend think of this tune as your special song?"

Nell fought against the tears stinging her eyes. "I think so."

"But you don't *know* so?"

Every speck of Nell's being wanted to say yes. She shook her head.

"This boyfriend—does he approve of your singing? Is he happy about your appearing on this radio show?"

"He's not standing in my way."

"That's not what I asked."

Nell met Madame's steely, unblinking scowl. "If you have a point to make, please don't beat around the bush on my account."

Madame rested her hands in her lap and paused, it seemed to Nell, to collect her thoughts, although probably just for show. This woman knew what she'd thought from the day she'd wriggled free of the womb.

"I've seen this a lot since the conclusion of the war. Our menfolk are as happy to be back as we are that they've returned to us. The problem is that they're expecting everything to be the same."

"Luke went through hell in the Pacific," Nell said. "Is it too much to ask that he come home to a cheeseburger, chocolate malted, and the girl he kissed goodbye?"

"Ah, yes, but are *you* the same girl he kissed goodbye?"

Nell wished there was a chair she could collapse into. Was Madame waiting for a response, or had her question been rhetorical? Botching "As Time Goes By" had thrown her. She didn't know what to think anymore.

"We womenfolk may not have fought at Normandy on D-Day," Madame continued, "or in the jungles on Guadalcanal, but the war changed us. We did jobs previously unavailable to us. Earned unheard-of salaries. What do they expect us to do now? Skip back into the kitchen? Bake another cake and tend to the children like nothing happened?"

Nell couldn't picture this woman stirring a bowl of cake batter, let alone toiling on a grimy production line welding bolts into airplane wings. But her point was valid.

"And now you're about to appear every week on a national radio station." Madame had softened her tone a little, which was more than Nell expected. "You're doing what most girl singers do when they reach a certain level of success."

"And what's that?"

"They sabotage themselves to make their men feel better." Luke's not that sort of guy, Nell tried to protest, but Madame cut her off with a stiff warning finger. "Resist the temptation, my dear. If this Luke fellow is jealous of your talent, or if he resents you finding your spotlight, it's better you find out now and save yourself the heartache. Nothing good comes from hiding your light under a bushel. Don't diminish yourself to suit some man's ego."

Nell wanted to clear the hell away from this woman with her patchouli oil, her dyed hair, and her stern admonishments. But only, she told herself, because deep down you suspect she's right.

"When I was performing in opera, I declined several lead roles because of the man I was seeing. I was too lovesick to see that my actions resulted in fewer and fewer offers. By the time his wife exacted her revenge, it wasn't hard for her to decimate what was left of my career. Vaudeville was a degrading step down, but it was the only open path. And then it died. Meanwhile, opera is alive and thriving. But not for me."

Madame stared along the body of the piano, mute and solemn.

Is the lesson over? Will Madame take me on as a client? Should I leave?

Nell was still deciding how best to extricate herself from what was supposed to have been a singing lesson but had somehow taken an abrupt right turn into an incomprehensible landscape.

"Stand with your feet apart, planted firmly on the carpet." Madame emerged from behind the piano. "Hands on hips. When you breathe in, hold it for one full second. When you sing a note, any note you like, push it out from here." She inserted her thumbs in a spot below Nell's ribs. "And when you do, hold it for as long as you can."

Nell nodded.

Madame held her thumbs in place. "And . . . IN!"

Nell breathed in as full a breath as she could manage with two bony thumbs poking her diaphragm. She counted a full second, then opened her mouth.

For a moment, Nell wondered if the note had emerged from

Madame. She had never made *that* sound. So rich. So full. So clear. It ballooned and swelled, pressing against the walls, the windows, and the framed opera posters.

"Keep going. Don't stop. Dig deeper."

Nell renewed her effort. The A-sharp above middle C grew even louder, stronger. Was it really coming out of her?

"See what happens when you refuse to hold yourself back?"

Short-winded and a little dazed, Nell nodded.

"Same time, next week?" Madame asked.

Nell scoured the room for her handbag, and spied it on a long, narrow mahogany table inlaid with a geometric pattern in gold leaf. She had no recollection of setting it down there, but could think only of escaping this place to digest what had happened in this over-stuffed room. She hoped she could make it to the lavender asters before her legs gave out from under her.

19

*L*uke's legs felt like they were made of wet sand. His arms, as well. Come to think of it, the rest of his body, too. What a rough night it had been. All that tossing and turning and glancing at his bedside clock over and over.

And when he had fallen asleep, he'd dreamed of the *Lanternfish*. Again. These days, it was all he ever seemed to dream about. In this most recent one, he'd been surprised to find his chair bolted to the floor of the radio room. In real life, he had no memory of his chair at all.

He lumbered into the department foyer as Justin, a freckle-faced kid promoted from the mailroom, materialized holding a Tiffany lamp and a Renaissance wooden candlestick. "Jumping Jehoshaphat!"

"I had a hard night," Luke mumbled.

"Mr. Warner's secretary called three times already."

It wasn't yet eight o'clock. "What did she want?"

Justin jabbed the candlestick at Luke. "You."

Oh, cripes. That didn't sound good.

"You're wanted in the big guy's office lickety-split. Them's her exact words."

"Have you made coffee?"

"You don't got no time for—"

"I suspect I'll need a bucket of it when I get back."

The no-nonsense bob on Warner's new secretary looked like something out of an early Warner Bros. musical. It didn't flatter her squarish face, but it was perfect for a busy secretary who spent her day corralling a loose cannon.

"There you are, Lieutenant."

"I came here as soon as I heard the words 'lickety-split.'" Luke hadn't expected his little joke to make an impact, but it elicited a sliver of a smile, so he pushed his luck. "Any chance you can preview what this is all about?"

"IS THAT VALENTI?" The ex-vaudevillian in Warner still knew how to project his voice.

The secretary bent at the waist. "Stick to your guns," she whispered. "He'll respect you more." She tilted her head toward her boss's open doorway.

Warner was on his feet, his hands planted on his desktop.

"I believe you want to see me," Luke said.

"What I want is to strangle the bejesus out of you," Warner snarled, "and plead justifiable homicide afterwards."

Luke cast his mind over the preceding weeks. The *Breakfast in Hollywood* show had been four months ago. The *Life* magazine interview? But that had been a rosy puff piece. "May I know the charges against me?"

Warner wiggled a fat finger at the chair Luke was clinging to. "Siddown." He flopped back into his own chair and hurled himself forward. "Why the goddamn stinking HELL would an employee of mine sell his life story to a rival studio? I should bounce you out the front gate for even talking to MGM, you infernal Benedict Arnold, you."

Ah, so that was it. The gossip grapevine had Chinese Whispered Adler's proposal into a formal offer.

"If I could, I—"

"Don't play games. Don't play innocent. And most of all, don't fuck with me."

Ladies and gentlemen, I give you Jack Warner, king of the bluster. "May I speak?"

"Make it fast because you're—" Warner narrowed the gap between his thumb and index finger "—this close to feeling my boot up your ass."

"You can't blame the competition for recognizing a cinematic story when they see one," Luke said, curtly as he could. "If Warner Brothers thinks my wartime experience would make a terrific movie, where's the offer?" He cupped his hands around his ears. "Hello? Is anybody there? Nobody from this studio has even raised the subject with me. So, when MGM put an offer on the table, you bet I listened."

Luke crossed his arms and stared at Warner, willing himself not to blink until the mogul spoke first. And when he did, the wrath had drained from his voice.

"Did you sign yet?"

"Not *yet*."

Warner pulled a fresh cigar from his desk drawer. Ripping off the cellophane wrapper, he sniffed as he ran it under his nose. "What's the offer?"

The bit with the cigar was pure performance. *I can afford a three-dollar cigar and you're just a punk from Props.* It did its job, though. Luke gulped. Had Marcus's offer been a fair one? Might he blow it by low-balling? Or high-balling? If the next sentence out of his mouth was a lie, did one of the most powerful men in movies have the means to learn what Marcus Adler had proposed? Probably. Had Adler been serious? The night at the Formosa had been more than a week ago, and nothing had arrived in the mail.

If Luke could boost MGM's offer by a few thousand bucks

more, it could match his inheritance—or maybe even better it.

"Twenty-five thousand," he told Warner, "plus an extra five for a 'Technical Consultant' screen credit." He had twisted his tone in such a way as to imply, "You're going to have to do better than that."

Warner kept his fleshy poker face immobile, but he couldn't disguise the furious blush creeping over his collar and inching toward his jaw.

"Thirty plus five. Legal will get a contract to you by week's end. Take it or leave it. I must have your answer, right here, right now."

Luke had thought his inheritance was more money than he ever expected to see in his lifetime. This offer was five grand above that. Of course he was going to accept it, but the rules of this game dictated that he pretend to carefully consider it. He let Warner sway in the wind for twenty-one seconds. "You've got a deal."

"Fine. Fine. We're done here."

Luke rose to his feet. "Just one thing."

Warner picked up the hefty crystal paperweight of a lighter and struck a flame. "Yeah?"

"I want Humphrey Bogart to play me."

"Where do you get off telling me how to cast my own goddamn pictures?"

"I think that—"

"John Garfield will go into this movie when he's done on *Humoresque*. Not that it's any of your goddamn business, you bald-faced chiseler." Warner thumped his desk blotter with his lighter. "Get the hell out of my sight before I ram this thing down your throat."

Luke backed out of the office, sped by the secretary, and didn't draw breath until he was standing in the wood-paneled corridor. "Sorry, Bogie," he muttered. "That's a battle you'll have to fight for yourself."

20

Nell twirled the stub of a chewed pencil around her fingers. The late morning sun flooding the department was starting to reflect on Taplinger's office window. In a few minutes, the glare would obscure his face and she wouldn't be able to gauge his mood. The guy wasn't much for getting worked up, which not only made him an intimidating poker player but also made it tricky for anyone trying to pick the right moment to quit her job.

She gulped some lukewarm coffee. Was she crazy to leave a steady paycheck to sing on a radio show that might get canceled without notice?

Maybe she should forget the whole thing.

She chomped down on her pencil hard enough to taste the lead.

But you'd love to be *Music from Hollywood*'s new resident singer. You haven't been studying with Cora very long, but you're already sounding stronger. Steadier. Louder. Imagine how you'll be in three months. Six months. A year. How much interest can you whip up for anemic program fillers? Not much, that's for damn sure. So go in there and tell him you're heading off into a brighter, more exciting future.

Nell pushed back her chair and bounded to her feet as Taplinger picked up his telephone. *When he's finished on that call, I'm going to march right in there—*

She sat down.

Luke thought it was a bad idea. Not that he'd said as much. What he had mentioned, though, was how the booming wartime labor market had cooled. If things didn't pan out at *Music in Hollywood*, how hard would it be for her to pick up a regular job again? It was okay for him with his gargantuan windfall, but how many brass rings did girls get a chance at?

Taplinger dropped the telephone into its cradle and sagged over his typewriter.

NOW! Up you get. The time has come. Taplinger said it himself. Pick a career and stick with it.

She marched up the middle aisle of desks and into his office, where he was making peculiar sounds, as though he were strangling a cat and hating himself for doing it.

"All okay?" she ventured.

He looked up, startled. "The truck transporting all the promotional materials for *Three Strangers* got wrecked in a twelve-car pile-up on the Arroyo Seco Parkway."

"How much did we lose?"

"Everything. The standees, lobby cards, those reproduction Chinese idols."

Months of work had gone up in flames. "*Three Strangers* comes out next month. We were supposed to ship it all out the day after tomorrow."

"We can do another run of the printable stuff, but we need to replace those display idols."

"Isn't that a lot of trouble for a B picture?"

Taplinger cocked a scornful eyebrow at her. "Haven't you heard? It's an A now." Nell resisted the urge to point out it was *his* job to tell her that. "You've got twenty-four hours to figure out something."

"Me?" *But I came in here to quit.*

"Your war-hero boyfriend works in Props, doesn't he? I suggest you make that your first stop."

* * *

"*Three Strangers!*" Nell barked out, breathless from the sprint. "Chinese idol! Which cupboard?"

Luke looked up from his paperwork. "Weren't you going to resign today?"

It was a fair question, and one she couldn't readily answer. Something about saving the day to get into the boss's good books so that they might come to an arrangement. "Those replicas we made for theater promotions, all destroyed. Terrible accident. Arroyo Seco. Show me where—"

"It's in the same one where we keep the falcons."

She followed him into the adjacent room, where he opened the metal cabinet doors and showed her the nineteen-inch seated Oriental figure of a slim Buddha, one hand resting in his lap, the other raised to his shoulder. She plucked it off the shelf; it had more heft than she remembered.

"Do Tony and Audrey have a telephone?"

"They got one when Avery moved in with them."

As the pain from Avery's busted hand ebbed, it had become clear he could no longer look after himself. Tony and Audrey had offered him the spare bedroom of the house they were renting, so he had gratefully, albeit reluctantly, moved in.

En route to his desk, she told him how Taplinger had tasked her with fixing the mess.

Luke snorted with contempt. "By this time tomorrow?"

When Avery came on the line, she babbled out the deadline they were now facing and steeled herself for the inevitable "It can't be done." Instead, he went quiet for too many excruciating seconds, then said, "I've got the mold for that statue under my bed. They're easy to duplicate if management isn't too fussy about the quality."

She clutched Luke's hand. "My orders are to come up with a dozen replicas. Taplinger said nothing about perfection."

"We can cook up the resin in Audrey's kitchen. It'll stink up the joint, so we'll have to make it up to her. I have enough black paint, but we'll have to buy tons of everything else."

Luke produced a pencil and turned over a purchase order.

"Okay. Shoot."

* * *

With the trunk of Luke's Ford Tudor now loaded with Avery's ingredients, they pulled out of the hardware store parking lot and onto Ventura Boulevard, which would take them to the house Tony had rented in Sherman Oaks.

"I have a confession."

Luke had been quiet since they'd dashed out of the studio. Nell wasn't sure she could handle many more plot twists today. "Should I brace myself?"

"I guess it's more of an admission."

Nell sat up straighter. "Of what?"

"That I should have told you it's been wonderful to hear how your voice has improved since you started studying with Cora Maddox."

Nell had upped her lessons to twice weekly, not because of the *Music from Hollywood* offer, but because she enjoyed them so darn much. Madame had made no comment, however, so doubt had started to creep in. Had all this work been worth it? Delight lifted her heart. "It has?"

"Not just your voice, but everything."

"Could you be more specific?"

"You're becoming more radiant every day, as though there's somebody inside of you moving from room to room, turning the lights on, one by one. I've been a fool to expect you to stick to your day job, and a schmuck for not being in your corner."

Had they been driving anywhere else and doing anything else, Nell would have asked Luke to pull over so that she could hug and kiss the living daylights out of him. "It means the world to me that you think so."

"When I left that meeting with Warner and was walking to your building to tell you, I realized how much you're enjoying your fame and how much you've blossomed under it. All I've wanted to do is run away from mine. But if old man Warner wants to pay me thirty-five grand for my story, maybe it's worth telling."

"So you're okay if I do leave the studio?"

"Choose whichever job makes you happy. If you want to quit, then quit—before we go to all this trouble, if that's what you decide."

She waited until a wailing fire engine raced past them. "But what if we get away with it, though?"

"Do you think it might make you indispensable in Taplinger's eyes?"

"Maybe indispensable *enough* to let me off work each Friday."

He drove for several blocks in silence. "*Yankee Doodle Dandy* was the biggest hit we've ever had."

She stared at him. "This conversation has taken a heck of a sharp turn."

"It came out four years ago. And since then, Cagney has made only two pictures in all that time."

"He keeps fighting for more money, so they put him on suspension."

"The star of their most successful picture, in a role that earned him an Oscar, and they'd prefer to stick him on the shelf instead of slinging him a few extra bucks."

Nell slipped her hand onto his knee. It felt warm through his uniform trousers. "You're saying nobody is indispensable."

"They'll always do what suits them." He slid his hand on top of hers. "You've done a first-rate job in PR, but they still took you off the A-list films. And now they've dumped this almost-impossible task in your lap. If we fail to deliver the goods, it'll be your fault. If we succeed, somebody else will take the credit for coming to the rescue."

Nell gazed at the passing stores. In the mad scramble to pull off the unpulloffable, she hadn't stopped to take in the bird's-eye view. "I suspect you might be more right than I want to admit."

"And there's something else," he added.

"Holy cow, Luke. I don't know how much more I can take."

"A certain missive has arrived."

Nell studied his impish I've-got-a-secret grin. For the first time since she watched him roll down the gangplank, she saw the Luke she had waved off to war. "Am I supposed to guess what—"

He tapped his right hip. "It's in my side pocket."

She fished out an envelope made from extravagantly creamy paper. The 'Bell, Amiss, and White, Attorneys-at-Law' return address in New York was engraved in gold. "Is this—?" She held it to her nose. "It even *smells* expensive." She opened the back flap, withdrew the check, and read the figure.

"Thirty-one thousand, nine hundred, and eighty-eight dollars." The amount tumbled out of her in breathy awe. "So many numbers!"

"Which we wouldn't be looking at right now if you hadn't been clever enough to write that song and talented enough to sing it on the radio." His lighthearted tone had dropped away.

"Wasn't that a good thing?"

"Yes and no."

"There's a 'no' part?"

He turned left onto a street that led up into the back of the

Hollywood Hills. "That special code, using every fifth word to inform you of my movements."

"What of it?"

"I broke a cardinal rule of security. If the enemy had cottoned onto it, I could've been drummed out of the service. Court martial. Dishonorable discharge. Public disgrace. The whole shebang."

Nell slipped the check back inside its gilded envelope. "How long has this been bothering you?"

"I avoided thinking about it until Mr. Warner put his offer in writing. What if they include our special code and what we were doing in the movie?"

"They won't if we don't tell them."

He threw her a sidelong look as he slid the envelope into his pocket. "Gossip is the gasoline that powers the engine of this town. Everybody knows everybody, and they can't wait to spill the beans. Especially when drunk."

"Are you having second thoughts about giving the money to Avery?"

"No," he said after a long pause. "It all seems to have evened out now that this movie lucre is coming."

She watched him squirm in his seat. "It's just that . . .?"

"I endangered the lives of my crew."

"You also saved them. Doesn't that even things out?"

They pulled to the curb outside Tony and Audrey's buttercup-yellow house. Nell would have preferred to hash out Luke's misgivings, but they would need every minute between now and this time tomorrow.

***

The door was already open; the aroma of chicken cacciatore filled the air. Audrey rushed along the hallway at them. "Avery brought me up to speed. What a disaster!"

"Thanks for letting us commandeer your kitchen," Nell said. "We'll be making a dreadful stink, I'm afraid."

"Forget about it. Stinks come and go. This is what families do when the going gets tough. Next Christmas, we'll laugh about the night we had to boil up gallons of resin in my biggest cooking pot."

"Which we'll ruin," Luke warned.

"I hope so!" Audrey said with a laugh. "It gives me a watertight excuse to buy a new one."

Avery joined them in the vestibule. His injured hand had contracted into a cluster of gnarled, withered fingers. "I called Tony; he's on his way." They trooped into the kitchen. "I've calculated the measurements for each batch." He snatched up the statue's mold from the counter. "Once it's filled, we'll put it in Audrey's Frigidaire while we concoct the next one. By the time it's ready, the previous idol will have cooled enough to paint. Any questions?"

Luke's comment about turning all her lights on came back to Nell. Avery seemed in brighter, higher spirits than at any time since the accident. He shone with joy, as though someone was following him with a spotlight. *You feel useful again, don't you? People need you, and only you can bring home the bacon.*

"Before things get crazy . . ." Luke held up the Bell, Amiss, and White envelope. "I want you to have this."

Avery stared at the golden address. "Those are my father's New York lawyers."

"Now might be a good time to put this in a safe place."

Avery kept his hands at his sides as Luke presented it to him. "There's no shame in changing your mind," he said. "It's a lot of money. And after all, Father left it to you."

"Did you know Warners have bought the screen rights to my war experience?"

"They're gonna make a movie out of the *Lanternfish*?" Audrey asked.

"I don't get paid until they officially announce it, but lawyers have been consulted and contracts drafted. It's the perfect solution. You get some money and so do I. Everybody wins."

Avery blinked rapidly, his eyes red and glistening. "When you offered this to me, I thought, 'Yeah, yeah, I'll believe it when I see it.' But now that it's here, I—you—your generosity... It floors me."

"Audrey said it best." Luke pressed the envelope into the palm of Avery's good hand. "It's what families do when the going gets tough."

Nell's heart melted. The Luke she had met so long ago had planned escape routes from a family that had once gone to a baseball game and forgotten him. But look at him now.

"I feel—I feel that—" Avery struggled to keep the tremor from his voice. "I can face the world again."

"Of course you can," Audrey said.

"It's such a battle, though. Every day. Sometimes it all feels so hopeless."

"Have you heard about Sam Goldwyn's next movie?" Nell asked. "*The Best Years of Our Lives* is about adjusting to life after the war. In one of the supporting roles, they've cast an Army vet who lost his hands. And now he's going to be in a big Hollywood movie. Point being, we don't know what's around the corner." She let her rhetorical statement hang in the air for a moment. "Meanwhile, we've got a diabolically long night ahead of us. Outside is a carload of stuff I can barely pronounce. How about we unload it so that when Tony gets here, we're at battle stations, ready to spring into action?"

21

Three days later, Luke was still picking flakes of glossy paint from his fingernails. A tiny splotch had lodged itself under the nail on his left pinkie and was clinging on tight.

"You haven't dug out that crud yet?" Justin asked.

"I think this chunk has taken up residence."

"A small price to pay for saving the studio's bacon."

Luke excavated deeper under his nail. "We hardly did that."

"You and Nell Davenport, a guy who got his hand crushed, and a hairdresser with a wooden leg cooked up a dozen statuettes in someone's kitchen. Overnight! The whole place is talking about it."

Luke gave up on the paint. "I had no idea."

"Probably because the Navy's got you running all over."

More and more lately, they had been sending Luke out on speeches to ladies' auxiliaries, Boy Scout troops, and Moose Lodge meetings. His first few had been like tottering along a rough hiking trail in poor light. It didn't help that he was telling these politely attentive folks about a night about which he retained only the barest fragments. But with practice, the verbal stumbles and shaking hands had abated.

He pointed to the prop requisition in Justin's hand. "What's that for?"

"Some extras over on *The Man I Love* got over-enthusiastic during the New Year's Eve scene and broke some vases. The set decorator wants four replacements. They have to be white and no more than a foot tall."

"I'll get them." He told Justin to mind the front desk and headed into the warehouse.

The wall of vases stood near the cabinet where the *Three Strangers* Chinese idol was stored. Luke had returned to it several times since "The Night of the Idols," which is how the five of them referred to the adventure, as though it were the title of their own movie.

He didn't know why he felt drawn to stand in front of the cabinet to study its contents: the gang of Maltese falcons, the original Chinese idol, some old-fashioned bottles of brandy and whiskey, several African tribal masks, Incan fertility statues, a wide assortment of daggers, a box of Egyptian ankhs.

One day he might figure out why it called to him like a Homeric siren, but until then, he stared and stared at the masks and daggers, wondering what he was missing.

He was about to close the cabinet when a flutter of déjà vu jarred him. It was similar to the day he'd heard a voice when he was putting away the ADAK ISLAND sign from *Appointment in Tokyo*. What was it the voice had said? He couldn't remember now. So much for that photographic memory of his. The hospital ship quack had told him this super-sharp memory might return one day. Yeah, well, it had been six months, so "might" was turning into "probably not" as far as Luke was concerned.

"Hello."

Luke yelped. "How long have you been standing there?"

"Long enough," Bogie replied.

Luke shut the metal door with a clang. "Walk with me. I have to get some vases to Stage Four." He snatched up a nearby soap box and led Bogie to the wall filled with vases of every conceivable color, shape, and size.

"Heard the news?" Bogie asked.

"That Nell and me and Tony and Avery are the talk of the lot? I still can't believe we pulled it off."

"Apart from that."

"You should have seen us: Avery supervising; Nell, Tony, and me running around following instructions; Audrey fueling us with chicken cacciatore, corned beef sandwiches, cookies, and coffee." He came to a set of four dark-cream porcelain vases, nine or ten inches tall. He picked up two in each hand and lowered them into the box. "You know what's funny? I'm blood-related to Avery and Tony, but they're not related to each other. But after going through that long, hard night, all three of us are like full brothers."

Bogie clapped a firm hand on Luke's shoulder. "You didn't have that growing up, did you?"

It wasn't the measuring, the pouring, the stirring, or the painting that Luke remembered most clearly. Frankly, it was all a blur. It was the spirit of camaraderie. A Princeton crew, rowing together in perfect synchronization.

"I'm happy for you, Valenti. I really am."

Luke went to lift the box of vases, but stopped. "What did you mean 'apart from that'?"

"I got called in to do a new set of publicity stills for *The Big Sleep* when the news came through: *The Last Submarine* got the official thumbs-up."

"The last what?"

"They've approved your movie, ya big dummy!"

"And they're calling it *The Last Submarine*?"

"On account of the *Lanternfish* was the last downed sub of the war."

This was like his inheritance: hypothetical and not worth

getting hopes up over—until it was. He set the box down. "A movie of my life. Can you believe it?"

"Frankly, kiddo, I can. What you did was remarkable. And even more remarkable?" Bogie added, poking Luke's chest. "Jack Warner has assigned it top priority, so other projects have been shuffled back down the pipeline."

"I want you to know that I fought for you to get the lead, but Mr. Warner wouldn't hear of it."

Bogie shrugged. "Garfield's ten years younger than me and everyone's talking about his *Postman Always Rings Twice*."

Luke picked up the soap box and made for the exit. "John Garfield playing me on the screen. It's like—like—"

"A scene from a movie?"

Luke laughed. "What about Nell? Is she—"

"Joan Leslie. *And* she'll be singing 'Every Fifth Word.'" They stepped outside into the brisk winter air. Bogie said, "As I recall, the studio doesn't pay you until the film is in production."

"That's right."

"So now that it is . . ."

Luke's mind was still galloping with visions of John Garfield playing him in a major motion picture, so he needed a few moments to cotton on. "We can move forward with Santana Productions."

"Bingo!" Bogie clipped Luke gently across the chin. "This calls for a celebration. Dinner at Romanoff's. You in your dress uniform, the girls in their fanciest dresses. Expensive champagne. The works."

"I can't go overboard, bubbly-wise."

"Why not?"

"I'm touring a VIP around the studio first thing tomorrow."

"Anyone I've met?"

"Remember Keaton Vance?"

The telegram had arrived the previous day telling Luke that Vance would be passing through town en route to Washington,

DC, and would love the chance to see him and maybe have a tour.

"Captain Stamina?" Bogie asked.

"He's Commodore Stamina now," Luke said, grinning. "But yes. The day of the parade was so crazy, we had no time to talk. Tomorrow's my opportunity to impress him."

"Show him that his confidence in you was justified?"

The stub of Luke's missing finger throbbed. Was it always this shade of purply red? He felt the pull of the cabinet of liquor bottles and fertility statues once more. "I'm declaring a two-drink maximum for tonight." He met Bogie's withering stare. "Okay, fine. Three. Then cut me off."

* * *

As he waited for Vance at the main gate, Luke wished he'd clocked a decent night's sleep. Or at the very least, had brewed his morning coffee extra strong. But he'd done neither, so he fidgeted with the hem of his wool jacket as he fought against the creeping tendrils of fatigue that burdened his joints and fogged his brain.

Bogie had guessed it right off the bat. Luke wanted to show Vance his faith in him had been vindicated. He'd never asked if Vance had broken, bent, or ignored any rules to get him into the service, and Vance had volunteered no information. But what would he make of Luke's character if he learned Luke had knowingly and deliberately defied one of the most important regulations of naval wartime security? How was Luke going to look him in the eye?

A black Cadillac pulled up and Vance stepped out, the gold embroidery on the black visor of his cap shining in the sun. "Lieutenant!" He snapped a casual return to Luke's salute and extended his hand as Luke approached. "So good of you to make time to show me around."

"Anything for you, Cap—er, Commodore—er, sir."

Vance smiled. "It's a hard habit to break, I know, but enough with the 'sir.'"

"But sir," Luke protested, "we're in uniform. I can't switch off—"

"That's an order, Lieutenant." He rubbernecked past the security gate. "Just you and me taking a stroll, right? It *is* okay to bend the rules once in a while."

Sticking to formality had been Luke's way of ensuring he didn't relax that little bit too much. He led Vance along Third Street toward the backlot. *It's okay to bend the rules.* Maybe he was worrying for nothing. He pointed out the props building. "That's where I work, but we'll save it for later."

"Remind me what props are."

"Anything on a set that an actor can interact with, such as a walking stick, a Zulu shield, or a candlestick telephone."

"Might it also be a statue of a falcon from Malta?"

Vance's eyes had taken on a mischievous twinkle Luke hadn't seen since that first time they'd encountered each other, when Vance had been sneaking out of Beatrice's boardinghouse room. Vance had had no choice but to look as embarrassed as any guy trying to make a discreet exit. It was nice to see that fellow again.

"It would," Luke replied. "And I'd be happy to show it to you." Any excuse to stare at those contents like a hypnotized zombie.

They ambled along the street, dodging racks of cowboy boots, gaggles of Wild West saloon girls, and a throng of dress extras in elegant opera finery. Luke walked him past the building where the cameras were housed, the machine shop where sets were built, and various soundstages where movies were being filmed. Thank God there was a lot to point out. The more he talked, the better he could tugboat the flow of conversation into safe harbors.

They crossed E Avenue and walked between the final two stages before Third Street opened into the backlot's landscaped park, and beyond that, Viennese Street. Vance slowed his pace as they approached a large poster advertising the upcoming KFWB Trans-Lux Flashcast news ribbon. "What's this?"

"KFWB is our radio station. This summer, they're adding an electric zipper on the Taft Building at Hollywood and Vine."

"Like the news ribbon on Times Square?"

"Mr. Warner decided the West Coast should get one, too. There'll be bleachers, a bandstand for Benny Goodman, as well as a bunch of stars. They'll even be closing off Hollywood's busiest intersection to traffic."

Vance kept his eyes glued to the poster and stiffened his spine. "Pulling out all the stops, huh?"

"It'll either be a glorious success or chaotic anarchy."

A grave silence, thick enough to cleave with a carving knife, enveloped Vance. Moments ticked by before he spoke again. "What's going on with you?"

Luke's breathing grew shallow. "Going on?"

"You're not the Luke Valenti I finagled into the Navy."

"War has a way of changing us all, sir." He doubted their conversation had taken a casual turn, so he'd added the 'sir' to return to a degree of formality.

"Don't be glib, son. Not with me."

Luke shoved his hands into his pockets in a vain attempt to stifle his escalating nerves. "I'm sorry, sir. I didn't mean to—"

"Keaton. My name is Keaton. Will you tell me what's on your mind, or shall I tell you?"

How could he know about the letters and the code? My V-mails to Nell were a handful among millions. He couldn't possibly—

"All right. Have it your way." Keaton turned to Luke. "You have the same squeak to your voice, the same fidgety hands, and the same skittish eyes of every junior-grade officer who has come to me, compelled to confess a transgression of some type or other."

So I'm as transparent as a pane of glass, after all?

Luke found the nerve to meet Vance's unblinking stare. "I thought I'd been doing a pretty good job of hiding them."

"You did." The commodore had shaded his response with a touch of benevolence. "And with someone else, you might have gotten away with it."

Luke sucked in a chestful of air so suddenly that it took him by surprise. He felt lighter. From what? Relief?

"Follow me," he told Keaton. "You'll get a kick out of this." He said nothing more until the two of them had arrived at the studio's pirate ship. "It's called the *Arabella*. Built for the Errol Flynn swashbuckler, *Captain Blood*. I've used this as a sanctuary for whenever I need to be alone."

Keaton nodded appreciatively. "I don't have all day."

Luke wished Nell were here. He clasped his hands behind his back so that Keaton wouldn't notice the strain blanching his knuckles. "You know that song Nell sang for me on the Hollywood Canteen broadcast?"

"And at Romanoff's on New Year's Eve."

"Right. Okay. Well. That song was inspired by the code I was using."

"Using?" Keaton asked evenly. "Code?"

"In my V-mails to Nell."

The commodore's sharp jawline had softened with age, but it momentarily took on its former edge. "Explain yourself."

"Nell and I had just met when I shipped out. I was missing her so terribly. Those shifts out at Montauk, they were so long. Especially at night. Sometimes I pulled a double. Sixteen hours straight. I was so lonesome."

"Get to the code, Lieutenant."

"I knew she'd be worried about me, wondering where I was, how I was." Luke raised his flattened palms. "I know, I know. All the girls who'd waved goodbye to their sweethearts were worried. But working as a cryptographer, I figured out a way I could ease her mind. You've got to remember, I was—"

"What, exactly, did you do?"

"I composed my V-mails in such a way that if Nell read every fifth word, she could decipher where I was and what I was doing."

"You relayed your movements. To a civilian. In writing."

"I did."

"And then she wrote a song that she titled 'Every Fifth Word,' thus broadcasting your now not-so-secret code to the entire world."

"That's right."

"During wartime!" A gang of nearby crewmen in paint-stained overalls looked up from Mexican Plaza, where they were planting fake orange blossoms. "Dammit, Valenti, I staked my reputation on your enlistment."

"Yes, sir. I'm keenly aware of what you did." Luke could barely manage more than a whisper. "But she only performed the song on that Hollywood Canteen broadcast because she'd received word of an unexpected inheritance coming my way. It was a huge amount of money and there was a strict deadline by which I needed to claim—"

"I'm a commodore of the US Navy!" Vance thundered. "A protégé of mine broke a—no, *the*—fundamental rule of security."

Dry-mouthed and clammy, Luke could only gape at him. What was he supposed to say? What could he say?

"Jesus, Lieutenant, you were a cryptographer. You, of all people —GODDAMMIT!" He punched the *Arabella* with the side of his fist. "Why the hell didn't you keep your trap shut about this?"

"Because—because—"

"Spit it out, for chrissakes."

"You insisted I tell you what was on my mind."

"You should have tried harder."

"It's just that now there's going to be this movie—"

"Are they using the song?"

"It was a huge hit."

Vance turned his back on the ship. "I can't let this slide."

The commodore was taking this confession as badly as Luke

had feared. But in an unexpected way, it felt good to confess his sin. It was time to push all his chips into the middle of the poker table.

Luke snapped to attention. "I was a cryptographer; I should have known better. I knew the dangers. I did it anyway."

"There's protocol I must follow. I'm going to have to kick this can upstairs."

"I understand."

"You could be court-martialed. Stripped of your medals. Drummed out on a dishonorable discharge. The *Lanternfish* hero in total disgrace."

"I chose poorly and am ready to face the consequences, sir."

Neither man said a word for a full two minutes.

"I can't make any promises," Vance said, his voice more tempered now.

"I know."

"The brass are going to do as they see fit. I can't begin to tell you how disappointed I am in you."

That one stung. Real bad. The razor-sharp edge of Vance's remark lacerated Luke's heart. "I'm so sorry, sir. More than I can say."

Vance pointed down Third Street. "If I walk to the end, is that where my car's waiting for me?"

"It is." Luke stepped forward. "Let me walk you—"

"I can find my own way."

Luke fell against the hull of the *Arabella*. He closed his eyes and didn't open them again until he was sure Commodore Keaton Vance was out of sight.

22

The CBS usher in the blue blazer rapped a knuckle against the dressing room door, where Nell's name was stenciled onto a square of white cardboard. He swung it open and pointed to a telephone in the corner. "If you need anything, dial one, one, three."

Nell waited until he had left. "They even have my name on the door!"

Luke helped her out of her coat and hung it on the rack next to a beat-up rehearsal piano. "It's official: You've hit the big time."

"And so has my handiwork." Tristan examined the hem of the pearl-gray dress he'd made especially for tonight. Gathering at the waist, it flared out when she spun around. "I don't care if this is radio and nobody'll see it."

Gus poked Tristan in the ribs. "That's not what you said in the car coming over."

"I underestimated how brightly our chanteuse would glow in it."

Nell felt like a star after she had put it on earlier that evening. So grown up! So elegant in these matching high heels that would probably kill her feet later.

She wished Bogie and Betty could have joined them, but the studio had rushed them into retakes for *The Big Sleep*, a picture they had finished filming a full year ago and now had to painstakingly recreate. The extra effort was to give Betty more screen time, so she hadn't complained. They had, however, sent two dozen red roses, whose perfume filled the room with elegance.

She fished from her purse the camera Avery had loaned her. He had overworked his crippled hand during "The Night of the Idols" and was still in considerable pain. Audrey had volunteered to stay with him and listen on the radio, so he'd told Nell to fill the whole roll of film. She handed it to Gus. "For the folks back home."

Luke threw her a knowing smile. He was the only one who'd seen that afternoon's telegram.

ALL SOUTH BEND WILL BE LISTENING STOP
WE COULDN'T BE MORE PROUD STOP
LOVE FROM THE WHOLE DAVENPORT CLAN STOP

There had been a time when she doubted that she'd ever get a message like that. But mail regularly arrived from home these days. Clippings from the *South Bend Tribune*. Photos of weddings, christenings, or Memorial Day picnics. Picture postcards of Lake Michigan vacations. How ironic that she had to move two thousand miles away to feel a part of the family. Naturally, they wouldn't approve of Nell sleeping with Luke without the benefit of clergy, so some topics were better overlooked. Aside from that, life had become a great big bowl of juicy, red cherries.

What a pity her resignation from Warner Bros. hadn't gone so smoothly. Having averted disaster with the *Three Strangers* crisis, she figured her chances might have been at least fifty-fifty that Taplinger would let her work five days a week with Friday afternoons off. But what she got was his "You're making a terrible decision" rant. Such a shame. Radio money was good, but the studio offered job security. Should she have dared to hope for the best of both worlds? No, she shouldn't have, as it turned out. Not even close. Taplinger had been so incensed, he had ordered her to pack up and get out.

Luke slid his arm around her waist as Gus focused Avery's camera. "You look sensational—even if I don't know what color it is."

He mentioned his color blindness so infrequently that she tended to forget he couldn't see them. "You're rather spiffy yourself, all decked out in your dress uniform—even if you don't know what color it is."

His smile had been empty of its usual warmth since his encounter with Keaton a few days ago. "I've screwed myself nine ways to Sunday," he'd wailed on her doorstep. She had waited until after she'd loosened his tie and fed him a double Kentucky Tavern to ask why. She had broken out into a cold sweat when she saw how her chart-topping song, the one that had led directly to *Music from Hollywood*, might result in his court martial. She wouldn't have blamed him for taking a powder tonight, but he had insisted on being there.

She squeezed his hand as Gus called out, "Say cheese!"

Hoagy pounded on the door. "You decent?" Nell told him to come on in. "I have news."

"Good or bad?"

"You know how you're singing 'Doctor, Lawyer, Indian Chief'?"

"I don't like how you asked that question."

"Here's the thing: I'm fine with you performing any of my songs, but Paramount sees it differently."

"What've they got to do with it?"

"They commissioned me to write 'Doctor, Lawyer, Indian Chief' for Betty Hutton to sing in *The Stork Club*."

"Which came out a month ago."

"It did, but Capitol Records won't be releasing Hutton's version until March. I told them you singing it was great publicity for the song, but Barney Balaban has gotten it into his head that we're stealing it out from under him."

It was fifty minutes to show time. What would Dinah Shore do? She would take this hiccup in her stride. Nell stroked one of the velvety-soft petals on one of the Bogarts' roses. "You wrote 'How Little We Know' with a simple melody and uncomplicated lyrics so that a novice could sing it, right?"

Hoagy's long face lit up. "You know it?"

"No, but I helped Betty learn it on the set, so we're halfway there." She jerked her thumb toward the piano. "Play it slowly so that Luke can take down the words. We've got ample time to go through the song seven or eight times.

"Will that be enough?" Gus asked.

Nell had rehearsed "Doctor, Lawyer, Indian Chief" close to forty times, so seven or eight wasn't nearly enough. "It'll have to be."

"Shouldn't someone tell the band about this?" Tony asked.

"Sacky is the producer; he's the one in the vivid bow tie. Arlo is the bandleader in the white jacket. GO!"

Tristan stepped close enough to rub his shoulder against hers. "What can I do?"

She tried to evict the thought that all of South Bend would be tuning in. This was the job she'd signed up for; she needed to roll with the punches. "You can hold my hand."

* * *

Nell wouldn't have thought of dressing all in white the day after her *Music from Hollywood* debut, but Kathryn Massey had recently reported how stunning Lana Turner looked in *The Postman Always Rings Twice*, currently filming at MGM. And so, when Nell had received the summons to appear in front of Jack Warner, she had looked in her closet and found she had the components for an all-white ensemble.

Appearing in front of a packed studio audience with Luke's scrawled lyrics in her hand had felt excruciatingly unprofessional. Dinah Shore wouldn't do that. Yes, well, Dinah had probably never performed a song she'd still been learning five minutes ahead of walking on stage. Let alone without flubbing a single line or note. So beat that, Miss Shore!

Warner's secretary used the rubber tip of her eraser to press a red button on her intercom. "Miss Davenport has arrived."

Warner's voice blasted through the speaker. "Send her in."

Nell's eyes went straight to Taplinger, who was seated in the other guest chair, staring at his shoes. What was this, an ambush? "Good morning." She ran her hands across her crisp skirt as she sat down.

"Miss Davenport!" Warner slapped the edge of his desk. "Hell of a job last night."

She strangled her snow-white purse a little more tightly. "You tuned in?"

"Just about busted my buttons when I realized you were singing one of our songs. I thought, 'Of course she is. That doll is a loyal Warner girl, through and through. What else would she sing? Some crummy second-hand Judy Garland ditty?' I said to my wife, 'That Davenport girl is a credit to the studio.' Ann agreed with me. Lemme tell you, that doesn't happen often."

Was she supposed to respond? Nell looked to Taplinger for a clue, but his footwear continued to fascinate him.

"The reason I've called you in goes without saying," Warner continued, "but it's best to make things clear."

"Being clear is always preferable."

"As long as you're employed here, I will only permit you to sing from our catalog."

As long as I'm employed here? Does he still think—?

"Like, for instance, any of the songs from those Busby Berkeley musicals. That gives you tons of choices."

Nell listed them in her mind: "You're Getting to Be a Habit with Me," "Shuffle Off to Buffalo," "I Only Have Eyes for You," "We're in the Money." Yes, she thought, but those movies were fifteen years old. Those songs were cute in their day, but weren't they a bit old-fashioned now?

"Somebody needs to let Leo Forbstein know that our Miss Davenport is to have full access to our catalog. You can do that, can't you, Robert?"

Taplinger looked up, a sheepish grimace torturing his face. "Yes, sir."

"I've got Errol Flynn's agent coming in soon, so if there's anything else you need, young lady, now's the time to speak up."

Could I? Should I? Dare I? Nell thought of Luke bargaining his way into a better deal. *If he can do it, I can.*

"There is a small thing." She angled away from Taplinger. "The demands of a radio show are heaviest on broadcast day. I was wondering if it might be possible to have Fridays off."

Warner glanced over at Taplinger. "You can manage without Miss Davenport one day a week, can't you? Especially as she'll be singing Warner songs. With all those millions listening, that's free publicity right there!"

Taplinger nodded. He still hadn't looked at her.

Nell shot to her feet. "Thank you, Mr. Warner." His handshake felt more like a dead fish than she was expecting. "I'll do the studio proud, I promise." She headed out the door without waiting for Taplinger to join her.

* * *

Nell ran into the props department. "Luke?" she called out. "LUKE?"

"At the falcon cabinet."

Nell picked her way around rocking chairs and billiard tables until she found him standing at a gray metal cabinet. He looked away from the jumble of contents and took in her dazzling white outfit. "Where are you off to? The Academy Awards?"

How delicious it was to describe her meeting, and how, afterward, Taplinger had admitted defeat, and even begrudgingly confessed how expertly she had handled herself. Luke half-turned his head toward the cabinet, his attention clearly drifting.

"Did I interrupt something?" she asked.

"You just missed Bogie."

"He was on the lot?"

"He'd come directly from Paramount."

"Enemy territory!" She jabbed him playfully, but he didn't respond.

"Wallis is prepping a Barbara Stanwyck movie, *The Strange Love of Martha Ivers*, and Bogie wanted him to run it."

Luke was speaking with a remote, preoccupied tone, as though he'd woken up not long ago and was still half-asleep. She hated how he had this Navy guillotine hanging over him, but there was nothing they could do until they learned whether or not anything would come of Vance's warning.

"Some acting pal of Betty's is making his screen debut in that picture," she said. "I don't remember his name."

"Kirk Douglas."

"Bogie doesn't think this Douglas guy is a potential competitor for Betty's affections, does he?"

Nell had been kidding around, but Luke failed to pick up on the flippancy in her voice. "The second female lead is an actress named Lizabeth Scott, who Columbia might cast opposite him in *Dead Reckoning*."

"Is that a bad thing?" Nell had to resist the urge to add, I can't tell from your daydreamy tone.

"This girl is a dead ringer for Betty, so Bogie wanted to check her out in case there were any issues that needed heading off at the pass."

"And are there?"

"He said she's a talented actress, and it's a way to give the public another Bogart and Bacall movie until *The Big Sleep* comes out."

"So it's a good thing?"

"A complicated thing. Going to Paramount to see an actress he might work with at Columbia while under contract at Warners. He's getting sick to death of being shunted around. I told him I could guarantee pulling him out of the dumps if he came over here." Luke smiled like he was Luke again and pulled a rectangular piece of paper out of his trouser pocket. Pinching each end between his fingers, he held up a check for thirty-five thousand dollars.

"Luke, honey! They paid you!"

"Which means you and I are about to become movie characters!" He refolded the check and slipped it into his pocket. "Won't that be a kick?"

Until this moment, the idea of Luke's story being made into a motion picture had been a pile of what-ifs, maybes, and somedays. Tons of movies that sounded great in a pitch never made it to the screen. And many of the ones that did fell short of expectations. So she had shoved all possibilities and anticipations into the shadowy backwoods of her mind, denying herself the thrill of being portrayed on screen.

Until now.

They went in for a long, passionate smooch.

When they came out of it, he said, "Full steam ahead on Santana Productions."

Oh. So he was still planning on going into the movie business? "Even more exciting!" Nell could tell that the enthusiasm she'd tried to inject into her response fell a little flat. Luke frowned. "Don't you think?"

"Yes, I do."

"But?"

"You could buy a house and have no mortgage." She made a one-shoulder shrug. "For Bogie, it's business as usual. But for us, it's a once-in-a-lifetime opportunity."

"Unless the profits from Santana movies equal *Casablanca* and *To Have and Have Not*."

A fair point. And besides, this was his money, not hers.

She cracked open the cabinet doors to find a disorganized hodgepodge of artifacts. "Is this a junk drawer for when you don't know where else to put odds and ends?"

"No," Luke said. "I like to . . . look at it."

He stands here and stares at stuff?

The third shelf down held an assortment of liquor bottles. Most of them had old labels pasted on them, designs she hadn't seen since her South Bend days. She picked up a bottle of brandy and cradled it in her left hand.

"My father wasn't much of a drinker, but he always maintained that brandy was the exception. I forget his rationale. Something to do with Christmas and Dickens and British traditions. Did I ever tell you he's an Anglophile? The British have a dessert called Christmas pudding, and it's—"

Luke ran a finger across the label. "Remy," he muttered, more to himself than to Nell. "It isn't a thing. It's a *person*."

Nell fought back tremors of alarm. Was the threat of a court martial getting to him more than she had supposed? "What is, darling? That bottle? You think there's a person inside?"

His face had paled to a ghastly gray, but his eyes were clear. "I've been preoccupied with this cabinet. Staring at it for weeks. Couldn't figure out why, though. The more I stared, the less I saw.

But then you come along and—" He tapped on the logo. "St. Remy Brandy VSOP."

"Are we talking about Saint Remy? The patron saint of, what, drinking in movies?"

He dropped his head to one side as though she'd conked him across the cranium with a lead pipe.

"Tell me what's happening, please, Luke. You're scaring me."

"You know when you're trying to think of someone's name? It's on the tip of your tongue. The glimmers are there, just past your fingertips."

Nell couldn't imagine what it must be like for him. Watching him struggle was hard enough. But talking to him now might hinder whatever was going on.

"Remy," he muttered again. "Oh my God, yes—it's a guy. I don't know anyone called Remy." Luke's head snapped back. "Tristan!"

"Remy is Tristan?"

"He knows Tristan."

"How do you know that?"

"Dunno."

"Remy is . . . who?"

"Dunno."

"Why is he important?"

"Dunno."

"I'm sorry, honey, but I'm not following this conversation too well."

Luke managed a watery smile. "Join the club."

She took his hand and held it to her chest. "Scraps of unrelated details come to you randomly. No pattern, no explanation, no rhyme or reason?"

He didn't respond for the longest time. "I've been dreaming about the *Lanternfish* more and more lately."

"Was this Remy guy on the *Lanternfish*?"

"No."

It was the most definite answer she'd gotten from him, so that was a clue. Wasn't it? "Or does Tristan know him?"

"I have a hunch he might."

"So, tonight we'll go see him, right?"

Luke nodded, but barely. "Please don't think I'm nuts."

"Hardly." She kissed him on the cheek and reassured him that they'd figure it out. "Meanwhile, I still work at Warners. Meet you here at six?"

He returned the bottle to its place on the shelf. "It's a date."

She dashed from the room, across the foyer, and into the brisk afternoon. No, she didn't think he was nuts, but later tonight, if Tristan stared as blankly at Luke as she had, all bets were off.

23

*G*us owned the biggest car—a sky-blue LaSalle convertible—so he had volunteered to drive everyone to The First Step, a nightclub on the easternmost edge of Hollywood, where Hollywood Boulevard crossed Sunset.

Betty unfolded her picnic blanket across their laps to keep them warm against the chill of the February evening. "Will someone please explain where we're headed, and why we're going there? All I know is it's called The Final Step—"

"Isn't it The First Step?" Luke asked.

"She's thinking of *The Last Submarine*," Gus said. "And congratulations, by the way."

It had been nearly a week since Luke had banked his check, but he was still grappling with the prospect of seeing himself portrayed on the screen by no less than John Garfield. "Thank you. I'll be signing autographs after the show."

"There's a show?" Betty asked.

Tristan twisted around to face the three in the back seat. "You need to brace yourself."

"Dare I ask why?"

Tristan looked beseechingly at Luke. "I know this is your story, but can I tell it?"

If it hadn't been for Tristan, Luke might be at home, tempted to bang his head against the bedroom wall, trying to dislodge the fragment of memory that explained why Remy referred to a person and not expensive Cognac. "The floor's all yours."

"Well, Miss Bacall," Tristan said, "there I was, reading the funnies in the *L.A. Times*, and in barged Luke looking like his ass was on fire. 'Remy! Remy!' he kept screeching at me. 'It's a person, isn't it? A PERSON!'"

"For the record," Luke butted in, "nobody was screeching. However, I will admit that my voice was raised a notch."

"He was all worked up because he couldn't figure out who Remy was. Which is when I, with the patience of Florence Nightingale, explained to him that he was probably talking about Remy Brandee-Whyne."

"Surely that's not her real name," Betty said.

"Heavens, child, she's not even a she."

"Come again?"

"Remy Brandee-Whyne is a female impersonator at The First Step, which is only *the* most fabulous nightclub in LA."

Betty shook her head. "Never heard of it."

Tristan reached over and patted her knee, "You're a long way from Ciro's."

"And I ought to brace myself because—why?"

Gus turned onto Franklin Avenue. Luke wasn't sure what to expect when they arrived, so he wanted to hear this explanation as much as Betty did.

"Remy Brandee-Whyne is famous for impersonating female celebrities. The first time I saw him, he was doing Tallulah Bankhead. The next time he was Joan Crawford as Mildred Pierce."

"His Marlene Dietrich is to die for," Gus put in.

"Word on the street is that he's laying 'em in the aisles doing—" Tristan batted his eyelashes at Betty "—Miss Lauren Bacall."

"NO!" Betty released an almighty screech of her own. "What if he spots me? What if he freezes? I don't want to spoil the fun."

Tristan dug out a curly blonde wig from a paper sack at his feet. "It's one of Joan Blondell's."

Gus braked at the traffic lights on Normandie Avenue. "We'll be there in ten."

A mixture of dread and eagerness warped Betty's beautiful face. "Should I?"

"I'm going to try talking to Remy after the show, so you'll be sitting alone in the parking lot for heaven only knows how long." He flicked Blondell's wig with a finger. "Nine minutes."

* * *

The First Step resembled an adobe house converted to a Mexican restaurant. Its flat roof featured a line of seven wooden beams jutting out two feet over thick walls painted sandy brown. The red light suspended over the lacquered oak front door tinted the tiles in welcoming pink.

But stepping inside was like entering a turn-of-the-century circus tent. The cherry-red walls led to a domed ceiling painted a dark shade of lapis lazuli blue, dotted with stars. A massive wrought-iron chandelier, at least ten feet across, looked like a prop from an Errol Flynn pirate movie. Wide streamers of all colors—butterscotch, mistletoe, cobalt, and fuchsia—hung from it in deep loops. Not that Luke could tell one color from the other, but as they reached the foyer, Nell described the scene as best she could. "Cherry-red" became "fruity-juicy," "lapis lazuli" became "big summer sky," and "butterscotch" became "candy sweet."

A buxom hostess dressed in a gypsy costume by way of Transylvania led them to a round table. It stood one row back from the stage, but provided Luke with a three-hundred-and-sixty-degree view of the gathering. And oh brother, what an audience.

It had never crossed Luke's mind that he had lived a particularly sheltered life. That is, until he surveyed the cross-dressers with hairy forearms, the pansies with their ambiguous is-he-or-isn't-she expressions of contrived boredom, the butch dykes with brilliantined hair and black leather bombardier jackets, and extravagantly dressed libertines sporting Oscar Wilde-esque frilly cuffs spilling out of their velvet coats.

Betty bumped her shoulder against Luke's. "You were smart to ditch your uniform."

Still a member of the US Naval Reserves, Luke was required to be in uniform when in public, but Gus had strongly suggested dressing in civvies tonight. With the threat of a court martial lurking beyond the horizon, flouting the rules meant he was taking an awful chance. However, now that he saw the kind of crowd that gathered in this place, he was glad he'd followed Gus's advice.

He tucked a stray lock of Betty's hair into her wig. "It's good Tristan brought Joan Blondell along. You might get away with it."

"Don't look now," Nell said, "but we seem to be the main event."

Most eyes in the joint had zeroed in on their table. Heads tilted. Lips murmured.

"I'm in a wig and Luke's out of uniform," Betty said. "That leaves you, Nell."

A pair of bon viveur Beau Brummel types in puffy shirt sleeves and striped ascots approached them. "We don't wish to disturb," the redhead said, "but aren't you Tristan Bannister?"

His friend, a peroxided blonde, elbowed him. "You mean Trixie Bagatelle."

Tristan cupped his hands around his chin like he was Mary Miles Minter. "Who? Me? Why, darlings, how kind of you to notice!"

Betty lifted her menu to cover her mouth. "Just when you think you're famous."

* * *

The floorshow was a spirited mixture of female impersonators who mimed to records or sang live to an accompanist at a midget piano. A magician dressed as Scarlett O'Hara on the left and Rhett Butler on the right followed a performer of indeterminate sex, who wowed the audience by juggling seven Raggedy Ann dolls.

The master of ceremonies came over the PA. "Ladies and gentlemen, and those who inhabit the netherworld in between, please welcome to our stage the one, the only—" the voice paused as a drumroll started up "—Remy Brandee-Whyne!"

The crowd erupted into a thunderclap of applause punctuated by wolf whistles as the room plunged into darkness. A spotlight hit the stage, revealing a woman decked out in a slinky black silk dress with a small hoop at the waist. It was an exact duplicate of Betty's costume in *To Have and Have Not*. Remy launched into a plaintive ballad called "The Fine Art of Bogart." It reminded Luke of Dietrich's "Falling in Love Again," but with wittier lyrics about falling in love with Bogie.

She followed it with a peppier Carmen Miranda–like pastiche about speaking the lingua franca while sipping hot Sanka on the streets of Casablanca. As the audience roared, it occurred to Luke that this Remy person would get the surprise of his life if he knew the real Lauren Bacall was right there in front of him.

"Pretty good, huh?" he asked Betty.

"Hysterical!" she half-shouted.

"I dare you to reveal yourself."

She shot him a look that said, *I couldn't—could I? I shouldn't—should I?*

"Double-dog dare you."

As the applause abated and Remy prepared for her next

number, Betty jumped to her feet and ripped off her wig. "YES, BUT CAN YOU SING 'HOW LITTLE WE KNOW'?"

The room sucked in a collective gasp as all heads turned toward her.

"How about you join me up on stage," Remy taunted, "and we'll put our lips together."

* * *

The club manager, a dapper gent with an impoverished aristocrat air about him, led them through the backstage area to Remy's dressing room.

Still in costume, he was standing when they walked in. "Oh, Miss Bacall!" he trilled. "I'm still shaking with sheer giddiness from getting to perform with you."

"Please," Betty said, "call me Lauren."

"Lauren Bacall asked me to call her by her first name!" He cradled his cheeks with his hands. "Since the moment I saw you in *To Have and Have Not*, I knew you were special. I hope to God you didn't take offense tonight."

"Offense?" Betty exclaimed. "I think you're sensational."

"Oh, Miss Bac—Lauren—I won't be getting no sleep tonight."

"Let me introduce my friends." Betty laid a hand on Luke's shoulder.

Remy's glossy lips soured into a sneer. "I know who *you* are."

Thrown by the abrupt shift, Luke wasn't certain what he should say. "I enjoyed your show so much." For all its blandness, his compliment only heightened Remy's resentment.

"You've got a hell of a nerve showing up here, Luke Valenti." He spat out Luke's name as though it were chunks of curdled milk.

Without the benefit of clever lighting, he came across less Bacall-y than he had on stage. But between his heavy makeup and styled wig, it was hard to determine how he looked in everyday life. "But why?" Luke asked. "I didn't even know you existed until a couple of days ago."

"Quit playing the innocent."

Luke looked at Nell, Tristan, and Gus; all of them looked as mystified as he felt. He asked the only question he could think of. "Does the name Christopher Walsh mean anything?"

Remy crossed his arms and shot Luke down with a glare he'd clearly learned from Barbara Stanwyck. "You know it does."

Betty ventured a step closer to Remy. "Could someone explain what's going on here?" She lowered her chin into a position the studio PR machine had dubbed The Look. "If only for my benefit?"

"For you, anything." Remy pulled out a copy of *Look* magazine from a voluminous carryall bag hooked around the back of his makeup chair. The cover featured a cherubic little boy under the headline YOUR LAST CHANCE TO AVOID ATOMIC DESTRUCTION.

"I haven't seen this issue," Betty said.

"Won't hit the newsstands until tomorrow," Remy said, flicking pages. "But the seamstress who makes my costumes is shacked up with a guy who works in *Look*'s LA office and got me an advance copy."

He held up a photograph of a couple in their late forties sitting on a loveseat with a cable-patterned rug slung over the back. The guy wore an ill-fitting dark-blue suit; his wife was in a shiny blouse with a tulip pattern that didn't flatter her thickening waistline. Neither of them had put much effort into smiling for the camera.

The headline demanded, WHO IS THE REAL HERO OF THE LANTERNFISH?

Remy flicked a surly nail at the caption and read it out loud. "'Roger and Arlene Walsh, Rockaway Park, Queens, New York.'"

Luke felt himself go pale. "Christopher's parents!"

"That's right, Lieutenant Hero. And although not stated

outright, they're carefully suggesting that their son was the actual hero of the *Lanternfish*."

"I never claimed—"

"It's *Christopher* who kept transmitting the SOS. *His* efforts lead to the rescue. Otherwise, the crew would have been sitting ducks for the Japs. Even worse, *you* insisted he remain at his station until it was too late."

"Give me that." Luke snatched the magazine from Remy.

He read the article's byline: Maxine Waterford. Wasn't that the reporter from *Life*? The one with the wind-blown hair and lively eyes? She'd seemed so nice. Had it all been an act? And now she had moved on to *Look*, where she had packaged a gross misrepresentation of the truth into a slick package of fiction.

As far as Luke could recall, at least.

Scanning farther down the article, he stopped at Mrs. Walsh mentioning the Brooklyn Bridge. A scrap of memory shook itself loose. Christopher had a picture of it taped to the wall. It was in color, he'd told Luke. Christopher had joked about how he preferred the Marine Parkway Bridge that connected Queens to Brooklyn, but it was the poor country cousin of New York bridges.

He handed *Look* back to Remy. "Just because it's in *Look* doesn't mean it's true."

"You tell me, then." Remy flung the magazine aside. "What happened when the *Lanternfish* went down?"

Here we go again. This won't bolster my case, but it's all I've got. "I hit my head that night. Got a severe concussion along with this." He raised his damaged finger for Remy to see. "Consequently, I have gaping blanks in my memory."

"So why should I believe anything you say?"

Why, indeed? I wouldn't if I were in your size ten pumps... which look horribly uncomfortable. Luke had no answer that would satisfy this guy, so he took a gamble. "I'm desperate to fill in the gaps, so if there's anything you can tell me about Christopher that might help me—"

"What, you mean like how his family would've hated the idea he was a fairy, so he left Rockaway before he got ran outta town."

The sharp notes from the trumpet player on stage bled through into the dressing room.

Wait. What? Christopher was a fairy?

"May I say something?" Nell had picked up the magazine and opened it again to the Walshes' interview. "According to this, Rockaway is deeply Irish, and therefore Catholic. Speaking as someone who comes from Catholic South Bend, Indiana, I'm aware that anyone who doesn't fit in is shunned." She paused to reflect for a moment. "Unless you're a priest. They get a free pass for everything."

An impenetrable expression flashed across Remy's face. Luke would have interrogated the guy on it, but Nell had more to say.

"The end of this article gives the impression that the Walshes would have kept to themselves except that Luke has sold his story to the movies for a huge amount of money, which they feel belongs to them."

"Pah!" Tristan jammed his hands on his hips. "They're doing all this for the money?"

But Luke was still stuck on Christopher being a fruit. "How did you meet him?"

Remy plunked himself down in front of his vanity mirror. "I can't see how that's any of your business."

"It's probably not, but I'm asking anyway."

"I need to take this makeup off before I claw it off." He opened a jar of Woodbury cold cream and sighed. "When I fronted up at the draft board, they tagged me with a 4-F. Denying I'm a homo was a waste of time, but I did object to being labeled a mentally ill moral degenerate."

"I got 4-F'd too." Luke wanted to establish common ground,

but regretted it when Remy threw him a look that seemed to say, *Yes, but not for being classified a moral degenerate.*

"I didn't finish high school"—Remy smeared a glob of cream across his face—"so the best job I could find was as a dishwasher at the Roosevelt. The pay was lousy, but I got to eat all the leftovers I wanted. In my spare time, I volunteered at the USO canteen at Hollywood and Cahuenga. I was still keen to do my bit for the war effort, even if they didn't trust me with a gun.

"So anyway, on a slow Tuesday night, Christopher came in, and my, oh my! It was like—" he found Betty in his mirror and gave her a playful wink "—being in a movie starring Humphrey Bogart and Lauren Bacall. He had a seven-day shore leave before shipping out to Pearl Harbor. I'll spare you the details, but let's just say it was an intense week in which we fell in love. I never knew it could be like that. I mean, not like *that*."

With Remy's thick stage makeup now removed, Luke could see this guy had an exotic, Hedy Lamarr "Take me to the Casbah" air to him, with almond-shaped eyes, full lips, and high cheekbones that half of Hollywood's leading ladies would have killed their agents for.

"His pass came to an end, and we had a tearful parting. Wept buckets, we did. Buckets and buckets."

"Did he write to you?" Betty asked.

"As much as he could. He was supposed to join the *Viperfish*—"

"The *Lanternfish*'s sister ship?" Luke cut in.

"Yep," Remy said. "How's that for irony? But at the last minute, the *Lanternfish*'s radio operator's appendix busted open. Christopher had none of the year-long training that most submariners get, and you had to be a volunteer, but he was the only one who stepped up to the plate."

Luke's mind was a slot machine, with wheels spinning and patterns falling into place. Volunteering on a submarine without the requisite qualifications. He and Christopher had shared that. He couldn't picture Christopher's face, but he heard his voice now. "We're lemmings," he had said with a laugh. "No common sense. All suicidal tendencies."

Betty theatrically cleared her throat. "Sorry to break this up, but I stupidly told Bogie I would be home by ten. It's almost midnight, and if I know him, he'll be climbing the walls."

After everybody had filed out of the dressing room, Luke lingered behind. "I work in the props department at Warner Brothers. In case you ever want to—" He shrugged. "Just in case." Luke kept his eyes forward as he exited the dressing room. He could, however, feel the heat of Remy's stare searing his back.

24

Nell waited for a break in the Sunset Boulevard traffic across from the CBS studios. Goodness, what an evening they'd had last night. A man dressed up as Lauren Bacall singing with the real Lauren Bacall would have made for a memorable time on its own. But all those dressing-room revelations afterwards! She'd been watching Luke's face as the memories had surfaced, one after the other. It couldn't have been easy, but surely it was better to know what had happened during the sinking instead of continuing to stumble in the dark?

Luke had been restless all night, wriggling around like the bed was made of rocks, which meant she'd had a poor night's sleep, too. And so now she had to perform "I Only Have Eyes for You." But there was one prospect that would help haul her through: her paycheck. And that was because now she could, at long last, pay off her wedding debt to her father. He'd told her several times that she didn't need to, and how her wanting to was payment enough. But reading between the lines of his now-frequent letters, she knew she'd earned his respect for taking responsibility for her actions.

Finally, a lull in the traffic. Nell dashed across the street. Don't think about those two thousand dollars, she told herself, stepping onto the curb. *It's an investment in future family relationships that—*

"Hello there."

The lead trumpeter from the Arlo Nash Orchestra was the one who'd improvised some snazzy notes to harmonize with her vocals during her debut. He always ducked out after the show, so she'd had no opportunity to thank him.

"Peyton, isn't it?" He nodded, but said nothing more. "There's fifteen of you, and when you all dress in tuxes, it's hard to, well . . ."

"Tell us all apart?"

"It doesn't help."

"At least you're trying. The vocalist in the first band I worked in back home in Madison sang with us nearly two years and never bothered to learn our names."

"You're from Madison? We're practically neighbors from across the lake."

"South Bend."

"How did you know that?"

He held the door open for her. "*Hollywood Reporter.*"

Nell wasn't clear how Kathryn Massey had dug up that morsel about her past, but it made a nice conversation starter with this trumpeter who'd helped her sound marvelous. "I've never thought of Madison and South Bend as being neighbors."

"As far as LA is concerned, we hail from the same neck of the woods."

In every big band or swing orchestra Nell had ever seen, it was always the trumpeters who had the Casanova reputation—especially the lead ones. There was an easy confidence about this Peyton guy. He didn't seem obnoxiously cocky, even though, with his broad shoulders, sky-blue eyes, sandy-blond hair, and relaxed smile, he had every reason to be.

They arrived at Studio Two, where the other musicians were

setting up. "You doing anything later?" he asked. "Maybe get a bite to eat?"

The Navy had booked Luke to give one of his talks near the USC campus south of downtown. With all the positive publicity he'd generated from the news about his movie, they weren't letting him sit around. He had hated the idea of public speaking for the first few talks, but nowadays he seemed to take it in stride. This morning as he'd been pressing his uniform, he was almost chipper at the idea of having his first brush with the Shriners.

But Peyton hadn't asked her out on a date, had he? Not a *date* date, at least. His tone had been too casually oh-and-by-the-way for that. Who knows how many of these evening speaking engagements the Navy would book Luke into. What was she supposed to do? Stay at home?

"Yes," she said, "that would be lovely."

Brittingham's Radio Center Restaurant was a brightly lit, ritzy diner with a cocktail lounge attached. It was in the same building as CBS's Columbus Square complex, so if anybody had seen Nell with Peyton, it wouldn't have looked as though they were clinking furtive cocktails in some backstairs hideaway with dim lighting and a gypsy violinist.

He jumped to his feet as she approached the booth where he was sitting and stepped aside to let her slide in. "You did a mighty fine job tonight."

She popped open her purse and dropped her gloves into it. "Thank you."

He cast a quick eye over the menu. "I was somewhat surprised when I heard that you'd be singing 'I Only Have Eyes for You.'"

"It's harder to sing than you might think."

"From 1934?" He made wide circles in the air with his hands as though to say, *It's a little old-fashioned, isn't it?*

"Mr. Warner has decreed I can only perform Warner tunes, so . . ." She circled her own hands in the air: *Whatcha gonna do?*

"Speaking of, I hear *The Last Submarine* is a go. How do you feel about Joan Leslie playing you on screen?"

"Strange, fun, disconcerting."

Their waitress arrived to take their drinks order. A Sidecar for her, an Old Fashioned for him.

"Strange, fun, and disconcerting, how?" he asked.

"Strange to see someone else playing me. Fun because I get to be a character in a movie. But disconcerting because who knows how they'll portray me."

"I doubt they would have cast Joan Leslie if they were planning on making you the villain."

His calm, casual manners put him in stark contrast with most guys in Hollywood, who fancied themselves as wolves on the make or radiated a hope that she could do them a favor. "I'm pretty confident the villains in this picture will be the Japanese." It was a tad warm in the room; she popped the front button of her poplin jacket. "It's possible I'm worrying unnecessarily. *The Last Submarine* is Luke's story. I'm only the home-front girl."

She wasn't altogether sure why she'd felt the need to insert Luke's name into this conversation. The first-date tingles between them were conspicuous only by their absence. This is a *non*-date. A couple of work colleagues getting dinner. That's all.

Why, then, did she feel like she was cheating on Luke? Because Peyton was handsome in a Randolph Scott sort of way? Not as good looking as Randolph—nobody was as attractive as that guy —but toward the Randolph Scott end of the scale.

It was time to change the subject. "What did you do during the war?"

"I spent it playing for a USO band. Bob Hope, mostly."

"That must have been memorable."

"You know when movies need to cover a long period and they show a series of quick scenes? What's that called?"

"A montage?"

"My war was a montage of getting squeezed into airplanes, crowded into trains, seasick on boats. Lots of hurrying and waiting. Cold coffee, stale cookies, and latrines I wouldn't wish on Himmler. It was nothing for us to drive two hundred miles in a jeep and give four shows to crowds of soldiers or sailors who laughed at every joke and applauded every note. The Nazis had to have been tracking Bob because they bombed three different towns we were playing in. Three!"

"How unnerving."

He lifted a dismissive shoulder. "It's amazing what you can get used to. We traveled all over both fronts, which means we got to see a terrible amount of death and destruction. Witness enough of that and you can't help but conclude that life is cheap. And short. And you never know when it's going to be taken away from you."

Nell wasn't sure how to respond to his breezy nonchalance. The way he talked about his war experience set him miles apart from Buzz Bryant, who wasted no opportunity to corner unsuspecting audiences with tales of his bravery on the stinking, sulfurous sands, fighting against the lurking Japs on Iwo Jima.

The waitress arrived with their drinks. As she set them down and told them she'd be back for their food order, Nell abandoned any doubts that Peyton saw this rendezvous as anything but a casual, post-work supper. Nobody asks a girl on an actual date and talks of death, destruction, and latrines he wouldn't wish on Himmler.

He raised his Old Fashioned. "Here's to . . . what should we toast?"

"Friends," she said. There, that was obvious enough, wasn't it? "Old friends, new friends, and friends we've lost."

"We all have those, don't we?"

She gingerly clinked his glass and took a sip. Her Sidecar barely touched the sides of her throat. "Now," she said, running a finger down the menu, "what looks good?"

25

When Luke met Greg Whitley out front of the Hill Street building in downtown LA, he noticed the guy wore a pinkie ring featuring a pair of intertwined boxing gloves. "You're a boxer?"

"The Navy's West Coast middleweight title two years running. Since the start of the war, it's all been fundraising exhibition bouts for the USO, or war bonds, or the Hollywood Canteen."

"Impressive. Do you—"

"Let's stick to the issue at hand, Lieutenant."

His deft deflection of Luke's attempted diversion showed that he wouldn't allow Luke to delay the inevitable.

When the summons had arrived by courier, Luke had been relieved. After waiting two months to see what might happen after Vance kicked the can upstairs, he was required to appear in front of a board of three admirals appointed to decide on the appropriate course of action. Did that mean a court martial? Dishonorable discharge? A stretch in the brig? The letter, typed on heavy stock US Navy stationery, hadn't stated, and Whitley didn't know because, as he had told Luke, "This is my first case where a Navy man ignored the loose-lips-sink-ships rule."

"Are you holding up?" Whitley asked.

"I was keeping a lid on it until about an hour ago on the streetcar coming in." Luke dug his hands into his pockets. "But they won't guess I'm about to stain my BVDs."

"Wrong tactic. And keep those hands out of those pockets at all times."

"Won't they admire a sailor who keeps his cool under pressure?"

"This is different. You're fighting to preserve your naval record. Displaying your nerves shows you would do anything to avoid tarnishing it. But—" Whitley raised a warning finger "—don't overplay it. The last thing you want is to come across like a weak-kneed sob sister."

* * *

Two rear admirals and a vice admiral were seated behind an oak table with flags—one American, one Navy—at each end. Luke positioned himself at the faint chalk mark on the floor, where Whitley had directed Luke to "stand at attention until and unless instructed otherwise."

Vice Admiral Crowther, a C. Aubrey Smith type with a chestful of ribbons, broke the tense silence. "Lieutenant Valenti, the vaunted hero of the *Lanternfish*." He spoke with such a resonant timbre that he could have understudied for Caruso.

"Yes, sir."

Crowther's "vaunted" had been an unexpected curveball. There would be time enough for trembling fingers and stammered words later. Luke had wanted to start out strong and confident, so he cringed when he heard a wobble in his voice.

"According to Commodore Vance's report, you admitted using a code in communication with your girlfriend. When writing to Miss—" he checked his notes "—Davenport, you devised your V-mails so that every fifth word, when pulled out of context and strung together, imparted information as to your activities and whereabouts."

The vice admiral hadn't posed a question, but Luke felt as though it was his cue to respond. He glanced at the woman seated at a stenograph machine. She stared unblinkingly back at him.

"Davenport?" one of the rear admirals asked. "She was the party to whom you were writing?"

"Yes, sir."

"The Nell Davenport who had a popular song out last year? 'Every Fifth Word,' wasn't it?"

"Yes, sir." Luke had stilled the quaking in his voice, but appearing before these stone-faced admirals was like facing Mount Rushmore.

"You, a naval cryptanalyst, used a secret code to tell your girlfriend of your whereabouts, which she incorporated into a famous song?"

"She didn't record it until after the war."

"She sang it on Armed Forces Radio, Christmas of forty-four," Crowther rebutted. "I was on the *Missouri*, bound for the Caroline Islands. The skipper allowed the broadcast from the Hollywood Canteen." He fixed Luke with a withering gaze. "Is my recollection accurate, Lieutenant?"

"It is, sir."

"Your code was used in a song heard across the world by millions of people. Not so secret, wouldn't you say?"

"Never in my wildest imaginings could I have conceived she'd use it to write a song."

"She wrote that song?" The question came from the other rear admiral, who had done nothing so far except look as though Luke had spent the morning burying his shoes in horse manure.

"Yes, sir. With Hoagy Carmichael." Luke watched the officer mouth Hoagy's name. From the man's raised eyebrows, Luke could tell he was impressed. "Miss Davenport and Mr. Carmichael became friends on the set of *To Have and Have Not*, when she was helping Lauren Bacall learn a song Hoagy had written for the movie."

The three grave faces told Luke they didn't give a tinker's damn about such inconsequential Hollywood hogwash. *Not during wartime, you insolent punk.*

"Did she write the lyrics?"

Vice Admiral Crowther had asked the question Luke dreaded the most. Luke felt breathless in the room's motionless air that smelled of dust and floor polish. "Yes, sir, she did."

"And coded into those lyrics, was there a message from her to you?"

Luke's shoulders ached from standing at attention. Couldn't they at least let him stand at ease? "Yes, sir."

Crowther's overgrown eyebrows bunched into a single thicket. "What was the message?"

Was it the Navy's concern what went on in the private lives of its men? Nell's message had had nothing to do with his performance as a US Navy Ensign—a performance that had garnered him a Purple Heart *and* a Navy Cross. Wartime or not, men were entitled to their personal lives. The Navy couldn't demand everything.

"Nell's message was of a private nature."

"Lieutenant Valenti, you are the property of the United States Navy, and as such, you have no private life." Rear Admiral Armstrong was a Hemingway man's man type: sun-weathered face, W.C. Fields drinker's nose, and the ability to deliver his reproach a notch above a harsh whisper. "Whatever life you have at this juncture is in the hands of this board. I order you to supply us with the gist of your girlfriend's message."

Jesus Christ, do they think Nell and I were swapping dirty mash notes? "It was a private matter separate from my naval duties. It had no bearing on—"

"The message, Lieutenant."

"And the sole reason she even took that route was because there was a strict deadline and it was the fastest—"

Crowther hammered the table with flattened palms. "Failure to give full and detailed testimony will result in an automatic court martial. Do I make myself clear?"

"Yes, sir."

"For the final time, Lieutenant, share with this board her message to you."

He'd given it his best shot. "She told me that I had come into a considerable inheritance."

"Why couldn't she have written that through normal channels?"

"The normal channels weren't working, sir. I received none of her V-mails. Not a single one. Time was running out. The day of the broadcast, I was at Pearl Harbor about to join the *Lanternfish*, after which I'd be incommunicado for long stretches."

Crowther huffed as he stacked papers that didn't need straightening. "Would your inheritance have vanished?"

"My grandfather stipulated I must claim it by the end of the war or the end of 1944, whichever came first. The broadcast was the week before Christmas, so I'd argue that Miss Davenport was downright clever to do what she did. I was able to contact the lawyers in New York before the *Lanternfish* sailed on its final patrol."

Luke added that last part to remind these three admirals that they weren't interrogating some random sailor. Naturally, they were familiar with the *Lanternfish*'s fate and his hand in it. But Luke kept his eye on Armstrong, who wore the gold dolphin pin indicating he'd been a qualified submariner.

"Lieutenant Valenti," Crowther said, "your inheritance—its magnitude, size, and stipulations—is irrelevant to this inquiry. The fact of the matter remains unchanged. You deliberately compromised the security of wartime communications for personal reasons. You, a trained cryptanalyst, were aware of the potential consequences of your actions had your *billets-doux* fallen into enemy hands. Is there anything further you wish to add in your defense?"

Luke studied the three faces, all of them grave as tombstones. What should he do? Throw himself on their mercy? Or remind them that thousands of wartime V-mails had been flying all over the world every week. What were the chances that the Japs would find his specific messages, realize they were coded, figure out the code to learn—what? That he was in language school in Boulder? Was it such a big deal? Crowther, Armstrong, and Dixon undoubtedly held the opinion that it was, indeed, a very big deal.

Sweat soaked Luke's armpits. He could feel it trickle down his sides. Thankfully, his jacket would hide this clammy mess, but he was in for one mighty uncomfortable streetcar ride home.

"I felt I was only bending the rules." Real Admiral Dixon emitted a derisive snort, but didn't follow it up with a cross-examination. "As a cryptanalyst, I knew the chances were infinitesimal that anybody would notice what I was doing. Even the Navy censors missed it. Knowing that I was easing my girlfriend's mind during my long absence was my motivation."

"Do you regret your actions?" Armstrong asked.

NO! Luke wanted to say. But would an outburst earn him a court martial? He was still weighing the pros and cons of being honest when a familiar voice rang out from the back of the room.

"Permission to approach and be heard as an *amicus curiae*?"

How long had Vance been there? Luke froze as Crowther told him that they would welcome his contribution.

Vance drew alongside Luke. "Commodore Vance, en route to Japan where I will soon begin preparations for the Tokyo War Crimes. May I proceed?" Crowther nodded. "Thank you, sir. I dropped by these hearings today to see if I could bring clarification to this prickly situation. While it's clear that Lieutenant Valenti here—" he landed a heavy hand on Luke's left shoulder, "broke strict naval regulations, I think it's also useful to point out that at no time did he transmit pertinent and/or secret and/or strategic information. Did you, Valenti?"

Unprepared for this question, Luke jumped slightly. "No, sir, I did not."

"It's now six months since the cessation of hostilities. Whether or not he contravened the rules, nothing of consequence resulted. We won the war. In fact, we trounced them. And a part of that trouncing transpired on the *Lanternfish*, due, in no small part, to the actions of Lieutenant Valenti.

"Furthermore, the US Navy has acclaimed him a war hero, as indeed it should. His actions saved an enormous number of lives. To strip Valenti of his honors and promotion would be admitting that a well-known and admired face of the Navy was a villain. And let us not forget that Warner Brothers is turning his story into a feature-length motion picture, which will be a PR windfall.

"In conclusion, I am here to assert my firm belief that, his actions regarding this matter aside, Lieutenant Valenti has been, and continues to be, a great asset to the Navy."

Somewhere around the part about stripping him of his honors, Luke had begun to feel lightheaded. His joints ached from holding himself rigid for so long. How could he have forgotten to unlock his knees? He needed to sit down, and soon, but that wasn't an option. He squeezed his cap even more tightly against his drenched armpit and steeled himself as Vance continued.

"I want the lieutenant to tell the board what he did with his inheritance."

Luke swung his head around and gaped up at Vance. But the commodore stared straight ahead and gave him no encouragement. Crowther rapped on the table, prompting Luke to return to face front. "I assume it's relevant."

Luke couldn't see how the fate of his inheritance was pertinent to these proceedings, but Vance had gone out of his way to be here, and to mention it.

"A few months ago, my uncle suffered a terrible accident in

which he lost the use of his right hand. He's an artist, so he also lost his livelihood, as well as his independence. Consequently, I gave him my inheritance."

"All of it?" Armstrong asked.

The hot slick of sweat had now spread across Luke's back. His shirt had adhered to his skin. Pretty soon, it would soak through his jacket. The outbreak hadn't reached his face yet, but that was only a matter of time. *Please let this be over before I drop to the floor like a sack of bowling balls.*

"I have the rest of my life to earn my way; he does not."

"Gentlemen," Vance continued, "I bring this up not to make Lieutenant Valenti uncomfortable, but to illustrate his upstanding moral fiber. His inheritance was substantial and yet he did not hesitate to provide for his unfortunate relative's future."

"I see." Crowther drummed the desk with his fingertips.

Armstrong screwed on the cap of his fountain pen and stowed it in the breast pocket of his blue service coat.

Dixon consulted his watch.

Were they done? Was it over? Could the three admirals please leave five minutes ago?

"Thank you, Commodore." Crowther scooped up his papers in a smooth motion. "You'll be hearing from us." He got to his feet and swept from the room, leaving the others to follow in his wake.

After the door closed behind Dixon, Luke counted out three seconds before he threw himself at the straight-backed wooden bench to his right and watched his sweat-soaked cap hit the speckled linoleum and skid out of reach.

26

For days after Luke's hearing, Nell wondered how men could be so stupid. Even smart ones like Luke. Why would anyone face such a trial having eaten nothing since the previous night? Add to it the pressure of having to *mea culpa* for his sins in front of three hangmen. Was it any wonder he'd nearly passed out?

Nor was it any mystery why he'd gotten loaded after Greg Whitley had called him to say that a severe rebuke was going onto his war record as a punitive measure, but that was all. No court martial. No dishonorable discharge. Vance's testimony appeared to have saved the day. All in all, a happy ending.

What a pity, she thought, the same couldn't be said for me.

She had been so pleased to be back in her PR job. At first. Singing one or two songs per week was hardly a demanding commitment. Having lots and lots of free time was terrific—in theory. But in practice? It was a bit of a yawn.

She jammed a pencil into the office sharpener and cranked the handle. Oh well. Trying to dress up a pedestrian program-filler like *Her Kind of Man* into a sparkly package was a good deal better than sitting at home reading *Modern Screen* and debating about taking up smoking to help pass the day. She pulled out the pencil to find that she'd sharpened half of it away and honed the nib down to a needle point capable of gouging out someone's eye.

"Nell, honey!" Paisley called out. "The boss has a couple of new assignments for you. Go straight in."

She went into Taplinger's office, where he motioned to a chair. "First up, *The Last Submarine*."

She felt herself brighten, despite herself. Something meaty! And an A-list picture! "I've got a slew of ideas for this one. Luke has an in with the Navy press office, so we could—"

"You can run all that by Buzz."

It took a moment for Nell to comprehend what her boss had told her. *Buzz*, because he was the lead agent on the movie in which *she* was a character? *The Last Submarine* was her own cotton-pickin' story!

"Oh, come on." She jabbed the air with a stiff finger. "I know he worked here before the war, that he had a tough time on Iwo Jima, and he deserved to get his job back. When you gave him *Of Human Bondage* and *Humoresque* and *Mildred Pierce*, I didn't complain because who gets which project is your call. But I have to draw the line."

The only movement on Taplinger's face was a single raised eyebrow. "You do, do you?"

"Robert!" She was taking liberties calling him by his given name, but doggone it, this was worth fighting for. "*The Last Submarine* is our story, Luke's and mine. Joan Leslie is playing *me*! If anyone deserves this project, *I'm* the one who—"

"In the first place, it's 'Mr. Taplinger' until I invite you to address me otherwise. And in the second place, you're too close to the material. I'm giving it to Buzz and you'll be his assistant."

In other words, his lackey on my movie. Well, that's just peachy. "Yes, sir."

"However, I do have a prominent project you'll be taking the lead on." That sounded more like it. Nell lowered herself back into the chair. "The unveiling of KFWB's news ribbon on the Taft Building."

"You want me to work up a PR campaign for an electric sign?"

"Mr. Warner wants us to go all out for the West Coast's first zipper. There'll be a stage for an orchestra, bleachers to accommodate a parade of Warner Brothers stars, and a live broadcast, with Mayor Bowron and Governor Warren."

What a very long way from the major motion picture features she loved to work on. She stared at her boss. *Just when I thought you couldn't demote me any further. The career I once adored is now a dead-end job.*

"I know what you're thinking, but let's look at your track record." Taplinger spread out the fingers of his left hand so that he could count them off. "The slapping Hedda incident; singing at Orry-Kelly's farewell; appearing on the Hollywood Canteen broadcast; having a hit record; becoming the resident vocalist on *Music from Hollywood*. You're unable—or unwilling—to stick to the PR axiom of never being the story. And in this case, the story *involves* you."

Taplinger had always clung to his dictum as though it were the Eleventh Commandment that Moses had somehow lost on his way down Mount Sinai.

A knock on Taplinger's door saved Nell from having to propose a counterargument.

"Sorry to interrupt," Paisley said. "I've got Abigail Hart from the art department out here. They're facing a strict deadline for the *Night and Day*, *Stolen Life*, and *Big Sleep* press kits. They can't move forward without your final approval."

Knowing an opportunity to beat a hasty retreat when she saw it, Nell leapt from her chair. Stepping out of Taplinger's office, she passed the art department girl. Her name didn't ring a bell, but gosh oh my, she sure looked familiar.

Back at her desk, she watched the girl through Taplinger's window. Where had she seen her before? It had been a long time since Nell had visited the art department. There had always been flunkies to do the running around. She was pretty enough to be in front of the camera. That hair, though. An odd but flattering darkish brown with a hint of cinnamon.

She watched Abigail make her way down the aisle, past all the desks, and out of the room.

"HELLO?" Buzz's voice shot at her like a cannonball. "Are you listening to me?"

Nell took her time turning her chair to face him. "Didn't hear a word."

"I asked you if that was Abigail."

"Yes. Why?"

"Dammit. I promised to give her these." He slammed a fist on a pile of papers. "You'll have to take them down there yourself. Do you know where the art department is?"

I've worked here for six years, she wanted to tell him. But she held her tongue, because, apparently, *she* was now the flunky.

As she gathered up the pile, she glanced at the first one. Holy moly! They'd already started work on the *Last Submarine* poster? It was clearly a rushed first draft. Nell would happily have bet that someone had lifted the typeface from a soapy Bette Davis picture. The faces of John Garfield and Joan Leslie were far from flattering. And worst of all, why was there no submarine?

Buzz tsked. "If I stood still like that on Iwo Jima, I'd be dead by now."

Nell gleefully imagined that she could remedy that problem right now, here in the office. Instead, she hugged the artwork. If they were going to demote her to flunky status, at least she could make it work to her advantage.

* * *

Indignation and resentment fueled Nell's marching footfalls.

I've lived through the plot of The Last Submarine, *but sure, give it to the guy who spends half his day staring out the window and the other half droning on about Iwo Jima. By all means, hand me a turkey like unveiling a sign because I've always got to BE the story. Why can't they admit what's going on: Boys looking out for boys.*

The art department filled the site once occupied by the gargantuan dressing room William Randolph Hearst had moved from MGM for his lady love, Marion Davies. The building that had risen in its place was as nondescript as its neighbors' stucco, which was painted a medium tan.

The smell of paint, ink, and heavy paper greeted Nell as she walked into an enormous room, almost as wide and long as the PR office.

Abigail was chatting with a beanpole of a guy in shirtsleeves and a bow tie he'd unraveled and slung around his neck. They were standing in front of a half-finished poster for the much-delayed next screen pairing of Bogie and Bacall.

Nell studied the girl.

Her updo into a bloom of curls wasn't a hairstyle everyone could get away with; it suited her, though. But had it always been that color? Nell stepped forward for a closer look as the skinny guy whispered into Abigail's ear. The girl reeled back, pretending to be shocked by compressing her lips into a thin wedge as she mocked disapproval.

Good God! It's her!

Replace the cinnamon with strawberry blonde, subtract four years, swap the white A-line skirt with a two-piece tartan suit and matching beret. YES! Nell was positive she was right. She drew closer as the guy was telling her that he needed to scrub his paint-splattered hands.

"Hello?" Nell said. "Abigail?"

The girl's facile smile faded; she dropped her eyes to the pile Nell was pressing to her chest. "Are those for me?"

"I'm Nell. From PR."

"You're not exactly anonymous around here." A measure of

wariness had left Abigail's voice, but not entirely.

"I used to be a script girl. One of the movies I worked on was *Casablanca*." She waited for a response, but the girl merely blinked slowly and deliberately, as though to say, *What of it?* Nell hesitated, then dropped to a whisper. "I was on set when a hopeful young girl was escorted into Michael Curtiz's office. It was the day when Humphrey Bogart and Peter Lorre had rigged up a loudspeaker, hoping to embarrass Curtiz into halting his practice."

Abigail hissed, "Follow me," and headed into a supply closet filled with tubes of paint, bottles of ink, and tall stacks of paper. She closed the door behind Nell, blushing bright as a lobster. "After all this time? You actually remember me?"

"I've thought of you often."

"Yeah, well—" Abigail's mouth splintered into a self-effacing smile—"I try not to brood."

"Can't say that I blame you."

"Mostly I think about how grateful I was that Bette Davis came along when she did. She was so busy cussing everybody out that it allowed me to head for the hills."

"I can only imagine how mortified you must have been."

"The bridge that crosses the LA river down the street... I hid under it and cried my eyes out. Do you remember that tartan suit I wore? I spent nine ninety-five for it at Mullen and Bluett so that I'd impress him. I ended up burning the damn thing in my fireplace." Abigail squinted. "Why would you have any reason to think of me?"

"I should've told Bogie to unplug the speaker. Or remind him that Curtiz might have deserved to be the butt of his practical joke, but two people would have been in that office. I was relieved when Bette Davis showed up, but I wish I'd been the one to give him what for."

Abigail laid a soft hand on Nell's forearm. "And get yourself fired? I knew what I'd said yes to when the casting guy brought it up. I told myself, 'I'm a tough little chickadee from the wrong side

219

of Fresno. I can handle this.' But as soon as Curtiz unbuttoned his trousers, my nerve deserted me. He was already—um, you know . . . so I had no choice but go through with it."

Now that Nell had had a chance to examine the girl more closely, she could see that, despite her delicate features and her elfin face, there was a peppy determination to her smile. Nell probably would have lost her job, but she could have raced after Abigail that day to check if she was okay. "But why the heck are you working for the studio that treated you so badly?"

Abigail's face softened. "When I got over it all, I saw that I'd been a fool to think I had what it took to make it as an actress. But I've always loved the movies, and so any job would have been fine. Entanglements with directors aside, being inside a movie studio thrills me."

Nell nodded sagely. Her own first day reporting for work at Warners had been one of the most exciting of her life. She'd bought a new set of clothes, too—a dark olive-green woolen suit she'd found on special at Sears. "Yeah, I get it."

"So I wrote to the personnel departments at all the studios, and would you believe the only one who responded was Warners? By then, I'd worked through all my revenge fantasies and thought it was funny. What's that line Bogie had in *Casablanca*? 'Of all the gin joints in all the towns in all the world, I had to hear from Warners.' As for that debacle with Curtiz, I presumed nobody knows, nobody cares, so what the hell. They had jobs going in the typing pool, the commissary, and the green department. I can't cook, and I can't keep a potted house plant alive longer than a week."

"How did you end up here?"

"One of the clerks dropped a Jobs-Opening memo on the desk of the interviewer. It was for a spot in the art department. So I talked about how I ran my high school's newspaper and how I had tons of experience in layout and mock-ups and printing. I didn't stop talking until he gave me the job."

"When did you start here?"

"How's this for irony: It was when Errol Flynn was facing those rape charges."

"But that was over three years ago!" Remorse weighed down on Nell. This lovely, spunky girl had been here all this time. "I prefer you as a strawberry blonde."

Abigail giggled and patted the rear of her updo. "Me too."

"You should change it back."

Her smile turned wistful. "It would be a relief to no longer color my hair."

Nell smiled and then looked at her watch. Her heart fell when she thought of the situation waiting for her back at her desk. Taking orders from Buzz Bryant and drumming up ballyhoo over an electric sign. Thank God she had *Music from Hollywood* to look forward to every week. Inspiration struck her. "How about you come over for dinner sometime?"

Abigail's lips formed a perfect "O" as she looked down at her hands. "If this is about making amends—"

"It's not." Truthfully, though, it was. And if Nell's daytime working life was going to be so dreary, her nighttime social life was going to need an overhaul. "I've been thinking of throwing a dinner party and would love you to join us. Do you have a boyfriend?"

"Not at the moment."

"Okay, then. I'll be in touch."

Nell stepped toward the exit, but Abigail stopped her. "Thank you for noticing me." Her voice trembled as she teetered over the words. "You've made me realize I've tried to make myself invisible for too long."

"Nobody should be made to feel that way."

Who are you talking to? Nell wondered as she walked back to her office. This sweet girl who's been under your nose all this time? Or yourself?

27

The March air chilled Luke's face as he surfaced from a jagged night's sleep. It sure was cold this morning. More like a January or a February cold. When he scratched his cheek, the fingertip came away slick with sweat. He slid another finger across his chest. It, too, was slippery and damp.

Oh, God. Not again.

He swung his feet onto the rug.

Enough's enough, already.

He mopped up his perspiration with an undershirt that he'd left heaped on the floor. He pulled on crumpled dungarees and a sweater and tottered into the kitchen to fill the coffee pot.

A snatch of nightmare flared in his mind. Christopher staring at him, his lips stretched into a snarl, hissing, "Who is the real hero of the *Lanternfish*? Who? WHO?"

Shards had been breaking the surface since The First Step. Slices of conversations about Coney Island, the food in the officers' mess at Pearl Harbor, and the relief of inhaling salty sea air after an eleven-hour dive.

He retrieved the Sunday *Times* from his porch and returned to the kitchen, where strong black coffee promised a cheerier morning. The striped metal bread box Tristan had given him as a house-warming present held a two-day-old apricot Danish. Better than no Danish at all. He slid it onto a plate, filled his largest cup, and dropped the *Times* onto the table.

Coverage of Winston Churchill's speech at Westminster College in Missouri filled most of the front page, quoting a foreboding term—"iron curtain"—that he had predicted would start a new era of hostilities he designated as "the Cold War."

A *new* era of hostilities? Hadn't the last one taken enough of a toll?

He arrived at "Hedda Hopper's Hollywood." The malicious columnist had made Nell's life hellish, so he was tempted to skip over her litany of innuendo, half-truths, and fabricated scandals. But Hollywoodites ignored her at their peril. At least it was better than iron curtains and cold wars.

Her first item described how chief censor, Joseph Breen, would soon be running a "refresher course" for studio executives, covering all points of the Production Code. Luke doubted any of those poor bastards needed reminding of the Breen Office's power to veto any part of any script.

His apricot Danish stayed half-eaten as he read the next item.

Oh, no.

Oh, crap.

Oh, shit.

Luke pulled out his LA City Directory and skipped to the Os. Tristan had mentioned Remy's last name was Owens. He ran his finger down the columns until he found the listing. Throwing on the first pair of shoes he came to, he swiped his car keys off the hall table and bolted outside.

Remy's apartment was the downstairs half of a shabby duplex off Western Avenue. It needed a lick of paint, and those desiccated azaleas clumped along the gravel path wouldn't have said no to a pitcher of water.

Luke struck the rusted palm tree doorknocker three times. A muted "Yeah, yeah, I'm coming" seeped through a window. Remy was still tying the sash of his frayed flannel bathrobe as he cracked open his front door. His black hair stuck out every which way; his eyes were narrow slits. "A little early for a social call."

"It's nearly ten," Luke replied.

"When you work till two in the morning, ten is like six for regular folks." He sucked his teeth. "I'd ask you what you want, but I think I can guess." Luke held up the *Times*. "Bingo."

"You can't take anything Hedda Hopper says as gospel," Luke protested.

"Ordinarily I wouldn't, but . . ."

But Hedda reinforced how Remy wanted to remember Christopher.

"Please let me in so that we can talk."

Remy gave Luke a wary once-over before leading him into a small living room with a loveseat and a tiny glass coffee table. Not counting a narrow, jumbled bookshelf, there was no other furniture. No decorations on the walls either, which surprised Luke. He had Remy down as a fan of the "More is better" style of décor.

"I'm making lavender tea," Remy announced from his galley kitchen. "Want some?"

Lavender tea sounded unappealing, but turning him down would have been a tactical error. "I'd love a cup."

As he waited for the kettle to boil, Remy checked his image in a hand mirror suspended from a hook next to the stove. "Jumpin' Jesus! I look like I've been electrocuted." He wetted his hands under the faucet and squashed the more prominent tufts onto his scalp.

Back at The First Step, Remy had still been wearing his wig and full makeup, and had afterwards been slathered with cold cream, so Luke had been unable to see how extraordinarily exotic he looked in the starker light of day. He had never seen a flawless complexion on a guy. And those almond eyes. As inscrutable as Anna May Wong's. Luke couldn't help wondering what the Warner lighting and makeup maestros might do with him.

Remy set down a pair of mismatched cups. "You're staring."

"Sorry. Didn't mean to."

"People have gawked at me all my life. At least now I get to charge for it." He let off a hollow laugh, leaving the impression it was a well-worn line.

Luke slapped Hedda's column onto the counter. "She claims to have followed up on that *Look* article about Christopher's parents."

"You think she hasn't?"

"Regurgitated, at best, would be my guess."

"That doesn't mean she's wrong."

"She wouldn't give a damn about you or Christopher or his parents except that *The Last Submarine* is now in production."

"Oh, yeah. Your movie. Talk about rubbing salt into the wound. Another exciting break for Luke Valenti. Whoopee. Lucky him."

Having narrowly avoided a court martial, Luke didn't feel lucky. "And even then," he continued, ignoring the jibe, "she wouldn't care much, but Nell is a character in the movie, and she's not exactly Nell's greatest fan."

"So," Remy said, the resentment in his face starting to thaw, "this is a way to stick her sharpest knitting needle into your girlfriend?"

"It's a theory. But I can guarantee you this: Hedda Hopper only cares about Hedda Hopper."

A plume of steam billowed from the whistling kettle. Remy poured the boiling water into a teapot with a zigzag pattern around its base. The sweet-tangy aroma of lavender filled the kitchen.

Luke paused to choose his words. "For better or worse, I've

become the face of the *Lanternfish*. I chafed under the title, at first. Especially when the Navy started booking me on speaking engagements to women's auxiliaries and Rotary Club lunches."

"It must be such a chore to talk about your bravery to adoring housewives and drunk insurance salesmen." Remy filled the cups and took them into the living room.

The guy was much more wary than he'd been at the nightclub. The excitement of hosting Lauren Bacall had coaxed him to let his guard down, but there was no Betty around today. Luke followed him into the living room and sat down on the sofa.

"My point being, the 'hero of the *Lanternfish*' title was the Navy's doing. They fed it to every press outlet on their list. Then suddenly I'm on the radio."

"Wailing like a baby. Yeah, I was listening."

"Falling apart in front of ten million people is not the laugh riot you might think." Luke ventured a glance to see if his joke landed. Remy tried to camouflage his smile behind the rim of his cup, but Luke caught it nevertheless. "The Navy didn't care that I was mortified. They insisted the public ate it up with a soup spoon. I haven't been separated yet, so I have to follow orders. They keep sending me out there. More adoring housewives, more drunk salesmen."

"Uh-huh."

"But I want to know if the story I spin at these speaking engagements is inaccurate."

Remy shrugged. "You were there, not me."

"The serious concussion I sustained that night punched big, gaping holes in my memory. Pieces of what happened have been coming back to me in fits and starts. But then in your dressing room the other night, they started surfacing more."

"Like, what, f'instance?"

"Christopher had a picture of the Brooklyn Bridge taped to the wall of—"

"HE DID?" Remy bent forward. "*I* sent him that. I didn't think he'd do anything with it because he asked for a different one."

"Marine Parkway Bridge."

"But I couldn't find one, which wasn't surprising because he called it the—"

"—poor country cousin of New York bridges."

Remy clutched at the folds of his robe. "You really did know him."

Luke sipped the lavender tea. Sweeter than he expected, but it wasn't the nastiest brew he'd ever tasted. "We were squashed in together every day, all during our watch."

Remy sighed a deep, leaden sigh as his eyes drifted around the sparse room and landed on a flattering photo of Christopher in a plain silver frame. "He was in school when Pearl Harbor was attacked, so he was exempt from the draft. And that was A-okay with his folks because he was the apple of their eye. But his conscience got the better of him, and he joined the Navy. His parents took it personally. All kinds of drama. Yelling, screaming, doors slamming, playing the offended card, playing the guilt card. Boy, oh boy. Every trick in the book to convince him to change his mind. After that, he couldn't get out of Rockaway fast enough. I don't suppose he told you any of this?"

Maybe Christopher had. Luke couldn't recall. He shrugged. "I'm sorry. I don't remember."

"After basic training and radioman school, they sent him to LA and gave him a weeklong pass."

"That's when you met at the USO club?"

"Yep." Remy's guardedness was falling away now; the sharp planes of his face began to thaw. "That night, I could tell it was his first time with a man. Turns out, it was his first time with anyone."

Remy rose and crossed over to the bookshelf to fetch a teak box carved with an interlocking pattern of doves. He withdrew a stack of V-mails bound with a white ribbon. "He mentioned you. Not by name, but didn't you share living quarters?"

227

"Bunks on a sub are stacked four deep—oh. Wait. The Pearl Harbor barracks." Luke could now picture the two-bed room they had shared. Comfortable mattresses. Scratchy blankets. A painting of Diamond Head, tacky and amateurish. "Submarine crews volunteer for a rigorous year-long training. Christopher and I didn't have that. We were outsiders, so we shared a room instead."

Remy gave him a look that Luke suspected contained more than a little envy.

"He loved the movies, so he was agog that you worked with Humphrey Bogart, and Bette Davis, and Errol Flynn." Remy let out a sly giggle. "I blow a gasket every time I think about meeting Lauren Bacall in the flesh."

Luke eyed the bundle of V-mails in Remy's hands. "Is there anything in those that might arm me against attacks from his parents or Hedda Hopper?"

"No." Remy hugged the letters to his stomach. "But maybe I can help you fill in the picture."

The tea had cooled now; sipping it gave Luke something to do until Remy broke the silence.

"Christopher wasn't in any old school," Remy said at length. "He was at St. Joseph's University in Yonkers."

"That's a seminary!" Luke said. Now that he could hear Christopher's voice, it wouldn't shut up.

What's it like to swim in the Pacific?
How does Humphrey Bogart act when he's not acting?
Do you go to Grauman's Chinese Theatre often?
Where's the best place to see movie stars?

Had Luke done most of the talking? Could he recall so little about Christopher because the guy had deflected attention away from himself?

"Rockaway Park is wall-to-wall Irish Catholics," Luke said.

"Christopher described his folks as the devoutest, God-fearingest churchgoers you'll ever meet. He said to me, 'When I told them I'd decided to become a priest, they couldn't have been more pleased than if I had told them I'd been elected Pope.'"

"Then he up and quit."

"And I quote, 'It was like the four horsemen of the apocalypse had come busting out of Jamaica Bay with Beelzebub bringing up the rear.'"

Luke had driven over here to find out as much about Christopher as he could, but this was more than he'd bargained for. He needed the crisp March air on his skin and some time to think all this through. "I'm sorry, but I have to go."

"Have I upset you? Was it the Beelzebub thing?"

The cup tinkled as Luke deposited it on the kitchen counter. "No, no. Thanks for the tea. I'll see myself out."

He was at the front door, his fingers gripping the handle, when Remy asked, "Could we stay in touch?"

"Absolutely." He meant it too, but for now, he needed to escape.

* * *

"Even though seminary students were exempt from military service," Nell said from Luke's passenger seat, "he signed up anyway? Bold move, Christopher Walsh."

Luke turned off Mulholland Drive and entered the twists and bends of Benedict Canyon toward the Bogarts' new hilltop house they'd bought from Hedy Lamarr. He had spent most of the afternoon hiking the dirt paths crisscrossing Griffith Park, thinking about what Remy had told him.

All through the long, monotonous nights he and Christopher had logged in the radio room together, he'd assumed the two of them had become as close as pals could be. But pals talk. They share. They listen. They ask. Had Luke spent all that time answering all those questions without once asking Christopher about himself? He'd left the priesthood. He'd disappointed his folks. He'd found love with someone who wouldn't be accepted by his church or his family or his friends. He must have been roiling on the inside.

"I don't know what it is about Remy, but every time I'm around him..." Luke rounded his Ford into a hairpin turn.

"More and more memories come back?"

"I wasn't the friend to Christopher I had been assuming. He took all that turmoil to his grave."

A lone streetlight shed a pale circle on a patch of dirt on the northern side of another tight curve. "Their driveway is the third on the right. As for Christopher, I'd imagine there's not much privacy inside a sub."

Benedict Canyon Drive stretched ahead of them. Privacy was all Luke had had growing up in Brooklyn. Sharing a three-hundred-foot-long tube with fifty other men was the opposite of that, and yet he'd taken to it without a moment's thought.

"You know that trumpeter from the Arlo Nash Orchestra I told you about?"

Yeah, I know. You mention him enough. And every time you do, my skin crawls and my chest tightens. And I'm not even sure why. Is there something you're not telling me? "What about him?"

"He's told me about his experiences trudging around Europe and the Pacific entertaining the troops with Bob Hope. He says there are no secrets in a pup tent. He says you and your tent-mate go through a lot together in a short amount of time. He says the bonds of those friendships go real deep."

"And that's without the threat of your tent sinking to the bottom of the Pacific." *Not that this is a competition, but it's not quite the same thing, is it? Tell that to your trumpeter the next time you see him.*

Nell told him to hit the brakes and shifted around to face him more squarely. "This bothers you a lot, doesn't it?"

What? Luke wanted to demand. *Me and Christopher? Or you and Peyton? Assuming there is a you and Peyton, which I have no* reason to assume other than my churning guts every time you bring up his name."

"This whole thing with you and Christopher and Remy," Nell prompted.

He nodded. "I assumed that when my memory started coming back, I'd be happier, more—I don't know… complete, somehow. But it has raised as many questions as it's answered." He kissed her left hand. "But fear not, I won't let it get in the way of having a good time. It's not every day we get to sit down to dinner with the Bogarts *and* Hawkses."

"Don't hold your breath," Nell said with a wicked smirk. "When Betty and I lived together, she was hardly the world's greatest cook."

Luke lifted his foot off the brake. "Let's hope she called in a caterer."

* * *

Betty greeted them in a sleek, body-hugging dress. She stretched out her arms. "Thank God you're here!"

"You said seven-thirty," Nell replied.

"The other two have been here since seven," she said, *sotto voce*, "and they were already a couple of drinks in. So was Bogie."

She led them down a short passageway and into a spacious wood-paneled living room with a wide brick fireplace, but where was the artwork? Knick-knacks? Mementos? It wasn't much different from Remy's tiny apartment.

Aside from a telephone-table-and-chair set in the corner, the only furniture in the room was a quartet of loveseats with mismatching upholstery in a square formation. At its center sat a circular wooden coffee table filled with hors d'oeuvres. As far as Luke could tell, they were untouched.

The same, however, could not be said for the four tumblers of whiskey.

"If it ain't the every-fifth-worders." Howard waved his fat cigar around like he was brandishing a semaphore flag on an aircraft carrier. He struck Luke as a more dapper John Huston, but he made no attempt to stand.

"I've heard a lot about you. I'm Luke Valenti."

Hawks's handshake was surprisingly feeble. "Everyone knows the hero of the *Lanternfish*. Pleased to meetcha. With any luck, we might get his songbird to warble us a tune."

A slender woman with a sophisticated air rose to her feet, a cloud of Chanel No. 5 shrouding her. In contrast to her husband's, her handshake was firm to the point of virile. "So glad to meet you." Slim Hawks greeted Nell with a cheek press and reassured her that nobody was going to make her sing for her supper.

"And besides, the movers dropped the piano." Bogie's diction sagged under the weight of a conspicuous slur. At least three drinks' worth, Luke guessed. He thrust a double whiskey into Luke's hand. "How long does it take for a piano to settle?"

"Give it at least six weeks."

"Lieutenant Lanternfish even knows about pianos," Howard declared. "Is there nothing he can't do?"

"I lived down the street from the neighborhood tuner," Luke said. "He worked on every piano between Bensonhurst and Coney Island."

The comment was enough to raise Howard's silvery eyebrows. "Brooklyn, huh?"

Luke hadn't known what to expect from the director of *Twentieth Century*, *His Girl Friday*, and *Sergeant York*, but it sure as hell wasn't this belligerent prick pickled in too much Old Forester. Luke's hopes about telling Bogie what he'd learned of Christopher were fading fast now that he could see how this celebrated director loved to dominate a room.

"Ignore the buffoon in the polka-dot tie," Slim said as Luke and Nell settled into an empty loveseat. "He's at his wits' end with how the studio is treating his movie."

"We're all frustrated," Betty said. "We shot it in late forty-four and here we are, March of nineteen forty-six, and they won't be releasing it for another five months."

"Mister Jack God-Almighty Warner is punishing you," Slim said. "What did he say in that memo? 'Word has reached me that you are having fun on the set. This must stop.' Christ, what a heeb. Sorry, hon. That doesn't apply to you."

Betty Perske's eyes flashed dimly before Lauren Bacall responded with an anemic nod of well-practiced gratitude. "And those impossible reshoots. How the hell were any of us supposed to know how we'd held our cigarettes twelve months earlier?"

Luke caught the furtive look that passed from Betty to Bogie. Between the end of *The Big Sleep*'s production and the reshoots, Bogie and Betty had gotten married. As payback, Hawks, who'd long had his extra-marital eye on Betty, abruptly sold her contract to Warners. Bogie hadn't revealed to Luke that this had strained their relationship with Hawks, but he hadn't needed to. Luke could see it for himself.

Not that he blamed either man. Betty was the complete package. Gorgeous but earthy. Funny but alluring. Smart but plainspoken. She was becoming everything that Slim Hawks already was, and more. No wonder Bogie had fallen hard. A while back, he had admitted that he'd behaved poorly during his previous three rotten marriages. But what he had with Betty had reset the clock. A do-over. Their marriage worked the way good marriages were supposed to. "I've cracked the marital code, ol' boy," he'd said.

So why then, Luke thought, do I feel like Nell and I are here to act as a buffer? When Bogie was with Mayo, he used to say, 'We're always on our best behavior when you're around.' Are we a cushion between the Bogarts and the Hawkses?

Normally, Luke wouldn't have minded. Anything to help out a pal. But not tonight. Not when his innards were still a whirligig from his lavender-scented coffee klatch with Remy. "I don't think you've got much to complain about," Luke said to Hawks. "You've done pretty well from *The Big Sleep*."

"It isn't even out yet," Hawks grumped.

"Warner paid you fifty thousand to purchase the screen rights, which you bought for ten."

"Oh-HO!" Bogie exclaimed with the glee of a five-year-old on Christmas morning. "Snookered in the top right pocket."

"Lieutenant Lanternfish got you," Betty said, straining to keep her tone light, "so no more complaining."

"You, too," Howard shot back. "*To Have and Have Not* did so well, Warner raised your weekly salary from three-fifty to a grand. I wouldn't have done that if I still held your contract."

"Is it always like this when you all get together?" Luke's interjection drove all four of them into abrupt silence. "I've had a grueling day, so if I'd known this was how it'd be, I'd have stayed home eating a grilled cheese sandwich and listening to *Tannhäuser*." He longed to jump on his bike and pedal down Argyle Road. But instead, he was stuck with this cranky bastard.

The other five froze in place, unsure what to say. Nor was Luke sure, but he sure felt better unloading this tension that had been pressing down on him all day. But now he'd ground all conversation to a halt. He looked up at Betty beseechingly. *Sorry to ruin your party.*

She winked back at him. *Think nothing of it.* Waving a hand over the untouched crab-filled celery sticks, pimiento cheese with crackers, and stuffed olives, she said, "Some of us might benefit from putting food in our stomachs."

"I am rather peckish, as the Brits might say." Howard pinched three olives by their toothpicks and held them aloft as though they were precious gems.

The testy atmosphere dissipated as their hostess talked about her plans to decorate their new home with a mix of Dutch, Early American, and French provincial furniture. She hated living in a house devoid of creature comforts, but this was her first home and she wanted to get the aesthetic exactly right.

She was talking about her ideas for the future nursery when Luke felt a sharp stick on his left temple. He looked down to find a stuffed olive resting in the creases of his crotch. He looked at Howard in time to see one of Hollywood's most respected directors pitch a second skewered black olive at him. It speared Luke between the eyes.

"Howard!" Slim cried out. "You might have stabbed Luke in the eye."

"Pah," Howard spat, waving his empty tumbler. "Let's save the drama for the screen." He lurched to his feet. As he went to step past Luke, he proclaimed his need to "usez-vous le pissoir bogartien." The director caught his foot on the table leg and stumbled with a guttural groan before trying to right himself. However, he over-corrected and toppled sideways. Mid-air, he twisted to the side and landed face down in the carpet.

"That's it." Slim stood up. "We're leaving." She rounded their loveseat and plowed her shoe into her husband's ribs. "You've embarrassed yourself enough."

Howard hauled himself onto his hands and knees, but could manage no further.

Luke hoisted him up. Hooking an arm around Hawks's shoulders—the man's breath reeked of all-afternoon whiskey—he frog-marched him to the silver Cadillac parked in the driveway.

"I'm so sorry he's made such a god-awful first impression." Slim held open the rear passenger door. "His last movie has been delayed and delayed, and *Red River* isn't coming together as easily as he expected. He wants to use this young actor, Montgomery Clift, but the kid's awfully intimidated by playing opposite John Wayne, and—"

"Will he regret his conduct tomorrow morning?"

"He'd better."

"We can't be at our best every single day." If we could, Luke thought, I'd have seen through Christopher's attempts to deflect attention. I would have listened to him all night long if that's what he'd needed.

She closed the door behind her prostrated husband. "I hoped we'd have a chance for a chat this evening. These aren't the circumstances I'd prefer, but here we are."

Luke couldn't imagine why Howard Hawks's wife wanted to talk to him, but her angular face had taken on a serious mien, highlighted by the glow of the dim moon.

She canted her head to one side. "Ever thought of writing a memoir?"

"No. Why?"

"I had lunch the other day with a writer friend who has an in with some muckety-muck at Simon and Schuster. The muckety-muck predicts a coming trend of memoirs by men who had extraordinary experiences during the war."

Yes, but most of them had full recall. Mine is better than it was six months ago, but it's still patchier than a moth-eaten quilt.

"I'm flattered, but my story will be covered by *The Last Submarine*."

"How much time did Albert Maltz spend with you?"

If this sharp, incisive woman could bring up the name of *The Last Submarine*'s screenwriter, she was no sit-on-the-sidelines director's wife.

"An afternoon in the commissary."

Slim raised a scornful eyebrow. "A few hours?"

"He was writing an action movie, not making a documentary."

"In other words, they're inventing the entire story. A book, on the other hand, could set the record straight."

"Sure, but I'm no author."

"I know a terrific ghostwriter. He'll help you shape the material. Maybe you can ride on the back of the movie onto the *New York Times* best-seller list. Wouldn't that be something to impress the old neighborhood?"

Howard pounded a fist against the window. "If we don't get home soon, I might have to barf everything onto this shiny new upholstery."

Slim pulled car keys from her clutch purse. "You'll think about it?"

"I will."

"*Serious* thought?"

Luke promised he would and waved her off as she and her cargo rounded a corner in the driveway and disappeared into the night.

The atmosphere in the living room had brightened up so much it almost felt as though someone had switched on all the lamps. He took his place on the loveseat as Betty continued with her story.

"So anyway, I hadn't a clue how Bogie would react to a surprise birthday party, so I invited the old gang from the Garden of Allah for a reunion. As soon as he came through the door, I handed him a drink and asked him to check the tub because something was wrong with the plumbing. I wish to God I had a camera to catch his reaction when he walked into the bathroom and found Mark Hellinger, Nunnally Johnson, Arthur Sheekman, Robert Benchley and God knows who else scrunched together in the bath with glasses raised, yelling 'Surprise!'"

"I was touched that people cared enough to show up," Bogie said.

"Of course they would," Luke told him. "You're Humphrey Bogart."

"To the world, maybe, but in here—" Bogie tapped his chest— "I'm Hump from the Upper East Side who had the misfortune to be born on Christmas day, so I never felt as though I had a proper birthday." He caught sight of Luke's pensive face. "Don't let Howard's behavior spoil the evening."

Luke related Slim's suggestion and asked them what they thought.

"I agree with her friend," Nell said. "Okay, so you haven't lost any limbs like your brother, but you've got a hell of a story, and *The Last Submarine* is only going to tell a small part of it."

Betty walked to the telephone table where a leather-bound address book lay. When she found what she was looking for, she wrote it on a pad along with Slim's home telephone number and handed the sheet of paper to Luke. "Tell her you're all in."

Luke slipped it into his pocket. There'd be time enough to think about that later. Meanwhile, he had barely touched his drink. He raised the tumbler. "Here's to new homes, new friends, and new opportunities. May they be in our future."

28

Jerry Wald's office lay at the far end of the administration building. The soles of Nell's new shoes slipped along the mottled gray and white linoleum floor that shone in the overhead lights.

She had spoken with Wald a bunch of times, as she'd worked on PR campaigns for his movies. But those had been brief, yes-or-no conversations. Now she needed a favor. Would he turn it into a quid pro quo at some point down the line? Probably. But it was important enough to approach *The Last Submarine*'s producer in person.

Through the open door behind the secretary's unattended desk, Nell heard him call out, "Is the Maugham playscript out there?"

A well-thumbed script with a dark green cover sat next to a typewriter.

THE LETTER

a play by

W. Somerset Maugham

. . .

She brought it with her into Wald's office. "Is this what you're looking for?"

"Somehow, I keep losing—Miss Davenport! Thank you, yes." He took the script from her.

"Remaking *The Letter*?" she asked.

"It's too soon, if you ask me, but with our upcoming *Of Human Bondage* remake, He Who Must Be Obeyed has decided that Maugham is all the rage. The fact that he's never read a word Maugham has written is beside the point. So we're now calling it *The Unfaithful*, and I'm casting two of my *Mildred Pierce* actors—Eve Arden and Zachary Scott—as insurance. Frankly, I'd rather be working on *Dark Passage*."

"I come bearing good news," Nell said, taking a seat. "Or fun, at least."

"I'll take fun any day of the week." He mopped his forehead with a white handkerchief. She saw no color in the face staring back at her. "*The Last Submarine*, I assume?"

"The *Music from Hollywood* team have had an inspired idea: they want Joan Leslie as a special guest to sing 'Shoo-Fly Pie and Apple Pan Dowdy' with me as a duet."

"I love it!" Wald threw up his hands; they were as pale as his face. "The real-life Nell Davenport singing with her screen counterpart. In fact, I'll go you one better and get my writers to dream up a skit."

Thanks to Cora, Nell's confidence in her voice had been growing week by week, but he was talking about performing comedy. Live on air. Probably with little rehearsal. That was a whole other sticky ball of wax that she hadn't bargained on getting stuck in.

"How about this for a premise?" Wald's fingers drummed feverishly as his creative juices flowed. "Neither of you knows what a Shoo-Fly Pie or an Apple Pan Dowdy is—hey, why are you looking at me as though you're Mata Hari and I'm the firing squad?"

"Mr. Warner has decreed I can only sing Warner tunes."

"What, like 'Honeymoon Hotel' and 'Shanghai Lil'?"

"His rule, not mine."

Wald planted his elbows on the desk. "We'll need to build a stronger case."

"Or I'll tell Sacky and Arlo to choose something else."

"Not on your life! Shoo-Fly Pie and Apple Pan Dowdy are funny names. It made the song work and it'll make the skit work. No, no, no, it has to be that one—hey! Isn't Peyton Sanders with Arlo's orchestra?"

Since their supper at Brittingham's a month back, the guy had often stopped by her dressing room to wish her luck on the broadcast. He'd never flattered her about how alluring she looked or how her shade of lipstick complemented her complexion. Nor had he backed her into a corner the way most wolves felt entitled to. He'd been the picture of gallantry at all times, making him either a one-in-a-million gentleman or the type of Romeo who played the long game.

"How do you know about him?" Nell asked.

"He was a big up-and-comer before the war. But he earned himself a stellar reputation appearing in all those USO shows alongside Bob Hope. Never missed a performance, always ready to perform, even when everybody else was out with dysentery, or trench foot, or hepatitis. One time it was down to him and Bob in a rainstorm in Belgium during the Battle of the Bulge. The brass said they didn't have to go through with it, but it was Christmas Eve and they insisted."

"He does come across as the dependable type," Nell said. Not to mention his boyish good looks and how his sandy-blond hair flops down across his forehead. I bet he could have any girl he wants.

"I'll tell my comedy guy to write a part in the skit for Peyton and his trumpet."

Oh, dear. Must you? "Sounds fun. But here's the clincher: We're talking about this week's show. So if four days isn't enough lead time—"

"No sweat." Wald fell back in his chair. "You'll have the script tomorrow morning."

"Well then, that settles that. Thanks so much." Nell stood, shook his hand, and marched back out into the corridor. Pulling off a comedy skit opposite an experienced performer like Joan Leslie was one thing. But to have to deal with a distraction like Peyton Sanders? *Damn, damn, damn. I should have told Sacky and Nash about Mr. Warner's rule and left it at that.*

* * *

Betty picked up the Westmore lipstick sitting on Nell's dressing room vanity. "What do you mean you haven't gone over the skit?"

Nell paced the floor. "They think comedy skits lose their spontaneity if they're rehearsed."

Deciding it wasn't the right shade for her, Betty put the lipstick back on the counter. "Before we roll, we've rehearsed the scene a couple of times. And it doesn't matter if we screw up; the director can always order another take. But on live radio? Sounds dangerous."

"It's a funny idea and a clever script. But I feel like I'm a Flying Wallenda and someone forgot to put up a net." Nell's fingers had twisted themselves around each other. She shook her hands loose. "Distract me."

Betty lit up a Pall Mall. "I had an ulterior motive in tagging along tonight."

"You're not here for moral support?"

"Of course I am. When Luke couldn't be here because he's talking to—who is it this time?"

The Navy had stepped up his speaking engagements ever since

the studio had announced *The Last Submarine*. When they had first started sending him out, he would pace the floor, note cards in hand, reciting his speech line by line, over and over. Nowadays, he skipped out, casual as a Sunday sleep-in, and returned home all keyed up, ready for some boudoir commotion, which suited Nell just fine.

"A convention of Navy contractors—the guys who make the buttons and levers and knobs."

"They sound like a hoot and a holler." Betty rolled her eyes. "At any rate, Bogie and I will be recreating *To Have and Have Not* on Lux Radio Theater. I was excited until I learned that we'll be performing live with zero rehearsal. It's all too seat-of-your-pants for my liking. Unfortunately, scheduling a migraine that night is off the table."

"So I'm your guinea pig."

"I'm here to observe and learn from a seasoned professional."

"Ha!" Nell laughed. "Me? Oh, please! Ten shows does not a seasoned professional make. And anyway, that's all been singing. This is more like acting."

"You silly goose." Betty stubbed out her cigarette in the triangular glass ashtray with the CBS logo stenciled into the bottom. "Has it occurred to you that you might be great? And that you're about to add another talent to offer producers? They're always looking for people who can do it all."

Joan Leslie appeared in the open doorway. "Hello there, real Nell Davenport!"

"Hello yourself, movie Nell Davenport."

They kissed the air to avoid disturbing their makeup. Joan giggled. "Isn't it absurd that real Nell and movie Nell work at the same studio and have never met?"

"That *is* crazy," Betty said.

"I was already working on *Two Guys from Milwaukee* when *Last Submarine* got pushed to the front of the line, so I'm shooting two movies at once."

"Even crazier."

"Not when my part wasn't terribly big because they preferred to stay on Luke's experience." Joan shucked off her fox-fur stole and hung it on the coat stand. "But then someone decided to enhance the love story."

"To make it easier to sell a war movie to women?" Nell asked.

Joan nodded. "Which means a beefed-up role for me, so I have no complaints. But of course you know all about this."

There was a time when Nell would have been the first to hear the latest rumors whizzing around the grapevine. Had she fallen out of the loop after her demotion to B pictures? God forbid anyone should keep her up to date on a movie that she helped inspire. "And on top of all that, they throw a radio appearance at you."

"Say no to *this* skit?" Joan asked. "Honestly, could it be any more hilarious?"

Nell felt Joan's optimism fill her with helium. Wald's writers had dreamed up a rapid-fire sketch filled with repartee that might have come from *His Girl Friday*. Nell's job this evening was to snap off a lot of syllables, sharp as a butcher's knife, for four and a half long minutes. But Betty was right. If she pulled it off, she could do pretty much anything.

"But while we're waiting, I have a favor to ask." Joan pressed her hands together in prayer. "Could you sing 'Every Fifth Word' for me? I want to get a feel for your intonations and how you hold yourself, because, you see, they're putting up the Hollywood Canteen set on Stage Seven this weekend."

They are? Another piece of information nobody has told me?

"You must be shooting the broadcast sequence soon." Those sorts of details made cute items for somebody's column. Was Buzz being petty?

"Monday."

"Knock, knock," a voice called from the corridor. "May I come in?" Arlo Nash walked in with an eager beaver look on his puss. "I have something I want you to think over."

"You have?" *What else do they want me to do? Yodel a Swiss mountain song while juggling cowbells? And couldn't it wait until after the show?*

"This summer I'm taking the orchestra on an eight-week, thirty-stop tour that will kick off with a fourteen-night engagement at the Cocoanut Grove in June. I need a girl singer and would love for you to join us. With all your PR expertise, I'm hoping you'll take on all the promotion as well, which is why I'm offering two hundred and fifty per week." Stunned into silence, Nell felt Betty squeeze her hand. "Besides all that, we'll be recording an album of ten songs. I'm still sorting through the choices, but I expect you'll be featured on at least eight of them, one of which will be 'Every Fifth Word.' How does that sound?"

Wonderful! Thrilling! A dream come true! "Can I have some time to think about it?"

"I'm expected on stage, so I'll leave it with you. Let me know what you decide." He dashed from the room at the same velocity as he'd entered.

Betty waited until he had closed the door behind him. "Are you nuts? What's to think about?"

Nell double-checked her makeup. "It would mean quitting my job."

"Sure. I mean, why would anyone turn their back on touring with Arlo Nash when they can toil thanklessly on B pictures, program fillers, and news zippers?"

Nell nodded, more sheepishly than she would have liked. "An album and a tour is exciting, but what happens after it's all over? I've already quit my job twice. There's no way Taplinger would take me back a third time."

"I get it," Joan said. "Warners has put me in less-than-stellar roles, but I started doing vaudeville during the Depression at the age of nine to keep my family from starving. My contract has given me the first financial stability I've ever known, and that's a lot to give up, even if the alternative takes your breath away."

The thought of Arlo's offer electrified Nell in the way her PR job used to, but hadn't in a long time. Didn't that count for something? Or should she be level-headed? Talk it over with Luke? Yes, she decided, that's what I should do. Think it through like a sensible adult. But for now, I have a once-in-a-lifetime chance to make a fool of myself in front of ten million people.

***

Nell rushed into her dressing room in a dizzy whirl. She hadn't stumbled over a single word, missed a cue, or stepped on any of Joan's lines. Rehearsal *did* kill spontaneity, as she'd suspected it would. She hadn't deviated from the script or improvised. That wasn't the challenge, nor had it ever been. The goal, she now saw, had been to slip along the high-wire tightrope of live broadcasting secure in knowing that she had what it took to go toe-to-toe with the best of them.

"Oh my stars!" Betty filled the doorway, flushed with elation. "Swear to God, Davenport, Roz Russell herself couldn't have spat out those lines with more verve."

"About thirty seconds in, I thought, 'Oh, wait, I *can* do this.'"

"I saw it, plain as day. You squared your shoulders, stiffened your spine, and stuck your chin out. I've got one question, though." Betty hesitated for a moment. "About halfway through that skit you started blushing."

"I did?"

"Beet-red. It was when the trumpeter joined you. Who is he, by the way? He's cute."

The moment came back to Nell like a slap in the face. "I was so absorbed in what I was doing that I forgot he was part of the act. When he threw in those funny trumpet sounds, it took me by surprise."

"But why the blush?"

"Jerry Wald laid it on thick about what a reputation he's got. As a musician, I mean. Real hot stuff, apparently. It's hard to not be impressed by his record. Especially when the guy's *so* good-looking."

Betty did a poor job of suppressing a smile.

Oh, crap. He's standing right there, isn't he?

Nell took a moment to collect herself. "Hello, Mr. Sanders."

"I stopped by to tell you how remarkable you were tonight."

Am I blushing? "Thank you." *I know I am.*

"I was also wondering if we could grab a bite at Nickodell. I can't get enough of their Turkey à la King." He stepped to one side. "Naturally, the invitation extends to you too, Miss Bacall."

"The God's honest truth is that I have an early start tomorrow. Louella Parsons is paying me a royal visit at home ahead of *The Big Sleep*'s release. I have to be on the ball, but thanks for thinking of me."

"Okay, so I guess it'll be a peanut-butter-and-jelly-sandwich dinner in my studio apartment. It's a good thing I enjoy 'em as much as I enjoy Turkey à la King!" He stepped backward into the corridor. "Some other time, then."

Nell turned back to Betty. "At least he had the decency to pretend he hadn't heard me."

Betty raised a sardonic eyebrow. "You know he was asking you out on a date, right?"

"No, he wasn't."

"But had to change his tune when he found me sitting here."

"We've had a late dinner—don't look at me like that. We were simply two co-workers sharing a meal."

"He's even better-looking up close," Betty singsonged.

"He didn't even hint at making a move." *Why did I drop my voice to a whisper?*

"Does he know about you and Luke?"

"Doesn't everybody?"

"Good point. Not that that's stopped any guy who has drawn breath since five thousand BC."

"Maybe he's lonely." Even Nell knew how hollow her suggestion sounded. The Peyton Sanderses of this world were rarely short of a dinner date. "Or maybe it's like what Joan Crawford said to me when I bumped into her in the ladies' lounge at the Orpheum."

"I can't wait to hear this."

"She said, 'If you're famous and pretty and rich, everybody assumes you have a date for Saturday night, so nobody ends up asking you.'"

"Are you saying that Peyton Sanders is the male Joan Crawford?"

Nell pulled a brush from her handbag and ran it through her hair. Grazing the bristles against her scalp calmed her. It also gave her time to wonder if she'd been naïve about Peyton's intent. "Do you think he's like Tristan and Gus?"

"Hardly!" Betty exclaimed. "Why? Do you?"

No, Nell didn't. But then again, she wouldn't have picked Gus out as a homo, either. Pangs of guilt pricked her conscience. As far as she could tell, he was a decent guy who deserved the truth. And she had a boyfriend who wouldn't love the notion of her going out with someone else, even if it was platonic.

"He's right about Nickodell," Betty said, handing Nell her purse, "I could go for a plate of Turkey à la King."

"I thought you had an early morning."

"And I thought you didn't want to encourage him."

"I don't—but, well, won't it be awkward if he's there?"

"You heard him. He's going home for peanut-butter-and-jelly sandwiches."

Nell hated the idea of Peyton having a sad dinner all on his lonesome. Maybe there was a way she could make it up to him.

By the time they had reached the Nickodell parking lot, she'd figured out how she could do exactly that.

29

Luke walked into the largest projection room on the studio lot with Nell, Bogie, and Tony, surprised to encounter so many of the front-office bigwigs scattered among the seating. When Jerry Wald had invited him to "see what we've got in the can already," he'd explained that although it was only three scenes, "they're humdingers I know you'll get a kick out of."

Pre-production on *The Last Submarine* had started in the middle of January; a month later, principal photography was under way. To minimize distractions, Curtiz had ordered a strictly closed set on Stage Seven, so it wasn't like Luke could wander in any time he liked. If they wanted him there, someone would ask.

Nobody had.

"Nervous?" Bogie asked as they found seats in the third row.

"Why should he be?" Tony asked. "He already knows what happens."

Nell stroked the back of his hand. "Are you?"

That conversation with Slim Hawks had been haunting him. *In other words, they're making up the entire story.* Whatever he was about to watch, it was going to be more fiction than reality. "It's not every day you get to watch yourself played on screen."

He looked around to see if John Garfield had shown up. It would have been nice if the actor had attempted to talk to him. Maybe he preferred to work up his own original character. And that was fine. But still.

"Did Wald tell you which scenes they're running?" Tony asked.

Nell shivered. "I hope it's not the part where you get clunked on the head and fall into the water."

A rowdy bunch of crewmembers who'd worked on several of Bogie's movies tumbled into the room. They shouted their hellos and fell into the nearest seats. The house lights dimmed as the curtains parted. The 5-4-3-2-1 countdown wound its way to zero before giving way to the *Lanternfish*'s cramped radio room, its black metallic boxes covered with knobs, dials, and gauges crowded all three walls. Thick wires snaked around Christopher's telegraph and his typewriter. Garfield sat closest to the camera, perched on a tiny stool and hunched over a white box, his face illuminated by a fluttering light.

Luke leaned forward, mesmerized by the cramped conditions, his backless chair, the way the light from his test model surveillance equipment pulsed.

"From Rockaway, huh?" Garfield asked the guy playing Christopher.

"Born and bred like a Nathan's hotdog."

"Boy, what I wouldn't give to be chowing down on one of those right now. 'Gimme all the fixins,' I'd tell 'em. Sauerkraut, mustard, da woiks. Pile it all on."

"You musta impressed those dames strolling along Riegelmann Boardwalk." Luke didn't recognize the actor playing Sparky, but he had nailed the Queens accent. "I can see it now. Some blonde glamor girl who works in Gimbel's ambles past. You've got sauerkraut, ketchup, and mustard dripping off you like you was an escapee from the local bughouse. And you're calling out, 'Come back, cutie-pie! You want a bite of my hotdog? There's plenty more where that came from!'"

It was a fun scene with playful banter, but as it played out, the real-life counterpart started up in Luke's head.

Luke had told Christopher when they got back to LA, they'd visit Finlandia Baths to prove that Bogie was a regular guy. Luke could see the awed look on Christopher's face, his eyes darting from side to side, his lips a perfect "O" at the prospect of sitting in a sauna with a star of Bogart's stature.

The action cut to the lookout on the high platform, alerting Captain Polk that Luke sighted the *Toyotomi Maru*. The news set off a frenzy of activity as the crew vaulted to their battle stations. It was a taut and gritty scene, accurately depicting the tension and claustrophobia.

Luke breathed a little easier when they cut back to the radio room, where the two actors now sat back-to-back, each man hunkered over his equipment. Over Garfield's shoulder, the set decorator had taped a picture of the Brooklyn Bridge.

Luke squirmed in his chair, his hands gripping the armrest.

It was *a* picture of the bridge, taken from the conventional angle at Old Fulton Street, looking toward Manhattan. But Christopher's was from Manhattan looking back at Brooklyn.

Luke kneaded his temples. He hadn't been able to visualize photograph in the *Lanternfish*. The sun's late-afternoon angle. The chain of yellow school buses lining the Brooklyn-bound side. The pointed arches.

Luke forced a heavy swallow.

Christopher chatters about riding his bike from Ninety-Seventh Street to Breezy Point Tip. The captain's voice calls out, Forward torpedo room, report your damage. The room sways as though it were drifting on the high seas. Japanese babbling, rapid and high-pitched. Now they're talking about the men crowded amidships. It's a hellship, the captain yells. Goddamn sons of bitches. The sound of gushing water. Men shouting. Alarms shrieking.

Luke steadied his breathing and forced himself to concentrate on the images on the screen.

It wasn't just the chairs and the radio room they'd recreated so meticulously. It was everything: the shape of the hatches, the dirty floors, the blotches on the ladders where paint had worn away. The camera panned across from the forward torpedo room, past the officers' quarters, and into the control room, where Polk was glued to the periscope's eyepiece. The layout, the equipment, the airless spaces.

Christopher's face appears, grim with determination. There's nothing more you can do, Garfield tells him. Follow me. Not yet, Christopher barks back. It's my job to SOS. We're on the surface, so I'm broadcasting in the clear, but I have to stay until a rescue vessel acknowledges. Luke tells Christopher there are plenty of ships out there. One of them is bound to be close by. Christopher replies, It's a big ocean. Get yourself topside. I'll see you up there.

Up on the screen, Luke follows the crewmen to the ladder.... He hears the chatter of gunfire and boom of cannons above him. He's halfway up the rungs. The *Lanternfish* takes another hit. The boat shudders. Luke loses his grip and plummets to the floor. He hears Christopher cry out in pain. He clambers over equipment and twisted metal to the doorway leading into the radio room. Christopher is sprawled on the floor, his left leg twisted at an awkward angle. Luke calls out his name. Christopher raises his head off the wet floor—or is it his own head that's wet?—and pierces Luke with his stare. It's what I deserve, he says, and lays his head down again.

Luke escaped his drawn-out déjà vu with his face damp and his finger stump throbbing. He could hear Christopher's anguished groan over the unfolding action. And what about that last thing? He deserved to what? Die? Why would he think that, especially if Luke were standing there? An even more horrifying thought occurred to Luke: Why didn't he pull Christopher free?

Nell whispered, "What's wrong?"

Luke jumped up. "I'll be back."

The cool night air whipped through his hair. He could still hear the sub's screaming alarm. The whoosh of water surging in. Feel the wind biting into his neck. No, it wasn't the wind. It was rope scratching at his skin. He could feel it looped around his right shoulder as he climbed up the conning tower ladder to the salty, fresh sea air as he reached topside. *There's still enough light to make out the silhouette of the machine gun on the cigarette deck. Nobody's shooting the Japs. I need to—*

"Sweetie?"

Nell's voice shocked him back into the present. Bogie and Tony were standing behind her, their faces creased with concern.

"Sorry 'bout that. Didn't mean to worry you. It's just that I . . . seeing it all . . ." The tremulous words mired in his throat and refused to budge.

Bogie landed a gentle hand on Luke's shoulder. "I've got a bottle of Four Roses in my dressing room."

Luke could picture Christopher's face now. The way fear had distorted it was almost grotesque. And how he'd said, It's a big ocean. Like he'd already surrendered. "A shot of Four Roses sounds good. But a double sounds better."

30

Nell pouted at her dining table. Now that she had laid everything out, it looked awfully cramped. "We'll be squished like sardines in a housing crisis."

Luke licked the wooden spoon he'd dunked in the mushroom soup. "Tasty!" he called from the kitchen. "How come you've never cooked this for me?"

"Because *Good Housekeeping* didn't publish the recipe until recently."

He let out a good-natured chuckle. "You read *Good Housekeeping?*"

What a relief it was to see Luke clown around again after that preview last week. Lord in heaven! Seeing Christopher sprawled out on the floor of the radio room had made him feel as though he'd been socked in the jaw, he'd told her. No wonder the poor guy had got roaring drunk afterwards. Nell had had the devil of a time cramming him into her car, and later onto his bed. But that was okay. Nobody's life was a Technicolor musical.

She removed the small vase of daisies from the center of the table and mentally crossed her fingers that she could read Luke as well as she liked to think. He'd never said out loud that he was jealous of Peyton. Or resented him. Or that he suspected that Arlo's lead trumpeter had any ulterior motives. However, she had noticed how his spine stiffened whenever Peyton came up in conversation or how he would sniff disapprovingly.

She joined him at the stove. "More salt? Pepper?"

"No."

"More mushrooms? Cream, maybe?"

He wrapped his arms around her waist. "Why are you so nervous about this dinner party?"

Because I've invited Peyton so that you can see there's nothing between us.

"Abigail will be in the same room with Bogie. Not that I intended to put the two of them together, but when I'd mentioned to Betty that I was throwing my first-ever dinner, she took it as an invitation."

Nell had grown up hearing Mother advise her five daughters that the goal of every hostess was to ensure her guests had a marvelous time. But how marvelous would this party be if Bogie recognized Abigail? Or would it be worse if he didn't?

"And besides, when I tell Mother about tonight, I'd prefer to avoid having to admit that I ended up burning down the kitchen."

"I can see the headline already: 'The Great Beverly Hills Fire of 1946.'"

"Isn't it time you went to the store for ice?"

He cocked an eyebrow at her. *I can't win with you, can I?* No, he probably couldn't. He tightened his hold around her. "I should skedaddle."

"And yet you're still here."

"I'm not budging until you acknowledge everything will go swimmingly tonight."

"Okay! Fine!" *No, it's not.* "It'll be a glorious success." *That remains to be seen.* "Please go before everyone shows up." *If only for the sake of my sanity.*

***

Betty raised her Old Fashioned. "If I'd known my old roommate could cook a complete meal by herself, I'd have insisted she did more of the cooking."

"In LA, girls' abilities in the kitchen aren't held in as high regard as they are in the rest of the country," Bogie added. "Am I right, Abigail?"

He'd barely taken his eyes off her. They had been running late, so Abigail and Peyton had already downed their first Old Fashioneds when the Bogarts had waltzed in, presenting a spray of white carnations that now permeated the room with its sweet perfume.

"You are," Abigail replied. "Back home in Oshkosh, if you couldn't cook a three-course meal by the time you were a high-school senior, people wondered what was wrong with you."

"You're from Oshkosh?" It was the first sentence Peyton had spoken out loud since he'd arrived wearing a tux. He'd taken one look at Luke in his pre-war, May Company, off-the-rack sport coat and declared himself more over-dressed than the presidential turkey at Thanksgiving. "I'm from Madison." He held up his glass. "Hello, fellow Badger!"

Abigail always wore her hair in a flattering updo, but tonight it framed her face and brushed the tops of her shoulders the way it had on that awful day on the *Casablanca* set. It hadn't helped Bogie recognize her; his mouth was still pinched in suspicion that he knew her . . . from somewhere . . .

Violet's booming voice followed her loud knocking on Nell's front door.

"Sorry I'm late." She sashayed into the room trailing a chartreuse feather boa behind her. "But I have the most exciting news." Luke handed her a cocktail which she downed in one mouthful. "I've spent all day screen-testing at Paramount for the lead in a movie about Sophie Tucker called *The Last of the Red Hot Mamas*."

"Violet!" Nell said. "How thrilling!"

"The front-office guys are losing patience with Betty Hutton, who my brand-new pal, Corinne in Costuming, tells me is becoming unmanageable. She said they let Hutton believe they almost replaced her with me in *Incendiary Blonde*."

"Weren't you Betty Hutton's stand-in for that movie?" Nell asked.

"I sure was. How awkward for her; how fabulous for me!"

"That's a Hollywood story if ever I've heard one." Peyton was sitting straight as a telegraph pole now, perched on the edge of his chair, wide-eyed from his first exposure to Violet's razzle-dazzle.

"Ain't it?" Violet said. "The whole idea is too *42nd Street* for words."

"You'd have been a knockout as Texas Guinan."

"Aren't you darling for saying that? Tell me your name again?"

See, Luke? Nell wanted to say. Not *everybody* knows who he is.

"Well, Mr. Sanders," Violet continued, "maybe you'll get to watch me as Sophie Tucker."

"Do you think they'll throw Hutton over for you?" Bogie asked. "She might be going off the rails, but she's still a big marquee name."

"It's the longest of long shots, but you've got to be in there taking your biggest swing." Violet ran her hand along her bright feather boa. "Buddy DeSylva told me that I was aces in front of the cameras, and *he* made Miss Hutton a star. So if I get called back for a full Technicolor screen test, I'll know I'm in the running. But listen to me prattle on."

"I have some news." Nell paused a moment to give everyone a chance to pull themselves from Violet's orbit. "Arlo Nash is taking his orchestra on a thirty-stop tour, kicking off with two weeks at the Grove, and has asked me to join them as his permanent singer. Not only that, but we'll be recording an album!"

The group broke out into enthusiastic applause as Bogie rose to his feet to make a toast about taking big swings and leaps of faith, especially when it meant quitting a regular job with a dependable paycheck.

"You're leaving Warners?" Violet asked. "Again?"

"The first time doesn't count," Nell replied. "But, yes, I've handed in my resignation."

"How did that crabby boss of yours take it?" Betty asked.

"Monosyllabically. 'Yes. Fine. Good.' I got more of a reaction out of Buzz Bryant."

"Who's that?" Peyton asked.

"A big deal in PR," Abigail put in. "Or used to be before the war. Sometimes I wonder if he left half his wits on the battlefield. You wouldn't believe the poster he approved for *The Last Submarine*."

Nell wondered why she hadn't heard about this. Granted, she had one foot out the door, but she still worked there. "He put the sub back in, didn't he?"

"Yes, but now it's at the bottom of the ocean."

"WHAT?" Luke slammed his tumbler down on the coffee table. It probably left a mark, but he was beyond caring. "The *Lanternfish*? Ten thousand feet down?" Abigail went to answer, but he was too upset. "Dead in the water? That's how this half-wit wants to show *my* boat? JESUS!"

"Don't worry," Abigail said, "my boss had a confab with his boss. They came up with a more inspiring version."

"You work at Warners, too?" Bogie asked.

"Art department."

"Is that why you look familiar?"

Luke crossed to the little sideboard where he'd set up the bar. His dark eyes darted like frantic bumblebees as he gulped a slug of whiskey. "This isn't the type of war movie where everybody dies in the end. What the hell was Buzz thinking?"

Nell would be asking that same question when she walked into the office on Monday. But that was two days away, and she needed a change of subject because the goal of every hostess was to ensure her guests had a marvelous time.

"You know what I'd love?" She swept her hand in a wide arc. "To see all your faces at my Cocoanut Grove debut. Knowing you're in the audience would mean the world to me."

"Of course we'll be there!" Betty said. "Wild horses, and all that. Couldn't be more excited for you." She elbowed her husband. "Right?"

Bogie broke away from staring at Abigail. "Uh-huh."

"It's hard to beat playing the Grove," Peyton said. "We're going to have such a terrific couple of weeks there."

"'We'?" Violet echoed.

"Yes, ma'am, I'm the lead trumpeter with the Arlo Nash Orchestra. Playing the Grove is the LA equivalent of playing the Palace in New York."

"As a former vaudevillian, you're talking my language," Violet said. "The audience dressed to the nines, ordering French champagne and puffing away on four-dollar Cubans."

"And," Peyton added, "you're up on stage knowing you're giving them a night to remember. That's what Nell has to look forward to, and I'm going to enjoy watching her soak it all up."

Nell felt herself blush. She was looking forward to making her Cocoanut Grove debut, too, but did Peyton have to add that bit about watching her?

"Holy Toledo!" Bogie prodded his index finger at Abigail. "You're that girl, aren't you?"

She narrowed her eyes warily. "I'm *a* girl."

"That day on the set."

"What day on what set?" Betty asked. "What girl?"

Bogie dropped his eyes to the carpet.

Nell saw now that she could have warned him, but she had wanted Bogie to figure it out for himself.

"We all played a part in Abigail's humiliation," he said quietly. "Each of us owes her an apology."

"Honestly, you don't," Abigail said. "It all happened so long ago."

Bogie lifted his gaze. "Lorre and I were so intent on sticking it to Curtiz that I never spared a moment's thought for the girl. Mission accomplished, Davenport. I feel like the biggest heel in Hollywood. And in this town, that's saying something."

Regret filled his face more than Nell had expected. She had failed—miserably—to consider what a sensitive man he was. *If anyone's a heel around here, it's me.*

"He'd barely even gotten started when Miss Davis came along," Abigail declared.

Betty's mouth was set into a frustrated pout. "Will someone tell me what we're talking about?"

"What were they called?" Luke hadn't budged from the makeshift bar. "Curtiz's Thursday Girls?"

"Tuesday Girls," Nell said.

Abigail's jaw dropped open. "*Girls?* Plural?"

Bogie snorted. "Every Tuesday, we had to stop working when he disappeared into his office with his chorine du jour. We rigged up that loudspeaker to shame him into stopping."

"I didn't think I was the only one, but he humped a different girl *every week?*"

Well, this is just peachy. Luke's angry. Bogie's embarrassed. Betty's confused. Abigail's humiliated. At least nobody's worried about Peyton making goo-goo eyes at me.

"Your prank with the speaker," Violet asked Bogie, "did it work?"

"Shockingly, yes."

"Think of it this way, dear." Violet patted Abigail's knee. "You were the *last* one."

"I shouldn't have had to be *any*one."

"Of course not. All men are all bastards all the time. I'm sorry you had to go through that, but thanks to *this* bastard —" she wiggled her fingers at Bogie "—you helped stop one first-class bastard dead in his tracks. You should be proud of that."

A hesitant I'll-take-your-word-for-it smile surfaced on Abigail's face as a pale shade of pink filled her cheeks.

"My mushroom soup needs tending." Nell fled to the kitchen, where she lit the gas under the pot. Was playing hostess always this nerve-wracking? She thanked God the main course was only tuna noodle casserole; she didn't have the wherewithal to manage anything more sophisticated. Luke's shadow fell across the floor. "You were right, honey," she admitted, keeping her back to him. "It doesn't need more salt, pepper, mushrooms, or cream. It's tasty, but it could do with extra oomph."

"Got any white wine?"

Nell froze. "There's some Chablis in the ice box if you think that'll help."

"According to my mother, wine always helps." Peyton opened the Frigidaire, pulled out the bottle, and popped the cork. "Not too much to overpower, but enough to zing."

"'Zing'? Is that a cordon bleu culinary term?" She made a Herculean effort to keep her voice light.

"Most certainly." He was at her side now; the aroma of Chablis filled the air. "It's a catch-all meaning to make everything lovely."

Was it her imagination or did he lean a little more heavily on the word 'lovely'?

He splashed wine into the pot.

"Shouldn't you try the soup first?" she asked him.

"You already said it was tasty."

"Well, yes, but—"

"All under control in here?"

Nell spun around. Luke was leaning against the doorjamb, his arms crossed, the corners of his mouth turned downward.

"We were debating whether the soup needed an extra boost," Nell told him.

"When I tried it a little while ago, it tasted perfectly fine."

"To wine or not to wine—isn't that the question?"

She faced Peyton for the first time since he had joined her in the kitchen. Instead of his usual Midwest handsomeness, he wore a dreamy-eyed expression paired with a tremulous smile.

Oh, brother. Don't tell me Luke's right.

31

Luke rubbed an oily rag along the barrel of the revolver Joan Crawford had used in *Mildred Pierce*. He didn't know who he should be furious at. Hedda Hopper was the obvious target. Using her column yet again to stir her witch's cauldron of even louder mock outrage over Christopher's parents. As if she gives a good goddamn about what happened on the *Lanternfish*. Someone needed to drive that woman over a cliff. And he wouldn't be the least bit upset if it were Peyton Sanders.

Maybe Hedda's vitriol had irked Luke so deeply because it had landed the same day his letter to the Walshes had come back to him, marked "Return to Sender." The message was clear: *We don't want to talk to you.*

He placed the revolver in the cardboard box and picked up two pie dishes. The metallic one bore the dents and stains of actual use; the clean white ceramic one would display better. If it had a crack or a chip in it, he might have selected it, but he chose the metal dish and deposited it next to the gun.

Okay, so maybe Sanders didn't deserve to be flung off a cliff with Hedda. It wasn't Nell's fault he went all goo-goo-eyed whenever he was around her. And okay, so that little domestic scene with the Chablis had been innocent enough. And granted, the mushroom soup had tasted better. But the rest of Nell's dinner party had gone off smoothly only because Luke had kicked off the conversation by asking everyone what they thought the top-grossing picture of 1946 was likely to be: *The Best Years of Our Lives*, *The Jolson Story*, or *The Big Sleep*. It hadn't been hard to defuse the tension in the room. Ask movie people for their opinions of movies, and you were off to the races.

He inspected a menu for Mildred's Fine Foods, Beverly Hills. The art department had created a two-page menu of chicken soup, chicken dinners, chicken pot pies, chicken salad sandwiches, and apple pie à la mode for dessert. Impressive for a prop whose only visible part would be its cover.

Sanders seemed decent enough, and if Nell's sole job was to sing on *Music from Hollywood* once a week, Luke would be okay with that. And if the orchestra played the Cocoanut Grove or the Catalina Island Casino, that was fine too. But this tour. Eight weeks on the road. A guy would have to be a chump not to worry about who got lonesome, and who might take advantage of that lonesomeness late one night when nobody was looking.

He picked up the rolling pin Mildred had used early in the picture when she was working her fingers to the nub. Unlike the metal pie dish, the pin looked fresh-from-the-store new. He added it to the pile.

Did he trust Nell? Of course he did. She was the most steadfast, dependable person he knew. And hadn't she stayed faithful to him the whole time he'd been away at war? Of course she had. Everybody knew that and so did he. But the knowing only made his insecurity all the more irrational—and his guilt over feeling this way all the more acute. He was only human, after all. But so was she. And that damned tour was going to have thirty stops. As far as he was concerned, that meant thirty opportunities for Mister Boogie Woogie Bugle Boy to charm and flatter his way up her sweater. Or down into—

Luke brushed the box aside. *Stop it. You'll drive yourself around the bend if you let that mental picture consume you.* He looked up to see a man in a dark pinstripe suit standing twenty feet away, a fedora in his hands. "Can I help you?"

"Lieutenant Valenti, I presume?"

Contrasting with the spiffy suit, the man's hair covered his ears and reached past his collar, twisting into curls spouting in all directions. After years of military crew cuts, it was odd to see a nest of budding spirals. "That's me."

"My name is Ethan Brophy. I believe Slim Hawks has spoken to you about the possibility of working together?" The cleft in his chin dug deep enough to give Cary Grant a run for his money.

"The ghostwriter. I was expecting you to call first."

"Normally, yes, but I had a meeting with Jerry Wald today. I wanted to pitch him the idea of adapting a novel called *Dark Passage* for *The Saturday Evening Post*."

"The one Bogie and Bacall will be filming?"

"Uh-huh." He motioned toward the box with his fedora. "What's all this?"

Luke wasn't *not* interested in Slim's suggestion, although even with the help of some arbitrary ghostwriter, writing a book seemed a formidable undertaking. But now a specific ghostwriter was standing in front of him, and seemed decent enough. Despite the badly needed haircut.

Luke balanced the pie dish on his fingertips. "Jack Warner has decided to throw a party for Joan Crawford, on account of how she won the Academy Award for *Mildred Pierce* but was ill the night of the ceremony."

"She wasn't too ill to be in full makeup when it came time to pose with her Oscar moments later," Brophy said with a twinkle. "And now she's furious with herself for staying home because she couldn't bear to lose."

"Translation: Mr. Warner wants to give her a memorable evening to keep his high-priced star happy."

Brophy picked up a stack of hardbound ledgers that Mildred was always poring over. "Props from the movie?"

"The Powers That Be tasked me with setting up a display centerpiece. Mr. Warner's office told me to leave room for Joan's Oscar." Luke took the ledgers from him and placed them in the box. "I'm required to build a tall platform for it so that she can see it at all times."

Luke had been looking forward to the challenge of taking a heap of otherwise unrelated items and arranging them into an attractive display around Joan's golden boy. And he wanted to do an especially good job now that Nell and the Arlo Nash Orchestra had been booked as the entertainment tonight.

"It's a long way from scrambling around a sinking sub, isn't it?" His shift to a more sympathetic tone had been subtle but unmistakable.

"Look, Mr. Brophy," Luke said. "I'm not sure I want to work on a book. The honest-to-god truth is that there are gaping holes in my memory."

"You can't remember the event that you're famous for?"

"More of it has come back to me over time, but it's fragmented and unreliable. If we have to pad it with invented details, it hardly seems worthwhile if the whole point is to set the record straight."

"Don't you think *The Last Submarine* will do that?" Brophy ran a cigarette-stained fingertip over the frilly edge of a starched waitress cap. "Last month there was a showing of three completed scenes. Did they bear any resemblance to reality?"

"Almost *too* real."

"Painful to watch, huh?"

The memory of that screening still made Luke's heart pound the inside of his ribcage. "You could say that."

"So the movie's not a complete figment of the screenwriter's imagination?" Brophy brushed a lock of hair from his face. His right earlobe was missing. Was it his equivalent of Luke's missing finger? These days, it was common to see guys with absent limbs, eye patches, scars, or limps and walking sticks. "All the more reason," Brophy said. "Even if it's accurate, it'll only be in theaters for, what, a week or two? Three or four if it plays well at Grauman's Chinese. But a book can stay in print for years, especially if it sells well. And it probably will if it can come out at the same time as the movie."

"As quick as that?"

"If we pull the lead out." Brophy produced two sheets of folded paper from inside his jacket and laid them on the table. "I took the liberty of preparing a contract. Typical boilerplate. It prohibits you from working with another writer to publish your story for a one-year period. However, there's a provision allowing either of us to exit the agreement at three-month intervals."

That sounded fair. "What's the other page?"

Brophy swapped the pages. The words "Simon and Schuster" filled the top. "I floated the idea past one of their editors. He was very interested and sent me this. It gives him first right of refusal, meaning we can only shop it around after he's passed on it. In my experience, though, if they insist on a first refusal, they smell a success."

"Thanks. I'll give it some serious thought."

Brophy watched with unvarnished disappointment as Luke folded the papers and tucked them into the back pocket of his khakis. "Keep in mind that the book I'm proposing will tell the full story. The *Lanternfish* part is compelling, of course, but so are your attempts to overcome your 4-F flaws, and how you refused to give up until you'd muscled your way into the Navy using your photographic memory and German language skills."

Luke had to hand it to him; he'd done his homework. Walking in here with two contracts wasn't a bad thing, as long as it didn't tip over into cockiness. Luke had seen enough overweening blowhards in the Navy to know those peacocks could rarely back up their claims.

Luke thought about Peyton Sanders. If the guy was trying to

muscle in, would Luke need to leave a longer-lasting impression on Nell as she sat on that tour bus with LA shrinking in the rearview mirror? No, he decided, it's not Nell I have to impress. It's Sanders.

"Thanks for stopping by."

* * *

He set up his *Mildred Pierce* display on the set of Joan's latest movie, *Humoresque*: a wood-paneled living room of a well-heeled New York socialite, featuring lots of elaborate candlesticks and fancy lamps. As members of the Arlo Nash Orchestra set up their instruments along the south side of Stage Fifteen, Luke had arranged the props he'd collected into what he hoped was an eye-catching presentation on a knock-off Chinese Chippendale table. It had taken longer than he'd anticipated; otherwise, he would have snuck backstage to wish Nell good luck. The rolling pin had proved to be a challenge to position—it kept threatening to roll onto the floor—so he'd swiped a pair of pewter salt and pepper shakers from the *Humoresque* set. They would keep the pin in place as long as nobody got drunk and decided to wield it like a Viking club and threaten to clobber Mildred's heinous daughter, Veda, with it.

"Nice job."

"Thanks." He moved the saltshaker a half-inch to the right, but the rolling pin shifted as he did, so he put it back. "Joan is bringing her Oscar, so I've built this—" he tapped the empty stand he'd fashioned out of a fishing tackle box from *To Have and Have Not*, which he'd covered in black velvet "—but holding my breath, I ain't."

"For the love of Mike, you big dummy," Bogie said, "look *up*."

He and Betty were standing next to Abigail, who hoisted Joan's Oscar aloft. "Ta-da!" The key lights above them made the gold veneer glow. "Joan walked into the art department half an hour ago holding it like it was the baby Jesus. She marched right up to my desk and announced I was the only person she could trust."

"The two of you are friends?" Luke asked.

"Never met her! I suspect my *Casablanca* story is getting out." Abigail lowered the Academy Award onto the fishing tackle box. "God, these things are heavy."

People were filling the set. Betty waved a manicured hand toward a pair of men near the entrance. "Why is Fred MacMurray here? And who's that with him?"

"He co-starred with Joan in her last MGM movie." The announcement came from Tristan, who had snuck up behind them. "The other guy was their director, Richard Thorpe. She invited them as a 'Screw you!' to MGM, who kicked her out after eighteen years—and then won an Oscar with her first Warner film."

"You sound like you're in the know," Betty said.

"Direct from the glamorpuss's mouth. I was with her while Tony did her hair. She claims to be nervous as hell."

"About what?" Bogie asked.

"Being the center of attention." Tristan kept a straight face for a whole second before bursting into laughter. He flicked the peak of Luke's Navy cap. "Don't you get sick of wearing the same khaki ensemble all the goddamn time?"

"I spend half my day dusting off grimy vases and hauling fusty sofas in and out of storage," Luke replied. "I'd sooner wear a uniform the Navy can replace for me."

"Which reminds me—Fleet Week is coming up in June. That's always fun." Tristan ran a knuckle along Luke's ribbons, pausing on his Purple Heart and Navy Cross. "Such a loyal Navy man through and through. You always did have that admirable quality about you."

"I don't know about that." Feeling his face redden, Luke looked away to survey the crowd. John Garfield had rushed through his scenes on *Humoresque* early so that he could jump into *The Last*

Submarine. He hadn't reached out, so Luke had been hoping for a chance encounter. Or failing that, an orchestrated one. His most likely opportunity would be at this sycophantic fawn-fest. Garfield was nowhere in sight. Kathryn Massey, however, was striding toward them.

"Nonsense," Tristan said. "Gus adores you for turning his life around. He hates to think where he'd be if you hadn't ignored his atrocious behavior and taught him to read."

It had been forever since Luke had thought about their first reading lessons at the back of the studio. Would Brophy include that type of thing?

"Hello, all." Kathryn looked fetching in a dark two-piece tailored to resemble a men's double-breasted suit, only huggier around the hips. It was the sort of outfit Joan wore whenever she played a spunky girl reporter or a cunning secretary on the prowl. She clamped a friendly hand on Bogie's shoulder. "I feel as though I failed to properly thank you for inviting Marcus and me to join you all at Romanoff's. We appreciated it so much."

"Are you still Hollywood's most godforsaken pariahs?" Bogie asked. "Or was that four hundred and twenty-three scandals ago?"

Early in the new year, Luke had bought a copy of that notorious roman à clef that everybody had been blathering about. He hadn't been at all impressed by *Reds in the Beds*, and was stumped by all the fuss swirling around it.

A playful smile twinkled Kathryn's eyes. "Marcus was right about your story making a good movie. From what I hear, *The Last Submarine* is shaping up to be a real nail-biter."

"It's still early days, but yes, those scenes were gripping, to say the least."

Past Kathryn, Luke spotted Ethan Brophy standing with a cluster of screenwriters. Was he better connected than Luke had assumed? Or merely skilled at talking his way into parties?

Luke had spent most of the day dithering over whether to

accept Brophy's proposal. It was a square deal, and he seemed gung-ho. If there was an obvious drawback, Luke couldn't see it.

Kathryn winked slyly at Luke. "Marcus knew there was little chance you'd take up his offer. But he also knew that when Jack Warner was made aware of it, he'd have to make you a better one."

Luke pulled his eyes off Brophy. "Why would Marcus do such a generous favor for someone he barely even knows?"

"Because he's that kind of guy." Kathryn threaded her arm through Luke's. "Sorry, folks, but I need a private word with the lieutenant." She led him to a quiet spot behind the display. "What can you tell me about John Garfield and Albert Maltz?"

Her question struck Luke as an odd one coming from a prominent Hollywood columnist. "Nothing you don't already know."

"I'm asking specifically in connection with your movie."

"Garfield might be playing me on screen, but we haven't swapped five words."

"And Maltz?"

"We spent an afternoon together. He grilled me about my experience, took a bunch of notes, but that's about it."

"Did he talk about his personal life?" Her eyes had taken on a brittle sharpness. "His background? Political affiliations?"

Aside from a few cursory details about Brooklyn, Maltz had restricted his questions to Luke's experiences aboard the *Lanternfish*. Why did Kathryn Massey care about any of this? The moviegoing public didn't give two hoots about screenwriters. Audiences preferred to believe that actors improvised their lines as they went along.

A fanfare blasted over the public address system as a spotlight fell on a doorway in the *Humoresque* set. Joan Crawford, resplendent in a floor-length gown of shimmering organza, wafted to a waiting Jack Warner, who greeted her with a kiss to a cheek. She pressed a hand to each side of her face as the surrounding crowd poured out its admiration.

"Thank you, thank you, thank you," she declared, as the

applause petered out. "I'm touched, truly I am. I knew Mildred was a gem of a role, but being the new girl on the block, I had to bide my time until my commander-in-chief cast me." She paused as Warner waved to his minions like a cross between Mussolini and Henry VIII. "But I didn't dare dream it would lead to an Academy Award and all *this!*" She flung out her arms, almost whacking Warner in the face.

The orchestra struck a flashy note led by a powerful trumpet. Luke glimpsed three intertwined initials—ANO—displayed on each bandmember's music stand.

The trumpeter held the note longer than Luke thought humanly possible. Sucking in a deep second breath, he launched into a lengthy arpeggio that sent his notes soaring.

This was not the mild-mannered Peyton Sanders who had suggested a liberal dash of Chablis to jazz up Nell's mushroom soup. This was the skilled trumpeter bewitching a difficult-to-impress crowd with his mastery of an instrument that seemed to exist as a natural extension of him.

Had he been that well-tanned at Nell's?

Had he looked that suave?

Or did he only radiate all that charisma when he dazzled people with his God-given talent?

After Sanders' extended solo, Nell strode on stage in a silk dress studded with diamantes that she'd bought for her upcoming run at the Cocoanut Grove. Catching the lights with tiny pinpoints, it looked ten times better up there than it had when she'd modeled it for him at home. She waved gleefully at the appreciative crowd, most of whom had known her and worked with her for years. Luke waved with both hands, but he was too far back for her to see him.

She reached her microphone and sang the first line: "Well, what do you know."

It was that Les Brown song, "My Dreams are Getting Better All the Time," which she had been rehearsing at home all week.

How come she'd never mentioned she'd be opening with it tonight? Before she got to the second line—"He smiled at me in my dreams last night"—Peyton joined her at the mike and kicked off into another brassy flourish of notes running up the scale and down again. Nell pulled an oh-my-gosh-where-did-*you*-come-from? face that may have fooled the audience, but Luke knew that face better than anyone here. She had rehearsed that mock-surprise expression, and she'd done it more than once. And he could tell that she had done it with Sanders; their split-second timing had been too tightly choreographed.

Back and forth they seesawed. She sang a line, he played eight bars. Back and forth. To and fro. Up and down.

Luke had to admit—and he hated having to admit it—those two had remarkable stage chemistry. They really did look as though they were having tons of fun up there, and their joy poured off the stage and spilled into the audience.

Unable to pull his gaze away from what was going on, Luke bit down on his lower lip. *You need to up your game. Don't be the dummy who wakes up alone one morning, flabbergasted that anyone could have lured away his girl.*

Their enchanting duo over, Peyton sat down as the orchestra segued into a jitterbuggy arrangement of "Flamin' Mamie." But Luke's eyes were now sweeping the crowd for a ghostwriter with shaggy hair.

32

The traffic signal on Vine Street turned red. Nell braked to a gentle halt and gazed past a Standard Oil gas station to the terracotta-tiled dome a block south of Melrose Avenue. She didn't know its name, but she could recognize a Catholic church from a hundred paces.

If she were a devout Catholic like her parents, she'd have stopped by, lit a candle, and recited a prayer for what she was about to attempt.

Recording all eight tracks in one day, four songs in the morning and four in the afternoon, seemed too much. "But it's how we do it," Arlo had assured her. "All it takes is focus, focus, focus."

The ten-foot globe on top of the RKO building on Gower Street looming into view meant she had two blocks to focus, focus, focus.

"Yeah, well, that's easy for Arlo to say," she muttered under her breath. "But he doesn't have to deal with a boyfriend jealous of your star trumpeter."

Had there been a connection between Peyton's performance at that apple-polishing jamboree for Joan Crawford and Luke signing with that ghostwriter? It wasn't like him to be so impulsive. Maybe the impetus hadn't been Peyton's trumpeting but rather that lovesick puppy-dog look he'd cast at her over the mushroom soup.

The sign—*5505 MELROSE AVE ~ DECCA RECORDING STUDIO*—appeared on the north side over a parking lot. She steered her Plymouth into the closest space, pulled the keys from the ignition, and closed her eyes.

Focus, focus, focus.

You know the lyrics. The melodies. The arrangements. All you have to do is nail the vocals. Preferably on the first take. Easy as rolling off a log, right?

Getting out of the car, she encountered Peyton halfway through a cigarette, pacing back and forth outside the entrance. With all the countless hours he'd spent on stage, Peyton Sanders got nervous? *This* guy?

"Good morning!"

He looked up like a startled prairie dog, albeit a slim-hipped one with great hair. "Do you have a spare minute?"

"Don't tell me Arlo's changed all the songs."

He smiled at her little joke. "We were so busy during rehearsals that I neglected to thank you for the marvelous time I had at your dinner party. And the food was terrific."

Nell doubted her mushroom soup and tuna noodle casserole had been anything to throw a parade for, but her carrot cake had turned out moist. *Always serve a top-notch dessert and go out with a bang, right, Mom?* "I'm so glad you could join us."

"It was my first home-cooked dinner in I can't tell you how long."

"Isn't the renowned Peyton Sanders inundated with offers?"

"Nah." His smile took on a glow, the sort that Nell suspected would compel Luke to bare his teeth. "Which made your invitation all the more endearing."

It was time to deflect. "Is there no special girl in your life?"

He crushed his cigarette butt under his heel. "Us musicians need someone who works the same schedule. That leaves nightshift girls or nightclub girls."

She tried not to read the "Like you, for instance" look in his eyes, but it was hard to avoid. Time to deflect the deflection.

"Do you hear much from your family back in Madison?"

He shook his head. "Dad died of TB when I was a senior in high school. Mom went a couple of years later when I was studying at the Boston Conservatory. The coroner said it was heart failure, but my sister and I think the actual cause was a broken heart. My folks were a pair of devoted peas in a pod. It's what I want to find when it's my turn."

So much for deflecting the deflection. Nell pulled at the door handle. "Shall we?"

* * *

Nell crossed Melrose Avenue feeling as though someone had tied a helium-filled balloon to the top of her head. Her feet were probably touching the asphalt, but she wasn't entirely certain.

Four down, four to go. The afternoon session still lay ahead, but the morning couldn't have gone better. She hit home runs with "Love Me or Leave Me" and a big-band version of "Stairway to the Stars." Both songs! In a single take! Another one—"Straighten Up and Fly Right"—had taken two, but only because Peyton had come in half a beat too early.

Ironically, it was "Every Fifth Word" that had given her the most trouble. Three takes! Heavens to Betsy, how embarrassed she'd been when she fluffed the chorus at the end. On the plus side, though, Arlo had tweaked the arrangement on the fly, and now it sounded better than it ever had.

She floated into the lobby of Lucey's New Orleans House. The place smelled of exotic foods simmered in rich, thick sauces with garlic and wine. She told the woman in the colorful dress that she was meeting someone.

"The actress with all the makeup?" the hostess asked.

A week ago, Violet had announced that Buddy DeSylva had set up the Technicolor screen test she'd been praying for. To their mutual delight, they'd discovered that it was to take place the morning of Nell's recording session. And with the Decca studios situated next to Paramount, a celebratory lunch at Lucey's across the street was in order.

The restaurant's décor packed a wallop. The dining hall was done out, wall-to-wall, ceiling-to-floor, in a violent shade of blood red. The carpeting, the tablecloths, the counter at the bar. Even the linen napkins were the exact same hue.

Violet was the only patron coated in more makeup than Tristan used to wear when he was flouncing around town as Trixie Bagatelle.

Nell slipped into the booth. "You look . . . um . . ."

"Like a hooker twenty years past her prime?" Violet sipped her beer through a straw, careful not to ruin her lipstick, which, Nell could see now, was the same shade as the surrounding bloodbath. "I had no intention of coming to lunch looking like—" she drew a circle in the air around her face "—*this*. I thought we'd be done by now, but they've decided to film a second scene."

"That's good, right? Screen tests are expensive."

"Especially Technicolor ones. So it means they're impressed. Oh, darling—" she seized Nell by the wrist—"it's more than I ever dreamed!"

Nell forced herself not to laugh at the incongruity of how lurid Violet looked in her garish makeup, thick as a circus clown's. But all the warpaint at Max Factor couldn't dim the optimism shining out of her. "I'm so thrilled for you."

"And even better?" Violet released her grip and tightened the edges of her black silk robe around her bosom. "Now that I've had a peek at the script, I'm convinced I can do a terrific job. I suffered through the end of vaudeville, exactly like Sophie did. This afternoon's scene comes when she's booked at the Palace, which was the goal of every vaudevillian. But it's the early 1930s, and by then, the theater reeks of decay, and she can see the writing on the wall. She's standing backstage, surrounded by fellow performers who are refusing to let go of the past." Violet pulled a crumpled page from her handbag and flattened it against the red tablecloth. "Could we run through it a few times?"

Nell's heart dropped a little. She'd hoped she could talk to Violet about this situation developing with Peyton. He'd had a brief solo in two of the songs they'd recorded that morning. Normally, he would remain embedded in the orchestra, but to capture them together at their best, Arlo had ordered Peyton's microphone to be set up next to hers.

More than once she had caught that same doe-eyed wistfulness. As the technicians had been setting up for the next song, he'd said to her, "You're a first-class singer. I hope you realize that." It wasn't a pick-up line that a cocky Don Juan would lay on a girl at a party. Nevertheless, it had made her blush. And feeling its heat had only deepened her embarrassment. He couldn't have failed to notice that she resembled a candy apple.

He had, however, been enough of a gentleman to turn aside. *You're not interested*, she'd told herself. *Not the slightest bit tempted. You have Luke, and Luke has you. But I'm only human and he's a good-looking guy—but unassuming, which makes him all the more attractive. What girl's head wouldn't be turned?*

Violet was bound to have had more than her fair share of unwanted attention, and would have answers to Nell's questions about what she should do. But she hadn't counted on today being a possible turning point in Violet's life.

"Anything to help you nab the role you were obviously born for."

* * *

After ordering their meals—Brochette of Chicken Livers for Violet and Tournedos Royale for Nell—they cleared their cutlery to one side. Nell held the script page in front of her. "And action."

"'Here's what so few people understand, so let me lay it out for you.'" Violet had dropped her regular accent—New Jersey by way of Savannah—in favor of Sophie's hard-living growl. "'Comedy and life are the same thing, my darlings. It all comes down to timing. Jobs, friends, opportunities, even lovers, there'll always be another one around the corner. Sometimes, they're the right one at the wrong time. Or the right time but the wrong place. The trick to steering through life—and comedy—is knowing it's the right choice *because* the right person has come along at the right time under the right circumstances.'"

Violet had infused her delivery with such heartfelt emotion that Nell looked up from the page, mesmerized by the woman's transformation.

"'Some jobs I've been right for,'" Violet continued, "'but they have shown up ten years too early. Some folks I was pals with in my twenties I wouldn't have given the time of day in my forties. It's the great, big, wonderful, gorgeous crapshoot of life. You get the biggest laugh of the night when you land the punchline in the *right* way at exactly the *right* time. It's always best to let it all fall into place. And that's why you shouldn't force life any more than you should force love.'"

Violet held her tell-it-like-I-see-it face in place, not twitching a muscle, until Nell realized she had finished.

"Oh, Violet!" Nell cried out.

"You're supposed to say 'Cut!'"

"I knew you were a great musical performer, but that right there was a skilled dramatic performance."

"Thanks, kiddo." Violet toyed with the Lucey's matchbook. "No matter how well written a monologue is, it's hard delivering it to a camera. But when I do it this afternoon, I'll picture you."

"I'm sure I was awfully distracting."

"Your face..." Violet reclined against the tufted velvet upholstery. "What a crazy quilt of emotions. You want to tell me what's going on with you, or will I have to gouge it out with an oyster knife?"

Nell waved away her concern with a fluttering hand. "Nothing, nothing. Not on the day of the biggest audition of your life."

"Waiter!" Violet called out. "An oyster knife, if you please."

"Uncle! I'm crying uncle!"

Violet kept up a poker face as Nell laid out her Peyton situation, then asked matter-of-factly, "Is there any attraction?"

"No. None at all."

"Mister Sanders is a nice guy in a town where nice guys are in short supply. Lemme ask you this: if Luke wasn't in the picture, would you be interested?"

"But Luke *is* in the picture," Nell protested. "Your question is theoretical and therefore irrelevant."

"So then, what are we talking about?"

"I have a jealous beau on my hands. I've never had one before and I don't know what to do. I don't even know why he's jealous."

Violet canted her head to the left and bunched her lips to the right. "You don't strike me as the idiotic type."

Nell stared at the woman she'd turned to when she was in desperate need of advice. "Excuse me?"

"Must I spell it out?"

Tears of frustration burned the backs of her eye sockets. "I think so, yes."

"After you play the Cocoanut Grove, you go on tour with the band, right?"

"Uh-huh."

"Peyton will be there, and Luke won't. For eight . . . long . . . weeks."

It took a moment for Violet's point to sink in. "I *am* an idiot! I never thought—never dreamed—Luke's got nothing to worry about."

"I know that and you know that. If you ask me, it's sweet that he's worried."

"How do you figure?"

Violet abandoned her straw and drank—deeply—from her beer. "The moment you let a fella take you for granted is the moment you surrender your upper hand."

"So I should let him believe that me and Peyton might—you know?"

"Listen to an old broad who's had to learn this lesson over and over—*and over.*"

Nell wanted to fly to the studio and set Luke straight, but instead she should let him fear the worst? Violet's recommendation didn't sit well with her. Not one little bit. But then again, Luke was her first jealous boyfriend. What did she know about these things? Especially when Luke hadn't said anything out loud. He was too stoic for that. All she'd had to go on were muted reactions and deafening silences. And quite frankly, she didn't know which was worse.

33

*L*uke stepped off the Rodeo Drive sidewalk and into The Tropics. Ah, so it was true. They really did spray fake rain onto a glass ceiling. Effective, too, in a close-enough-is-good-enough way.

The maître d's bamboo-covered podium was unattended, so he ambled into the main room. Coarse nets roped like spider webs along the walls. Fishing rods and taxidermied trout hung here and there. Phony palm trees bracketed each doorway. A faintly sweet smell—honeysuckle? frangipani?—pervaded the atmosphere. Luke suspected the cigarette girl surreptitiously sprayed perfume from time to time. The place reminded him of a bar he'd run across in Honolulu. Makuahine's wasn't as big, though, and had been far more crowded with servicemen.

It was not, however, a typical Bogie haunt. Those frou-frou cocktails with paper umbrellas didn't sound like Bogie's speed. The only thing he liked in his booze was ice cubes.

A trio of see-no-evil, speak-no-evil, hear-no-evil wooden monkeys dangled from the ceiling above Bogie. A near-empty glass shaped like the torso of a well-stacked hula dancer sat in front of him. Perched on his head was an old trilby. Grimy at the peak and slightly crushed around the brim, it had seen rosier days.

Luke took off his Navy cap and dumped it on the table. "You surprise me," he said, dropping into the empty chair.

"This place?" Twin plumes of smoke escaped Bogie's nostrils. "Wouldn't have been my first choice, but Delmer loves it."

Delmer Daves had been conscripted to direct Bogie and Betty's next picture, *Dark Passage*. Luke guessed rendezvousing away from the studio suggested Bogie was planning to weigh in on the aspects of the story he didn't like too much.

Luke glanced at the cocktail menu.

Miriam Hopkins' Rum-Gum and Lime

Rita Hayworth's Karanga

Lana Turner's Untamed

Luke ordered a Dorothy Lamour's Sarong from a passing waiter, and waited for Bogie to bring up the reason he'd asked to meet.

Bogie drained his glass. "I hear *The Last Submarine* is racing along."

"Curtiz closed the set, so it's a moot point."

"I'd love for your story to have been Santana Productions' first movie. How fun would it have been for me play to you and Betty to play Nell? And *I* would give you full access."

"Maybe Curtiz did me a favor. Look at how I reacted to those scenes. I didn't even make it to the third one, so even a recreated *Lanternfish* might reduce me to a blithering mess."

"I've never seen you look so pale as you did that night. I wouldn't be in a rush to repeat that, either." Bogie was slurring his words. That hula dancer hadn't been his first. "Listen, I have news. You know the post-war backlog gumming up the works at City Hall?"

"The one that's prevented Santana Productions from being registered?"

"They got to our application."

"Are we official?"

"We are indeed."

Finally, some good news—especially after the heart-to-heart Nell had insisted on last night. Dorothy Lamour's Sarong arrived in a translucent green tiki god with a pineapple wedge dunked into a muddy concoction. "Here's to swinging into action," Luke said.

"I'm shooting *Dark Passage* and *Dead Reckoning* back to back, so I wanted to talk about gathering material. Novels, plays, magazine short stories. Hell, I'd option a kid's fairytale scribbled on the back of a Chinese laundry bill if it was a decent yarn."

"But the big studios have teams of people reading everything prior to publication."

"Which is why we need to get inventive."

Luke sipped his Sarong. Boy howdy, it was strong. He guessed it was fifty percent rum, with banana and mango flavoring blended in to help soften the rum's uppercut. "How about we zero in on magazines and books published more than, say, a year ago?"

"Whatever's in that pagan brew, it helps you to think like a movie exec. Okay, so Santana Productions' Rule Number One: Don't act like a front-office pencil-pushing prick who thinks he knows what makes a viable movie because someone told him he could be Gary Cooper's twin."

Luke's head was already spinning. "Should I be writing down these rules?" he asked.

"There's only two."

"What's the other?"

"Be unfailingly honest." Bogie lifted his battered trilby. "Starting now."

He nearly always wore his toupée, so seeing the man's scalp virtually barren of any hair came as a sobering shock.

"What did you do, catch bowling-ball-itis?"

Bogie's craggy face fell. "We've been trying for a baby, but the natural way wasn't working, so I've been taking hormone treatments to nudge things along. The doc's confident it'll work, and if it does, that's great. But meanwhile, it's causing my hair to fall out even faster than it was." He clamped the trilby back onto his head. "At this rate, who the hell knows what'll come first—fatherhood or winning an Erich von Stroheim look-alike competition." A wide smile broke out. "And yet I've never been happier because after three disastrous walks down the aisle, I doubted I could ever make a go of the marriage game. But then the right person for me showed up and everything has fallen into place. And do you know why?"

"Because you're famous and she's fantastic?"

Bogie socked him with a pretend whack to the jaw. "Because we have trust. We have our scraps. Sure we do. But do you know what Lizabeth Scott looks like?"

"Isn't she the girl Columbia has cast opposite you in *Dead Reckoning*?"

"A dead ringer for Betty. The face, the hair, the voice. The whole package. Now, you'd think Betty might be justified for feeling jealous over my spending three months working with her mirror image."

"And is she?"

"No! Why? Because—"

"You've got trust."

"Exactly. I've given her no reason to be jealous, but people are people. Jealousy is a natural human trait. But not when you've got trust. Y'see?"

Yes, oh yes, Luke saw, all right. This tropical tête-à-tête was nothing but a good old-fashioned set-up. In less than forty-eight hours, Violet had spoken to Nell, who'd told Betty, who had blabbed to Bogie, who had taken it on himself to reassure Luke that he shouldn't be jealous of anyone from the Arlo Nash Orchestra.

"This is about a certain trumpeter, isn't it?"

"And here's me thinking I'm the master of nuance."

"Nell mentioned her conversation with Violet." Luke forced a mouthful of Sarong down his throat. Dammit to hell and back, jealousy wasn't the type of response that a man-to-man powwow could subdue, no matter how stiff the drinks. "I wish he wasn't so good-looking, so charming, so talented."

"This is Hollywood, Lieutenant." Bogie struck a match to light the Chesterfield he'd inserted into the corner of his mouth. "There's always bound to be someone more good-looking, more charming, more talented."

"So I'm supposed to let all that go?"

"Hell, no!" He blew the smoke into Luke's face. "You park it in a dim corner of your mind that gets no light, no warmth, no water, until you forget about it and it dies from neglect."

"Is this the part where you tell me it's easier said than done?"

"I don't want to see you burn through three noxious marriages before you understand how good you had it with Nell."

That's what it all came down to, wasn't it? Recognizing he had the best thing that had ever happened to him when he had it, and not after he'd smashed it into a million pieces.

"When are you meeting Delmer?"

Bogie consulted his watch. "Three-quarters of an hour."

"Do we have time for another—" Luke waved at Bogie's empty glass. "—whatever that was?"

"A Paulette Goddard's Captain Blood."

"Seriously?"

"Either that or Sonia Henie's Celestial Delight."

"You should be insulted that they don't have a Humphrey Bogart's Gin Joint."

Bogie laughed out loud, catching the notice of the bartender. "That's one for the suggestion box."

Luke waited until after Bogie had gestured for another round. "Thanks," he said quietly.

Bogie's silence was his reply.

Luke loosened his black necktie. If he was going to tackle a second Sarong, he'd need to be better prepared.

34

The mirror in Nell's Cocoanut Grove dressing room was taller than the one she had grown used to at CBS. It was wider, too. She examined her left profile in the full-skirted dress she'd found at Bullocks Wilshire. It was Kathryn Massey who had suggested she go see her friend, who worked as a seamstress in the exclusive dress salon.

Gwendolyn had access to an eye-popping buffet of gowns, including the one Nell wore. She loved how its bateau neckline scooped across her chest, and the way it cinched into a princess bodice. The print was a brave choice: large, vivid ivy leaves against delicate rose pink. Nell wasn't convinced she could get away with it until Gwendolyn had encouraged her to try it on, advising, "Stage dresses call for boldness." When Nell had worried that the hem might catch on microphone cables or other hidden booby traps, Gwendolyn had chopped it off to mid-shin.

Doubts continued to creep in from the edges, however. Those ivy leaves looked more severe than they had at Bullocks. Would the spotlight emphasize their intensity? Would the audience notice only her dress?

Three rapid knocks broke Nell's preoccupation. The door swished open. Bubbles of laughter and chattering filtered in from the main room. "The protective fellow at the—oh, wow."

Luke's bug-eyed response told Nell that the ivy dress had been the right choice. She twirled around so that the skirt flared out. "You like?"

He went to kiss her on the lips, but remembered the lipstick-before-performing rule and redirected it to her cheek. "I love."

"Is everyone seated out there?"

"All fourteen, plus your seat at the head of the table. We're so near the stage that if you pop a button, one of us will catch it."

Knowing that her dearest friends were close at hand was a comfort. "Terrific!" But Luke gave no response beyond a pensive face. *Please tell me this isn't the Peyton business again.* "Or not?"

"It's Violet."

"Oh, dear. They're giving the Sophie Tucker movie to Betty Hutton?"

"And now Violet's out there getting pickled."

"In other words, she's had a little too much?"

"Your singing teacher is sitting next to her. She told me she knows how to handle Violet, but let's face it, the broad is a handful."

A handful of loaded Violet wasn't on Nell's Cocoanut Grove debut wish list, but it was better to be forewarned. It was twenty minutes to show time. "Anything else?"

"Yes." A hesitant tone had crept into Luke's voice. "Buzz Bryant is here."

That was not a name she'd been expecting to hear tonight. "Who's he with? Taplinger?"

"An older couple."

"His parents?"

"No," Luke replied soberly. "Christopher's."

"The Walshes are *here*?"

Luke nodded. "Christ knows what Buzz is up to."

"Maybe he's not up to anything. Maybe he's . . ." But she couldn't dream up a scenario where Buzz Bryant was acting out of the kindness of his heart.

After she shooed him from the room, she returned to the mirror to check her dress one last time. Yes. The ivy print was perfect. She looked so glamorous. Hmmm. Too glamorous? Done up like this, she barely recognized herself these days. It felt as though the more successful she became as a singer, the more glamorous she had to be, and the more she feared slipping away from the person she truly was.

A few weeks after *To Have and Have Not* had come out, Nell and Betty went clothes shopping at Saks on Wilshire Boulevard. It was the first time Nell had witnessed a knot of fans besieging her. "I'm just Betty Joan Perske," she'd said later in the car, "but everybody treats me as Lauren Bacall."

Nell had laughed at the time, but looking in this flattering mirror encircled with lights, Nell understood Betty's objection. She wondered if the price she had to pay was too high. *No! This is no time to let doubts creep into your mind.* "Stage dresses," she reminded her reflection, "call for boldness. Let's go out there and be BOLD."

* * *

Still breathless from the applause, Nell wafted into her dressing room. She had instructed everybody that she would meet them at the table, but she wished now that Luke or Betty or Cora or *someone* could have been here to greet her. All she was left with was her own reflection in the mirror as she unfastened the hook at the top of the side zipper and wriggled out of her dress. "Maybe you ought to always go with bold-print dresses," she told her other self.

How silly to think a dress could have helped her sing. But it had boosted her confidence as she felt the embracing warmth of her baby-pink spotlight. It had melted her jitters like sun on a springtime snowfall as she stepped up to the mike to croon "Straighten Up and Fly Right." And, of course, the cheers from the rowdy crowd at the front table may have helped.

She hung her gown back on its hanger and buttoned herself into a smart, sleek cocktail dress made of plum-colored taffeta with magenta ruffling around the décolletage.

It was Cora who deserved the credit. The woman presented herself as though she were a superannuated prima ballerina thirty years past her peak, but Nell suspected all that dyed hair and thick eyeliner was for show. She had drawn out Nell's talent bit by bit, note by note, phrase by phrase, song by song. The Nell Davenport who had walked into her apartment four months ago couldn't have walked onto the stage tonight and delivered a show like *that*.

Hunger pangs gnawed at her innards as she slipped into her three-inch heels. She should have eaten a light snack, but hadn't been willing to take a chance that her stomach might run riot halfway through her set. She wouldn't make that mistake again, because now she could eat half the Cocoanut Grove menu.

She checked herself in the mirror. The plum dress had been Gwendolyn's suggestion, too. That gal sure knew her stuff.

The Cocoanut Grove's resident band was deep into "Fascinating Rhythm" when Nell reached the table. All fourteen of them treated her to a standing ovation, peppered with hoots, hollers, and hoorays.

"Settle down before you get us thrown out," she hissed as she took her seat. "The show is over."

"Nell, Nell, *Nell!*" Betty exclaimed. "When I think of that night we stood on that Mulholland Drive overlook, who'd have guessed I'd be watching you sing at the Grove like a goddamn nightingale? I'm speechless!"

"If anyone deserves a round of applause, it's this lady." Nell gestured extravagantly to her singing teacher, who had gone easy on the eyeliner tonight: it had taken ten years off her.

Her fingers teeming with oversized jewelry, Cora waved away Nell's compliment. "You came to me with a natural talent in need of a guiding hand. That's all."

"Babycakes, lemme tell ya." Violet sloshed martini onto her bulging bosom that she'd squeezed into a strapless gown. "You were so doggone charming, I coulda listened to you all night long. When that album comes out, I'll be first in line to buy it."

Nell's stomach screamed for food. She looked around for a waiter. "I'll set one aside for you."

Cora pinched the stem of Violet's glass and steered it onto the table. "Some water, Violet dear? Coffee?"

The band plunged into "String of Pearls." Luke extended his hand. "May I have the first dance with the lady of the hour?"

"The lady of the hour is so hungry she might pass out." The eagerness on Audrey's face was hard to miss. Tony was thriving on his prosthetic leg these days, but the dance floor was his no-man's-land. "Take Audrey for a spin?"

Audrey was on her feet before Luke could make his offer.

Nell caught the eye of the only unfamiliar face at the table. His thicket of black curly hair gave him away. "You must be Ethan," she said. "How's the book coming? Is Luke giving you enough background to go on?"

"It's a crossword puzzle." He had to raise his voice to be heard above the band. "Clues. Solutions. Interlocking facts. Unreliable memories. Surprising twists." He smiled genially. "We'll get there."

A sharp knowing filled the man's eyes—Nell bet they didn't miss much—contrasting with his unruly, almost bohemian hair.

She tilted her head toward Abigail, who was critiquing with Tristan and Gus the wardrobe choices of a woman on the dance floor.

"Miss Hart," Ethan said, taking Nell's hint. "Care to dance?"

Abigail was as eager to join the throng as Audrey had been. With no menu-carrying waiter in sight, Nell slipped into the seat beside Bogie that Abigail had vacated. She picked up an unused fork and attacked his leftover Roast Long Island Duckling. "Did Luke tell you about Christopher's parents?" The duck was *a l'orange*; the citrusy bite tingled her mouth.

Bogie nodded. "That couple with Buzz looks like every Rockaway native I've ever seen."

"I've never met this Buzz Bryant you lot are always talking about," Betty said. "Where are they?"

"Half a dozen tables from the maître d's station," Bogie said, "under the palm tree with the monkeys hanging paw to paw."

Betty rubbernecked the room until she'd found them. "Christopher's parents aren't Lieutenant Valenti's greatest fans, but maybe they'll talk to you."

"With Buzz sitting right there?" Nell asked.

"What if I ask him for a dance? What's he going to do? Refuse me?"

She was right. No red-blooded male this side of Peking would turn down an opportunity to cheek-to-cheek it with Lauren Bacall.

Nell finished the rest of Bogie's duck as Betty sauntered to Buzz's table. The guy decamped with scarcely a nod to his guests.

Nell finished Bogie's meager leftovers, then weaved through the tables and papier mâché palm trees and approached the couple. Christopher's mother wore a one-size-fits-all dress that she'd probably bought from Klein's, and had decorated with a green-glass brooch tasteful in its restraint. The father wore his Sunday-best suit, neatly pressed but fraying at the cuffs. They both displayed the smiles of people who could hardly believe where they were.

"Hello," Nell said. "I thought I'd come over and introduce myself. I'm—"

The man's agreeable smiled disappeared. "We know."

Nell gripped the back of the unoccupied chair. "What I meant was I'm the girlfriend of—"

"The hero of the *Lanternfish*." Mrs. Walsh subjected Nell to a withering once-over.

"So-called," her husband added.

"Mr. and Mrs. Walsh, Luke and I want to explain—"

"Soft soap us, you mean." Walsh crossed his arms and rolled his jaw around as though he were working his way up to spitting at her. "Not interested."

"In that case, why did you come to the Cocoanut Grove? Did you not know I was performing tonight?"

"We did."

"Did it occur to you that Luke might be here?"

"Naturally."

"Then why—"

"We preferred to see what you two snakes looked like in person."

"We're not—"

"Good evening, Miss Davenport."

"I only wanted to—"

Walsh shot to his feet so quickly that Nell reared back. Hint taken. No need to cause a scene. Especially on an otherwise sparkling success of a night.

Returning to the gang, she flagged down a passing waiter. "I'll have the Monterey Sole with potatoes and broccoli au gratin. And wine. White. I don't care what it is as long as you can get it here fast." As he headed for the kitchen, she chanced another look at the Walshes' table. Neither of them was talking, but instead stared at their folded hands.

***

Several hours later, Nell felt warm and gooey from the combined effects of the Monterey Sole, an excellent pre-war Chablis, and the constant flow of table-hopping admirers. By the time the final well-wishers had bid her good evening, Nell and Luke were the last ones at their table.

"I think it's about time I drove Little Miss Belle of the Ball home." Luke took her hand and led her toward the Grove's glass doors with the palm trees etched in gold. "It's been a magical night. I hope you enjoyed yourself."

"Every bit of it. Except for—you know." He stopped walking abruptly. She followed his flinty gaze to where Buzz was draping a rabbit-fur wrap on Mrs. Walsh's shoulders. "We're their two least favorite people in the world. Why would they stick around?"

They followed the trio into the Ambassador Hotel's expansive lobby. Near the reception desk, Buzz adopted a formal pose as he shook each of their hands before heading outside.

Luke charged forward, still holding Nell's hand. "We should give it another go." The couple were still standing where Buzz had left them. Spiteful resentment froze their faces as Mrs. Walsh shielded herself with a cloth handbag.

"May we have two minutes of your time?" Luke asked.

It was a more gracious approach than Nell would have chosen. She would have kept talking, but Luke paused to give them a chance to take in the real Luke Valenti and not whatever noxious picture they'd formed in their heads.

"It's late," Mr. Walsh said.

Luke crept a half-step forward. "I wanted to acknowledge how it's perfectly understandable that you feel Christopher should be the hero of the *Lanternfish*." He paused for another diplomatic moment. When it became obvious they had no rebuttal, he continued. "Please believe me, I'd give anything for Christopher to have survived, and for him to be hailed as the hero. That blasted title, "Hero of the *Lanternfish*"—it was shoved on me by the Navy, the press, and the studio. I didn't ask for any of it. I just wanted my life back."

Mr. Walsh's shoulders slackened an almost imperceptible notch or two as his wife's handbag dropped to her side. Nobody said a word as a hotel bellhop marched past them and announced a call for Mister Samuel Haversham.

"Tell them about the photo." Nell nudged Luke. "In the radio room."

"Christopher taped a picture of the Brooklyn Bridge to the wall of the radio room. Whenever he looked up, there it was, reminding him of home."

Mr. Walsh clasped his wife's hand as disbelief clouded his face. "We thought he didn't care about where he came from, or his heritage, or his past. He took off for war and we never heard from him again. We've got nothing of his. Not even his Purple Heart." Mr. Walsh bowed his head as though in pain.

"We called the Navy to see if we could get it," his wife continued. "They told us to put our request in writing."

"Did you hear back?" Nell asked.

"Months later, we got a letter saying they had forwarded Christopher's Purple Heart to his listed next-of-kin, and as far as they were concerned, the matter was now closed. When we told Mr. Bryant that, he said, 'Doing our bit for the war effort is all the Navy cares about and as far as the Navy's concerned, it's time for us to get lost.'"

If the Navy had dispatched Christopher's posthumous Purple Heart to his next-of-kin, why hadn't his parents received it? The post office would never be so careless with such a precious keepsake. This was their dead son's medal. Who else would—

The bellhop passed them by. His calls masked Nell's soft gasp.

Christopher had changed his next-of-kin from his parents to Remy.

Nell stole a glance at Luke, who she could see was one step ahead of her.

He reached into the wide coat pocket of his uniform jacket. When he withdrew his hand, he had bunched it into a fist.

"The Navy can be frustratingly bureaucratic." He unfurled his fist to reveal his Purple Heart. "I don't know why they thought I was Christopher's next-of-kin. I wasn't his anymore than he was mine, but an anonymous paper shuffler decided otherwise."

Luke gently took Christopher's mother's hand and placed the medal in her palm. "And now your son's Purple Heart is where it belongs."

Blinking like a bewildered owl, Mr. Walsh turned to Nell. "This is what you wanted to tell us? That Lieutenant Valenti had it all along?" It seemed cruel to contradict him. Not when his weather-beaten face and threadbare suit told the story of a man whose life had brought few pleasures. "Neither of you is how Mr. Bryant described."

Nell and Luke looked at each other again: *Well, now, that's a topic for discussion on the drive home.*

Nell feigned a yawn. "You were right," she said from behind her raised palm, "it's getting late."

"Can you recommend a Catholic church?" Mama Walsh asked. "We wish to have Christopher's medal blessed."

"St. Vibiana's in downtown LA," Luke replied. "Any taxi driver could take you there."

The hesitation in their faces was easy to decipher. "Or," Nell said, "we could drive you."

"That'd be awfully decent of you."

Nell wasn't sure what Buzz Bryant was up to—or why—but she knew she and Luke ought to seize any opportunity to neutralize whatever spiteful nonsense he'd fed this unsuspecting couple. She walked to the nearby elevator and pushed the call button. "What room are you in?"

"Four-eighteen."

"We'll be in touch. Good night."

They waited until the elevator had swallowed the Walshes

whole. Nell squeezed Luke's arm as hard as she could. "You, Mister Lieutenant Hero of the *Lanternfish*, sir, did a very fine thing."

He wrapped his hand over hers. "We lied to them."

"You gave them peace of mind, and that's more important."

35

Luke picked up the battered stereoscope he'd spent nearly two days tracking down for *Life with Father*, currently in production on Stage Fourteen. He positioned his face in the viewfinder. A hand-colored three-dimensional vista of New York sharpened into view. The finest carriages money could buy waited along Fifth Avenue curbs out front of robber-baron mansions. It was a far more sedate version of midtown Manhattan than Luke had ever seen, but would have been familiar to Aunt Wilda.

"Knock, knock."

Luke pulled his face out of the stereoscope. "You're early."

Ethan's curly locks grew shaggier every time Luke saw him. "I have exciting news to share before we tour the submarine set with your pal. I thought it best to get it out of the way because you said he might be nervous."

For weeks, Luke had been gently brushing aside Remy's veiled requests to visit *The Last Submarine* set. Even now, more than a month later, Luke could almost feel the grit of those previewed scenes scraping his teeth. How would someone like Remy, who

299

always led with his emotions, react to the real thing? Talk about inviting disaster.

With the end of production drawing closer, Remy's requests had become more forthright until he had worn Luke down. "Be at Props on the dot of noon," Luke had told him. "Twelve-oh-one will be too late."

Ethan glanced at the clock. It read eleven fifty-three. "Lately I've been reading *The Loss of the S.S. Titanic: Its Story and Its Lessons*, and I came up with a title for your memoir: Fateful Night."

Luke rolled it around in his noodle. Mysterious, foreboding, exciting. "Very evocative."

"And in other news—" Ethan's eyes glittered with glee—"*The Saturday Evening Post* has offered to serialize."

"My memoir? In the *Post*?"

"Better than that—you're going to be *on* it."

Luke tried not to squeal like a prepubescent Girl Scout. "Come again?"

"On the cover. And we're not talking some crummy photographer with a second-hand Graflex. They're hiring an artist to paint your portrait." Ethan splayed his hands on the wooden countertop as though to brace himself. "Norman Rockwell."

"NO!"

"YES!"

Luke had suffered through weeks of remorse after he'd signed that publishing contract for the wrong reasons. That is, until he recognized that Ethan was taking greater care to chronicle his story than *Last Submarine*'s screenwriter had ever shown. On top of which, he'd come to enjoy the guy's company. However, the thought had never entered his head that it might lead to being painted by the most famous commercial artist in America.

Luke's folks were unlikely to read an entire book—but a magazine article? He pictured his father showing off the *Post* to every friend, relative, and neighbor on the Valenti family Christmas card list, his proud smile stretching from Brooklyn Heights to East Flatbush. Yes, they'd read that.

Possibly.

* * *

Luke's mind was still so ablur from the Rockwell news that he barely took in Remy's nonstop prattling as the two of them walked to Stage Seven with Ethan.

"I'm sorry," he said to Remy, "what was your question?"

"If you're the technical consultant, how come you haven't seen the set?"

"My screen credit is window dressing. Also, Curtiz ordered a closed set so that he could shoot as fast as humanly possible."

"But the whole picture's about you. He wouldn't make an exception?"

Yes, Luke wanted to say, he probably would have—if I'd asked.

But he hadn't been keen to revisit the worst night of his life—even a wood-painted-as-metal ersatz version. When whispers had begun to spread that *The Last Submarine* was shaping up to be a gripping account of Luke's fateful night, a germinating kernel of curiosity had taken root. Its tendrils were still worming their way to the surface the evening of the preview. After that, Luke had shied away from the idea. But during the intervening weeks, the fear that he might later kick himself had grown greater and stronger.

"Curtiz can be quite the despot when he wants to be, which is most of the time," Luke replied. "When he closes a set, it stays closed."

They headed up C Avenue. Remy bounced along on the balls of his feet. "I'm glad you convinced him to change his mind."

Now that the film had reached its final week of production on time and on budget, the movie's assistant director had guessed that Curtiz was no longer so particular. "But just to be sure," the

AD had told Luke, "wait until twelve-fifteen, when we've broken for lunch."

It wasn't until Stage Seven loomed in the distance that the butterflies of apprehension began to romp around deep inside Luke's guts. He slowed his pace.

"Something wrong?" Ethan asked.

"I was thinking about the speech I gave at the Ebell Women's Club yesterday."

Remy's face fell into a sneer. "Somebody needs to tell them that the war's been over for nearly a year. It's about time *somebody else* got on with his life."

Luke didn't disagree, but all these talks were part of Greg Whitley's PR plan to counter the Walshes' claim that Luke has stolen the title of 'hero of the *Lanternfish*' from their son. These days, though, he enjoyed giving his speeches—especially his presentation at the Ebell. Maybe because it had taken place in a beautiful ballroom with a hundred respectful women, who had asked insightful questions about his Japanese training, his time at Pearl Harbor, and how it felt to hear his girlfriend sing to him over the radio. He had driven back to the studio filled with the contented glow of knowing he'd done a fine job representing the Navy to an appreciative audience.

Or was it different now because he'd spent time with the Walshes? The previous weekend, he and Nell had taken them to St. Vibiana's, where the priest had blessed the Purple Heart. Luke had peppered their conversation throughout the day with spontaneous-sounding questions that had been anything but. By the time they'd returned to the hotel, it had become clear Buzz Bryant had gone out of his way to convince them that Luke had snatched Christopher's limelight for himself.

The three of them entered the soundstage as the crew was evacuating for the commissary. The assistant director flagged them down.

"Curtiz saved the sinking scenes till last because we'll be

drenching everything and everyone. It involves a lot of complicated one-take shots, so it's now-or-never time." He gave Luke's companions—a long-haired rake and a pale phantasm in flimsy silk pants—a wary once-over. "You'll have the run of the place for the next half-hour. Make the most of it, but be careful." He pointed to a janitor in white overalls working along the length of the sub. "We had an accident this morning. One of the grips walked through a big grease puddle and traipsed it across the set."

The *Lanternfish* stretched from the southwest corner of the soundstage to its northeast counterpart. The cutaway set had bisected the sub as though it were filleting a deep-sea halibut, from the forward torpedo room, through the officers' quarters and the periscope, to the galley and crew mess, the engine room, and finally the aft torpedo room.

This, Luke could see, was no jerry-rigged substitute for the original.

His pulse throbbed in his ears. He had assumed the authenticity they'd achieved in those bleak preview scenes was through the movie magic of lighting, special effects, and masterful editing. But now he saw that from the bolts around the midship access hatch to the pale-yellow faceplate of the master gyro compass, this chillingly accurate replica was everything he could recall about the sub that had been his home for all those interminable months at sea.

Remy's breath grew fitful. Luke stole a sideways glance. The guy was keeping himself in check by burying his fists in his pockets, the knuckles of each finger dimpling the silk.

"How're you doing?"

"Where's Christopher's chair? I want a sense of his day-to-day life before . . ." He blew out a ragged breath until he'd emptied his lungs. "And then perhaps I can put all this behind me." He gave out a hiccupy laugh. "Dear God in heaven, I hope so. I'm not too good at letting go."

"You see the periscope? Christopher's radio room is the first one to the right."

Ethan waited until Remy was out of earshot. "Wasn't Sparky's real name Christopher?"

Luke nodded.

"So this little elf was Sparky's . . . ?"

Luke reckoned Ethan was worldly enough to fill in the blanks. He nodded. "As in 'not for publication.'"

"Got it." Ethan took off to inspect the forward torpedoes, leaving Luke to join Remy in the radio room. The paint job was still fresh; its heady tang filled his senses.

Oh, and look. There's his picture of the Brooklyn Bridge.

Although this one was shot from the opposite end, both it and Christopher's had been taken in the fall. The gentle, warm autumnal light was similar.

"What's that for?" Remy asked.

The radio room's fourth wall was made of glass and hung on sturdy brass hinges. Above their heads, out of view, and therefore out of frame, were two wide-mouthed pipes that opened straight down. They were the only extraneous details not in the original *Lanternfish*. It took Luke a gut-churning moment to realize the glass wall would enable them to seal off the room and film "Christopher" at his desk, tapping out the SOS as those pipes flooded it. It was the last visual image Remy would want. Luke was looking around for a distraction when he heard a gurgling, strangled sound.

Remy had flattened his palms against the thick glass as though he were holding it back. His face rested against it as his gasping breaths fogged the glass. "They want us to watch the water fill . . ." He flinched when Luke laid a hand on his right shoulder.

"You want to leave?" Luke asked.

"Is there some place I could go for a bit of privacy?"

"John Garfield's dressing room is in the northwest corner—"

Remy sprinted away.

Luke had helped the set decorator locate the two thinly padded chairs. He wasn't aware how accurate the set designer's selections had been until he saw them in position. It wasn't only the chairs they had recreated so accurately; it was every doohickey and gizmo, gauge, lever, and knob. Christopher's typewriter was in the exact right place and his earphones hung on the hook near where the actor's left shoulder would be.

A metallic clang sounded on the concrete floor as the janitor reached the radio room. "Damn grease," the guy muttered. "Can't promise I'll get it out by the time them folks return from lunch."

Luke ran his fingers along Christopher's workbench. They'd even matched the green linoleum. Christopher had called it "diseased seaweed," but Luke argued it was closer to "gangrenous cabbage."

A whiff from the janitor's bucket wafted past him. A stinking pall of bleach burned his eyes. He closed them, waiting for it to pass, but it only intensified, pressing against him like a damp, heavy blanket. His knees were going to buckle any second now. He dropped into his chair with a leaden thud.

Christopher's voice, clear as a record, tells Luke he'll follow, but not yet. It's my job to keep sending the SOS. I'm not hearing any noise on the line. Could be my radio's gone kaput. Could be I'm broadcasting okay, but can't hear responses. I'm staying until someone acknowledges.

But seawater's rapidly rising throughout the whole boat, Luke shouts. It won't be long until it's up to our waists.

Yeah, yeah, I know. Panic slurs Christopher's voice. And I know how high it has to reach to short-circuit my radio.

There are plenty of our ships out there, Luke insists. One of them is bound to be close by—

It's a big ocean, Christopher cuts in. Get yourself topside and

I'll see you up there. Or in the drink. Whichever comes first. Now GIT.

Luke can feel the cold seawater sloshing against his ankles as he scrambles to the ladder that leads topside. He can hear gunfire and the boom of cannons. He's halfway up the ladder when the *Lanternfish* takes another hit. The boat shudders. He loses his grip and plummets down.

He's a bit dazed but hears Christopher cry out in pain. Back in the radio room, he finds him sprawled on the floor. Luke steps through the hatch to pull Christopher to his feet. He's only got one foot inside when a pungent odor permeates the air. There's no escaping it.

Seawater has flooded the sub's batteries, creating chlorine gas. It's heavier than air, so it'll affect Christopher first down there on the deck. At high levels, it can kill. The two of them need to get out *right now*. Luke grabs at Christopher.

STOP! Christopher yells. NO!

The thickening gas stings Luke's eyes. They weep hot tears. He reaches out, groping for Christopher. His pal pushes him away. I'm done for, Luke. Save yourself. There's nothing for me out there. I'm going down with the ship. It's what I deserve. GO NOW!

The wailing alarm seems to grow louder. Emergency signal. Abandon ship.

No man left behind, Luke growls. Especially not you. Take my hand. I'll pull you up.

I've hurt my knee, Christopher yells over the shrill horn. Real bad. It'll be easier to haul me up using rope. There's some near the ladder.

The gas—Luke's lungs feel like they're shrinking. Barely breathe. Barely see. He stumbles toward the ladder. The water laps at his knees. The *Lanternfish* shudders again. Luke catches hold of the ladder with one hand, and finds a loop of rope with the other. He turns around. Christopher is on his feet, hands pressed against the frame of their watertight door. Save yourself.

DON'T! Luke lunges forward to stop him from locking himself inside. He reaches the door a fraction of a second too late to stop it from closing. The middle finger of his left hand is still in the doorway. It slams with a violent CLANG! that ricochets through Luke's body.

He looks down at his finger. Top half missing. Blood gushing.

He starts to cough. The gas. So dense. The rough rope scratches his neck. He still has it looped around his right shoulder. He climbs the slippery rungs of the conning tower ladder. The cold sea air nettles his face as he shinnies topside. A near-full moon casts the vast churning Pacific in a bright silvery light.

Luke slumped in the radio-room chair. Planting his elbows on his knees, he buried his face in his hands as he battled to recover his breath.

The desperate plea in Christopher's voice still rang in his ears. *It's what I deserve.* Why did Christopher believe he deserved to die when Luke could have pulled him free? It would only have taken them another few seconds. No man left behind.

Luke's finger was now throbbing worse than it had in a long time. He lifted his head off his hands to examine it. *All this time, I thought it'd been shot off when I reached the gun deck. But it had been Christopher slamming the hatch so that he could . . .* Luke looked away. It was too awful to think about.

"You're as white as a sheet."

Luke shook his head to clear his mind. "I'm okay," he told Ethan.

"I've got a meeting downtown, so I have to get going. Hell's bells, Luke, did you get run over by a forklift?"

Luke forged an I'm-perfectly-fine smile. "Let's chat later."

. . .

Luke walked into Garfield's dressing room and found Remy at the makeup mirror smoothing down his hair. "Feeling better?"

"I needed to collect myself."

The chaotic jumble of recollections still crowded Luke's mind. The frigid seawater. The torment in Christopher's eyes. The anguish in his voice. Rope scratching his neck. His severed finger.

Remy reached him in three strides and threw his arm around Luke's shoulders. "We could both do with some fresh air."

The early summer sun felt sharp and astringent. What a relief to get out of that dark, dank set. Luke wasn't as steady as he'd have liked, but few benches lined the alleys between soundstages, so he guided them toward the pocket of privacy he knew best.

"Tell me," Luke said, "was Christopher serious about becoming a priest? Or was he doing it for his parents?"

"There's a question from out of left field if ever I heard one."

"I have my reasons."

Remy took his time to respond. "Did being in Christopher's radio room jog a memory?"

How could Luke tell this guy what had happened during those last minutes?

"You know how you wake up from a dream, but the details slip through your fingers? It's all a mishmash, but Christopher's plans to become a priest had something to do with it."

They stopped outside Stage Fifteen and watched a crew of carpenters assembling a Small Town, USA–type of house for a new Shirley Temple picture.

Remy said, "Christopher's folks weren't going to be satisfied until he was serving in the Vatican."

"That's a lot to lay on a kid's shoulders."

"No foolin'. But then the war came along, and he saw his escape hatch."

"He wanted out?"

"He knew he'd be disappointing his parents real bad, so he played nice. Told 'em this was only for the duration."

The Walshes' willingness to believe that their beloved son had been the genuine hero of the *Lanternfish* made more sense now. As they rounded the corner of the soundstage, the *Arabella* pirate ship loomed ahead.

"Remember that song from the Great War?" Remy continued. "'How Ya Gonna Keep 'em Down on the Farm After They've Seen Paree?' Christopher said the farther New York was in the rearview mirror, the more relieved he felt."

Luke pictured himself and Christopher crammed into that little cocoon, dials lit, needles swaying, the clatter of Christopher's typewriter keys, the occasional squawk through Luke's earphones. All those hours. Verbal word games. Crossword puzzles. All those Hollywood stories Christopher made him tell. And not a peep about what he'd left behind.

Luke led Remy up the *Arabella*'s gangplank. "Did he talk about the seminary? His parents' ambitions for him? Any of that stuff?"

"Are you kidding? Letter after letter, it was all he talked about."

They sat on Captain Blood's berth. That bleachy stench still swarmed Luke's senses. Would he ever be rid of it? "Was Christopher tormented about leaving the priesthood?"

"Not at first. More and more as time went on, though." Seconds ticked by before Remy was ready to continue. "He hated disappointing his parents, and failing to live up to their expectations. I've never had much of a family life, so I didn't get it. But those waters ran real deep with him."

Luke knew a thing or two about disappointing one's family. If only Christopher had hinted about what he'd been going through, maybe Luke could have eased the burden.

"And then there was the whole other issue. You know. Guys." Remy kicked off his white Keds and wriggled backward until he could lean against the wall. "Until we met, it was all speculation. But from that first night, we couldn't get our fill of each other."

Luke thought of their final few days in LA leading up to him shipping out. He and Nell had tumbled into bed at every opportunity. Usually right here on this berth. "Because the future was so uncertain?"

"Yeah, that. Also because he'd been trying not to think about bedding a man, and here he was doing it. And enjoying it. But feeling guilty about enjoying it so much."

"Sounds like torture."

"That's what the flood of V-mails was about."

"Pouring out his heart?"

"One letter would be about breaking free from his old life. In the next one, he'd be more religious. More fervent. Faith! Church! Prayers! Bible! And then he'd swing all the way back again." Remy tsked. "I guess that'll happen when you live under the constant threat of annihilation."

On the Mexican Plaza backlot set behind the pirate ship, a band was rehearsing on tinny instruments Luke had located for the producer of a B picture program filler whose name he'd already forgotten.

"I have something to confess," Remy said, his voice barely audible over the trumpets and guitars. "Out loud."

"Go on." Luke sat up straighter. "Get it off your chest."

Remy's head fell backward, hitting the wooden wall behind them with a dull thud. "I'm a *terrible* person!"

"You must be good at hiding it. I've seen no sign of this alleged terribleness."

"All those letters Christopher sent me, grappling with life-and-death issues… I never wrote back."

Luke was glad "La Cucaracha" drowned his gasp. "How come?"

"I didn't even make it to the eighth grade. The only reason I passed the seventh was because my teacher pitied me."

"Are you saying you can't read or write?"

"I'm no dummy!" The wobble in Remy's voice betrayed his conviction. "But my mom worked two jobs, six days a week. I was such a chatterbox everybody assumed I was swimming along fine. But all that reading-writing-'rithmetic? I couldn't cotton on to any of it. When I put pen to paper, anybody'd think I was a backward four-year-old."

Luke thought back to when he'd first met Gus; it hadn't occurred to him then that a swaggering loudmouth like Hell O'Farrell's son couldn't distinguish his vowels from his consonants. This slim, pale, hollowed-out soul next to him was so utterly different, and yet he faced the same self-doubts. "Christopher never heard from you?" he said gently.

"I felt so inadequate. This guy might end up serving in the stinkin' Vatican. He could do so much better than a dishwasher." He sat forward now, his elbows on his knees, staring at nothing.

Ninety percent of Navy life was nothing like how they showed it in the movies. They only depicted histrionic highlights. Torpedoes firing. Messages arriving. Tempers blazing. Occasionally, Gene Kelly or Frank Sinatra might break out into a peppy dance. Mostly, it was an endless drudge of repetitive tasks. That's why mail call was often the high point of a sailor's week. None of Nell's V-mails had reached him, yet every time he heard the words "Mail call!", his hopes had soared until the chief yeoman had distributed the last envelope.

"Christopher needed a shoulder to lean on." Bitterness and recrimination filled Remy's voice. "All he got from me was stony silence."

"If you're a terrible person," Luke said, "I am, too."

"Don't make me laugh."

"Christopher and I spent weeks and weeks sitting as close to each other as you and I are now. He was going through all that angst and I never detected any of it. I was too busy trying to impress him with stories about having champagne cocktails at Ciro's and filming *Casablanca*."

"Who doesn't want to hear those stories?"

"Not at the expense of making sure your best bud is doing okay."

"You didn't know," Remy said. "Stop beating yourself up."

"I will if you will."

But Remy didn't react with a lighthearted quip the way Luke had hoped. Instead, he said, "Tell me a good memory."

"Of Christopher?"

"I need to know his last few days weren't bleak and hopeless."

"What makes you think they were?"

"I suspect he had a death wish." The next words came out in a frenzied delirium. "I dream about him a lot. We're together, but underwater. He weighs me down and his hands are always slick with oil. His fingers slip from mine and I'm powerless to stop him from sinking. Even as the dark ocean is swallowing him, he tries to comfort me."

"How?"

"He says something like, 'Everything's okay, Rem. Everything's how it's supposed to be.'"

Luke could hear Christopher's voice almost as clearly as he could hear the band outside. *It's my fate to go down with the ship. It's what I deserve.* Remy was right, but would it make him feel better?

"Christopher loved his job," Luke said. "Typing his messages. Checking his readouts. Monitoring the airwaves. He would have sat at his desk all day and night if the CO had let him."

"What was he doing the last time you saw him alive?"

"Three dots, three dashes, three dots."

"Isn't that Morse code?"

"SOS."

The second-rate mariachi band had sounded like they'd been slapped together with adhesive tape and desperation. Thankfully, though, silence fell now as they finished their inept squawking. Remy looked around the cabin, taking in the moth-eaten curtains bracketing the sloop's rear window. "Where the hell are we?"

"They built this for *Captain Blood*."

"Sweet Jesus, am I sitting on Errol Flynn's bed?"

"Yes," Luke admitted with a laugh. "I suppose we are." Pain

jolted up the stump of his half-finger and deep into his palm. He massaged it, but the throbbing intensified.

The image of the steel door fired up in his mind. He closed his eyes, wincing as it slammed on his finger.

I've been assuming I lost it when I manned the topside machine guns, dispatching Japs to their maker. But all I did was get it caught in a door. If that isn't the ultimate joke, I don't know what is.

His eyes flew open.

His shoot-out with the enemy was why the Navy had awarded him the Purple Heart. And probably his Cross, too. But that wasn't how it had happened. He'd received his medals under false pretenses. Protocol was very clear.

I have to give them back.

But that would mean he'd have to explain why. And *that* would involve recounting Christopher's actions that night. What about the movie? And the book deal? So much was riding on the version of events he'd been telling everyone. He'd repeated that version so often to so many people he'd almost come to believe it himself.

"Finger still giving you trouble?"

Luke rested his head against the wall. "From time to time."

Remy fidgeted with a loose button on his shirt. "If it hadn't been for Christopher, you and I never would have met."

"I'm glad we have. Even if you *are* the most terrible person this side of Jack the Ripper."

Remy snorted. "I didn't say I was that bad."

"No, you didn't." *But what about my Purple Heart? I can't ask the Walshes to return it. I'd rather face those Japs again, in the middle of the night, in the middle of the Pacific, in the middle of a sinking.* "Could be I was thinking of myself."

36

Nell stepped onto the Santa Monica pier, still brimming with the zest that always filled her after a singing lesson. Was it the deep-breathing exercises? The exhilaration of reaching a previously unobtainable note? Nell had long since given up trying to figure it out. Better, she decided, to fly on the euphoria for as long as it lasted.

The pier was surprisingly busy for a Tuesday afternoon. She hummed her latest conquest—Hoagy's "Ol' Buttermilk Sky"—as she dodged young mothers with strollers, weather-hardened sailors, pretty girls still hoping to insert their foot inside Hollywood's door, traveling salesmen taking a break from hawking hair rollers and theater candy, and—oh, look. A familiar face.

She skulked a circuitous path across the long shadows cast by the turrets of La Monica Ballroom until she could see what this young woman was sketching.

It was the view facing north up the wide expanse of sand. A road known as the California Incline angled steeply to Route One, which hugged the coast. The girl had included the accurate number of palm trees along the cliff, but at the far left, she'd inserted an imaginary three-ring circus tent topped with orange pennants flapping in the sea breezes.

"Should I get my eyes checked?"

"Oh!" Abigail Hart whirled around. "I thought I'd been caught for not returning to work after my dentist appointment."

"You're so talented," Nell told her. "Professional level. Even that tent you slotted in."

Abigail dropped the sketchbook cover over her illustration. "God forbid Warner Brothers art department trusts me with more than gluing captions and washing out calligraphy nibs."

Her artwork reminded Nell of Luke's lighthouse sketches, not that he'd done any since he got back from the war. He wasn't at Abigail's level, but it would be a shame if he'd given it up altogether. She told herself that she ought to bring it up with him tonight. It was a safe subject after the events of the previous couple of days.

After he'd returned home from visiting the *Lanternfish* set, she had arrived at his place with a veal casserole to find he'd already plowed through a tumbler of Kentucky Tavern. As dinner had cooked in the oven, he told her about the torturous déjà vu he'd undergone as Remy sat weeping in Garfield's dressing room. She had listened to stories she'd never heard, such as the hand-painted sign the sonar guy had hung in the forward torpedo room: FRESH FISH SERVED DAILY. Evidently, 'fish' was Navy slang for torpedoes—Luke hadn't mentioned that either. Later, someone named Blinkeroo had printed FREE DELIVERIES underneath it, a lark that had earned him a rare chocolate-and-peanut-butter cupcake from the galley.

In the days that had followed, he'd grown clearer, somehow. As though the sun had reached through a tiny clearing in a winter storm cloud. And yet . . . but yet . . . somehow . . . she sensed a hesitation fettering his outpouring of tales and recollections. Almost as though he was filling their dinner conversation with everything but that one detail he couldn't bring himself to share.

Not that she was about to complain. Afterwards, he had taken her to his bed, where he'd brought renewed gusto to his lovemaking.

Abigail packed away her art supplies. "Where are you headed?"

"No place in particular. I'm here to enjoy some seaside time before schools let out and the beaches are invaded."

They strolled toward the far end of the pier, where a pair of fishermen in tattered dungarees had drooped poles over the railing.

"You made the right choice leaving Warners," Abigail told her. "With Buzz dripping poison in Taplinger's ear every chance he gets, I'm impressed you lasted as long as you did."

Dripping poison? "I never figured out why he got himself so worked up over me."

They reached the pier's end. The anglers stared into the ocean, mute as dime-store mannequins, listening to the waves crash into the pilings.

An intriguing should-I-or-shouldn't-I hesitation crept across Abigail's face.

"What are you not telling me?" Nell asked.

"Does it matter now that you've quit?"

"Tell me everything and tell me immediately; otherwise, I'll toss you into the drink."

One of the nearby anglers snorted. Nell and Abigail shuffled along the railing until they were out of earshot.

"He's furious over *The Last Submarine*," Abigail said. "Positively seething."

"But why? Are you sure?"

Abigail nodded as though she were deliberating over breaking a confidence. Nell waited for her to conclude that yes, she should.

"A pal of mine works in the Owl Drug Store on Hollywood Boulevard at Sycamore. She gets me extra fries on the side. I was there a couple of months ago when Buzz walked in with some pal of his. Madder than a hornet, he was. Ranting about how *he* should be the big war hero at Warners. *He* should be the one with a movie made about his experience on Iwo Jima. But then along came Luke Valenti with his goddamned *Lanternfish*, and that was the end of that. Even worse, he got assigned to handle PR for *The Last Submarine*—the last picture he wanted to work on."

The onshore breezes were chillier than Nell had anticipated. She wrapped her arms around herself for warmth. "So he's a six-foot-two bunch of sour grapes?"

"The ever-lovin' sourest. And his pal sat there being Buzzard's punching bag."

"Who was he?"

"A screenwriter is my guess. He talked about how he'd worked up a treatment outlining Buzz's Iwo Jima experience, but all that work was for nothing. They also talked about someone called Rene Gagnon. Ever heard of that name?"

"I don't think so. What was the context?"

"The pal told Buzz, 'You're not Rene Gagnon, so it seems pointless running around town trying to convince people you are.' Buzz got all hot under the collar. He did *not* want to hear it." The wind whipped the ends of her scarf across her face; she grabbed them together and held them against her shoulder. "So I dropped in on the research department and asked them if they knew who this Gagnon guy was."

"And?"

"Get this: You know that famous photo of the Marines hoisting the flag on Iwo Jima? Rene Gagnon was the guy who ran it up Mount Suribachi."

"It wasn't Buzz?"

"Did you know the famous flag was the *second* one raised that day?"

Buzz had been lying this whole time? "There was *another* flag?"

"The first one went up earlier that day. That's the one Buzz carried up the hill. But nobody cares because the second one was bigger, so it made for a more spectacular photo, which is why it's more famous."

"So . . ." Nell struggled to gather her thoughts in light of this revelation, "Buzz . . . is . . ."

"Trust me, Buzz 'the Buzzard' Bryant is a dirty, lying, rat bastard, master bamboozler worthy of nobody's consideration. You're going on to greater things, while he's stewing in a rancid soup of his own resentment."

* * *

The foyer of the Beverly Theatre struck Nell as an interior decorator's idea of a bazaar in a clandestine corner of the Far East. "What did you think?" she asked Luke.

"Of what?"

She halted when she noticed he had lagged several steps behind her. "Did the postman not even ring once for you?"

They stopped in front of the CURRENTLY PLAYING display case. John Garfield was shown in profile, his arm wrapped around Lana Turner, who wore a tight tangerine dress. Nell was surprised they hadn't depicted her in that infamous two-piece white romper with matching turban that everybody had been talking about.

"I liked it," he said absently, then caught himself. "They burn up the screen like nobody's business." He ran his eyes down the display. "She's never looked sexier."

"Neither has he." Nell tapped the glass near Luke's alter-ego. "Are you still thinking about how much Buzz resents us?"

"I'm wondering if that's why he approved a poster for *The Last Submarine* with no sub in it." He pushed himself away from the cabinet when he spotted someone behind Nell. "This is a pleasant surprise."

Kathryn Massey and Marcus Adler were holding hands, which surprised Nell more than seeing them at a movie theater.

"We've been hoping we might bump into you," Marcus said.

"You two hadn't seen this movie yet?" Nell said. "It's been out since January."

Kathryn raised her hand. "Guilty as charged. I've been hinting for months about those persistent rumors flying around that John and Lana Turner were going at it hot and heavy during filming, but somehow I didn't get around to it. So I wanted to see if any of that chemistry ended up on the screen."

"I think we can all agree it does," Luke said.

"And then some," Kathryn added.

"Hold the phones," Nell said. "What did you mean that you've been hoping to bump into us?"

Kathryn and Marcus exchanged a grave look. "The Brown Derby is around the corner," she said. "Free for dinner?"

* * *

It didn't escape Nell's notice that Kathryn asked the maître d' for a quiet booth and ordered a round of Singapore Slings for the table.

"You guys come here often?" Kathryn asked.

"This is where we had our first date," Luke replied.

"Evidently it went well."

"As a matter of fact, we discovered Ingrid Bergman was dining alone and invited her to join us. We were shooting *Casablanca* and she was miserable because Bogie wasn't giving her much to work with, which came as no surprise because he was dealing with Mayo and all that that implies."

"He's a different person with Betty, isn't he? When he brought her to the Garden of Allah in the lead-up to getting married in Ohio—"

"Can we save the chit-chat for later?" Nell broke in. "I'd rather get back to how you were hoping you'd bump into us." That same heavy look passed between them again. "What's the big mystery?"

"Not so much a mystery as a . . ." Kathryn spun the Brown Derby matchbook between her fingertips until she settled on "tip-off."

"About what?" Luke asked.

"I was in my boss's office the other day and clapped my little peepers on a list he'd drawn up—" she tossed the matchbook aside "—of people he suspects are commies and pinkos."

"Based on what?" Nell asked.

"He's got a deranged bee in his bonnet about how all these commies are swarming Hollywood."

"Are they, though?" Luke asked.

"No!" Marcus interjected. "Despite what you might read between the dingy pages of *Reds in the Beds*."

"So this list," Nell said. "He's publishing it in the *Reporter*?"

"When I challenged him on it, he got all cagey. Refused to even so much as hint at his plans. What that tells me is that he will, but when he judges it's the right time to wreak the most damage."

"To whom?"

Kathryn scooped up the matchbook and started flipping it over again. "He might strike off some names and add others," she said, lowering her voice. "Or he might decide 'The hell with it' and publish it intact. Who knows? The list I saw named nearly forty people. I doubt they're all commies or pinkos, but statistically speaking, some of them probably are."

"It's not illegal to be a member of the Communist Party," Nell pointed out.

"Not yet, anyway," Marcus added.

"But here's what you need to know," Kathryn continued. "Three of the names that stuck out were John Garfield, Albert Maltz, and Michael Curtiz."

"The star, screenwriter, and director of *The Last Submarine*."

All four of them were silent as cadavers when a waiter arrived. The chatter of their fellow diners washed over them as he slid their Singapore Slings onto the table, paused a moment as though to ask if they were ready to order, but thought the better of it.

"Is there any chance it could be true?" Luke asked. "Not all three, obviously. But just one of them turning out to be a commie could scuttle our picture."

Marcus pushed his horn-rimmed glasses onto his head and rubbed the bridge of his nose. "Last night I attended a cocktail party thrown by a Russian writer, Konstantin Simonov. It was aboard a Soviet ship in Long Beach with a bunch of prominent Hollywood people, including Chaplin. And Garfield was there too. The party degenerated into a free-for-all. You'll be hearing about it in the papers tomorrow."

Kathryn tsked dismissively. "It took Wilkerson all of four seconds to hear about it, and another three seconds to give it a name: 'the Simonov Affair.' As far as he's concerned, it bolsters his theory, and so now Chaplin and Garfield are at the tippy-top of his list. Naturally, Hedda's going to have a field day. She's had her knives out for Chaplin for years. And now it's Garfield's turn."

"And Curtiz?" Luke asked. "Was he there too?"

Marcus shook his head.

"But he's on Wilkerson's list," Kathryn said, "because he directed *Mission to Moscow*, which was a jingoistic-level slice of pro-Russia propaganda."

"We made that when the Ruskies were our allies," Nell protested. "Of course the picture was pro-Russia. We all were!"

"If you're looking for logic, you're in the wrong booth."

So, Nell thought, pretty much everybody is a low-down, dirty skunk. Including Buzz. *Especially* Buzz. How often did I have to listen to him droning on and on about Iwo goddamned Jima, and it wasn't even true. Abigail's right, she decided. I'm better off without that job.

"From what I hear, Jack Warner wants to release *The Last Submarine* as soon as possible," Kathryn continued. "Wilkerson might not publish his list until after it comes out, in which case you can all relax. But I wanted you to be forewarned."

"You might want to tell Bogie," Marcus said.

"Don't tell me he's on the list," Luke said.

"No, but Hedda's been dogging him for years about being a commie—or a liberal, which in her mind amounts to the same thing. If Garfield gets accused, and you're good pals with Bogie, as well as being played by Garfield, both of you could find yourselves tainted with the commie brush."

"Guilt by association?"

"There goes your movie. There goes your war-hero reputation. There goes your singing career."

Luke turned to Nell, worry creasing his face. "We need to tell someone about this. Taplinger would be easier to see than Warner."

"No, no, no!" Kathryn threw up her hands. "I'm the only one who's seen Wilkerson's list. I told him he's playing with fire and an op-ed like that might end up burning *him* to a crisp instead. We had quite a dust-up over it. Still, this might all be for nothing. He might change his mind and drop the whole thing. But in case he doesn't, I thought you ought to know."

"Thank you," Nell said. "We appreciate that."

Kathryn lifted her glass in a toast. "Let's move onto a cheerier subject. Did any of you see that skywriting plane a couple of weeks ago? The one that wrote 'THE OUTLAW,' followed by two giant circles, each dotted in the center?"

"Who didn't?" Nell asked. "Poor Jane. I'd be mortified if my boss did that to me."

"Aren't you forgetting who owns her contract? When Howard Hughes is your boss, you have to be ready for anything."

* * *

Nell waited until they had passed the Chateau Marmont near the eastern end of the Sunset Strip before she asked Luke what she had been wanting to ask him all evening. "Is there anything you haven't told me about that day on the set of *The Last Submarine?*"

"Like what, fr'instance?"

"I don't know. I wasn't there." Her retort came out more snappish than she intended. "Just a feeling I've been getting, is all." There. That was better, albeit possibly too little, too late.

"It took a lot out of me," he said, after a protracted pause. "And now I wonder if the next time I smell bleach, I'll be thinking, 'Ugh! What else have I forgotten that's about to punch me in the neck?'"

"So there's nothing I need to know?" She shouldn't be pushing him this hard, but she couldn't help it. The prospect of Billy Wilkerson's list was starting to unravel her. If it ended up capsizing everything, she needed reassurance there were no secrets between them.

"I didn't say that."

To push him any harder was crossing a line, so she sat mutely with her hands folded in her lap.

Luke pulled to the curb outside the Garden of Allah Hotel and hit the brakes. The yellow-tinted glow from the neon sign spilled across them. She kept her eyes on the traffic inching past Schwab's.

"I hate that you can read me like a book," he said. "And I love it, too."

"You're not that hard to read—which is one of the things I love most about you."

He held up his injured finger and twisted it to the left, to the right, and back again.

"Is it getting worse?" She gulped. "They're not going to amputate the rest of it, are they?"

He assured her they weren't, then wryly added it might be easier if that were the case. She couldn't imagine what could be worse than amputation, but whatever was coming, she guessed she ought to get a sturdy grip on herself.

"I didn't lose my finger the way I've been assuming," he said. "It got stuck in a slamming door."

"Must have been a hell of a door."

"They're made to lock into place to cut off flooding, so yeah, they could stop a herd of stampeding bison."

"You got your hand caught in one? Sounds horrible."

Another long, excruciating pause. "It is—when your best pal shoved it hard as he could so that you'd have no choice but to leave him to go down with the ship."

"Didn't he send you to fetch the rope?"

"It was a distraction."

"You could have pulled him free, but he locked—oh, no."

"He never intended to get out alive."

"But that's—"

"Imagine if I told his parents."

"His very *Catholic* parents." The blazing headlights of an enormous truck filled the car as it roared past. "So it wasn't some stray Jap bullet." Even in the murky light, Nell could detect the apprehension stippling Luke's face. "Submarine hatch or Japanese slug —does it make that much of a difference?"

"I wasn't awarded my Navy Cross because somebody slammed a door on me." Luke's right knee bobbed up and down compulsively. "In theory, I'm supposed to give back my medals."

"But *The Last Submarine*—"

"It climaxes with the scene outside City Hall where Captain Stamina presents me with a medal for personal injury in the face of enemy fire—which we now know is a great, big, fat lie."

"Have you told Ethan about this?"

"*The Saturday Evening Post* and the Rockwell cover are a big deal for him. How could I burst his bubble? And on top of everything else, now I have to worry about this *Hollywood Reporter* list. What if it turns out all three of them are commies?"

The two of them sat there in silence, each of them sorting through the wide range of possible outcomes. None of them ideal.

"You should think about telling Ethan," she said. "It's only fair he knows that what he's writing isn't accurate. It might not be a big deal. It probably happens all the time—especially in celebrity memoirs. Don't forget, this town is built on misdirection and reinvention. He might shrug and say 'Big whoop-de-doo.' But it'll be an informed whoop-de-doo." She was relieved to see his spasming knee settle down. She flicked a fingernail at his steering wheel. "It's getting late and I'm plum tuckered out."

He thanked her as he brought the engine to life. Focusing now as he was on rejoining the Sunset Boulevard traffic, he failed to notice how her encouraging smile faded from her cheeks.

37

"Let me get this straight, Luke, ol' chap." Bogie eased his foot off the gas when Sunset Boulevard curved to the left as they entered Beverly Hills. "Tokyo Joe didn't shoot your finger off? You got it caught in a *hatch*?"

"It's called a door when it's *inside* a sub," Betty chided him. "And you pride yourself on being a sailor." She turned to Luke and Nell in the back seat. "It must have hurt like all get-out."

"Holy crap on a cracker, Valenti." In the rearview mirror, Bogie shot Luke one of his taunting leers. "And all this spilled out because you smelled the janitor's bleach?"

"They say the sense of smell is the strongest driver of memories," Betty put in.

"I remember those warnings about how seawater in batteries produces chlorine gas," Bogie said. "It was a big deal in our safety drills."

"They had batteries back then?" Betty asked. "Didn't you have to row long, wooden oars like they have in those biblical pictures?"

"My wife, the comedian. And they wonder why I drink." Bogie flicked his cigarette out his window. "Seriously though, Luke, what a horrible kick to the Balzac when it all came flooding back."

"The question is," Nell said, "does he give back his Navy Cross?"

"HELL, NO!" Bogie bellowed.

"I second that," Betty added. "What's done is done."

"So you're still okay about being in business with a fraud?" Luke asked.

"I'm not in business with your naval record, bucko."

Despite the rogue's gallery of gangsters and lowlifes he'd played on screen, the Humphrey Bogart that Luke knew was a man of high principles and lofty ideals. Luke liked to believe their friendship could withstand this recent revelation, but he had wanted to know for sure. He squeezed Nell's hand in relief.

"Speaking of which, how goes the search for potential material?"

Outside the car, the lights of the Beverly Hills Hotel twinkled in the early summer dusk. "You'd think that with all the novels, the plays, the short stories and magazine articles out there, it'd be easy to find a property to develop. But either there's no love interest, or it needs to be shot on location, which jacks up the budget, or it has a good opening scene but no story, or it's already been done, or someone's snapped up the rights already. I might have to recruit you as a reader."

"Just say the word."

"The main sticking point is distribution. Jack Warner'll hit the roof when I don't renew my studio contract so's I can start my own film company. So distributing through Warners is out. I must say, Harry Cohn's been swell while I've been filming *Dead Reckoning* at Columbia. I'm tempted to pitch a deal to him. What are your thoughts on that, *partner?*"

A rush of pleasure tingled up Luke's spine. *Partner?!* In a strictly legal sense, yes, they were. But Luke assumed Bogie would take the lead on all decisions. So being asked what he thought about distributing Santana Productions' movies through Columbia caught him off guard.

"Everybody says Cohn's an ass. Is there much point in jumping from one to another?"

"Warner is a buffoon who thinks he's a genius. Cohn's never forgotten he's a pool hustler who made good. But when he strikes a bargain, he sticks to it."

"That might suit Cohn," Luke said, "but will it benefit Santana in the long term?"

Luke's question gave Bogie pause. "And that," he said, after a moment or two, "is why I asked you to be my partner."

"Just promise me one thing. Our movies won't take twenty months to come out like *The Big Sleep*. You guys started filming before the Battle of Leyte Gulf, before Iwo Jima, before the Battle of the Bulge. And the movie still isn't out yet."

"Trust me," Bogie said, "we're all furious—Howard more than anyone—that Warners have dragged their feet. But they had so many war-themed movies in the bank that they felt they needed to burn through them first."

He merged onto Whittier Drive, then veered onto Linden.

"I hear Bugsy Siegel's girlfriend has taken a house on this street," Nell said. "Anybody know which one?"

"Nope," Betty responded. "And I don't want to. We almost didn't come to this preview. I mean, what if Bugsy invites himself over?"

Bogie parked the Cadillac across from the Hawkses' bricked driveway. Slim had invited "around twenty of our nearest and dearest" for tonight's *Big Sleep* showing. Several cars gleamed in the moonlight, all of them shiny-new and top-of-the-line pricey. She answered the door in a snug, knitted two-piece ensemble that showed off her athletic body. She angled her head over her right shoulder and called out to the rowdy gathering behind her. "The stars have arrived!" She backed into the foyer. "We engaged a bartender for the evening, but he's run to the store for extra ice. A certain numbskulled husband underestimated the inebriates we've summoned for tonight's clambake. The bar is in the living room. It's the size of Grant's Tomb, so you can't miss it."

The crowd was the effervescent mix Luke had envisioned. Statuesque women who had failed to set the screen on fire pretended to listen to husbands in expensive Sy Devore suits droning on and on about box office rental statistics and back-end points. Luke recognized a few faces who had appeared in previous Howard Hawks pictures, but the others looked like dwellers of legal offices and bank headquarters.

Around a half-hour after they'd arrived, Luke glimpsed Slim through the open kitchen door. She stood at an island arranging circles of pale cheese on saltine squares.

"Good evening," he said, "and thank you for recommending that ghostwriter."

"I look forward to reading the book."

"Ethan hasn't shown me any pages yet, but promised he'll meet the deadline."

"Who's Ethan?" Slim snapped a quartet of saltines and added them to the plate. "Your Simon and Schuster editor?"

"He's the writer you recommended." Luke stared at her blank, uncomprehending face. "Isn't he?"

"The man I suggested was Michael J. Reed. He's been eking out a subsistence in a cheap apartment down the misbegotten end of Hollywood Boulevard."

"What does he look like?"

Slim placed pickles cut into triangles on each slice of cheese. "Tall. Rangy. Intellectual. Like an undernourished Tennessee Williams. Judging from the distress on your face, I'd guess that doesn't match the chap you're working with?"

Luke gripped the edge of the kitchen counter, its glazed tiles cool to the touch. "It does not."

"I'm sure there's a perfectly reasonable explanation."

Luke hoped there was, but he was due at Norman Rockwell's

studio first thing in the morning and wouldn't have a chance to telephone Ethan until late that evening.

"You're happy with this writer?"

"I am." *Whoever he is.*

"So everything's worked out for the best." She picked up her platter and asked if he wouldn't mind taking the hors d'oeuvres around, reminding him it was a nifty way to meet people, and if he didn't care for them, he had a perfect excuse to keep circulating.

He stared at the triangular pickles sitting on circular cheese atop square crackers. Who had he been spilling his guts to? When he showed up tomorrow at the address Ethan had given him, would Norman Rockwell have heard of him? Was there even a manuscript?

* * *

Luke sprinted down the central corridor of the main building of the Otis College of Art and Design, his dress Navy cap in hand. The campus had been easier to locate than the studio where Rockwell was ensconced as the current artist-in-residence. He was late by only ten minutes, but Greg Whitley had warned, "Mr. Rockwell takes his work seriously and expects the same of his subjects."

The guy was staring at the clock inside Studio C when Luke knocked on the doorjamb. "This place is so big that a map in the parking lot would be handy for newcomers."

When Slim had described her writer friend, she could have been talking about Rockwell. The artist's handshake was unexpectedly and disappointingly flaccid. "You're here now." He led Luke to a ballet barre with a three-pronged hat rack behind it. At around chest height, he had tied a large feather duster so that it rested horizontally.

"I ought to warn you that my pliés and jetés are a little rusty."

Rockwell stared at him as though he'd spoken in Swahili. "All you need to do is look heroic."

Sheesh. So much for injecting a bit of humor to warm things up. This is the man who has painted some of the most emotionally stirring images of the past fifty years? Luke stood at the barre. "Sorry I was late, but it's summertime and there are no roaming students who I could ask directions from."

"I was disoriented the first few days I was here, so I understand." Rockwell's tone had softened, but his long, thin face remained mired in an inert scowl. He gestured at the barre. "It'll be the *Lanternfish*'s gun deck railing in the finished painting."

Luke canted his head toward the hat rack. "And this?"

"The conning tower next to the topside machine gun you manned when you let the Japs have it."

Machine-gun bullets had been crowding Luke's dreams. The weight of them in his hand. The sound of the brass casings slapping the deck. The acrid stink of hot metal. The vibrations running through his hands and up his arms as he anchored his thumbs on the V-shaped trigger.

Rockwell approached the barre, his broad forehead crinkling with concentration. "Here's what I want. You've run through your ammo. Your left arm is resting across the railing like this." He draped Luke's arm on the barre. "Hang your fingers down so that we can see the half-finger. That's it. Right hand to your hip. Right leg straight. Bend the left one. A little more." Rockwell stepped back. "Yes. Perfect."

"In case it makes a difference, I wasn't in this dress uniform."

Rockwell tapped his chin with a lead-smudged finger. "What were you wearing?"

"Standard-issue, beaten-up chambray Navy shirt rolled past the elbow, khaki shorts, canvas deck shoes. And an untrimmed beard. After the fourth week at sea, you give up caring. Who are you trying to impress? The guy in the bunk eight inches above you, who belches in his sleep all night?"

That provoked a smile. Not a face-splitter, but wide enough to soften the angular edges of Rockwell's lean face. "I tried to enlist in the Navy during the Great War, but they rejected me because I was ten pounds underweight."

"I know how their rejection stings," Luke said.

"I've had to squeeze this assignment in between the others I've got lined up. But when I read your profile in *Life* magazine, I thought, 'Yep. I get it.' I wiggled around it too."

"How?"

"Stuffed my bazoo with doughnuts, bananas, and as much milk as I could stomach. Did the trick, though. It's a fine feeling, isn't it, hearing them say, 'Welcome to the US Navy.'"

Had that been the reason for Rockwell's initial hostility? He didn't have time for this project, but had rearranged his busy schedule only to find the joker couldn't be punctual?

"It sure is," Luke told Rockwell. "How about I lose this jacket, untuck my shirt, and roll my sleeves up?"

"That would be helpful." Rockwell returned to the easel he'd set up next to a small table covered in pencils and tubes of oil paints.

"Sorry to be running later than the White Rabbit!" Ethan strode into the studio, hatless, with a pad and pen in one hand, and a necktie stenciled with apples in the other. He stuck out his hand for Rockwell to shake. "I'm Ethan Brophy. We spoke on the phone."

As Rockwell treated Ethan to a dead-slug handshake, Luke removed his uniform coat. "What are you doing here?"

He hoped the terse tone might convey his indignation, but it sailed over Ethan's head. "The *Post* wants me to pen an intro to the *Fateful Night*'s serialization. I thought, 'What could be better than to witness the painting of the cover?' But don't mind me. I'm here to gather atmosphere and a few facts."

"Facts, huh?" Luke yanked his shirt out of his trousers and

pulled off his necktie. "Is that another word for 'truth'? Because I'm not convinced you're familiar with the concept."

Confusion flitted across Ethan's face. "Hasn't there been a free flow of information between us since day one?"

Luke bent over the ballet barre and adopted the pose Rockwell had composed. "Has there?"

The scratching and scraping of Rockwell's pencil filled the silence that yawned between Luke and Ethan—or whatever his name was.

"Honesty is an interesting word choice," Ethan said, "given how prominently your stump is on display. Is the hat rack a thirty-caliber or a fifty? Maybe the four-inch deck cannon?"

Confessing the real events of that night had seemed the right thing to do, but that was before Slim had asked "Who's Ethan?" Had the two of them been alone, Luke would have pounced. But with Rockwell standing there, he swallowed the clever retort he itched to fling back.

Rockwell's hand swooped and slid around the canvas. "If you've come up with a better idea, now's the time to speak up."

"We're just kidding around," Luke said.

Rockwell's face fell into a stern reproof. "I heard wittier badinage at FDR's funeral."

"And I heard an interesting twist when I was at the Hawkses' place." Luke saw Ethan's shoulders twitch. "Slim was surprised to hear I've never heard of Michael J. Reed."

There was a long pause. "Some answers require lengthy explanations."

"Lieutenant!" Rockwell barked. "Stop dropping your chin. Remember, you're looking at the *Toyotomi Maru*."

"My war record might be sunk, too, if I continue to trust it to the wrong people."

"You haven't," Ethan said thickly.

"Mr. Rockwell, I'm sorry to interrupt." A young girl in a black beret hovered at the doorway. "You've got a phone call in the main office. Long distance. Indianapolis. Someone from *The Saturday Evening Post* insisted I come get you. It appears there's a problem with your Statue of Liberty cover. Something about the workmen on the torch."

Rockwell threw down his pencil. "Gentlemen, I'll be back as soon as I can. Whatever beef you two have going on, please take this opportunity to settle it during my absence." He strode out of the room.

Luke straightened up. "Is your name even Ethan?"

"I don't blame you for being upset. I would have confessed sooner or later."

"Or only when cornered?"

"Here's the God's honest truth: I've been sharing a crappy little apartment with Mike ever since I mustered out. I had no money; he had a comfortable couch. I spent months and months trying everything I could think of to get a foothold in the business. Nothing worked. Nothing took hold. I've had trouble settling down after they released me from the Army hospital after Monte Cassino."

"You were with the Thirty-Fourth?"

Sailing endless stretches of empty Pacific had provided Luke with plenty of time to catch up on news. The actions of the 34th Infantry Division in the mountains around Monte Cassino southeast of Rome were renowned as one of the most admirable accomplishments of the entire war, and had opened the way to the Allies liberating the Eternal City.

Ethan nodded. "Going through a deathtrap like that affects you." He tapped his right temple. "I could get nothing started. Then Mike caught a terrific break punching up *Road* scripts at Paramount. He was pulling in six times what he had been earning, so he moved out. I was alone, broke, and living in a dive I couldn't afford when Slim Hawks called. She explained why she was calling and gave me all the details."

"And you thought, 'Mike doesn't need the job' and you saw your chance."

Ethan flinched. "I was planning to tell you, honest I was, but I wanted to wait until after I'd finished the manuscript so that you could see for yourself before you canned me."

"But you haven't shown me a damned word this whole time."

Ethan rushed to the barre as though it were the *Lanternfish*'s last life preserver. "The brutality of war, it never left me. Since I was discharged, I've avoided thinking about anything connected with that miserable slugfest at Monte Cassino. But I hadn't thought about how being stuck in a rut was connected to avoiding my war experience—until you came along. Writing about someone *else's* war has been unbelievably cathartic, and has led to new opportunities, including a book contract with Simon and Schuster and the possibility of a job at *The New York Times*' LA bureau." The man's face was lit up like a Sunset Strip billboard. What was Luke supposed to say to this guy who had been through Monte Cassino and survived intact?

"I mean, we're talking about *The New York* goddamn *Times!*" Ethan's curls shook as his head bobbed with enthusiasm. Luke glimpsed the chunk missing from the lower half of his left ear. Okay, so maybe the guy hadn't survived Monte Cassino wholly intact.

Rockwell loped back into the room. His eyes bounced from Luke to Ethan, standing on opposite sides of the barre. "Have you two reached a détente? May I proceed with the job at hand?"

Ethan raised his eyebrows at Luke. *Have we?*

"Let's get on with it." Luke resumed his pose. "Someone in this room is waiting to hear from the *Times*."

38

With its sparsely clad chorus girls and comics skirting the legal side of blue, Florentine Gardens wouldn't have been Nell's first choice to launch the Arlo Nash Orchestra recording. But Arlo was poker pals with the owner, so she had kept her misgivings to herself.

In her dressing room mirror, the diamante-dotted peach dress she'd taken a chance on at the I. Magnin store on Wilshire looked as bright as the orange sherbet at C.C. Brown's, and the good Lord knew how it was so vivid it verged on garish.

"Stop second-guessing your outfit." Betty fanned away her cloud of cigarette smoke. "It looks great."

The clock above the clothes rack showed six forty-five. "The promo materials should have been here by now." She looked at Luke. "Should I be worried?"

"Because they're fifteen minutes late?"

"Because Buzz is in charge of them." Nell had already suffered the indignity of watching Taplinger put Buzz in charge of PR for *The Last Submarine*, but now that she was free of Warner Brothers altogether, she couldn't help resenting how she was still reliant on him to do his job properly. Would she never be free of this self-serving baboon?

Luke jumped up from his chair as though Tony had lit a firecracker under it. "Come on," he said to his brother, "let's go scouting." Leaving the dressing room door open, they rushed into the organized bedlam of the backstage area.

"Those three standees were in the foyer when I came back from lunch this afternoon," Abigail said. "All Buzz had to do was make sure someone from the delivery pool picked them up. I should've stuck around instead of hotfooting it over here."

"It's not your responsibility," Nell told her. "I'm glad you've joined us."

The girl had a calm, almost serene way about her. Nell imagined it would be difficult to throw her off-kilter. Maybe it was how she'd been able to get through that *Casablanca* situation.

"These standees," Bogie said, lighting a fresh Chesterfield from the butt of his wife's, "what are they of?"

"There's a five-foot-by-five-foot version of the album cover, the *Last Submarine* movie poster, and a reproduction of the Norman Rockwell portrait Luke posed for last week." She glanced at the empty doorway. "We're cutting it awfully fine. I go on at seven-thirty."

Abigail stuck her nose into the corridor. "Luke's coming!" She stepped aside as he appeared, carrying a painter's easel under one arm and the album reproduction in the other.

"One out of three is better than nothing," Luke said.

"Where's Tony?" Audrey asked.

"One of the chorus girls out there used to be at Warners. She begged him to fix her hair." He tapped the enlarged album cover. "Looks good!"

The album's name—"Swinging on a Star"—blazed across the top in crimson. Beneath it lay *The Arlo Nash Orchestra* against a large gold glittering star. In the bottom right corner, a photo of

Nell with the caption "Vocalist Nell Davenport and her #1 hit, *Every Fifth Word*, as featured in Warner Bros.' *The Last Submarine*."

Somehow, Jerry Wald had squeezed a tidy pile of bucks out of someone's budget. They had come at a hefty price, so she was relieved to see what a fine job the studio had done. As the orchestra's PR manager, tracking down the other two was up to her.

"I wish I had Buzz's home telephone number," she said. "With Warners sponsoring this launch, Taplinger's bound to ask questions if they're absent from the publicity photos. And that's not a conversation I relish."

"Would it be helpful to know Buzz lives up the street from here?" Abigail asked.

"How do you know that?"

"One of his first assignments was the *Of Human Bondage* remake. He fumbled the ball by missing a *Variety* deadline. I was the poor sap ordered to traipse down to his place so that he could deliver them himself and explain why they were late."

"How about you and I run up there now?" Luke suggested. "Knock on his door. See if he answers."

Abigail shook her head. "No sirree. He flew off the handle like *I* was the one who screwed up. I've avoided him ever since and I'd prefer to keep it that way."

"You'll be faster alone, anyway." Nell turned to Abigail. "Do you remember his address?"

"No, but his street is only two blocks east. North side of Hollywood Boulevard with a shoe repair on the corner. His building's on the left, with three miniature palms out front. Name on the mailbox. You can't miss it."

Nell pushed Luke out the door. "Run!"

Was it always going to be this hard on the tour, too? She had assumed that once they'd hit the road, they would settle into a routine where the only challenge was finding their hotel each night in a strange town.

"Everything okay?"

Arlo walked in with Peyton trailing behind. Peyton was in the standard penguin suit that all the band members wore, but Arlo had gussied himself up in one of his snappier pinstripes, his graying hair pomaded back, and radiating the type of aftershave balm that signaled he'd had a professional shave within the last hour. He stood in front of the album cover. "My goodness, didn't this turn out well? And the others?"

"Missing," Nell admitted. "But we're on the hunt."

Arlo frowned. "Warners shelled out a lot of clams for tonight. They'll expect their money's worth."

Bogie swung to his feet. "You've got a pair of Warner stars right here. Betty and I would be more than happy to pose for the press. Not to toot my own horn, you understand, but a photo of us will ensure the Arlo Nash Orchestra and Florentine Gardens get splashed around the columns tomorrow morning."

"I'm all for getting splashed anywhere and everywhere."

This statement came from a man in a shiny suit, reeking of brilliantine. He ran Florentine Gardens with a fawning zeal that might've worked well on some of those chorines in the wings, but he made Nell's skin crawl.

"The other two standees haven't showed up yet," Arlo explained. "In case they go AWOL, Mr. and Mrs. Bogart were offering themselves up as a distraction. Being Warner Brothers stars, they would—"

"But John Garfield and Joan Leslie star in that submarine movie," the manager said. "Why aren't they here? Especially Garfield. The press—"

"NO!" The word shot-putted out of Nell.

Mr. Brilliantine's reasonable suggestion sailed too close to Billy Wilkerson's red-tinged wind. He hadn't published his list of commies yet. June was ticking by fast, but with any luck, *The Last Submarine* might come out before he catapulted that bombshell into the skies over Hollywood.

"Suit yourself," he said. "I have a house to open, so I'll leave you to it."

Nell waited until he was out of earshot. Her gaze bounced from face to face. *Crap, crap, crap. I have to tell them. Sorry, Kathryn, but I can't risk it.* "Keep this under your hats—and I mean good 'n' tight—but John Garfield is a liability. I have it on good authority that Billy Wilkerson is planning to publish a list of people he suspects are commies. Several names connected with *The Last Submarine* are on it."

"Garfield's one of them?" Bogie asked.

"It is. And if his photo is circulating—"

Betty snorted. "I bet Buzz Bryant isn't on that list. He'd happily sink a bunch of careers."

"But *The Last Submarine* is a Warner picture," Peyton said. "Whose side is Buzz on?"

"I can guarantee you Buzz Bryant is on Buzz Bryant's side," Abigail said. "If you ask me, it's no coincidence that the two missing standees are the movie poster and the portrait of its hero."

Abigail's observation was circumstantial, but convincing. This was also a guy who'd worked in publicity for years and knew how to attract maximum attention.

Luke flew back into the room. "I found his place."

"And?" Nell pressed her hands together as though in prayer.

"He wasn't there. But the building supervisor saw Buzz lug some posters into a *Hollywood Reporter* truck."

"See?" Abigail said. "He's up to something. It might have nothing to do with that list—"

"You told them?" Luke asked, wide-eyed.

"The suggestion came up to get John and Joan in here to stand in for the missing artwork," Nell explained, "so I had to put the kibosh on that."

"Hello in there," Tony called from the open door. "A gaggle of press are loitering out here and looking antsy."

Nell checked in the mirror for lipstick on her teeth. "Time to sparkle, people!"

She asked Luke and Peyton to haul the huge album cover into the wings as she greeted the knot of press. "Gentlemen! Hello, and thank you for coming out tonight." She searched for familiar faces of columnists and photographers she had dealt with during her studio PR days, but she'd met none of these people. How had everything changed so quickly?

Playing hostess, she shuffled herself and Luke, Bogie and Betty, Arlo and Peyton in as many combinations around the album cover as she could invent. It wasn't hard to decipher Arlo's simmering pout. The Bogarts' long-awaited screen re-teaming ensured that most of the spotlight swung away from Nell and the Orchestra. Though unhappy the Bogarts were hogging the lion's share of the limelight, Arlo was also smart enough to know that grabbing hold of the coattails of the nearest movie stars was the best way to publicize the album. He was lucky Bogart and Betty were here at all—*and* willing to pose.

"Hey, Nell." Peyton drew up behind her, close enough that she could feel his breath on her ear. "Half-hour to show time."

"We've got a show to do," she told the reporters, "so you should go find yourselves a table."

She shook a few hands from some of the guys, and accepted break-a-legs from others—honestly, who *were* these people?—and, discreetly as she dared, shepherded them toward the door that led to the main room.

As she turned toward the stage, she glimpsed a figure slipping through the gaggle of showgirls in their skimpy daisy costumes. He had Buzz's bulky frame, but the lights hadn't come up yet. It might've been him. But what was he doing backstage when he'd last been seen loading the missing standees into a *Hollywood Reporter* van?

She wasn't due on stage until fifteen minutes into the program. She had time to investigate.

Don't be ridiculous, she told herself. Who are you? Nancy Drew? And what, exactly, are you going to do? Sneak around in your high heels because some stagehand resembles the guy who hates your boyfriend? And what happens if you catch your new sparkly dress on a stray nail? There'll be no time to change into the back-up outfit—not that you brought one.

She wended her way past the bags, crates, and props until she arrived at the burgundy velvet curtain hanging behind the bandstand. She gingerly lifted it off the floor and peered under it.

It was him, all right. No mistake. Okay, Nancy Drew. What now? She thought of Luke and everything he'd been through. She ducked inside the backstage area.

Buzz Bryant stood ankle deep in a jumble of cables and wires, too distracted by studying each one, following its route, to notice her. He stooped over and picked up a gray cable with a thin orange stripe. He reached around to his back pocket and pulled out some sort of tool. Nell squinted to see it better, but he was still too far away. She chanced a couple of cautious steps forward. A silver blade glinted in the stage lights. He was holding a pair of sturdy wire cutters. Worse than that, he held her microphone cable. The jackass was out to sabotage *her*.

She followed the cable in his hand through the tangle of wires carpeting the floor to the rear of the stage, where it snaked under the backdrop curtain. She reached it in three steps, grasped it with both hands, and yanked it with all the force she could summon. The cable whipped through his fingers, catching him off guard. It dropped to the floor along with the wire cutter.

"What the—?" He turned to glower at her. "You."

"Yes, me." Nell threw back at him. "I know about the standees, and I know about the *Hollywood Reporter* van."

He picked up the wire cutters and snipped them at her menacingly. "If these can cut cables, imagine what damage I can do to a pipsqueak little girlie like you."

She threw back at him, "You don't scare me." It was all bluster and swagger, of course. Those wire cutters looked sharper and sharper with every step closer he took. What could she do to stop him? Pitch a shoe? The heels were sharp, but she'd have to be a better pitcher than Spud Chandler if she were to hit the bastard where it would do the most damage. And besides, they were expensive, and she'd had them dyed to match her dress.

If she didn't do something, though, he'd keep coming at her.

"As soon as I figure out the rest," she taunted, "I'm going to blab it to anyone who'll listen. Starting with Taplinger."

It did the trick—with only ten feet to spare.

Buzz jabbed an accusing finger at her. "I'm not done with you."

"I suggest you take a hike—"

"Nell!" Peyton's voice rang out. "We're about to start."

Buzz shot her a resentful glower before spinning around and lumbering toward the far end of the stage.

Peyton stood at the backdrop curtain, a trumpet dangling from his fingers. "Who was that?"

"I'll explain later." She plugged her microphone cord back into its socket and picked through the tangle of cables until she reached him at the curtain.

"Do we need to call security? Do you want to delay the show? Because if you—"

She hushed him with a menacing finger as she headed for the curtain. There was no way in hell she'd give Buzz the satisfaction of missing her cue.

39

The day after Nell's launch party, the headline on page three of Luke's *Hollywood Citizen-News* read:

ARLO NASH SWINGS ON A STAR
And his cute vocalist, too!

Nobody in the packed audience would have guessed that mere minutes prior to her entrance, Nell had been threatening some crackpot. What a trouper, singing the dickens out of those songs as though she hadn't a care in the world. But Luke had known something had gone astray. He'd noticed the brittle piquancy lacing her voice as soon as she'd launched into "Straighten Up and Fly Right," and how she'd doggedly refused to look at him until she was halfway through "Every Fifth Word."

It hadn't been until the drive home after the show that Nell had told him of her backstage encounter with Buzz. He had threatened to turn his car around and head back to the son of a bitch's apartment, but Nell had had enough by then. "What're you going to do?" she'd asked him. "Pound on his door in the middle of the night, wake up all the neighbors, one of whom will call the cops. Suddenly it's a three-ring circus at two o'clock in the morning. Who needs that?"

A better tactic, they'd decided, was to confront Buzz in front of witnesses. But he hadn't reported for work. Nor had he called in sick.

Luke turned the page to a report on how Bugsy Siegel had bought a parcel of land from Billy Wilkerson in the gambling town people had been talking about lately, Las Vegas, where they planned to open a casino. Luke was still wondering who on earth would drive all the way out to the Nevada desert just to play a hand of cards when his phone rang.

"Good morning, Lieutenant." Luke's body jerked involuntarily when he heard Jack Warner's secretary on the line. "You've been summoned."

"I suppose that means immediately?"

"Is there any other time?"

* * *

When Luke walked into Warner's office, the mogul had set his mouth into a flat line. "We want you to explain yourself."

The "we" he was referring to was Nell's old boss, Robert Taplinger, and Blayney Matthews, the taciturn head of studio security who'd been chummy with Gus's father and whom Luke wasn't inclined to trust for a moment. Luke took Warner's third guest chair, sifting through the possibilities of what he was here to explain himself about.

The Last Submarine?
Fateful Night?
Rockwell portrait?
Those missing standees?

Why would any of these developments have angered Jack Warner so much that he'd summoned Taplinger and Matthews, too?

"Well, sir," Luke prevaricated, "if you could be a little clearer—"

"For chrissakes, Valenti, how long have you known about this blacklist?"

The only surprising facet of Wilkerson's list was that it had remained a secret for as long as it had. "As far as I know, it's not a blacklist, per se. Nobody is forbidding—"

"Why the hell didn't you tell me, or Taplinger, or Matthews what you knew? Be careful how you answer that. Your job hangs in the balance."

Sitting at the apex of the Hollywood food chain, Warner might have heard about Wilkerson's list from any number of tattletales keen to curry favor. But instead, he'd come to Luke. Luke couldn't imagine how anybody could have overheard that conversation at the Brown Derby, but Hollywood walls contained a thousand ears. Or had the snitch eavesdropped on Nell at the Florentine Gardens?

"Out with it," Warner demanded. "You think we've got all morning to hold a staring contest?"

Kathryn had been clear that neither Luke nor Nell could tell anyone about the list. That was all very well in theory, but Nell had had to tell the gang in her dressing room. She could trust them, but could Luke trust this ogre and his boot-licking lackies? Nope, nope, and nope.

"It was an accidental eavesdropping in a stall in the Brown Derby men's room."

"Yes? And?"

Luke should have known better than to hope his vague confession would have satisfied his boss. "I don't know there's much more I can tell you without reading between the lines."

"Start reading," Matthews growled.

"From what I could gather, it appears that a list is being drawn up."

"A list of?"

"Pinkos and commies. Actual and suspected."

"Drawn up by who?" Matthews asked.

"It would only be pure conjecture."

Warner spluttered impatiently. "Then I suggest you conjecture before my patience runs out."

Sorry, Kathryn, but these guys are the three most powerful men on the lot. I have to give them something. A name pinged around Luke's mind. "Buzz Bryant."

"BUZZ?" Taplinger yelled. "That's a hell of an accusation, Lieutenant. He's been with us since Cagney in *The Public Enemy*. What makes you suspect it's him?"

"For starters, he hasn't shown up for work today. Hasn't called in sick. Completely disappeared."

"S'at true?" Warner snapped at Taplinger.

"Maybe he can't get to a telephone." Taplinger's suggestion came out limper than a used rubber.

"He was healthy enough last night," Luke said, "when he showed up at Florentine Gardens and tried to sabotage the Arlo Nash record launch."

"That's who Nell Davenport sings with, isn't it?" Matthews asked.

"Correct. And Buzz tried to attack her before the show."

Luke expected Taplinger to explode with accusations that he was being outrageous and ridiculous. He remained mute and motionless, though, so Luke continued. "Nell had organized a greet-the-press photo opportunity in front of the enlarged version of the album cover."

"I saw the pictures this morning." Warner snapped. "Everything looked fine."

"Two other standees were made: the *Last Submarine* poster, and a reproduction of my Norman Rockwell portrait. But they went missing. When I learned Buzz's apartment wasn't far away, I ran up there. The building manager told me he saw Buzz put them onto a truck owned by—" Luke paused for effect "—*The Hollywood Reporter*."

Warner and Taplinger didn't bother to cloak the chagrin that passed between them.

"Looks to me," Luke said, "as though you have added two plus two."

Taplinger cleared his throat. "Those missing standees were recovered early this morning."

"May I ask where?"

"In the trash cans out back of one-twenty-four West Sixth Street."

"In downtown?" Luke asked. Well now, the plot had thickened like old glue. "It shouldn't be hard to learn who has offices in that building."

Matthews crossed one leg over the other and rolled an unlit cigar he'd been holding between his fingers. "The headquarters of the LA branch of the Communist Party."

"Are you a commie?" Warner's question came at Luke in a resentful growl.

"Absolutely not." Luke ran a finger around the cuff of his Navy jacket to underline his point. "But even if I was, I'm not your primary concern right now."

"Keep talking," Matthews said.

"John Garfield, Albert Maltz, and Michael Curtiz are likely to appear on Wilkerson's list. If that happens, the *Lanternfish* might sink all over again."

40

Nell took Luke's arm as they stepped out of La Monica Ballroom and onto the Santa Monica pier. A sea breeze blew through the cloudless summer sky, lifting her wide-brimmed hat. "Whoa! I should have gone with a turban."

They stopped at the railing and took in the majestic sight of battleships, destroyers, aircraft carriers, gunboats, cruisers, and frigates fanning out across Santa Monica Bay.

The anticipation of Fleet Week had been building in LA for months. It was a chance for civilians to tour various ships and glimpse into how their husbands, boyfriends, brothers, and sons had experienced the war. The crews seized a rare opportunity to enjoy the delights and attractions of a large city. Being in Los Angeles made it all the more delightful and attractive, not just for the smartly dressed uniformed sailors but for every single girl between Santa Monica and San Bernardino.

But one specific vessel had kicked Nell's publicity generator into motion—thanks to Tristan. She and Luke had been on a double date with him and Gus, wolfing down hot fudge sundaes at C.C. Brown's, when Tristan had asked Luke, "Did you know the *Lanternfish*'s sister ship will be in town for Fleet Week?"

"The *Viperfish* will be here?" Luke had blanched whiter than his vanilla ice cream. Visiting a movie mock-up had sent him tumbling down a rabbit hole of unearthed memories, so what might crop up if he toured an exact twin? Nell hadn't been sure. But the promotional opportunity had been too good to ignore, so she had organized a concert by the Arlo Nash Orchestra, featuring the girl portrayed by Joan Leslie in *The Last Submarine*, which was set on the *Lanternfish*, whose sister was moored at Santa Monica pier during Fleet Week.

Ordinarily, it would be an event the Warner PR team would put together. But Buzz was now MIA, so Nell had taken charge and asked questions later.

They had completed the daunting sound check. With room for five thousand people on their hard maple wood dance floor, La Monica was the biggest ballroom on the West Coast. Unless she played Radio City Music Hall one day, it would likely be the biggest crowd she would ever play, so every detail had to be right on the money. Checking the acoustics had taken them longer than she had expected, but Luke was a patient man with plenty to read.

Walter Winchell had broken the news that the mysterious author of *Reds in the Beds* was Clifford Wardell, the head of Paramount's writing department. By lunchtime Wardell had been fired. According to Tristan, the pulpy novel's NJN movie studio was a thinly veiled MGM, which meant that its writing department head, a senior member of the Communist Party called Eugene Markham, was a veiled Marcus Adler. So Hollywood's eyes were turning MGMward. If Wilkerson were going to publish his list of alleged commies and pinkos, wouldn't he do it now?

"Look!" Nell pointed to the steps that led down to where the *Catalina* steamer picked up day-trippers.

Luke nodded, but said nothing.

"Is it weird for you to see the *Viperfish* here?"

"It's like seeing a ghost ship."

"It's open for public inspection." She ran her finger along the ribbons pinned to his uniform, and around his Navy Cross. "Free admission to military personnel."

"What if there's a guy in the radio room who's a dead ringer for me?"

He had tried to pose his question in a light singsong, but Nell could tell it was an effort. He backed away and headed across the pier toward the rollercoaster, and she followed. They watched as the lead car crawled over the top, then plummeted into a steep dip.

"Sometimes I wonder if Ethan had the right idea, not wanting to think about the war ever again," Luke said.

"You're not looking forward to *The Last Submarine* opening?"

"A glitzy premiere of a movie all about us? It doesn't get any more exciting than that. I hope it's good, and earns good box office, but I'm ready to think about something else."

"Like Santana Productions?"

"Bogie said he might recruit me as a reader. I keep offering, but I suspect he considers himself a more experienced judge of material."

"Which he is," Nell conceded. "Or maybe he's set on being the one to find his very first independent project. Give him time."

Luke was still taking her advice on board when a familiar face approached them.

"They told me at La Monica I might find you out here."

Kathryn Massey was holding onto her straw cartwheel hat the same way Nell was. She looked a little pale and was wearing only one glove.

"Good God!" Nell exclaimed. "Winchell's kicked your hornet's nest, hasn't he?"

"He's a creep whose main concerns are scoops, headlines, and rumors. In that order. I want to think his comeuppance will trip him up any day now, but I'm not holding my breath."

"How's Marcus bearing up?" Luke asked.

"The bigwigs are grilling him as we speak." She let the screams of roller coaster riders blow past them. "I volunteered to cover your show today because I wanted to tell you that it's happening tomorrow."

"Wilkerson's list?" Nell asked.

"He was at Santa Anita yesterday, so I snuck into his office and read the galleys for his *TradeView* column. He's calling it *A VOTE FOR STALIN*. It's more of a general warning about the spread of communism in the film industry, so it's not as bad as I feared."

"That's good, right?" Luke asked.

Kathryn seesawed her hand. "While I was there, I also saw an early draft of a follow-up article in which he lists actual names of screenwriters he believes are commies."

"And?"

"Albert Maltz was on it."

Drat it. Maybe the public wouldn't care that *The Last Submarine* had been written by some guy they'd never heard of whose name had appeared in a trade paper they didn't subscribe to.

"Mr. W. got all worked up after someone discovered missing standees in the Communist Party's trash. I should tell you—"

"*The Last Submarine* poster and my Rockwell portrait?" Luke asked.

"How did you know that?"

"Because they were last seen in a *Hollywood Reporter* van."

"Interesting." Kathryn blinked several times. "What's the bet he's pulling so-called evidence from any tenuous direction he can? At any rate, I've now got seven hundred phone calls to make before your show, so I need to find a secluded telephone booth far from all this commotion."

"The Georgian Hotel has a bank of phones in the lobby," Luke said.

Kathryn thanked him and hurried off.

"For someone with all that going on," Nell said, "she's remarkably composed. I wonder, though, if she noticed she's missing a glove." She caught Luke staring at the *Viperfish*. "Tempted?"

"I was thinking about Buzz."

"You think he'll pop up here?"

"Cranks like him seldom stay hidden for long."

They crossed to the northern side of the pier, where only seven people were waiting to enter the submarine. Without comment, Luke launched himself down the steps and joined the line.

"Do you suspect he'll try something?" Nell asked when she caught up with him.

"The *Lanternfish* is at the bottom of the Pacific." Luke rubbed the stump of his missing finger. "He might see the *Viperfish* is the next best thing—JESUS!" He inspected his stump more closely. "It's killing me."

The sailor stationed at the forward hatch saluted Luke, but didn't appear to recognize him. The metal ladder taking them into the bowels of the ship was narrow and hostile to high heels, but not irksomely long. Nell stepped off it and looked around.

Oh, my. How cramped it was down here. Barely enough space to turn around. And a hundred different corners, shelves, levers, and knobs to bang one's head on, whack an elbow, or stub a toe.

Luke rested a hand against a silvery-gray torpedo stowed in its rack. "The length of these things surprised me." He sounded so far away. "Twenty feet, six inches. No wonder they can blow holes the size of a delivery van in their targets." He landed the side of his fist against a section of the wall at around shoulder height. "On the outside is the bow plane. We lost ours in the first Japanese strike. The first one crippled us. The second one killed us."

He swallowed so hard that Nell could see his Adam's apple bob up and down.

A pair of giggly shopgirl types started down the ladder. Luke led Nell into the adjoining room.

"The wardroom." He rapped his knuckles on a rectangular table fixed to the floor with a thick metal pipe. "It's where the officers eat." Biting down on his lower lip, he stared at it longer than he needed to.

Holy cow, how did those men stand being squished into this tin can? Talk about cabin fever. No room. No privacy. All the while knowing that you can't climb up to the surface for a breather because there's two hundred feet of water above you and God only knows how many feet below. Nell sniffed at the metallic tang in the air. Iron mixed with paint mixed with oil. *How did they breathe this air? Not to mention the collective stink of fifty men without a woman to keep them in check.*

She shivered. "What's next?"

They stepped into a larger room. Finally, some breathing space. Luke tapped a shiny metal tube. "Above us is the conning tower—"

A sailor in his dress white uniform jumped out from behind the periscope. "Warner Boy!"

Luke's face glowed with delight. "Jigs, you old so-and-so!" He slung an arm around Nell's shoulders. "This is my Nell! Honey, this is Jigs. He was our radar guy, and one of the first faces I saw when I came to on the hospital ship."

"*The* Nell? Pleased to meetcha." He pumped her hand.

She smiled, looking back and forth from him to Luke. "Jigs. Warner Boy. So everybody really did get a nickname?"

"Only the ones we liked," Jigs replied.

Nell watched a slow-motion double-take sprawl across Luke's face. *How could he have lived in such close quarters with so many men and not know they liked him?*

The giggling salesgirls and their boyfriends joined them in the periscope area. With Luke now shooting the breeze with his crewmate, Nell stepped into the next chamber.

It was the radio room.

Packed wall-to-wall with equipment, leaving little floor space, it created a stifling claustrophobia that weighed down on Nell. She thought of how Luke sensed the vibrations through his back when Christopher spoke. Whenever Luke had talked about it, she'd thought how constricting it must have been. So stifling. But now she understood that this kind of proximity could also build such a tight camaraderie with someone that you'd do anything for them. Luke was lucky to have experienced that—even if the outcome had been so dreadful.

Nell swiped a palm across her forehead; it came away sticky and moist. Was this how claustrophobia felt? She shuffled past the washroom and showers, and through the engine room, where she was relieved to find the ladder leading to the aft access hatch. Climbing onto the deck, she drank in the fresh sea air.

The line to tour the *Viperfish* was now a checkerboard of Navy uniforms and pretty girls in light summer dresses. Farther down, a band played rousing military marching music. Behind them was an elaborate backdrop of bunting, flags, and banners flapping in the breeze.

Nell returned to the pier and stood against the railing that faced the wide ribbon of sand stretching north to Malibu. Jumping June bugs! Sailing on a submarine was even more dismal than she had imagined. How did those fellows not go screwy? She now understood how well those *Last Submarine* preview scenes had captured the grittiness of day-to-day life. If the rest of the movie were as realistic, it was going to make one hell of a picture. All the more reason to ensure it escaped the stink of communism.

"Hello in there?" Tony's voice scuttled Nell's thoughts.

"I told you!" Carol said. "She didn't even see us."

Tony's daughter wore a bright yellow cotton dress. "I'm so sorry," Nell told her. "How did I miss your pretty outfit?"

It wasn't just Tony and Carol who had approached her. Audrey was with them, and Avery, too. He was gussied up in his best Sunday suit, and held a hefty brown cardboard cylinder, the type PR departments shipped posters in. "What have you got there?"

"I'll present it to you after the show."

"Please don't make me wait. I've been down there." She

pointed to the *Viperfish*. "Gave me the heebie-jeebies, so I need some perking up."

Avery removed the cardboard stopper and pulled a canvas from the cylinder. He unfurled it and asked Tony to hold the other end.

He'd painted her bathed in a golden-pink spotlight on the stage of the Cocoanut Grove wearing Gwendolyn Brick's ivy-print dress. "My debut!" She clapped her hands together. "Oh, Avery! It's gorgeous. But—wait. Did you paint this? Your right hand... it's—the doctors—"

"Those quacks said nothing about my left one. I used to be somewhat ambidextrous back when I was a little kid. But those horrible nuns would scream, 'Using the left hand is a sign of the devil!' They beat it out of me until I'd forgotten."

"You've taught yourself to be left-handed again?"

"Honestly, I can't believe how quickly it came back."

Nell rolled up the canvas and inserted it back into the cardboard cylinder. "I'll treasure it forever."

"I've got something to show you too," Tony said. "Only this one ain't so fun." He produced a handwritten leaflet on light blue paper.

"Do NOT go see *The Last Submarine!*" the flyer read. "It is written by and directed by and starring COMMUNISTS. It is a STAIN on the patriotic record of our WAR HEROES. Read tomorrow's *Hollywood Reporter* to learn why."

"There's more on the other side."

Nell turned the page over.

"Do NOT go see Nell Davenport perform in La Monica Ballroom today. She's TAINTED by the same brush. We didn't fight long and hard in WWII to hand America over to COMMIES!"

Nell cast her eyes around the pier. How did she not notice so many people were holding the same handbill? A couple of passers-by, an almost matching pair of priggish bluenoses, lanced her with looks of loathsome condemnation.

Nell rattled the flyer. "Where did you get this?"

"From a Third Division Marine out front of the ballroom."

She slapped the cylinder into her palm. "Luke's down in the *Viperfish,* catching up with a Navy buddy. Could you stick around and tell him I had to go prepare for my show?" She kept her face lowered as she plowed into the crowd.

In his dress blues with the gilt buttons and white belt, it wasn't hard to spot Buzz. But he'd been out of the Third Division for more than a year, so what in tarnation was he doing in his uniform? It wasn't a hard question to answer: He wanted to be conspicuous as he dispensed his poisonous flyers.

He caught sight of her and ducked inside La Monica. By the time she had entered the main room, he hadn't yet reached halfway across the vast dance floor. She yelled, "STOP!" but he ignored her. "YOU YELLOW-BELLIED, PANTY-WAISTED COWARD!"

That did it.

He spun around. "I'm a lot of things, but a coward isn't one of them. I'm a proud Marine who fought on Iwo Jima—and survived."

Nell advanced closer. "Not every man's story can be told, Buzz."

"Luke's can. In a movie. And a book. *And* he gets to be painted by Norman Rockwell. He got everything!"

"Luke didn't go looking for any of that."

"Yeah, yeah." Buzz looked like he was about to fire a wad of spit at her. "I know what you told the Walshes."

"And I know what *you* told them."

"THE GODDAMN TRUTH." He lifted his fistful of homemade flyers and shook them above his head. "Commies are trying to take over the country. We have to nip it in the bud. Starting with *The Last Submarine.*"

"But—"

"Billy Wilkerson knows what I'm talking about."

"Yes, but does Wilkerson know what *he's* talking about?"

"Just wait till the *Reporter* comes out tomorrow. That man has more guts in his big toe than all the braggarts and swellheads in this town put together."

Buzz was going to do whatever he wanted, but, Nell realized, she should try to take those poisonous flyers away from him.

"It's easy to have guts when you're the one with the printing press. All those names, Buzz, they're real people. With lives and careers and families."

"They should have thought of that before they joined the Communist Party."

She inched forward. They were thirty feet apart now. Maybe less. She only needed to be close enough to grab his flyers and fast enough to rip them into pieces. "Wilkerson had better have photos of their membership cards or he'll have a bunch of libel cases on his hands."

"He's got truth on his side."

Nell was close enough now to see the hysteria in his bloodshot eyes. When was the last time this lunatic had slept? He reminded her of some of the returned veterans she'd seen at Wadsworth. Tony and his pal, Hollis, had pulled through their experience better than this guy.

Just get his flyers. Stay calm. Stay collected.

"Wilkerson doesn't have the right to assassinate reputations any more than you have the right to hand out these!" She shook the flyer Tony had given her. "They're in your handwriting, which is the legal requirement of libel." She rattled his flyer some more. "There's no Communist Party membership card with my name on it."

"You don't need one if you're a pinko commie fellow traveler," Buzz retorted. "I knew you were trouble the day I came back to the studio. You, with your smug attitude, your chumminess with Humphrey Bogart and Lauren Bac—"

"You dumped my standees in the Communist Party trash cans,

didn't you? That's called 'character assassination,' which is slander. Crime number one. And this—" she held up his flyer "—is written down, which is libel. Crime number two." She could see the ire rise in his face, so she kept talking. "Crime number three: You tried to cut my microphone cable."

"Look who's throwing around slander now!"

"The charge for that would be breaking and entering with malicious intent." Nell wasn't certain it was an actual crime, but it sounded convincing.

"Quit being so melodramatic. What a prima donna you are. You and your bogus *Lanternfish* hero."

"Luke may not have been the sole hero of the *Lanternfish*, but he sure as hell deserves some of the credit."

"Of course you'd say that," Buzz sneered. "Your type is always lying." He hitched up his dark trousers. They seemed to bag around his hips like they were several sizes too big for him. His jacket sleeves reached halfway along the back of his fist. Was this even his uniform?

"Did you mention 'lying'?" Nell marched forward, halving the distance between them. "Let's talk about how you never carried that famous flag in Iwo Jima."

A fat vein throbbed in the middle of his scarlet forehead. "I was *there*. *I* carried the flag. *On* Iwo Jima. *Up* Mount Suribachi. All the way to the *top*. What would you know about it, anyway? Sleeping soundly in your comfy widdle beddy-byes a thousand miles away when I was slogging through stinking sand and bloated corpses, not knowing if my next step would be my last."

"I didn't say you weren't there," Nell shot back. "Yours was the first flag. The one *nobody* cares about because it's not the second one. The *famous* one."

"THAT'S A DIRTY, FILTHY LIE." Buzz knew how to project his voice; it echoed off the cavernous ceiling arching overhead.

Nell curled her lip into an expression she knew would rub his pride worse than sandpaper. "You figured 'I can dazzle them with the glory of my war record. These dummies tucked in their beds won't know the difference. I can spin them any story I want because that's what I do best.'"

"NO!"

"'Heck, if I tell it often enough and convincingly enough, Warners might even make a movie out of it.'"

Buzz's blotchy face flushed a deeper shade of red. "NO! NO!"

She felt the heat of white-hot anger radiating from her scalp. So much for staying calm and collected. It might have been different if this fraud had been telling the truth all this time. But he'd chosen instead to plant himself smack dab into one of the biggest victories of the war. Being the PR maestro that he was, he'd done a masterful job of convincing everyone that he had been there. Almost everyone.

"You missed out on making history by a couple of hours, and it drives you nuts." The confined quarters aboard the *Viperfish*, with its stale air and narrow spaces, came back to Nell in a rush. "You should be ashamed of yourself badmouthing people. Luke risked his life amid actual danger."

They were within striking distance now. Buzz clenched his right hand into a fist.

"What's your plan?" she goaded him. "To punch a girl?" Buzz pulled his fist back. *The hell you will, you big phony*. She gripped the thick cardboard cylinder like a baseball bat and swung it around, as hard as she could. It caught him squarely on the side of his head, sending him sprawling to his knees. The stack of flyers soared into the air.

"If you're such a tremendous war hero," she yelled, whacking him across the chest as the handbills cascaded around them, "where's *your* parade?" Across his shoulder. "Show me *your* key to the city." Straight down onto his head. The force opened a wide crack in the cylinder. "ASSHOLE!"

The ruptured tube was ripped from her hands. Out of the corner of her eye, she saw Buzz scramble to his feet and charge toward a side door. "Get lost," she yelled after him, "you lousy fraud." She looked around to find Luke and Peyton standing beside her. "Where'd you two come from?"

Peyton jacked a thumb at the door leading backstage. "Are you okay?"

Luke blinked away the shock in his eyes. "I'd say she's more than okay."

Nell looked at the broken tube in Luke's hands, then threw herself at his chest. He wrapped his arms around her and whispered "My hero" into her ear.

"What on earth—?" Avery's voice came from somewhere behind Luke. "What's happened to my painting?"

Oh, no! Nell pushed herself free of Luke's embrace and retrieved the battered cylinder. "I got carried away. He made me so mad. It was in my hands. I just—"

"You used it to pummel the bejesus out of him?" Avery popped the top and extracted the canvas.

"Please tell me I haven't damaged it."

Avery unfurled the painting. "I don't see any cracks."

Peyton peered at Avery's portrait over Tony's shoulder. He studied it some more before making a suffocated croaking sound. "Try as I might, I still can't get over how much you look like my sister."

"Wait. What?" Nell swiveled slowly around, taking in Peyton's declaration. "Your *sister*?"

"Uh-huh. Not just the way you look, but your spirit, your humor, the way you approach life."

"And you never thought to mention it?"

"I know I should have said something before now, but there never seemed to be a good time to bring her up." Peyton attempted a smile, but it trembled at the edges. "She was an Army nurse. Bravest woman I ever met. Spent practically the whole war in Europe. But she died in a surprise skirmish during the Allied march to Germany. I didn't even get to bury her. Not a day goes by I don't think of her."

"Gosh, Peyton," Nell said softly. "I'm so sorry to hear that."

"Being around you, it—" His voice cracked. He drew in a steadying breath. "It felt like I had her back with me because you're so similar." Peyton could only pull his gaze away from the picture when Avery carefully rolled it up again. "Only recently did it occur to me that maybe you thought I had a crush on you." She made a feeble attempt to deflect his suggestion, but he held up his hand to stop her. "As it happens, I do have a crush."

"Anyone we know?" Luke asked.

Peyton took a moment to gather himself. "I don't suppose you know if Abigail is single?"

41

"May I take a moment to recap what I missed?" Tristan trickled maple syrup over the flapjacks Luke had cooked using a recipe Nell's mother had sent. "While you were down the hatch catching up with your shipmate, little Miss Joe Louis was pummeling the fake hero of Iwo Jima with a portrait that one-armed Avery had painted, which Peyton thought was of his sister?"

"Yep," Luke said. "And then Joe Louis got up and sang her heart out to five thousand people."

Nell took the miniature ceramic pitcher from him. "The show must go on."

"After we dumped Buzz's horrible flyers in the trash, I showed everyone the *Viperfish*."

Seeing Jigs had come as a shock—a diverting one, though. Luke had forgotten how his old shipmate had been an irrepressible chatterbox. He loved to chew over the glory days of his wartime experiences, how his hometown, Joplin, Missouri, had thrown him a parade, how he'd signed up again after the war, and the irony of getting assigned to the *Lanternfish*'s sister boat.

When Luke had emerged from the *Viperfish*, he'd still been a little groggy from the onslaught of nostalgia. Not just from the blitzkrieg of Jigs's reminiscences, but from glimpses of objects he hadn't given much thought to during his time on the *Lanternfish*. The shape of the switches on the forward drain manifold. The color of the grips on the number one periscope. Far from the gut-wrenching crack-up he'd feared with every step down the ladder, the inspection had felt more like revisiting a familiar scene, like standing on the platform of the 50th Street subway station back in Brooklyn.

He had also expected to find Nell waiting for him on the deck beside the aft hatch, not fighting hand-to-hand combat. His first instinct had been to rush to her rescue, but in his dash across La Monica's dance floor, he saw that if anything needed rescuing, it had been Avery's painting.

"And how about Wilkerson's column!" Tristan brandished a forkful of pancakes. "*A Vote For Stalin*. He was throwing gasoline on a mountain of kindling, and he knew it."

"I suspected Kathryn was being alarmist," Nell said, shaking her head, "but she was right. I still can't believe he named actual names of some of the most respected screenwriters in the industry."

"Warners should be thankful Maltz was their only screenwriter he included," Gus put in. "How was the mood at the studio yesterday?"

"The joint was swarming with rumors about how Jack Warner had turned into Mount Vesuvius," Luke said. "It seems he had called Wilkerson and thought he'd talked him out of publishing the column."

"Can you imagine the yelling and the screaming and the vase-throwing?" Nell asked with a sigh. "I'm glad I'm not working in studio PR anymore. What a nightmare. I haven't bothered with any of this morning's columns, but I'm sure Louella, Hedda, and Sheilah have all shared their two cents' worth."

Luke hadn't read them either. He was still too buoyant over

what Jigs had said when Luke had confessed that he felt he'd let Christopher down and that he wished he'd been a better shipmate. Jigs had whacked him across the shoulder. "We admired you for volunteering to serve on a submarine even though you didn't have our twelve-month training. That took guts, and plenty of it. And you never blew your own horn for working at a movie studio and being friends with Bogart. And that's aside from how you learned of incoming torpedoes in enough time for us to take evasive action. Not to mention how you tried to save Sparky."

Luke had grabbed onto the periscope's hand-grips to calm himself. "You saw me?"

Jigs had lowered his voice. "I was the sonar guy. Us and the radio guys are the last to evacuate. I was snatching up my essentials when I noticed you."

"Did you see him stop me?"

Jigs's eyes had drilled Luke, apprehension contorting his face. "I've seen it before. Signs of someone who wanted to go down with the ship." His gaze had drifted down to Luke's stump, where it had lingered for a moment. "You were a first-class crew member, and I'd be proud to sail anywhere with you."

Minutes later, as Luke had stepped off the *Viperfish*, he could feel his doubts about that night and everything that had sprung from it ferment into a quiet pride.

Tristan stabbed at his stack of pancakes. "I've read every word all the columnists had to say about Wilkerson's editorial."

"Let me guess," Nell said. "Hedda beat the hang-all-commies drum until her arm withered to a stump."

"That dried-up old prune is as predictable as Joan Crawford slapping her co-star halfway through a picture. Louella and Sheilah surprised me, though."

"They're anti-Wilkerson?" Nell asked.

"They're anti his threats of reprisals for simply belonging to a political party."

"And Kathryn Massey?" Luke asked, refilling their coffee cups. "What did she say?"

"She talked about the proposed merger of Universal with International Pictures, and the upcoming unveiling of KFWB's news ribbon. In other words, she avoided Wilkerson's rant altogether."

"Wouldn't you?" Nell asked.

"I suppose."

"Gee, guys," Luke interjected, "wouldn't it be nice to have breakfast without all this melodrama?"

"Dear, sweet Luke!" Tristan batted his eyelashes like he was Pearl White in *The Perils of Pauline*. "If you want your hot cakes without a side order of drama, you're in the wrong town."

Luke jumped when his new telephone rang in the living room. One of these days, he'd get used to hearing its sound. "Burbank House of Hot Cakes."

"Luke? Is that you? It's me, Jerry Wald."

Oops. "What can I do for you at nine-fifteen on a Sunday morning?"

"The Wilkerson bombshell." Wald spat out his words. "In light of his insinuation, I've ordered our editors to work around the clock. They'll have a decent cut ready by tomorrow morning, so I've scheduled a screening."

"You want me to be there?"

"I want all key personnel to assess it for elements that could be thought of as anything less than one hundred percent pro-America, pro-war effort, anti-enemy, anti-commie, anti–any damn thing that might cause us distress at the box office."

That's rich, Luke thought. Neither you nor anyone on your team has asked me for my recollections, or my advice, or my participation beyond an afternoon with your suspected commie screenwriter. But now the picture's in trouble, suddenly I'm key personnel?

But it seemed petty to quibble. He wanted *The Last Submarine* to succeed. What if there was a problem only he could spot, and he wasn't there to catch it?

"Sure," he told Wald. "What time and where?"

* * *

Almost a hundred people had gathered in the lobby of the Warner Theater on Hollywood Boulevard.

"When Wald said 'all key personnel,'" Luke whispered to Nell, "I thought he meant a dozen."

"That was twenty-four hours ago," she murmured. "The rumor mill's been spinning so hard, I'm surprised it didn't fall off its spindle. At least the only *Last Submarine* person Wilkerson named was Maltz. We're lucky he excluded Garfield and Curtiz." She executed a slow three-hundred-and-sixty-degree whirl. "But who's to say there won't be a second, longer list? On the bright side, we get to see the movie!"

Had he not visited the *Viperfish*, Luke doubted he could have sat through the whole thing. But he was a different person now and was excited to watch his life play out on the screen. 'Excited' wasn't the right word. More like—he settled on 'eager.' When Wald had said he wanted Luke's objective opinion, Luke had assured him that he would get exactly that. But as he stood in the packed lobby, he wondered how impartial he could possibly be.

"Holy smoke," Nell muttered. "They're all here: John Garfield and Joan Leslie, Curtiz, Jack Warner. You see that knot of suits Taplinger's talking to? They're all from Legal." She nodded toward the staircase. "Maltz has shown up. Gutsy move."

Luke spotted four familiar faces scattered around the lobby, which smelled of stale popcorn and expensive aftershave lotion. "You know it's a big deal when the typeset quartet are all here: Hedda, Louella, Sheilah, and Kathryn."

Ethan appeared from behind the thicket of lawyers. "Quite a turnout." He reconnoitered the growing crowd. "I talked my way in because the *Post* wanted to cancel the article and the Norman Rockwell cover."

"Because of one editorial that offers zero proof?" Nell asked.

"I don't want to dismiss them as Midwest fuddy-duddies, but they are gun-shy over even the whiff of a controversy. But I convinced them to hold off on a final decision until I've seen the movie and can report back." He did a double take. "Do you know Kathryn Massey from *The Hollywood Reporter*?"

"Why? Is she marching over here?"

"Should I disappear?"

Kathryn had joined them before Luke could respond. "Just one thing I need to know. And please be honest with me, even if it's not what I wish to hear."

"Sure," Luke said.

"Did you tell Jack Warner what I told you at the Brown Derby?"

"I promised you I wouldn't."

She acknowledged his response with a tense smile. "I needed to ask because everything escalated too quickly to wrangle damage control. I fear this is going to get a lot uglier and I'm trying to figure out how this has all come about."

"You might want to ask Buzz Bryant about that," Nell said.

"Buzz Bryant?" Kathryn looked aghast. "Are you talking about *Bailey* Bryant?"

"I don't know." Luke shot Nell a look that said, Way to go, pinning your leak on Buzz. "Are we?"

Nell shrugged. "I've never heard anyone refer to him as anything other than Buzz."

"The one who's worked in your PR department since forever?"

"Yes, that's him."

"Oh, brother," Kathryn muttered under her breath. "He and my mercurial boss got their start at Famous Players-Lasky in New York. When Wilkerson moved to LA to set up his own film studio, Buzz came with him. But they couldn't make a go of it, so he had to find work elsewhere, which is when he landed at Warners. Wilkerson has had it in for the moguls who succeeded where he failed and has been dirty on them ever since."

Luke thought of the *Hollywood Reporter* truck that had spirited away the missing standees. "Are Buzz and Wilkerson still friendly?"

"Oh, yeah. Poker pals and boozing buddies."

"He hasn't shown up for work in the past week, but if you can track him down, ask him a few pointed questions."

"Watch your step, though." Nell drew circles in the air around her temple. "He's gone a bit crackers."

The manager announced over the PA that the theater was ready and would everybody please file into the auditorium as the picture would start in ten minutes.

Kathryn told them she ought to rejoin her *Hollywood Reporter* contingent and melted into the river of people entering the theater.

A third of the way down the stairs, Luke and Nell found Avery and Tony were already saving their seats. Neither of them had worked on *The Last Submarine*, "but how could we pass up seeing your picture?"

As the lights dimmed, Luke's apprehension swelled. Maybe this wasn't such a great idea, after all. Had he talked himself into being ready? Nell's hand slipped on top of his. "Remember how you felt after visiting the *Viperfish?*" she whispered. "This'll be the same. I promise."

She had no right to promise any such thing, but he needed a personal cheerleader more than he'd realized. He squirmed down in his seat. *Enjoy it, Valenti. It's all about you.*

And he did. The first twenty minutes breezed through his time monitoring German transmissions at the Montauk station, transferring to the language school in Colorado, boarding the *Lanternfish* in Pearl Harbor, and getting chummy with his shipmates.

But then they came to the scene where Garfield heard the

Japanese word for 'torpedo' and the sub came under fire. The destruction of the bow plane hadn't sealed the *Lanternfish*'s fate, but it had been the first nail in its coffin. The scene was every bit as gripping and gutsy as any in the preview. Using extreme close-ups and stark lighting, Curtiz had achieved the grim claustrophobia inside a submarine as alarms shrieked and the danger mounted.

He had, in fact, recreated it a little too vividly. Luke felt his heart push against his throat. Seeing the *Viperfish* hadn't helped. Nor had hashing over old times with Jigs. He needed to get out for a couple of minutes to shake off his nerves and clear his head. He whispered, "I'll be back" into Nell's ear and hurried up the aisle.

He had not, however, counted on coming face to face with Greg Whitley in the empty foyer. "What are you do—"

Every other time they'd met, Whitley's uniform always been laundry-fresh, his hair trimmed, his shoes polished to a high shine. But not today. Someone had jerked the knot of Whitley's necktie halfway around his collar. The bottom jacket button was missing, and a four-inch rip gaped open along his left lapel.

"Have you come from a bar fight?"

Whitley slid his tie back into place. "I was running late because of my Fleet Week duties, so I dashed in here already agitated. And then I found the Wild Man of Borneo waiting to ambush me."

"Who?"

"That lunatic, Buzz Bryant."

"Buzz? Is here?"

"Live, in person. I wrestled out from under him, got to my feet, and asked what the hell was wrong with him."

"What did he say?"

"He ranted on and on about how I was part of the problem."

"What problem?"

"Favoring you and the *Lanternfish* over him and Iwo Jima. And how all of your motion picture glory should have been his, but I'd siphoned it over to you instead."

The hairs on the back of Luke's neck stood up. "Did you?"

"Hell, no. I had him pegged as a crackpot from the get-go, so I've been playing nicey-nicey with him. But my patience ran out today. I told him he was being ridiculous because nobody cares about the *other* guy who carried the *other* flag up Suribachi."

"You knew about that?" Luke asked.

"Of course I did. So when I reminded him he'd missed out on making history, oh boy! It's been a long time since I've seen a man lose control of himself so fast. Fists flying. Insults. Screaming."

Luke flicked the torn lapel of Whitley's bespoke lieutenant commander jacket. "Didn't realize he was taking on a middleweight champ, huh?"

A quiet smile emerged on Whitley's face. "He may claim to be a battle-hardened Marine, but mine were the fists doing most of the flying."

And I'm sure they left more of a mark than Nell's cardboard tube. "Where did you last see him?"

"Sprawled out on the sidewalk." Whitley headed for the auditorium doors. "You coming?"

Luke told him he'd be along in a minute.

Hollywood Boulevard was deserted, but Luke had hurried outside in time to see someone disappearing along Wilcox Avenue. Was it Buzz? He couldn't be sure. At the corner, he caught sight of a door closing at the top of a flight of stairs halfway down the block. Luke took them two by two. The door opened into a short, dimly lit corridor. A closed door stood at the far end with a sign: *PROJECTION ROOM*. Halfway down, Buzz was pulling something from his jacket. It took Luke a moment to identify the pair of wire cutters Nell had told him about on the day of their La Monica fracas.

The door closed behind Luke, throwing the corridor into semi-darkness. "What do you plan on doing with them?"

The seam where Buzz's sleeve met his jacket had unraveled, but he didn't appear to have noticed. "Cut you to shreds."

"You might get lucky and pull off a button or two. But there's no way I'll let you draw blood."

"Not personally, ya dope." He held the cutters at arm's length and snipped them menacingly. "The you on the screen."

"You're editing me out of my own movie with a pair of wire cutters?"

"Jesus, Valenti. Dumber'n a dead dog." He jerked his head toward the projection room. "I'm gonna snip-snip-snip the only print of *The Last Submarine* until it's a useless pile of celluloid."

This guy was certifiably out of his cotton-pickin' mind. "Why bother?" Luke asked. "Our editors can piece together another one."

"But that'll take weeks, which will give Wilkerson time to publish his list."

"He already did, Buzz. Yesterday, he—"

"His *full* list. A whole bunch of people are about to get what's coming to them."

Without those pruning shears, Buzz was Samson after a haircut. But Marines saw a lot of close-quarters conflict. Luke had no such training, nor did he have Whitley's boxing skills. Then again, he wasn't as desperate, rabid-eyed, or unhinged as Buzz appeared to be.

The door behind Luke opened, letting in a flood of sunlight. "Hey there."

It was Avery.

Luke kept his eyes on Buzz. "What is it?"

"Nell sent me out to look for you so that she could stay with Tony."

"Is he all right?"

"He's not faring so well watching a realistic war picture."

"But he was okay when we saw those three scenes."

"Compared to you, maybe. But I got the impression he was glad we left early that day. Say, what's going on here?"

"Buzz plans to shred the only copy of *The Last Submarine*."

"Does he now?" The floorboards creaked as Avery stepped forward.

At least it was now two against one—even if one of them had a bum hand.

The swell of violins from Max Steiner's score penetrated through the floor from the theater below. The boom of a timpani drum gave way to a series of discordant staccato notes from a loud oboe. Luke guessed that an intense scene was unfolding on the screen and wondered how Tony was coping. He felt Avery's warm breath brush his neck.

"One of the ways I trained myself to use my left hand," Avery whispered, "was to toss quarters into a cup. Got real good at it. Very accurate. A lot of force."

Buzz grunted. "You two cripples can have yourselves a chit-chat, but I'm here to do a job."

Luke wasn't sure what Avery had meant about tossing quarters until he had shunted Luke to one side, his left hand drawn back. A silver quarter caught the overhead light as Avery pitched it down the corridor. It thwacked Buzz square on his forehead.

Buzz lunged, the sharp point of his wire cutters jabbing the air. "I'm a fucking Marine," he hissed. "You think you can bring me down with a bunch of lousy—"

Avery's next projectile struck Buzz's left eye with a dull thud. The one after that hit his right eye.

Avery ripped off his right shoe; the metal tip on the heel glinted in the overhead light. "I go high, you go low." They catapulted themselves forward. Avery swung his shoe in a wide arc above his head as Luke landed on his left foot and kicked out with his right. It nearly clipped the cutters, but missed by only inches. He stumbled to the side, pressing his hands to the wall. He spun around and aimed his best attempt at an uppercut at Buzz's wrist.

It missed its target, but collided with his forearm. Buzz grunted again, but the impact wasn't enough to loosen his grip.

Luke looked up. The tip of Avery's shoe had gouged out a chunk of Buzz's forehead; blood oozed down his nose and pooled in the corner of his mouth. He didn't seem to notice, though. His eyes blazing, Buzz flipped the cutters so that he could wield them like a dagger. Luke flattened himself to the wall. As Buzz thrust downward, Avery threw himself in front of Luke. He let out a guttural howl and dropped to the floor.

The shears remained in Buzz's grip, the tip now slick with blood. Buzz disappeared into the projection room as Luke sank to his knees.

A dark, wet patch bloomed near Avery's left shoulder. He swallowed hard and forced out a series of rapid breaths.

"Lie still," Luke told him.

Avery shook his head. "Go after the bastard."

Luke cradled Avery's head in the crook of his arm. Below them, the *Lanternfish*'s shrill alarm rang out. The bloodstain seeping through Avery's shirtfront grew to the size of a dinner plate. "Not when you took one for the team."

A tremulous smile. "Think of it as… payback for… the inheritance." Avery looked down at his chest to take in the slowly growing blotch. "It's not as bad as it looks. I swear." He jutted his chin at the projection room door. "There's only one copy of the movie, so take care of that first. That's an order, Lieutenant. GO!"

Luke set Avery's head on the wooden floor and scrambled to his feet. He threw himself against the door and it banged open. Inside, the projectionist was sprawled on the carpet, motionless, his legs flung out at awkward angles.

Next to him, two empty film cans lay discarded, snippets of celluloid cascading onto them like autumn leaves. Buzz stood to one side, holding giant loops of film in one hand as the other one snipped and shredded.

"Oh, Buzz," Luke murmured. "What have you done?"

42

Nell and Luke stood at the end of Brownstone Street and kept their eyes on the entrance to the executive dining room of the studio commissary. "How do we know Curtiz is there?" Nell asked.

"Because Tony has been doing Alexis Smith's hair on *Night and Day*—"

"Which Curtiz is directing, but how do you know he's in there right now?"

"Because Alexis told Ann Sheridan what a swell job he did on her for *Of Human Bondage* and that she should request him to work on her for *The Unfaithful*."

"But Vincent Sherman is directing that," Nell said.

"Yes, and then he's going to direct her in *Nora Prentiss* right after that. He wants his leading lady to be happy—"

"And a well-coiffed leading lady is a happy leading lady." The pieces were starting to fall neatly into place now.

"And so Vincent Sherman is having lunch with Curtiz to ask if he minds swapping hair and makeup people."

"Curtiz doesn't strike me as the type who gives a hoot who does hair and makeup on his stars."

"He doesn't, so it's an easy ask—"

"That makes Curtiz feel like the great benefactor granting wishes to lesser directors." Honestly, Nell thought, the egos on these men should be in some psychiatric textbook somewhere.

Had they been hunting down Michael Curtiz for any other reason than the one they were there for, Nell might have been tempted to stick a quick knife in on Abigail's behalf. He'd probably walked past her a million times and not even noticed her. Nell no longer worked at Warners, so what did she care? But that's not why we're here, she scolded herself. This is not the time or place.

"Tell me again how you're going to ask," Nell said. "It doesn't hurt to practice these—" The dining room door swung open. Nell held her breath, but it was only Otto Preminger. "I wish I smoked. Apparently it's very relaxing."

Luke suppressed a laugh. "Let's survive the next ten minutes first." He ran his finger down the crease along his pant leg. He'd taken great care to press his uniform this morning, so it was sharp enough to cut paper. Nell took it as a sign he was as nervous as she was. "Just keep talking until—there he is!"

Curtiz and Sherman stepped out of the commissary and onto First Street. The two men were smiling. A good sign. And shaking hands. Another good sign. Sherman waved Curtiz goodbye and headed toward the western side of the lot as Curtiz headed toward the recording studio. It wasn't far, so they didn't have long.

Nell and Luke charged at him. "Mr. Curtiz?" Nell called out. "May we have a word?"

Curtiz had stopped to light a Montecristo cigar. "I have a busy afternoon." He kept his eyes on the flame of his lighter, but he hadn't told them to beat it.

"This won't take long," Luke said.

Slipping the lighter into a pocket, Curtiz looked at them for the first time. "Oh, it's you two."

"Yes," Nell said, as lightly as she could manage. "We were hoping—"

"Yesterday's preview. Ach! Such a train wreck." He liberated an uninhibited belch. "Your friend, the one who got stabbed. Is he okay?"

Luke nodded. "Avery will be sore for a while, but the emergency room doctor said he'll recover."

"All four of them." Curtiz shook his head sorrowfully. "Louella, Hedda, Kathryn, Sheilah. They had to be there, didn't they?"

"Don't forget," Nell said, "there's no such thing as bad publicity."

"In that case, why don't you go back to the PR office and call all four of them and remind them of that? Oh yes, that's right—you don't work here anymore."

"But I do—" Luke took over—"and we wanted to make a suggestion."

Curtiz's gaze turned glacial. "*You* are going to tell *me* what to do with *my* movie?"

Nell wished she could remind him that while he might be Warners' most valuable director, he was still a salaried employee, and all movies on the Warner Bros. lot belonged to Jack Warner. And if she could waltz into the big boss's office, she would. But as Curtiz had pointed out, she no longer worked here.

"Like I said—" Luke ran his thumbs down the undersides of his lapels to underscore a point that might go completely over Curtiz's head—"it's just a suggestion."

"You've got thirty seconds."

"You're right to fear that those four columnists are probably going to report about yesterday's disastrous preview, but if we—you—can give them some good news, maybe it'll even things out."

"Such as?"

"Dedicate the movie to Christopher Walsh."

Curtiz sucked on his cigar and raised his chin toward the clear sky. "Uh-huh."

Luke glanced at Nell. *Should I keep going?* Yes, she nodded, don't stop now.

"Sparky saved as many lives as I did that night," Luke continued. "I've been lucky enough to get a whole movie made about me. The least we can do is remember Christopher this way."

"And perhaps," Nell said, "under his name, you could say something like, 'As well as all the Navy personnel and American POWs whose lives were lost the night of the sinking of the *Lanternfish*.'"

Curtiz shot a plume of gray-white cigar smoke at Nell and Luke. Maybe he'd been aiming above their heads. If he had, he missed.

Luke leaned back half a step but didn't fan away the smoke. "You might want to keep in mind that your screenwriter and your star are about to be implicated in Billy Wilkerson's anti-commie campaign."

"My picture is very patriotic," Curtiz snapped.

"A dedication would emphasize that patriotism even more."

"As we all know," Nell put in, "Jack Warner is the most patriotic of all the movie moguls. And more importantly, the most publicly supportive of the US military. If you go to him and ask that a dedication—"

He flicked away a chunk of cigar ash. It missed Nell's cheek by mere inches—not that he noticed. "*The Last Submarine* is my movie. I won't ask him. I'll tell him."

Nell looked at Luke. *Our work here is done.* "Thank you for your time, Mr. Curtiz. We won't keep you any longer."

She hooked Luke by the elbow and frog-marched him back the way they'd come. They didn't look back and didn't speak again until they were back on Brownstone Street.

43

*L*uke took Nell's hand as they dodged the cars and trucks jamming Hollywood Boulevard to a standstill. "You know what Bogie asked me yesterday? He said, 'What if nobody shows up?' I thought he was kidding and laughed. But all I got was silence, and I thought, 'Uh-oh. He's serious.'"

"Humphrey Bogart gets his footprint ceremony outside Grauman's Chinese, and nobody showing up is his most likely scenario?" Nell rolled her eyes. "Honestly, that man."

They shouldered through the onlookers as the setting sun cast long shadows across the checkerboard of odd-shaped blocks. In the center, a man in a beret ladled wet cement into a rectangular tile.

As absurd as it was to imagine that nobody would care about Bogie's ceremony—did Warners have a bigger male star right now?—it was the same humility that had helped Luke decide to invest in Santana Productions. Would he have done it with someone as reckless as Flynn? Or as testy as Cagney? Not a chance.

"He still can't see himself as a romantic leading man. Or grasp that he nabbed his beautiful leading lady. Or that he could be so happy with her. Or she with him."

"Betty told me she fully expected to have to knot his necktie today."

They found a spot at the western end of the forecourt, where the *Centennial Summer* poster hung in the CURRENT ATTRACTIONS box. Everyone from the little girl in an outmoded Shirley Temple dress to the old-timer with red wine stains on his wrinkled tie had shown up this evening. The forecourt couldn't hold many more people, so the inevitable pushing and shoving would be starting soon.

"I'm surprised you didn't wear your uniform," Nell commented.

"I didn't want to detract from Bogie's big moment."

"But Navy regulations dictate personnel must always be in uniform."

"I've had a long talk with Greg Whitley. Once *The Last Submarine* comes out, my value to the Navy is bound to nosedive. So I asked him, 'What does a guy have to do to get kicked out?'"

"Did he laugh in your face and tell you that you're never getting out?"

Luke spied an usher cracking open the theater's front door and peering at the thickening crowd. "He said, 'All you have to do is fill out a form.' So I called him a rat bastard for not telling me it was that easy, and threatened to hang him up by his BVDs if he didn't send me that form pronto."

Luke's time in the Navy had been a far cry from what he had expected when he pestered Captain Stamina to help him enlist. If he'd known back then what lay ahead of him, he might not have fought so hard. But now that he was nearing the end of his stint, he was glad that he'd weathered all those storms, literal and figurative. The way he saw it, he had only one more hurdle to clear.

"Did you read Mr. Warner's press release?" he asked Nell.

"I was busy all morning packing. Abigail has lent me her traveling trunk. It's got hangers and drawers and even a secret compartment." Nell snorted. "And guess who was with her when she dropped it off."

Luke didn't need to look at Nell to know mischief filled her face. "She and Peyton are officially dating?"

"I think it's safe to say they are, which is bad timing, seeing as how he's leaving LA on Friday."

"Any pointers for Abigail and me on how to contend with being stuck on the home front while our sweethearts are on a tour of duty?"

He tossed her an acerbic smile, which she pretended to be shocked by.

"She sketches lighthouses, by the way."

This was news. He'd never met anyone he could share his specific hobby with. "It's about time I got back into that."

"As for those pointers you asked about, you could write to me," she said. "Lots and lots and lots of letters."

"Coded?"

"Scented."

"With what?"

"The bottle of Drucker's aftershave standing on your dresser next to the tour schedule I typed up."

"Thought of everything, haven't you?"

"I try, but after this Friday, you'll have to figure out the rest of it on your own."

Those two words. *This Friday.* It left only three more days. Luke felt the weight of apprehension bear down on him. Determined to get in as many kisses as he could before waving her off on the bus, he pulled her to him and kissed her on the lips. A pair of prepubescent girls in parochial school plaid uniforms nearly choked on their half-suppressed giggles.

"Maybe I'll spend the whole time you're away going shopping," he said.

"For what?" she threw back at him. "Civvies? Come to think of it, now that you'll be mustering out, you could do with a new wardrobe. You didn't sink all your *Last Submarine* money into Santana Productions, did you?"

"No," he reassured her. "I held some back for. .. essentials."

A cheer swelled when Bogie and Betty emerged through the front doors of the auditorium, he in a dark suit and matching tie, she in a two-piece black suit with three-quarter sleeves. They waved as Sid Grauman guided them to the block of fresh cement.

"Look at that lit cigarette Bogie's holding. He must be nervous if he's willing to risk dropping ash into his cement, where it'll stay trapped forever."

Bogie took a sharpened stick from Sid and kneeled on the velvet-padded gantry to gouge his message into the cement.

"Did he tell you what he plans to write?" Nell asked.

"We brainstormed a few ideas, and settled on 'Sid, may you never die till I kill you.'"

"Cute. Dark, but cute."

Bogie drove his hands into the bottom right corner, then stood up to display his grimy palms. "Sid didn't warn me about his cement," he yelled at the crowd. "It's COLD!"

The gathering applauded their appreciation as he stepped onto the cement. He whispered into Betty's ear. She crouched down and yelled, "The skinny little runt isn't heavy enough to make an impression!" Everyone laughed. She shifted her weight forward and pushed down onto Bogie's lucky shoes.

Sid helped her to her feet and handed Bogie a small towel. Once his hands were clean, Bogie threw an arm over Sid's shoulder. "It's amazing to be invited to leave my mark outside this man's world-famous theater." He gave Sid an extra squeeze, then took Betty's hand. "It also means the world to me that you all came to witness one of the most exciting events of my life. THANK YOU!"

Yes, Luke thought, Humphrey Bogart is one happy man.

* * *

It was a fraction past eight o'clock when Luke and Nell approached the maître d's podium at the Roosevelt Hotel's restaurant opposite the Chinese. "We're here to join Mr. and Mrs. Bogart," Luke told the tuxedoed gent.

The maître d' told them that the Bogarts hadn't arrived yet, but he'd reserved the corner table to ensure they "remained as undisturbed as possible on a forecourt ceremony night."

He led them on a circuitous route through the maze of diners. Their waiter had already deposited a tumbler in front of each chair. "Mr. Bogart requested that drinks be waiting."

Nell took a seat and sniffed at her glass. "Manhattans." She deposited it back into place. "Tell me what the press release said."

"Oh, *that*." Luke interlaced his fingers. "'A masterpiece of glossed-over half-truths.'"

"Drafted by Taplinger, no doubt."

"He said when *The Last Submarine* started screening in front of a live audience, it was obvious the film wasn't working."

"Did he say why?"

"Nope. Just that as a consequence, they are now recutting the picture." Luke ran a fingertip around the rim of his glass. If the Bogarts were going to be delayed—surely autograph hounds had swamped them?—he and Nell might be stuck staring at these drinks for an eternity. "I sure hope they include that dedication. You kind of have to admire Curtiz's willingness to tell Jack Warner what to do." Were these the sorts of decisions he'd face at Santana Productions? Bogie had never clarified whether he wanted Luke to be an active part of decision-making. Was he merely a silent partner?

Reverential applause rippled through the restaurant. The couple of the night waved graciously until they reached the table.

"Are those our Manhattans?" Betty dropped onto her chair.

"Look!" she said to Bogie, waving a hand at the glasses. "They listened."

Luke had planned on making a long-but-not-too-long, flowery-but-not-too-flowery speech to mark the occasion of what he knew was a high-water mark in Bogie's eyes. But before he embarked on it, Bogie ducked his head under the table and announced, "And they delivered it!"

Luke eyed his drink with the thirst of a man lost in the Sahara. "Delivered what?"

Bogie reappeared holding a cardboard box. "Business first, pleasure second."

Business *before* booze? This was a first.

Bogie opened the flaps and pulled out six books. "No wonder studios have whole departments going through everything they can lay their hands on. I still haven't found anything, not even in *Black Mask*, so I went to the Pickwick Bookshop this morning and got these." He straightened them into a neat stack. "Apparently, I'm thick as ten planks because I needed nine hundred years to realize I didn't have to do this alone. Not when I've got one of the smartest people I know on my team."

I'm not *the money-man silent partner.* A tingle of excitement charged up Luke's spine as he stared at the pile of books.

"Take your pick of whichever ones you like," Bogie prompted. "Or you can eeny, meeny, miny, mo."

Luke felt the heat of stares from neighboring diners. He took the top two novels and the bottom one.

"Which ones did you get?" Betty asked.

Luke read the title of the first book. "*Plausible Deniability.*"

Bogie lit a Chesterfield. "A national guardsman is murdered behind the Capitol Building in DC and his brother-in-law tries to hunt down the killer."

"That sounds intriguing," Nell said.

Luke looked at the second book. "This one's called *The Dream Builders.*"

"For the record," Betty chimed in, "this one's my favorite."

"It's set in a movie studio during the early silent era," Bogie said. "A director named Cedric G. deVille—"

"In other words, Cecil B. DeMille?"

"—by way of the south side of Chicago, is trying to figure out how to direct a motion picture while his two romantic leads are romancing each other's spouses." He tapped the third book, titled *Retaliation*. "This is my favorite. It's about the airmen in the Doolittle air raid on Tokyo four months after Pearl Harbor."

Luke said, "*Plausible Deniability* sounds like a Bogie movie. *Retaliation* does too, but an expensive one. Maybe we'd be better off starting with a smaller story."

Bogie smiled with the satisfaction of someone who'd backed a hundred-to-one winner of the Kentucky Derby. "We'll know better when you've read your three and I've read mine." He dropped his novels back into the box and slid it under his chair. "Maybe none of them will be right and we'll have to go back to the drawing board. But somewhere out there is the right story. All we have to do is find it."

Luke picked up his cocktail. "Can I make my toast now?"

Bogie did the same. "Make it brief. I'm thirsty."

"First of all, congrats on being immortalized." He could tell Bogie was about to mock himself with a self-deprecating wisecrack, but Luke cut him off. "Being asked to jam your feet into wet cement is a big deal in this town. It deserves acknowledgment."

Bogie raised his glass higher as though to say, *Thanks, cheers, and let's drink.*

"Also, to our chanteuse, who's about to embark on quite the adventure. I'm sure she'll be a spectacular success, and we can't wait to hear all her stories when she gets back."

Nell blinked her eyes, shiny with tears, as she mouthed the words, "I love you."

He mouthed his reply, "I love you, too."

"Are you done yet?" Bogie urged. "Can we drink now?"

"Third, thanks to Betty for making Humphrey DeForest Bogart happier than he ever thought he could be."

"Thank you," Betty said, "but trust me, the pleasure's all mine."

She made a comical salute at him, but before she had a chance to snatch up her cocktail, Luke deftly commandeered her left hand and brought it closer. "I've never had a chance to inspect your engagement ring." He rocked it from side to side so that the huge diamond could catch the overhead lights. "That sure is one impressive rock. Where did you get it, Mr. Bogart?"

Bogie snorted. "If you hadn't been dumb enough to invest in Santana Productions, maybe I could send you there."

"It's probably better if I shop around," Luke said, mildly.

"You don't even wear a Navy pinkie ring," Betty said.

"Wait a cotton-pickin'—" Nell gripped his forearm. "What are you saying?"

"I told you before that I'd spend the time you're away going shopping." He shot her an impish wink. "You're the one who assumed I'd be shopping for clothes."

Her shocked expression was exactly what he was hoping he'd see. Until this moment, he wasn't sure Nell even wanted to get married. They'd never talked about it. But he was pretty sure he'd just given her something to think about for the next eight weeks.

Taking advantage of a rare moment of speechless astonishment, he continued. "After I came back from the war, it took me a while to realize the world's a different place now. A whole lot less predictable—but in a good way. So whatever's in store, good, bad, or indifferent—" he raised his glass "—here's to the four of us."

Tapping their cocktails together attracted the attention of everyone close enough to hear the chime of glass. The couple in a booth to the left, well-dressed, in their sixties, with abundant gray hair, raised their glasses in silent camaraderie. To the right, four young women, all of them pretty and decked out in costume jewelry, followed suit.

As Nell, Bogie, and Betty downed their Manhattans, Luke

paused. This December it would be five years since he'd landed in LA with three days' worth of cash in one hand and a hollow falcon in the other. Where had that wide-eyed Brooklyn boy gone? It doesn't matter, he decided. It's the future that counts. Looking over at Nell, he knew he was in for a lot of glorious tomorrows.

THE END

Did you enjoy this book?

You **can make a big difference.**

As an independent author, I don't have the financial muscle of a New York publisher supporting me. But I do have something much more powerful and effective, and it's something those publishers would kill to get their hands on: a committed and loyal bunch of readers. Honest reviews of my books help bring them to the notice of other readers. If you've enjoyed this book, I would be so grateful if you could spend just a couple of minutes leaving a review.

Thank you very much,

Martin Turnbull

AUTHOR NOTE

As with most historical fiction, *You Must Remember This* is a blend of fact and fiction. To help you sort out which parts were real and which I invented, here are some clarifications.

Fletcher Bowron, who appears in Chapter 5, when Luke is presented with the key to the city, was Los Angeles's mayor from September 26, 1938, to June 30, 1953, which at the time made him the city's longest-serving mayor.

Breakfast in Hollywood was a very popular morning radio show created and hosted by Tom Breneman. It aired on three radio networks, NBC, ABC and Mutual, and ran from 1941 to 1948 under several names and at several locations. In 1945, Breneman opened his own eponymous restaurant on the west side of Vine Street, north of Sunset Boulevard, and broadcast from there until his premature death from a heart attack in 1948.

In Chapter 13, Bogie says: "An actor needs something to stabilize his personality, to nail down what he really is, not what he is pretending to be." I was paraphrasing an actual Bogart quote: "An actor needs something to stabilize his personality, something to nail down what he really is, not what he is pretending to be. Sailing does it for me."

Report from the Aleutians (1943) was a 45-minute documentary produced by the US Army Corps, and was directed and narrated by John Huston. You can find it on YouTube.

You can also find *Appointment in Tokyo* (1945) on YouTube.

The *Music from Hollywood* was a real radio show that ran from 1937 to 1950.

The scene at the Melody Lane restaurant in which Gus talks about watching Carmen Miranda give an impromptu concert on V-J Day is based on a real event. When celebrations broke out on August 14, 1945, to mark the end of WWII, Carmen Miranda gave an impromptu performance on the back of a convertible at the corner of Hollywood and Vine.

In Chapter 8, Nell goes to Hoagy Carmichael's home. You can see photos of his house in the digital photograph collection of the Huntington Museum near Pasadena, California.

In Chapter 10, Nell and the gang listen to Nell's recording at Wallichs Music City. It stood on the northwest corner of Sunset Boulevard and Vine Street, Hollywood, where it opened in 1940, and quickly became one of the go-to music stores in Los Angeles.

In the mid-1940s, when this story plays out, long-playing records had not yet been developed. Back then, an "album" of ten songs was made up of a set of five records, each with one song per side. For a typical album from 1946, see *"Blue Skies* (Decca album)" on Wikipedia.

Radio KFWB's Trans-Lux Flashcast news ribbon actually existed on the Taft Building on the southeast corner of Hollywood and Vine. It was unveiled to much fanfare on August 6, 1946.

The novels that Bogie picks up with an eye to turning one of them into the first movie produced by Santana Productions—*Plausible Deniability*, *The Dream Builders*, and *Retaliation*—were my own invention. However, Bogart's production company, Santana Productions, was a real entity. In all, it produced seven movies between 1949 and 1953, all of which were released through Columbia.

When Joan Crawford was nominated for an Academy Award for her role in *Mildred Pierce*, she didn't attend the ceremony held on March 7, 1946, at Grauman's Chinese Theatre out of fear that she would lose. She should have gone, though, because she won the Oscar for Best Leading Actress. The party in Chapter 31 to celebrate it on the set of *Humoresque* was, however, my own invention.

"The Last of the Red Hot Mamas" was a Sophie Tucker song, but there was never a movie made about her. Betty Hutton did, however, star in a movie about Texas Guinan called *Incendiary Blonde*.

Lucey's New Orleans House, where Nell and Violet meet for lunch in Chapter 32, was a real place on Melrose Avenue, across from Paramount Pictures movie studios. It's not to be confused with Lucy's El Adobe Mexican restaurant, which currently exists on the same block.

The Tropics on Rodeo Drive in Beverly Hills, where Luke meets up with Bogie in Chapter 33, was a real bar that opened in 1936, and was one of the earliest of the Polynesian places. In 1953, it was purchased by one of Lana Turner's former husbands, Steven Crane, and turned into The Luau.

In 1946, after trying unsuccessfully for some time to conceive a child with Lauren Bacall, Humphrey Bogart underwent hormone treatments to improve their chances. Eventually they worked—their first child, Stephen, was born in January 1949. Bogie was over the moon at the prospect of being a father, but it was at the expense of his hair, most of which fell out as a result of his treatments. Fortunately, he had some excellent toupees and the services of Verita Thompson, who knew how to maintain and position them so that we oblivious moviegoers would never suspect he was wearing a hairpiece.

Those of you who have read my Hollywood's Garden of Allah series might like to know that the dress with the ivy print that Nell wears for her Cocoanut Grove debut in Chapter 34 is the same dress that Gwendolyn caught her boss wearing in *Reds in the Beds*. It didn't suit Herman Dewberry, but it was perfect for Nell!

The reference that Kathryn Massey makes in Chapter 36 to Howard Hughes's publicity stunt for *The Outlaw* actually happened. During the spring of 1946, he hired a small skywriting plane to fly over Pasadena and skywrite the words THE OUTLAW, followed by two giant circles, each dotted in the center.

I set the scene in Chapter 37, where Luke and Nell go with Bogart and Bacall to the preview of *The Big Sleep* on Linden Drive, in Beverly Hills because I couldn't determine exactly where Howard and Slim Hawks were living during the summer of 1946. At some point, Hawks was living in a house on Linden, so I set the scene there. By then, Hawks, Bogart, and Bacall were frustrated with the delayed release of *The Big Sleep*. Warner Bros. had a backlog of war pictures that they wanted to burn through first, so even though principal photography had finished on January 12, 1945, and additional scenes were filmed a whole year later during January 1946, the movie didn't get released until August 1946. It was, however, worth the wait because the picture was a huge hit and cemented Bogart and Bacall as a favorite screen couple. At the time of Chapter 37 (June 1946), Bugsy Siegel was living at 810 N. Linden, which is where he was assassinated on June 20, 1947. It was on that same street that, on July 7, 1946, Howard Hughes lost control of an airplane he was test-flying and crashed into several houses on the west side of the street. This incident was depicted in Martin Scorsese's movie, *The Aviator* (2004).

Also in Chapter 37 is the scene where Luke poses for Norman Rockwell. At the time, the Otis College of Art and Design in Westlake near MacArthur Park invited Rockwell to be their artist-in-residence during the winter months. His studio was in Stockbridge, Massachusetts, so it must have been a nice change to work in temperate winter weather. The college is now known as Otis College. The story about Rockwell stuffing himself to make the minimum weight requirement for WWI is true. He painted "Working on the Statue of Liberty" in 1946. I don't know exactly when he completed it, but as that chapter takes place in June 1946, I figured I had a 50/50 chance of being historically accurate. You can learn more about it on "Working on the Statue of Liberty" on Wikipedia.

As readers of my Hollywood's Garden of Allah novels will know, Billy Wilkerson was the owner/editor of *The Hollywood Reporter* in which he wrote a regular editorial column called TradeViews. On July 29, 1946, under the inflammatory headline *A VOTE FOR JOE STALIN*, Wilkerson printed the names of eleven members of the Screen Writers Guild whom he accused of being "avowed Leftists and sympathizers of the Party Line." These were the first names on what would eventually become the infamous Hollywood blacklist, a subject he would go on to write about many times in the ensuing years. Albert Maltz was not included in the July list; however, Wilkerson did include him on a more extensive one that he published on September 12 of that same year.

The Last Submarine was a fictitious movie of my own invention, but Albert Maltz wrote or contributed to a number of memorable movies, such as *This Gun for Hire*, *Destination Tokyo*, *Mildred Pierce*, and *The Robe*.

The USS *Lanternfish* and its sister, the *Viperfish*, were my own invention. In real life, the last downed US submarine of World War II was the USS *Bullhead*, which was sunk by Japanese aircraft on August 6, 1945, the same day that the Allies dropped an atomic bomb on the Japanese city of Hiroshima.

In real life, Bogie's footprint ceremony outside Grauman's Chinese Theatre took place on August 21, 1946, while 20th Century-Fox's *Centennial Summer* was playing. To create a more cohesive narrative, I shifted the ceremony to a few weeks earlier.

ALSO BY MARTIN TURNBULL

The Hollywood Home Front trilogy
A trilogy of novels set in World War II Hollywood

Book 1 - *All the Gin Joints*
Book 2 - *Thank Your Lucky Stars*
Book 3 - *You Must Remember This*

Chasing Salomé: a novel of 1920s Hollywood

The Heart of the Lion: a novel of Irving Thalberg's Hollywood

The Hollywood's Garden of Allah novels
Book 1 – *The Garden on Sunset*
Book 2 – *The Trouble with Scarlett*
Book 3 – *Citizen Hollywood*
Book 4 – *Searchlights and Shadows*
Book 5 – *Reds in the Beds*
Book 6 – *Twisted Boulevard*
Book 7 – *Tinseltown Confidential*
Book 8 – *City of Myths*

Book 9 – *Closing Credits*

*R*ave reviews for Martin Turnbull's *Hollywood's Garden of Allah* series:

What a marvelous series! I tore through all nine books in record time and plan to go back to the beginning and start over! Thank you so much for this grand treat!

I loved this whole series, I'm sorry it had to end, but the reading was worth it! One of the best book series I have ever read!

If you start The Garden of Allah series from the beginning you will be treated to not only a great story but an accurate history of Hollywood from the 1920's Silent Era through the mid-1950's. I highly recommend this series of books for your total enjoyment.

I would give every one of the nine books more than 5 stars. This was a wonderful series that I wish did not have to end. I LOVED reading this series! They were so well-written, thorough, detailed, and really really interesting. I would love to read more, as I enjoyed these characters so much, and loved learning about the development of the industry and the area.

Martin Turnbull not only entertained me, but he gave me a respect and love for movies, actors, actresses, writers, directors, studios, and everything that contributed to the development of our entertainment industry.

What a great series of books! Anyone who loves movie history has to read these. I really felt I was part of of the friendship with

Marcus, Gwen, and Kathryn, and shared every emotional roller-coaster ride.

~oOo~

See the Hollywood's Garden of Allah novels
on Martin Turnbull's website.
~oOo~

Be the first to hear about new books and other news - sign up to my mailing list - http://bit.ly/turnbullsignup
(I promise (a) I won't fill your inbox with useless drivel you don't care about, (b) I won't email you very often, and (c) I'll never share your information with anyone. Ever.

ACKNOWLEDGEMENTS

My heartfelt thanks to:

Jennifer McIntyre, my editor, for her keen eye, unfailing humor, and the willingness to debate every last letter and comma placement.

Steve Bingen, who provided me with detailed photos and maps of the Warner Bros. studio lot in Burbank, California.

My beta readers: Vince Hans, David Fox, Beth Riches, and Steven Adkins for their time, insight, feedback and advice in shaping this novel.

I'd especially like to thank John Luder, who generously shared his deep knowledge of World War II and the U.S. military. His input gave the manuscript a degree of gritty realism it had previously lacked and went a long way toward giving the reader a more authentic experience of life during WWII and the immediate post-war era. I would also like to thank Gene Strange who patiently guided me through four—yes, that's right, *four*—outlines of this novel, and who refused to let me settle for "That'll have to do" and continued to push me to "Nailed it!"

My proofreaders with the best eagle eyes in the biz: Bob Molinari, Susan Perkins, and Leigh Carter.

Book cover by Damonza

ABOUT THE AUTHOR

A lifelong love of travel, history, and sharing his knowledge with others has led Martin Turnbull down a long path to authorship. Having made the move to the United States from Melbourne, Australia in the mid-90s, Martin staked his claim in the heart of Los Angeles. His background in travel allowed him to work as a private tour guide--showing off the alluring vistas, mansions, boulevards, and backlots of the Hollywood scene. With stints in local historical guiding with the Los Angeles Conservancy as well as time on the Warner Bros. movie lot, Martin found himself armed with the kind of knowledge that would fly off the very pages of his future works. As a longtime fan of Hollywood's golden era and old films, Martin decided it was time to marry his knowledge with his passions and breathe life back into this bygone world.

The product of his passions burst forth in the form of Hollywood's Garden of Allah novels, a series of historical fiction books set during the golden age of Hollywood: 1927-1959. Exploring the evolution of Hollywood's most famous and glamorous era through the lives of its residents, these stories take place both in and around the real-life Garden of Allah Hotel on iconic Sunset Boulevard. Although Martin's heart belongs to history, his energy remains in the present, continuing to put his passions on paper and beyond.

CONNECT WITH MARTIN TURNBULL

MartinTurnbull.com

Facebook: facebook.com/gardenofallahnovels

Blog: martinturnbull.wordpress.com/

Goodreads: http://bit.ly/martingoodreads

Amazon author page: http://bit.ly/martinturnbull

Be sure to check out the **Photo Blog** for vintage photos of Los Angeles and Hollywood on Martin's website: martinturnbull.com/photo-blog/

To hear about new books first, sign up to my mailing list:

http://bit.ly/turnbullsignup

I won't fill your inbox with useless drivel or I email you too often or never share your information with anyone. Ever. (And you can unsubscribe at any time. No hard feelings.)

Made in the USA
Columbia, SC
15 December 2023